"Andr...ul
blend ....st-
plain-...g
as a g...
—*.......ews*

"An engaging and satisfying tale of life, loss, and love."
—*Booklist*

"Mary Kay Andrews's novels have become a summer
staple like a new .... *Times*
bestselling autho................................. cocktail of romance, ...
—.........*server*

"This is her bes.................................. of the
strengths we have come to expect from this audacious
and beguiling author." —*Huffington Post*

"A court-ordered therapy session is the site of the action
in Andrews's zesty, amusing latest." —*People*

"Mary Kay Andrews blends heartache and hilarity in a
story line filled with surprises." —*Southern Living*

"If there were a literary genre dedicated to great beach
books, the novels of Mary Kay Andrews would set its
standard for excellence."

—*Cape Gazette*

Spring Fever

"If you're making a list of 'must-read' books, this one
should be at the top." —*Huffington Post*

"A winsome love story and compelling family drama; an idyllic small-town setting and surprising twists and turns." —*Booklist*

"Andrews delivers a satisfying read that will leave a taste as tangy, delicious, and sweet as an ice-cold bottle of Quixie soda." —*Kirkus Reviews*

"A very Suth'n novel . . . full of intriguing plot turns by colorful characters." —*Seattle Times*

"Charming . . . a perfect mix of humor, romance, and quirky loveable characters." —*The Times News*

Summer Rental

"Mary Kay Andrews spins a beach-blanket sizzler around three lifelong friends . . . a warm-weather treat that has a lot going for it, not least the sunny forecast that summer love can blossom into a four-season commitment." —*Publishers Weekly*

"Andrews writes another charmer with a picturesque Southern setting and winsome female characters." —*Booklist*

"[R]eaders of *Summer Rental* will stay glued to their sandy beach chairs waiting to see what happens next." —*The Christian Science Monitor*

"Secrets are shared, a mystery woman appears, love may be in the air."   —*People* magazine

"[T]his is prime beach-read material."
                                    —*Daily Record* (Gannett newspapers)

"*Summer Rental* is like a great day at the beach. You don't want it to end. Enjoy a vacation any time of the year with the ever-delightful Mary Kay Andrews."
                                    —Susan Elizabeth Phillips,
                                    author of *Heroes Are My Weakness*

"The bright and breezy plot of *Summer Rental* delivers just the right combination of sexy romance and warm friendship."   —*Chicago Tribune*

"*Summer Rental* is just a delight to savor. The lively cast of characters is complex, genuine, and strong, and the interplay between the long-term friends is heartwarming."
                                    —*Times Record News* (Texas)

"You will relate to the women and their relationships as you laze through the pages . . . and you will smile, chuckle, and maybe even get a little misty-eyed."

                                    —Examiner.com

"Andrews is at her warm and funny best . . . [She] excels at creating the kind of characters readers can relate to, and she has a fabulous sense of humor to boot."
                                    —*Library Journal* (starred review)

ALSO BY MARY KAY ANDREWS

Ladies' Night

Mary Kay Andrews

St. Martin's Paperbacks

LADIES' NIGHT

Copyright © 2013 by Whodunnit, Inc.
Excerpt from *The Weekenders* copyright © 2016 by Whodunnit, Inc.

All rights reserved.

For information address St. Martin's Press, 175 Fifth Avenue, New York, NY 10010.

Library of Congress Catalog Card Number: 2013009101

ISBN: 978-1-250-13062-4

Our books may be purchased in bulk for promotional, educational, or business use. Please contact your local bookseller or the Macmillan Corporate and Premium Sales Department at 1-800-221-7945, ext. 5442, or by e-mail at MacmillanSpecialMarkets@macmillan.com.

Printed in the United States of America

St. Martin's Griffin trade paperback edition / May 2014
St. Martin's Paperbacks edition / May 2017

St. Martin's Paperbacks are published by St. Martin's Press, 175 Fifth Avenue, New York, NY 10010.

10 9 8 7 6 5 4 3 2 1

In memory of my brother, John Joseph Hogan,
who left this world too soon.
Miss you, Johnny.

Ladies' Night

1.

If Grace Stanton had known the world as she knew it was going to end that uneventful evening in May, she might have been better prepared. She certainly would have packed more underwear and a decent bra, not to mention moisturizer and her iPhone charger.

But as far as Grace knew, she was just doing her job, writing and photographing Gracenotes, a blog designed to make her own lifestyle look so glamorous, enticing, and delicious it made perfectly normal women (and gay men) want to rip up the script for their own lives and rebuild one exactly like hers.

She peered through the lens finder of her Nikon D7000 and frowned, but only for a moment, because, as Ben had told her countless times, a frown was forever. She made a conscious effort to smooth the burgeoning wrinkles in her forehead, then concentrated anew on her composition.

She'd polished the old pine table to a dull sheen, and the available light streaming in from the dining room window glinted off the worn boards. With her right hand, she made a minute adjustment to one of the two deliberately mismatched white ironstone platters she'd placed on a rumpled—but not wrinkled—antique French grain-sack table runner. She replaced the oversized sterling forks, tines pointed down, at the edge of the platters. Should she add knives? Maybe spoons? She thought not. Spare. The look she was going for was spare.

Edit, edit, edit, she thought, nodding almost imperceptibly. Less was more. Or that's what Ben always claimed.

Now. About that centerpiece. She'd cut three small palmetto fronds from the newly landscaped driveway . . . No, she corrected herself. The builder's Web site referred to it as a motor court. The palmettos were giving her fits. She'd arranged them in a mottled, barnacle-crusted pale aqua bottle she'd plucked from a pile of random junk at the flea market the weekend before. They should have looked great. But no. They were too stiff. Too awkward. Too vertical.

Grace replaced the palmettos with a cardboard carton of lush red heirloom tomatoes. Hmm. The vibrant color was a good contrast against the nubby linen of the runner, and she loved the lumpy forms and brilliant green and yellow stripes on some of the irregularly shaped fruits. Maybe, if she placed the container on its side, with the tomatoes spilling out? Yes. Much better.

She grabbed a knife from the sideboard and sawed one of the tomatoes in half, squeezing it slightly, until seeds and juices dribbled out onto the tabletop.

Perfect. She inhaled and clicked the trigger on her motor-driven shutter. Click. Click. Click. She adjusted the focus so the pale gel-covered seeds were in the foreground. Now, she zoomed out, leaving the tomatoes as red blurs, so that the old ironstone platters were in focus, their age-crazed crackles and brown spots coming into sharp relief.

"Very pretty," a voice breathed in her ear.

Grace jumped.

Ben rested a hand lightly on her shoulder and studied the vignette.

"Is that for tomorrow's 'Friday Favorites' post?" he asked.

"Mm-hmm," Grace said. "I tried the palmetto fronds and, before that, a basket of seashells, and then some green mangoes, but I think the tomatoes work best, don't you?"

He shrugged. "I guess."

"What?" Grace studied his face, as always, craving his approval. "The tomatoes don't work for you?"

"They're nice. In an artsy-fartsy kind of way," he said.

She pushed a strand of light brown hair off her forehead and took a step back from the table. She'd spent an hour putting the table together, and she'd been fairly pleased with the effect she'd achieved. But Ben didn't like it.

"Too country-cutesy?" she asked, glancing at her husband. Ben's trained eyes missed nothing. He'd been in the ad business forever, and no detail was too small or too insignificant. It was why they made such a great team.

"It's your blog," he reminded her. "And your name is on it. I don't want business stuff to impinge on your editorial freedom. But . . ."

"But what? Come on. I'm a big girl. I can take it."

"The Aviento folks sent us a big crateful of pieces of their new fall line," Ben said, hesitating. "Treasures of Tuscany, the new pattern is called. It's for the giveaway you're doing on Monday. I was thinking maybe you could put the tomatoes in one of those bowls they sent."

Grace wrinkled her nose. "That is seriously the ugliest pottery I have ever seen, and it looks about as Italian as a can of Chef Boyardee."

"You don't have to set the whole table with it. Just maybe put some of the tomatoes in one of the bowls. They *are* spending a lot of money advertising with us now, and it would be good if they could see their product . . . you know."

"Stinkin' up my 'Friday Favorites' tablescapes," Grace said, finishing the sentence for him. "Did you promise them I would use it editorially? Tell me the truth, Ben."

"No!" he said sharply. "I would never try to influence you that way. But would it hurt to maybe try a couple shots with one of the bowls. Or a plate?"

"I'll try it out. But if it looks as crappy as I think it will, I'm not going to run it. Right? I mean, you promised when we monetized the blog, we wouldn't be whoring me out by using the advertisers' product in a way that would compromise my aesthetic."

"It's your call," Ben said, picking up one of the tomatoes and examining it. "These are weird looking. What kind are they?"

"Don't know," Grace said, gently taking the tomato from him and replacing it on the table. "J'Aimee picked them up at the farmer's market."

"Kid's got a good eye," Ben said. He glanced back at the table. "How long before you're done here?"

"Maybe an hour? I guess I'll try some shots with the Aviento stuff. Then I need to edit, and I've still got to actually write the piece." She glanced down at her watch. "Good Lord! It's after six. I've been piddling around with this tabletop for hours now. Why didn't you say something?"

"Didn't want to interrupt the genius while she was at work," he said. "But since you brought it up, is there any actual food to go on these pretty plates?"

"Nada," she said apologetically. "I'm sorry. I completely lost track of the time. Look, I'll just take a couple more shots with the Tuscan Turds, then I'll run down to Publix and pick up some sushi. Or maybe a nice piece of fish to grill. I can have supper on the table by seven. Right?"

"Finish your shots," Ben said easily. "J'Aimee can pick up supper."

"No, I'll go. I've had J'Aimee out running errands all afternoon."

Ben dropped a kiss on her forehead. "That's what assistants are for, Grace."

"But I hate to bother her," she protested. "She just went back over to the apartment an hour ago."

Grace gestured in the general direction of the garage, which was at the back of the "motor court." J'Aimee, her twenty-six-year-old assistant, had been living in the apartment above the garage since she was hired three months earlier. Her battered white Honda Accord was parked in the third bay, beside Ben's black Audi convertible.

Their builder had referred to the apartment as a mother-in-law suite, or even a nanny suite. But Grace's mom lived only a few miles away on Cortez and she wouldn't have moved to this "faux chateau," as she called it, at gunpoint. Ben's mother lived quite happily down in Coconut Grove. And since the fertility specialist still couldn't figure out just exactly why Grace couldn't get pregnant, the apartment, for now, was the perfect place to stash an assistant.

"Finish your shoot," Ben said, settling the matter. "I'll walk over there and roust J'Aimee. In fact, I'll ride to Publix with her."

"Thanks," Grace said, going back to her camera. "You're the best."

Ben gave her a gentle pat on the butt. "That's my girl," he said.

Grace went into the kitchen and found the heavy wooden crate with the Aviento shipping label sitting on the polished black granite countertop, pausing, as she always did, to flick a crumb into the sink. She hated the black granite. Even the tiniest fleck of sea salt showed up on it, and she seemed to go through a gallon of Windex every week, keeping it shiny.

But Ben and the builder had ganged up on her to agree

to use it, after the granite company offered the countertops at cost in exchange for a small ad on Gracenotes.

She was soon immersed again in her work, barely reg-
istering the familiar roar of Ben's car as it backed out of
the garage. Grace looked up in time to see that he'd put
the Audi's top down. He did a neat three-point turn and
gave her a carefree wave before he sped down the driveway, his forearm casually thrown across the back of the
passenger seat, and J'Aimee's long red hair flowing gracefully in the wind.

Ben reminded her of Cary Grant in *To Catch a Thief*, a
golden boy, elegant, aloof, mysterious, maybe even a little
dangerous? She reflected briefly on how unfair life really
was. At forty-four, Ben was six years older, but you'd never
know it from looking at him. He never gained weight and
never seemed to age. He kept his tennis tan year-round.
His gloriously glossy dark brown hair still didn't show a
speck of gray, and the faint crow's-feet around his eyes lent
him the look of wisdom, not imminent geezerdom.

Grace, on the other hand, was beginning to spend what
she thought of as an alarming amount of time on maintenance. At five-four, even five extra pounds seemed to go
right to her butt or her belly, and she'd begun coloring her
sandy-brown hair two years earlier, at the suggestion of
Ruthanne, her hairdresser. Her face was heart-shaped, and
only thirty minutes in the Florida sun left her round cheeks
beet-colored, giving her even more of the look of a little
Dutch girl when Ruthanne got carried away with the blond
highlights. Ben insisted she was still as pretty as the day
they'd met six years earlier, but they both knew that with
Grace's blogging career about to take off, she would have
to be that much more vigilant about her appearance.

Blogging? A career?

If anybody had told her two years ago that she'd make
a living out of journaling her quest for a more beautiful

life, she would have laughed in their face. And if anybody told her that she would become enough of a success that Ben would quit his career to run hers? Well, she would have politely written that person off as a nutcase.

But it was all true. She and Ben were on the very verge of the big time. This house, a 6,500-square-foot Spanish colonial located in a gated golf-course community had been one of the subdivision's model homes, and the builder, whose wife was an avid Gracenotes reader, had given them an incredible deal on it in exchange for a banner ad across the top of the blog. Most of the expensive upgrades on the property—the landscaping, the pool and spa, their amazing master bath—had also been trade-offs for advertising.

She'd always loved writing, and had tinkered with photography for years, but once the blog took off, it had somehow caught the eye of magazine editors and television producers. In addition to having their own house featured in half a dozen magazines, writing, photography, and decorating assignments had begun coming her way. She'd become a contributing regional editor for *Country Living* and *Bay Life* magazines, and next month, they were going to start working with a production company out of California to shoot a pilot television show of Gracenotes for HGTV.

All because of her silly little blog.

She couldn't say why she awoke so suddenly. Normally, Grace fell asleep the moment her head hit the pillow, and she slept so soundly Ben often reminded her of the time she'd slept through Hurricane Elise, not even stirring when the wind tore the roof totally off the screened porch of their old house in a slightly run-down Bradenton neighborhood.

That night was no exception. She'd retreated to her office after dinner, writing and rewriting her Gracenotes post and fussing over the photographs before, finally, shortly before eleven, pushing the SEND button and crawling into bed beside her already-slumbering husband.

For whatever reason, she sat straight up in bed now. It was after 1:00 A.M. Her heart was racing, and her mouth was dry. A bad dream? She couldn't say. She glanced over at Ben's side of the bed. Empty.

She rubbed her eyes. Ben was probably downstairs, in the media room, watching a tournament on Golf TV, or maybe he was in the kitchen, looking for a late-night snack. Grace yawned and padded downstairs, already planning her own snack.

But the downstairs was dark, the media room deserted. She went out to the kitchen. No sign of him there, either. The kitchen was as spotless as she'd left it three hours earlier, after finishing up the last of the dinner dishes and packing up the faux-Tuscan pottery. Not even a cup or a spoon in the sink.

Grace frowned, and this time she didn't bother to worry about wrinkles. She checked the downstairs powder room, but the door was open and there was no sign of her husband. She ran back upstairs and peeked inside the two guest suites, but they were empty and undisturbed. She walked slowly back to the bedroom, thinking to call Ben's cell phone. But when she saw his cell phone on his dresser, along with his billfold, she relaxed a little. And then she noticed the keys to the Audi were missing, and her heart seemed to miss a beat. She went to the window and peered out, but saw nothing. There was only a quarter moon that night, but it was obscured by a heavy bank of clouds. The backyard was wreathed in darkness. She couldn't even see the garage.

"It's nothing," she told herself, surprised to realize that she was talking out loud. She shrugged out of her night-gown, pulling on a pair of shorts and a T-shirt, slipping her feet into a pair of rubber flip-flops. "He's fine. Maybe he's out by the pool, sneaking a midnight cigar."

The sandals slapped noisily on the marble stairs, the sound echoing in the high-ceilinged stairway. She ditched them by the back door, carefully switching off the burglar alarm before stepping out onto the back patio. She paused, put her hand to her chest, and could have sworn it was about to jump out of her body.

"Ben?" She kept her voice low. It was pitch black, except for the pale turquoise surface of the pool and the eerie green uplights on the date-palm clusters at the back of the garden. Cicadas thrummed, and in the far distance, she heard a truck rumbling down the street. She crept forward, her hands extended, edging past the pair of chaise lounges perched at the edge of the patio, feeling the rough-textured coral rock beneath her feet.

Gradually, her eyes adjusted to the dark. There was no glowing cigar tip anywhere on the patio or the garden. She glanced toward the garage. No lights were on in J'Aimee's upstairs apartment, and the garage doors were closed. Was Ben's car there?

For a moment, a train of scenarios unspooled through her imagination. Ben, passed out, or even dead, at the wheel of his car, an unknown assailant lurking nearby. Should she retreat to the house, find some kind of weapon, even call the police?

"Don't be an idiot," she murmured to herself. "You're a big girl. Just go look in the garage. You live in a gated community, for God's sake. The only crime here is dogs pooping on the grass."

She tiptoed toward the garage, skirting the electronically controlled metal doors, heading toward the side door, trying to remember whether or not it would be unlocked.

Luckily, it was. The knob turned easily in her hand, and

she stepped inside the darkened space, her hand groping the wall for the light switch.

And then she heard . . . heavy breathing. She froze. A man's voice. The words were unintelligible, but the voice was Ben's. Her hand scrabbled the wall for the switch. She found it, and the garage was flooded with light.

A woman squealed.

Grace blinked in the bright lights. She saw Ben, sitting in the driver's seat of the Audi. He was bare-chested, his right hand shielding his eyes from the light. His hair was mussed, and his cheeks were flushed bright red.

"Grace?" He looked wild-eyed.

And that's when she realized he wasn't alone in the car. Her first instinct was to turn and run away, but she was drawn, like a bug to a lightbulb, to the side of that gleaming black sports car. The top was retracted. She looked down and saw that distinctive mane of flame-red hair.

J'Aimee, her loyal, invaluable assistant, was cowering, naked, making a valiant effort to disappear into the floorboards of the car.

"What the hell?" Grace screeched as she yanked open the passenger-side door.

"I'm sorry, Grace, I'm so sorry," J'Aimee blurted, her eyes the size of saucers.

J'Aimee's clothes were scattered on the floor of the garage, and, come to think of it, that was Ben's shirt—his expensive, pale-blue, custom-tailored, monogrammed, Egyptian cotton shirt that Grace had given him as a birthday gift—that was flung over the Audi's windshield.

With the passenger-side door open, Grace saw, at a glance, that her husband was nearly naked, too—if you counted having your jeans puddled down around your ankles as naked.

For a moment, Grace wondered if this was some bad

dream she was having. Hadn't she just been asleep a moment earlier? This couldn't be happening. Not Ben. Ben loved her. He would never cheat. She shook her head violently, closed her eyes, and reopened them.

But this was no nightmare. And there was no mistaking what she'd just interrupted. Suddenly, she felt a surge of boiling hot rage.

"Bitch!" Grace cried. She clamped a hand around J'Aimee's upper arm and yanked her out of the car in one fluid, frenzied motion.

"Ow," J'Aimee whimpered.

Grace flung her against the side of the car.

"Stop it," J'Aimee cried. Her face was pale, with every freckle standing out in contrast to the milky whiteness of her skin. For some reason, Grace, in an insane corner of her mind, noted with satisfaction that J'Aimee's breasts were oddly pendulous for such a young woman. Also? Not a real redhead.

"You stop it!" Grace said, drawing back her hand.

"Jesus!" J'Aimee screamed. She raised her arms to cover her face, and for a moment Grace faltered. She had never hit anybody in her life. She dropped her hand and glared at the girl.

"Now, Grace," Ben started. He was wriggling around in his seat, trying in vain to surreptitiously pull up his pants. "Don't get the wrong idea. Don't . . ."

"Shut up, just shut up!" Grace shouted, her eyes blazing. For a moment, she forgot about J'Aimee. She flew around to his side of the car, but before she could get there, Ben had managed to slide out from under the steering wheel, zipping up his pants as he stood.

"How could you?" she cried, raining ineffective punches around his head and shoulders. She was aware that her high-pitched shrieks sounded like the howls of a lunatic, but she was helpless to stop herself. "You? And J'Aimee? My assistant? You were screwing her? Under my own roof?"

He easily caught her fists and held them tight in his own. "No!" Ben lied. "It's not what you think. Look, if you would just calm down, let's talk about this. Okay? I know this looks bad, but there's a logical explanation."

"Like what? The two of you snuck out here to the garage while I was asleep and you decided to have a business meeting in your car? A clothing-optional meeting? And suddenly, J'Aimee decided to give you mouth-to-penis resuscitation? Is that the logical explanation for this?"

"Calm down," Ben repeated. "You're getting yourself all worked up . . ."

Grace saw a flash of movement out of the corner of her eye and looked over just in time to see J'Aimee scoop up her clothing and make a run for it.

"Oh, no," Grace said. "You're not getting away from this." J'Aimee darted out the door, and Grace went right after her.

"Stay away from me," J'Aimee cried, running in the direction of the house. "I'll call the police if you come near me . . . It's aggravated assault."

"You don't know the meaning of aggravated," Grace shouted. She flinched when her bare feet hit the lawn, damp from the automatic sprinklers, but ran after J'Aimee, who was surprisingly slow for a young woman unencumbered by clothing. She picked up her speed until she was only a few yards behind her former assistant. She reached out to try to snatch a handful of J'Aimee's hair, but her prey danced out of reach.

"Don't you touch me," J'Aimee cried, backing away. "I mean it."

But Grace was quicker than even she expected. She

managed to grab J'Aimee's arm, and the girl screamed like a stuck pig.

Lights snapped on at the house next door. A dog began barking from the back of the property.

"Get away," the young woman screeched, dropping her clothing onto the grass and windmilling her arms in Grace's general vicinity. "Get away."

Now they heard the low hum and metallic clang of the garage door opening. Grace glanced over her shoulder to see Ben come sprinting out of the garage. "Are you insane?" he called. "For God's sake, Grace, let her go."

In her fury, Grace turned toward her husband, and in that moment J'Aimee slipped out of her grasp. While Grace watched, speechless, J'Aimee scampered, naked, around the patio. A moment later, she'd disappeared behind the thick hedge of hibiscus that separated the Stantons' property from their nearest neighbor.

"Go ahead and run, bitch!" Grace screamed. "You're fired. You hear me? Your ass is fired!"

Ben was walking slowly across the grass, his hands raised in a cautious peace gesture. "Okay, Grace," he said, making low, soothing sounds at the back of his throat, the kind you'd make to coax a cat out of a treetop. "Oh-kay, I know. You're upset. I get that. Can we take this inside now? You're making a spectacle of yourself. Let's take it inside, all right? I'll make us some coffee and we can sort this out . . ."

"We are *not* going inside," Grace snapped. "Coffee? Are you kidding me? You think a dose of Starbucks Extra Bold is going to fix this? We are going to stay right here. Do you hear me?"

"The whole neighborhood can hear you. Could you lower your voice, please? Just dial it down a little?"

"I will not!" His calmness made her even crazier than she already felt. Grace megaphoned her hands. "Hey, people. Neighbors—wake up! This is Grace Stanton. I just caught my husband, Ben Stanton, screwing my assistant!"

"Stop it," Ben hissed. "I was *not* screwing her."

"Correction," Grace hollered, lifting her voice to the sky. "She was blowing him. My mistake, neighbors."

"You're insane," he snapped. "I'm not staying around listening to this." He turned and stomped off toward the house. "We'll talk when you've calmed down."

"One question, Ben," Grace called, running after him. She grabbed him by the shoulder to stop his progress. "You owe me that."

"What?" He spun around, rigid with anger. She noticed three small love bites on his collarbone. Hickeys? Her forty-four-year-old husband had hickeys? A wave of nausea swelled up from her belly. She swallowed hard.

"How long? How long have you been fucking her?"

"I'm not . . ." He shrugged. "Come inside. All right?"

"How long?" Grace felt hot tears springing to her eyes. "Tell me, damn it. This wasn't the first time, was it? So tell me the truth. How long?"

"No matter what I say, you won't believe me," Ben said quietly.

"Tell me the truth and I'll believe you," Grace said.

"No," he said softly. "Not the first time. But we can fix this, Grace."

"Fix it?" Grace exploded with pure, white-hot rage.

"Fix it," she said, lifting her voice to the heavens. "He's been screwing her for a while now, and he thinks we can fix it."

"That's it," Ben said. "I won't stand here and let you humiliate me like this."

"Don't you dare walk away from me," Grace called.

"I'm gone," Ben said. True to his word, he stalked away toward the house.

She raced to the back door, to discover that he'd locked her out.

"Let me in, damn it," she screamed, pounding on the kitchen door.

Nothing. She kicked the door. Still nothing.

She looked around for something, anything, to break the glass in the door. Just then she spied the heap of clothing J'Aimee had discarded in her hasty escape.

Grace scooped up the clothes and returned to the back patio. She craned her neck in the direction of the hibiscus hedge, hoping she might spot J'Aimee's bony white ass back there, hiding in the foliage or, better yet, being gnawed on by the neighbor's dog, a vicious-tempered chow mix named Peaches. But nothing moved in the shrubbery.

She had an idea. She stepped onto the patio and found the light switch for the outdoor kitchen, with its granite counters and six-burner gas-fired barbecue.

Earlier in May, her Gracenotes blog had dealt with barbecues.

Mr. Grace and I are fortunate to live in Florida, where grilling season never ends. But just because we're dining outdoors doesn't mean I serve burnt hot dogs on spindly white paper plates. I love to spread a white matelassé bedspread diagonally across our glass-topped patio table and anchor it with a pair of heavy black wrought-iron candelabras, or, if it's a windy day, I'll place votive candles in old Mason jars anchored with a layer of bleached-out seashells. Especially for casual occasions like this, you do not have to have a set of matched plastic dishes. I'll let you in on a secret: I hate matchy-matchy! Instead, I have an assortment of mismatched Fiestaware plates picked up at junk shops and yard sales over

the years, in bold shades of turquoise, green, pink,
yellow, and orange. Paired with silverware with
ivory-colored Bakelite handles, and oversized plain
white flour-sack dish towels bought cheap from Ikea,
and a bouquet of brilliant zinnias cut from the gar-
den, they telegraph the message to guests: the fun is
about to begin!

Speaking of fun, Grace chortled as she tossed J'Aimee's clothes—a T-shirt, pair of shorts, bra, and pink thong panties—onto the counter and then reached into the stainless steel bar fridge and found herself a perfectly chilled bottle of Corona. She didn't really like beer all that much, and there were no lime slices handy, but she'd just have to make do. She uncapped the bottle and took a long, deep swig, and then another. She pushed the IGNITE button on the front burner and the blue flame came on with a satisfying whoosh.

The beer wasn't bad at all. She took another sip and tossed the panties onto the burner. The tiny scrap of synthetic silk went up in flames and was gone in a second or two, which was a disappointment. The shorts made a nicer display, and she watched the blaze for two or three minutes, reluctantly adding the T-shirt and then, after another five minutes, the bra. The bra, which had heavy padding, smoldered for several minutes, sending up a stinky black fog of smoke.

She looked around for something else to add to the fire, and remembered Ben's shirt, still draped over the windshield of his Audi.

Ben loved expensive things. But Grace, raised above her parent's working-class bar in the nearby fishing hamlet of Cortez, could never quite get comfortable with the luxury goods that her husband had grown up with as the pampered only son of a Miami bank executive. The day she'd bought the shirt at Neiman Marcus, for $350, she'd walked away from it twice, finally forcing herself to pull the trigger and buy the damned thing.

Grace stood in the open doorway of the garage, scowling at the Audi. If the shirt was Ben's favorite, the Audi, a 2013 Spyder R8 convertible, was beyond his favorite. It was his obsession. He'd bought the Audi without consulting Grace, right after they signed the pilot deal with HGTV. Ben wouldn't disclose what he'd paid for the car, saying only that he'd "worked a deal" on it, but when she checked the prices online, she'd discovered that the thing retailed for $175,000! She'd somehow managed to swallow her resentment over not being included in the decision to buy the new car, telling herself that if Ben, who handled all the family finances, thought they could afford the car, then she shouldn't worry.

She walked around to the driver's side, snatching the shirt off the windshield. Looking down, she noticed the keys were still in the ignition.

The next thing she knew, she was using the shirt to wipe down the bucket seat's leather upholstery—just in case. She slid beneath the wheel and turned the key in the ignition, smiling as the powerful engine roared to life.

Ben didn't exactly prohibit her from driving the Audi, but he didn't encourage it either, telling her it was "a lot of car" for a woman and pointing out that her experience driving a stick shift was limited, although she'd learned to drive on her father's beat-up manual-transmission Chevy pickup.

Maybe, Grace thought, she'd just take the Audi for a spin around the neighborhood. Wouldn't that just fire Ben's rockets? She hoped he was watching from one of the upstairs windows. He'd have a stroke when he saw her behind the wheel. She eased the car into reverse, carefully backing it out of the garage.

Maneuvering an expert three-point turn, she was about to head down the driveway when the kitchen door flew open.

"Grace!" Ben yelled. "What do you think you're doing?"

"Going for a drive," she said cheerfully, raising the Corona in a jaunty salute.

"The hell you are," he barked, walking toward her. "You've been drinking and you're in no shape to be driving. Get out of my car."

"Your car?" she raised an eyebrow.

"You know what I mean," he said. "You've had your fun. This is taking things too far."

Too far? Grace revved the Audi's engine and slammed the car in first, screeching past Ben, who was a shouting, raving blur. Now she was at the edge of the patio, knocking over chaise lounges and the wrought-iron table with its jaunty green umbrella. The limpid turquoise surface of the pool was straight ahead. She closed her eyes, held her nose, and stomped the accelerator. The shock of the water was a final reminder. This was no nightmare. She was awake.

2.

Grace had grown up living above a marina, but she was only an okay swimmer. Still, she could dog-paddle and manage a serviceable backstroke when the occasion demanded. The shock of the cold water disoriented her momentarily, but seconds later she managed to kick herself free of the Audi and power up to the surface, blinking and gasping for air.

As soon as she surfaced, the enormity of what she'd just done came crashing down. She pushed her hair from her eyes and saw Ben, standing at the side of the pool, staring down at her, wild-eyed and more agitated than she'd ever seen him. "Jesus, Grace!" he shouted. "My car! What have you done to my car?"

He wasn't alone. A uniformed police officer stood at his side, training a large flashlight over the pool. Grace wished she could dive back down to the bottom, maybe hide in the Audi's trunk. Just until things got a little less crazy.

"Ma'am?" The cop was young, with close-shorn hair and a look of concern that was noticeably absent from her husband's face. "Are you all right?"

Grace coughed and brushed a strand of hair from her

face, dog-paddling to stay afloat. "I'm all right," she said cautiously, flexing her toes and examining her hands just to make sure. Not a scratch, she thought, which pleased her. After all, she was homicidal, not suicidal.

"You're not all right," Ben snapped. "You're fuckin' nuts."

"Ma'am, could you come out of the water now?" the cop asked.

Grace looked around the backyard. "Where's the slut?" she called.

The cop looked confused. "Who?"

"J'Aimee. The slut. I'm not coming out if she's still here."

"Who's Jamie?"

Grace jutted her chin in Ben's direction. "Ask him." Her legs were getting a little weary from all the dog-paddling, so she floated onto her back and stared up at the sky. It was a gorgeous evening. The clouds had cleared, and the stars sprinkled in the deep blue heavens looked so close she felt she might just reach out and pluck one. It was too bad she couldn't just float here for a long time, enjoying this view.

"Sir?" she heard the cop say.

"It's not Jamie, it's J'Aimee," Ben said. "And she's our assistant. The woman my wife assaulted earlier this evening. Grace chased her off. I don't know where she's gone."

"Our assistant?" Grace said. "I thought she was my assistant. Of course, that was before I found her assisting you earlier this evening." She turned to face the cop. "I caught them, doing it, right there in the garage. In the front seat of the Audi. So you see why I want to make sure she's gone, can't you?"

The cop was blushing now, which made him look even younger. He coughed and crossed his arms and looked over at Ben. "Is that correct?"

"No, it's not correct," Ben said. "My wife thinks she saw something she didn't, and now she's blown everything completely out of proportion."

"Blown!" Grace called, her legs pumping underwater, her voice abnormally gleeful. "You got that right, buddy. Only I wasn't the one doing the blowing, was I?"

"You're disgusting," Ben said. He turned to the cop. "She's been drinking, obviously."

The cop gave Grace a stern look. "Ma'am, have you been drinking?"

"I had half a beer," Grace said. "You want me to take a Breathalyzer? Want to draw some blood?" She held her arm above water, as though he might tap a vein right there and then.

While he was considering that, the radio clipped to his shoulder began to crackle. He turned his back to her, spoke into it briefly and then turned around again.

"I think you need to come out of that pool now," he told Grace. He turned to Ben. "You told the dispatcher you were afraid she might get hurt. Or hurt somebody else. Are you still concerned about that?"

Ben shrugged. "I suppose not."

"What about you?" the cop asked Grace. "Did your husband strike you, or threaten to harm you in any way?"

"Not really," Grace admitted.

"What about this J'Aimee person? Do I need to get a statement from her?"

Grace swam to the shallow end of the pool and pulled herself up on the coral rock patio. The May night was warm, but she shivered as the water streamed off her body.

Ben's voice was low. "That won't be necessary."

"I want to get a statement from her," Grace called, standing up. She pointed toward the hibiscus hedge. "She went that-a-way."

Her teeth were chattering and she hugged her arms around her torso. "Excuse me," she told the cop. "I'm just going to get a towel to dry off."

Grace found a thick yellow and green striped beach towel in the cabinet at the edge of the patio and wrapped it around herself. She took another towel and wound it around her head, turban-style. Suddenly, her legs felt weak. She sat, abruptly, on the edge of the only chaise lounge she hadn't mowed down on her way to the pool.

The young police officer looked down at her with an expression of unspeakable pity. "Are you sure you're all right? You didn't hit your head or anything?"

"My head is fine," Grace said, tears springing to her eyes. She couldn't say the same of her heart. Her chest felt like it might explode.

"What happens now?" Ben said, his voice gruff. He was standing ten yards away, keeping his distance so her craziness didn't rub off.

"Unless one of you wants to file a complaint, nothing happens," the cop said. "I'd suggest you take your wife inside and get her some dry clothes."

"She can get her own clothes," Ben said.

"Also, considering the, um, circumstances, I think it would be best if you did not both spend the rest of the night here," the cop went on. He looked over at Ben. "Maybe you could call a friend? Or get a motel room?"

"I'm not going anywhere!" Ben said, outraged. "This is my home." He looked over at Grace. "Besides, I can't exactly leave, since my car is currently resting on the bottom of the pool."

"Don't worry, I'm going," Grace said, struggling to her feet. She glanced in the direction of the house. She could see the lights she'd left on in their bedroom, and the kitchen light, too. The house looked enormous, like something she'd seen in a magazine layout. Or a real estate ad. It didn't look real to her. Not like a home. Nothing like a home.

The cop looked from Ben to Grace. His radio crackled again. "Are we done here?"

"We're done," Grace said wearily.

Ben stomped off in the direction of the house. A moment later, he switched off the exterior lights, throwing the yard into sudden darkness. The cop gave a nervous cough, but he didn't leave. He switched on his flashlight, but held it down at his side.

"Um," he said, and she could see that he was blushing again.

"I swear, I'm not going to do anything violent," Grace said. "I'd just like to tell you that, for whatever it's worth, I'm really a very normal, peace-loving person. I've never, ever done anything like this before."

She peered at his face, to see if he believed her.

"Look," he said hesitantly. "I didn't want to say this in front of your husband. But I'm a big fan of your blog."

"You read Gracenotes?" Grace wasn't sure if she should be embarrassed or flattered. "Really?"

"Oh yeah. I even subscribe. My girlfriend and I just moved in together, and we're fixing up our place, and we both really enjoy Gracenotes. Next weekend, we're even going to paint our bathroom ceiling the same color you painted your powder room."

"Waterfall? That is so sweet!"

"Well, we're going to cut the strength fifty percent, like you suggested in your blog," he said. "But Amy, that's my girlfriend, she's already painted the walls Cloud Cover. How do you think that will look?"

"It'll be great," Grace assured him. "That's one of my favorite whites. And Benjamin Moore is an excellent paint. I use it all the time."

Am I really discussing paint colors with a cop? Within an hour of my life imploding?

"Great," the cop said. He reached into his pocket and brought out a business card. "Hey, uh, I'm sorry about tonight. Don't quote me, but I kinda don't blame you for what you did with his car. I mean, what kind of douche bag does something like that?"

"The kind I'm married to, apparently," Grace told him. She took the card, and he held up his flashlight so she could read it. "Officer Strivecky."

"Pete," he said. "My cell phone number is on there, if you need me again tonight. I'm on shift until seven, okay?"

"Okay," she said, touched by his kindness. "Thanks for not arresting me."

"You've got a place to go?" he asked. "It's really not a good idea for you to stay here."

"Don't worry," she said, feeling a shiver run down her spine. "I'm just going to throw some things in a bag, and then I'm gone. My mom lives over on Cortez. I'll head over to her place. You couldn't pay me to spend another night here, now that I know what's been going on right under my own nose."

"I could hang around," Pete Strivecky said, gesturing in the direction of the house. "Make sure he doesn't try anything tricky."

"He won't," Grace said. "He's a douche bag, like you said, but he's not a dangerous douche bag."

He turned to go.

"Officer Strivecky? Pete?"

"Yeah?" he said, pausing at the edge of the pool, glancing down at the submerged Audi.

"Do you mind if I ask how old you are? You look too young to be a police officer."

He laughed. "I get that all the time. It's the red hair and

freckles. I'm twenty-six. Been on the force for three years now."

"Twenty-six," Grace said wistfully. "So young . . ." She nodded her head in the direction of the house. "Seems like a long, long time ago."

"Yes ma'am," he said.

She had an idea. "Hey. Send me a photo of your bathroom after you're done, will you? For the blog? I'd love to see how it turns out."

"I'll do that," he said. "And you take care."

An open bottle of Chivas Regal stood on the kitchen counter. She could hear the sound of the television coming from the media room. The door was firmly closed, but he'd turned up the volume on the surround sound, and she recognized Bruce Willis's voice. He was watching one of the *Die Hard* movies again. For Ben, watching the bad guys blow up buildings and try to shoot down airliners just never got old.

She ran up the back staircase to their bedroom. On her side of the his-and-hers bathroom suite, she peeled out of her sopping wet shorts and T-shirt, stopping only to drape them neatly over the towel bar beside her Jacuzzi. She grabbed a cosmetic bag from a drawer in her dressing table and swept in some random toiletries: her shampoo and conditioner, deodorant, and her vitamins. Her hand hovered over the Clomid pill bottle. She'd been scheduled to start her second round of the fertility drug at the start of her next period, in two weeks.

It had taken Grace two years to talk Ben into seeing a fertility specialist. An only child herself, she'd always wanted children. Ben claimed to want them, too, although he didn't see why they couldn't just "wait and see" if she'd get pregnant what he called "the natural way." Finally, two months ago, he'd relented. "Now or never," was the way Ben looked at it.

"Never," Grace said now, tossing the pills into the trash. She wondered if he'd already started sleeping with J'Aimee when she'd begun taking the Clomid. But she couldn't think about that right now. What was done was done. And she—and Ben—were done.

Standing in her walk-in closet, she dressed quickly in a pair of white jeans and a favorite navy-blue knit top. She slid her feet into a pair of Jack Rogers sandals. Opening a suitcase on the top of the island that housed her folded clothes, she dumped a handful of random things: panties and bras, some shorts and tops, and a pair of jeans. She threw her running shoes and socks on top of the clothes, then zipped the suitcase.

Grace stepped into the bedroom and looked around. One last time, she told herself. At the silver framed photos of her and Ben in happier times, at the paintings she'd collected and hung on the walls, at the gorgeous custom-made linen drapes. It was the nicest room she'd ever owned, and she was getting ready to walk right out of it.

She found her purse on the tufted velvet bench at the foot of the bed and slipped the strap over her shoulder. Picking her suitcase up, she made her way back down the stairs. She stopped in her office, shoving her laptop computer and a handful of file folders into an oversized tote bag. She dumped her camera bag on top, hefted the tote onto her other shoulder, and made her way awkwardly to the kitchen door.

The Chivas bottle was gone from the kitchen counter and the door to the media room was still closed. From within, Bruce Willis was kicking ass and taking names.

Grace paused by the door. She raised her hand to knock, but changed her mind. She went out the kitchen door, walked to the garage, and got into her own car, a four-year-old Subaru. "Now or never," she whispered aloud.

3.

Grace was idly switching channels on the big wall-mounted television at the Sandbox, her mother's bar on Cortez, a spot only seven miles, but light years, away from Grace's house on Sand Dollar Lane.

"Leave it on channel four," Rochelle said. "Please."

Grace gave her a look. "You know I always watch the morning news on four," Rochelle said. "I hate that weather guy's hair on channel eight."

Grace gave a martyred sigh and did as she was told, turning back to her mother's favorite channel, just in time to see a reporter standing in front of her very own front yard.

"Holy crap," Rochelle whispered. "Is this what I think it is?"

"Good morning," said the reporter, a black woman who'd been a local television mainstay for as long as Grace could remember. Camryn Nobles. Grace stared at the television. How the hell had Camryn Nobles gotten past security?

"I'm at the exclusive gated community of Gulf Vista on

Siesta Key, where police were summoned this morning to what they termed an escalating case of domestic disturbance. But what makes this story newsworthy, in fact, fascinating, is that the principals involved in the incident are a nationally known domestic goddess—and her husband—or is it safe to say, soon to be ex-husband?"

The camera panned to show a pale-pink stucco two-story Spanish colonial revival mansion with red tile roof sprawling across a swath of emerald green lawn dotted with colorful beds of tropical flowers and half a dozen black-and-white Sarasota County sheriff's deputy cars, as well as a fire truck, an emergency rescue ambulance, and a large black tow truck. A traffic helicopter from the Tampa CBS affiliate droned overhead.

"You're a media event," Rochelle said, and Grace shot her another look.

"If these palatial house and grounds look familiar to many of you," Camryn Nobles said, her voice lowering to a confidential tone, "it's because this is the home of lifestyle blogger Grace Stanton, who writes the wildly popular Gracenotes blog. The house has been featured in numerous national publications, and Ms. Stanton has been a frequent guest on network shows like *Oprah, Ellen,* and, yes, even the *Today* show, and of course our own *Suncoast Morning!* where she's been practically a fixture over the past two years, as a lifestyle expert."

Now Camryn was talking again, strolling around to the side of the house, down a long coral-rock driveway toward the rear of the Stanton mansion.

"Grace Stanton is a successful interior designer and a hometown girl who grew up in modest circumstances in nearby Cortez," Camryn said. "After moving to South Florida and marrying, she had a thriving design practice before moving back here to the Suncoast in 2009. Husband Ben, forty-four, was an advertising executive who gave up

his career two years ago in order to devote all his energies
to maximizing his wife's burgeoning lifestyle business.
Grace and Ben Stanton are fixtures on the local social
scene; in fact, they hosted a charity party for the local children's shelter right here in this lovely poolside setting
back in October. But authorities say this bucolic scene
turned ugly sometime after midnight. Here's the tape police have released, of the panicky 911 phone call they re-
ceived at one fifteen A.M. from Ben Stanton. And we want
to apologize to our viewers, in advance, for the somewhat
graphic language in this tape."

*"Yeah, I'm gonna need some assistance here. My, uh,
my wife, she's out of control."*

The female 911 operator sounded bored. *"Sir, are you
in physical danger?"*

*"What? I don't know. She went crazy on me. I've never
seen her like this. Look, I think you better get an officer
over here before she does hurt somebody."*

Shrieks were clearly audible in the background. And
then came Ben Stanton's muffled voice.

*"Grace, what are you doing? This isn't funny. Are you
crazy? What the . . . Get the hell away from there!"*

In the background came the sound of a car door slamming, then a high-powered motor revving, tires squealing
across pavement. And then, a loud splash.

*"Christ! Grace, what the hell have you done? Jesus
H! . . ."*

"Sir? Do you have a life-threatening situation there?"

Stanton's voice, when he came back on the line, was
grim. *"If she hasn't already drowned, I'll kill the bitch
myself."*

"Turn it off, please," Grace said, turning her back to the
television.

Rochelle dialed down the volume, but she kept watching.

Camryn was back on camera, walking toward a patio

area lined with a lush hedge of sea grapes. Graceful coconut palms and hibiscus shrubs were scattered about the
patio, which included a fully outfitted kitchen and thatch-
roofed tiki bar.

The reporter gestured in the direction of a two-story,
three-bay garage. "The police won't say what sparked the
altercation between Grace and Ben Stanton last night, but
I spoke off camera to a neighbor who claims to have overheard what she termed 'a spirited exchange' between the
married couple last night. That neighbor says the source of
the problem was Mrs. Stanton's stunning twenty-six-year-
old female assistant, who has been living in a garage apartment on this property for some months now. The neighbor
also says that in the early morning hours before dawn today, that assistant, whose name we aren't divulging, fled
in terror through that hedge." Camryn pointed to the sea
grapes, "wrapped only in a beach towel."

"Neither of the Stantons were available for comment at
airtime," Camryn went on, still walking toward the patio,
"But despite the lack of witness statements, or cooperation
from the parties involved, there are some simply inescap-
able conclusions we can draw about what went down here
last night."

The camera pulled back to show a three-car garage,
with all three parking bays empty, and then panned over
toward the swimming pool, a shimmering free-form turquoise oasis set on a patio of more coral rock. The shallow end of the pool had coral rock steps that descended
into a separate, enclosed whirlpool spa. And the deep end?

Camryn Nobles stood at the edge of the pool and looked
down, the camera following her gaze. A lime-green canvas beach umbrella floated tranquilly on the surface of the
water, as did four chartreuse vinyl lounge cushions. Totally
submerged and barely visible beneath the water was an
ominous-looking oblong black form.

"And that," Camryn said, her voice somber, "appears to be Ben Stanton's 2013 Audi Spyder convertible, which retails for approximately 175,000 dollars."

Rochelle Davenport pointed the remote control and finally, mercifully, clicked it off.

"You really drove a car worth 175,000 dollars into the pool?" Rochelle asked her daughter.

Grace shrugged. "I doubt he paid that much for it. Knowing Ben, he worked some kind of advertising trade-off with the dealer."

"This is just so unlike you," Rochelle said. "I mean, I don't blame you for what you did, but it's just so not you."

"Temporary insanity," Grace said. "That's the only explanation I can think of."

"You could have drowned," Rochelle said. "Did you think of that? You'd have left me a childless widow."

"And then Ben could have collected on that two-million-dollar life insurance policy we bought last year," Grace muttered. "I gotta change that."

"It was a dumb thing to do," Rochelle insisted. "Seriously."

"I couldn't have drowned. The top was still down," Grace said, suddenly returning to her normal, logical self. "I guess it got kind of hot in that garage, while she was . . ."

"Giving him a blow job?" Rochelle said helpfully.

"Yeah. In the front seat of the Audi."

"I also can't believe Ben just let you drive it into the pool," Rochelle said. "How exactly did that happen?"

"I can't discuss that right now," Grace said, staring moodily into her iced tea glass. "It makes my head hurt."

Rochelle reached behind the bar for the industrial-sized bottle of ibuprofen she kept there, shook two into her hand, and handed them to her daughter.

"Thanks," Grace said, swallowing the pills. "Have you

got any food around here? I've always heard that heartbreak kills your appetite, but I haven't eaten in twelve hours, and, I swear, I could gnaw my arm off right now."

Rochelle pushed one of the plastic laminated menus across the bar.

Grace looked down at the Sandbox menu, which, as far as she knew, hadn't changed in at least fifteen years. "Buffalo wings. Stuffed potato skins. Stuffed potato skins with Buffalo-wing sauce. Onion rings. Fried oysters. Fried shrimp." She looked up at her mother. "Seriously? How are you still alive, eating this stuff all this time?"

"I don't eat this crap," Rochelle said, nonplussed. "You kidding me? I'd be big as a damned house."

She allowed herself a satisfying glance in the mirror over the back bar. At fifty-nine, Rochelle was proud of her still-trim figure. She took good care of herself, slathered herself with sunscreen before taking her two-mile walk along Bradenton Beach every morning, colored her hair a soft brown at home, and allowed herself a single glass of heart-healthy red wine or the occasional beer most evenings. She'd quit her pack-a-day smoking when Grace was still a baby, and her doctor said she had the bone density of an eighteen-year-old.

"I microwave myself a nice Lean Cuisine for dinner, usually. And for breakfast, I juice."

"You juice? As a verb?"

"Don't get snotty with me," Rochelle said. She nodded at the oversized Oster blender on the back bar. "Felipe, this real nice Mexican guy, comes in here with his soccer team on Sundays, his mom runs a produce stand at the Red Barn, and he brings me all kinds of fresh produce. Spinach, kale, chayote, strawberries, pineapples, mangoes. Herbs, too. I like mint and ginger. I put it in with everything."

"That doesn't sound too bad, actually," Grace admitted.

"You got anything like that you could fix up for me? Not kale," she said, wrinkling her nose. "But any of that other stuff?"

"Sorry," Rochelle said. "I used up the last of the fresh stuff this morning. I could maybe make you a sandwich. Would a BLT offend your delicate sensibilities?"

"That'd be great," Grace said, resting her cheek against the bar and folding her arms over her head. Her shoulders heaved, and she let out a muffled sob. It was the first time Rochelle had seen her cry since she was a teenager, and it wrenched her heart just as it had back then.

Rochelle hesitated, but then reached over and smoothed her daughter's mussed hair. "Don't worry, sweetie. We'll fix this. We'll figure it out."

Grace raised her head and looked at Rochelle, tears streaming down her cheeks. "Fix it? That's exactly what Ben said, 'we can fix this.' And then he admitted it wasn't the first time. How do we figure this out, Mom? I loved him. I thought he loved me. But it was all a lie. Everything was a lie. What do I do now?"

Rochelle handed her a paper towel. "Blow your nose. Dry your tears. Eat something. And then we'll call your Uncle Dennis and take the bastard to the cleaners."

"Uncle Dennis is a real estate lawyer," Grace said, sniffling. "He doesn't do divorces."

"No, but he's been divorced twice himself, so he'll know who we should call, and who we should avoid."

Grace took a gulp of tea. "I'm not even sure I want a divorce."

"You're kidding," Rochelle said. "You caught Ben having sex in your garage with your assistant, who he's surely been screwing at your house all these months, and you're not sure it's over?"

"I don't know," Grace wailed. "This is not the way I thought my life would go. I don't understand any of this.

I thought I would have a forever marriage, like yours and Daddy's."

Rochelle considered this, started to say something, then changed her mind. Now was not the time.

"Have you talked to Ben since last night?"

"No."

"Any plans to talk to him?"

Grace shrugged. "I've got to go over there and pick up some more clothes pretty soon. And I'll have to figure out what to do about the blog, and the HGTV pilot and all the rest of it."

Rochelle busied herself putting together her daughter's sandwich. She popped two slices of bread into the toaster, slapped some bacon on the griddle, and picked up a fat red Ruskin tomato from a bowl on the back bar. She had the knife poised to slice it when Grace spoke up.

"Could you peel that, please?"

Her mother shot her a look of annoyance. "I fixed you a million BLTs in your childhood, and now, suddenly, you have to have your tomatoes peeled? La-de-damn-da."

Grace stood up and came around the bar. "Never mind. I'll make it myself if it's that big a deal."

"It's not a big deal. I just don't get why it's necessary. The peel has the most vitamins."

"That's not true," Grace said flatly, taking the knife from her mother and proceeding to pare the skin from the tomato.

Rochelle stood back with her hands on her hips. "Who says it's not true? It's absolutely true."

"According to who?"

"I forget," Rochelle said stubbornly. "Maybe I heard it on one of those cooking shows."

Grace shook her head and reached into the refrigerator for a head of lettuce. She peeled a leaf from the head and gave a martyred sigh.

"What now? You don't like my lettuce?"

"I'm just not crazy about iceberg," Grace said. "Romaine is so much tastier. And prettier, not to mention better for you, since we're talking about vitamins."

"I like iceberg," Rochelle said, her tone frosty. "It's what I've always bought. It was always good enough for you up until now."

Grace fixed her with a look. "Are we going to get into this again? I'm sorry, Mom, if I like nice things. Sorry if it somehow offends you that I outgrew my childhood taste for Kraft macaroni and cheese and frozen Tater Tots and casseroles made with cream of mushroom soup and canned onion rings. And Asti Spumante." She shuddered involuntarily at this last listing.

"That chicken casserole used to be your favorite," Rochelle said. "You insisted I make it for your birthday dinner every year."

"I was a kid," Grace said. "I grew up and my tastes changed. Refined, if you will."

Rochelle rolled her eyes and built the sandwich. She placed it on a plate, deftly cut it in half on the diagonal, and handed it to Grace.

"Thanks," Grace said. She took the sandwich and moved back to her barstool, chewing slowly.

Rochelle wiped the bread crumbs from the cutting board. "This split-up could get pretty messy, pretty fast, you know. Ben is involved in every aspect of your business. You can walk away from him, but can you walk away from everything you've built up in the business? Not to mention the house?"

Grace shrugged to indicate she had no answers, and kept chewing.

"Counseling?" Rochelle offered. Grace shook her head violently and took another bite of her sandwich, and then a sip of her iced tea.

"All right," her mother said, glancing meaningfully at the neon Budweiser sign that hung over the mirrored bar back. "It's after eleven now. My lunch trade is gonna start trickling in here pretty soon."

"I can take a hint," Grace said, finishing off the last of her sandwich. She pushed the empty plate aside and stood. "I'm gonna go upstairs to my old room and try to get some work done. I'm doing a giveaway of this hideous Tuscan pottery on Monday, and I've got to write that blog post and figure out what I'm writing about tomorrow."

She picked up her laptop case. "You've got Wi-Fi, right?"

Rochelle wrinkled her brow. "I guess. They hooked up some kind of Internet doohickey when I changed cable providers back in the spring."

"Password?"

"Who knows?"

"Never mind, I'll figure it out myself," Grace said. She headed for the stairway that led to the family's upstairs living area, and then stopped and poked her head around the doorway. "If Ben calls here looking for me, you haven't seen me and don't know where I am."

"Gotcha," Rochelle said. "I hope he does call. I'll give the son of a bitch an earful."

"Thanks," Grace said, offering a wan smile. "It's good to know you've got my back."

"I do," Rochelle assured her. "I'm your wingman, right?"

Grace pushed the bedroom door open with her hip. She'd decorated the room herself, at the age of fourteen, and not one single thing had changed in all these years.

She'd been in her Laura Ashley phase then. She'd longed for the pink and white striped wallpaper she'd seen in a *House Beautiful* layout, but with no money to spend, she'd laboriously taped and painted pink stripes over the cheap knotty pine-paneled walls that her mother had previously slathered with white paint. Grace found a crappy $9.99 faux-mahogany four-poster bed at the Salvation Army and painted it white, then stenciled a sappy design of green vines, pink daisies, and blue ribbons across the headboard.

Grace kicked at the worn and stained beige wall-to-wall carpet on the floor. She'd begged and pleaded with her father to let her rip up that carpet—the same stuff that covered every surface in their apartment, but Butch had been adamant. "Do you know how much money I spent on this stuff?"

She settled onto the faded pink chintz bedspread and opened her laptop, clicking onto the logo for Gracenotes. She reread the post she'd written the previous evening, which seemed like something from a previous life. There were already forty-seven comments posted. Had any of her readers seen the news about the flamboyant scene at her house? She decided against reading the comments. Maybe later.

Instead, she concentrated on writing Monday's post, going ahead with the topic she'd already settled on a week ago: how and where to find great deals on discounted designer home fabrics. Soon she was typing away, copying and pasting images of favorite fabrics and room settings, copying Web site links, losing herself in the process of creation.

When she looked up from her work, she realized that two hours had passed. Her cell phone, lying on the nightstand, had not rung, and no beeps had signaled an incoming text message. She'd halfway expected Ben to call, either downcast and contrite, or furious and full of threats. The silence seemed ominous. No matter. She glared at the phone, daring it to ring. She would not call him. Not ever. Let the swine call and beg her to come crawling back.

Grace went back to her work. She checked for typos, misspellings, links that didn't work, pictures that were improperly sized. Finally satisfied with her work, she pulled up the Gracenotes blog page, and clicked on the sign-in and password buttons.

A red highlighted italicized sentence flashed on the screen.

Invalid password. Try again?

She frowned and winced as she retyped the password. *GracenBen4ever.*

Invalid password. Check for misspellings?

Not possible. She typed the word again, with the same results.

Reset password?

She checked her e-mail, waiting for the message to alert her that her new password had been sent. But when she opened the e-mail, she stared down at the message in disbelief.

New password may not be reset. Invalid username. Please contact technical support if you believe this message has been sent in error.

She fumed and dialed the number provided, waiting on hold for ten minutes. Finally, a young man who identified himself as Hans came on the line.

"Hello," she said briskly. "My name is Grace Stanton, and I write a blog called Gracenotes. I've just spent half an hour trying to get access to my dashboard so I can write a new post, but I keep getting error messages, and, finally, I got a message telling me that I can't set a new password, because I have an invalid username. But it's not invalid. I've been writing this blog for three years under the same name. So I can't understand what is happening."

"Let me just check that," Hans said. She could hear his fingertips flying over a keyboard. "Just a moment," he said, putting her on hold.

A moment later he was back on the line. "Mrs. Stanton?"

"Ms. Stanton," Grace said pointedly.

"Right. Um. The thing is, you don't have access to the blog dashboard."

"I know that," she said sharply. "That's why I'm calling you. Because I need access. It's my blog."

"Wellll," he said. "From what I can tell, the domain owner has changed the user sign-on and password. That would explain why you're locked out."

"That can't be," Grace said, feeling her face get hot. "I'm the domain owner. The blog is Gracenotes. I'm Grace Stanton."

There was a long meaningful silence on the other end of the line. "Actually," Hans said, "according to our records, the domain owner is Ben Stanton. And apparently, he's changed the access."

"He can't do that," Grace cried. "Change it back. It's my blog. I started it, I write it, I own it. And I want you to change it so I can have access to my own blog."

"I'm sorry, Ms. Stanton, but I don't have the authority to do that," Hans said. "Now, is there anything else I can help you with?"

Downstairs, in the bar, Rochelle was pouring a longneck Sweetwater Pale when she heard an unearthly shriek coming from the direction of upstairs.

Frank, a mailman who'd just come off his shift, gave her a questioning look.

"My daughter," Rochelle said apologetically. "She's having some marital issues."

4.

Three days had passed since Grace had walked out of the house on Sand Dollar Lane.

They were three of the longest, most miserable days of her life. During the days, she tried to help out around the Sandbox, working behind the bar, waiting tables, even doing a brief stint as a short-order cook, until her mother unceremoniously fired her from that job after she caught Grace substituting ground turkey for ground chuck in the bar's signature Sandbox burger.

"I know you mean well," Rochelle said, ordering her out of the kitchen. "But my customers don't care about saturated fats or sodium or antioxidants. They just want a big, greasy, salty burger on a puffy, white, highly processed white bun. With maybe a slab of gooey yellow cheese on top. And they definitely don't want a side order of smug advice about healthy dining."

Evenings, Grace locked herself up in her bedroom, spending hours writing blog entries she couldn't even post. When she finished writing and editing, she slipped out to the second-story deck overlooking the Cortez marina. Growing up, she'd hated that marina. She hated the stink of the diesel fuel burned by the boats and the shrill cries of seagulls wheeling overhead as the shrimpers and commercial fishermen returned to the docks with their catches. She'd hated the greasy water lapping against the seawall, and the constant ebb and flow of fishermen and regulars who regarded the Sandbox as their home away from home.

Most of all, Grace hated the fact of where she lived. In high school, the guys she dated thought it was awesome that she lived right on the water, and above a bar! But she didn't want to live on a marina. She wanted a regular suburban house, with a grassy green lawn, and although she loved her parents, she longed for a father who worked in an office and wore a necktie, with a mother who stayed home and played bridge and got her hair done every Thursday.

The only ties Butch Davenport owned were bolo ties, which he wore with his ever-present violently colored Hawaiian shirts. As for Rochelle, who cut her own hair, Grace was fairly sure she didn't even know how to play bridge, although she was a demon at pinochle.

For some reason, the sights and sounds of the marina, and the bay that flowed beneath the weathered gray boards of the docks, were now oddly comforting. When sleep wouldn't come, and it rarely did, she crept out to the deck, in her nightgown, and sat for hours, her knees tucked to her chest, staring off at the sparkling black water and the shadowy hulks of the fishing vessels tied up at the dock.

That first morning Grace had moved home, Rochelle found her like that when she arose at seven to make coffee.

Her mother sank into the chair next to her, wordlessly handing her a steaming mug. Grace nodded her thanks and sipped.

"Gonna be another hot day," Rochelle said finally, looking at the pink-tinged sky.

"Hotter than the hinges of hell," Grace agreed, repeating one of Butch's favorite sayings.

"You sleep any?" Rochelle asked.

"A little," Grace lied.

"I've got some Ambien, if you want," her mother offered.

Grace stared at her, shocked. The only drugs she'd ever known her mother to take were baby aspirin.

"Don't look at me like that," Rochelle said. "The doctor gave 'em to me, after your daddy died. I only took the one. Slept for fourteen hours straight, and when I finally did wake up, I'd eaten most of a pecan pie somebody brought to the house after the funeral. I looked it up on the computer. It's a real thing. Sleep eating, they call it. Hell's bells, I eat enough when I'm awake. I don't need a pill that makes you eat a whole pie without even remembering it."

Grace was forced to smile.

"You hear anything from the asshole?" Rochelle asked.

"Not a word," Grace said.

"Are you okay for money?" Rochelle asked.

"For now," Grace lied.

Rochelle knew it for the lie it was, but didn't call her daughter out on it. Instead, she sighed and gave Grace a sideways glance. "I think you better give your Uncle Dennis a call."

When she couldn't access her blog, Grace reluctantly called Ben, leaving a voice mail when he didn't pick up. Three days later, Ben still wasn't returning Grace's phone calls. But he'd been a busy little worker bee during that time. He'd changed the PINs for their joint checking and savings accounts, and although she'd gone to the bank in person, twice, and argued with the branch manager, she still couldn't make them understand that her estranged husband was freezing her out of her own hard-earned money. He'd canceled her AmEx and Visa cards. And when she'd gone to her gym to try to work out some of her frustrations in a Zumba class, she'd been greeted with the unwelcome news that her membership had been terminated, since the gym was no longer able to debit her checking account for her fees.

"Call Dickie Murphree," her Uncle Dennis said, when she finally got him on the phone. "I finally got smart and hired him the second time around. He's the best divorce lawyer in town. Didn't the two of you go to high school together?"

"Dickie! Of course," Grace said, her black mood lifting, just a little. "That's a great idea. Dickie took me on my first real car date. I haven't seen him in a couple years."

"Give him my best when you call," Dennis said. "And tell him I hope I never have to see him again. No offense."

She called the law offices of Murphree-Baggett-Hopkins twice a day, for two days in a row, each time asking the receptionist to please have Dickie call her about an urgent matter.

"He's in court," the receptionist told her. "I know, but I'm an old friend," she said, giving the woman her maiden name. Might as well start getting used to it again, she thought glumly.

Things really were getting pretty dire.

As much as she dreaded another confrontation, she had to talk to Ben. Aside from business matters that had to be settled, she needed more clothes, her treasured interior design books and magazine files, and the macro lens for her camera. Also panties.

Finally, she decided on an ambush. Grace dressed carefully for the outing, as carefully as she could considering the fact that her hastily packed suitcase contained three faded T-shirts, two pairs of yoga pants, her jogging shorts, and a pair of skinny white jeans that she hadn't actually been able to fit into in two years.

Now though, the jeans zipped with ease. Heartache, she thought ruefully, was the ultimate diet aid.

She tried calling Ben one more time, and when her message went directly to voice mail, she resolutely got behind the wheel of the Subaru and drove the ten miles to Siesta Key, her stomach roiling so badly that once, a mile from the house, she had to pull off onto the side of the road to barf on a white oleander bush.

On the way over, Grace rehearsed her lines.

"Hello, Ben. I know you've been avoiding me, and you're probably still furious about me driving the Audi into the pool, but hey! I'm still furious about finding you and J'Aimee doing the nasty in the front seat, so why don't we just call it a tie and figure out a way to get through all this with some courtesy and civility?"

She thought that was an excellent opener. And she would follow it up by letting him know that he would absolutely HAVE to unfreeze the bank accounts and credit cards and restore her access to the blog.

"It's my business, Ben. It's called Gracenotes, for God's sake. Your preventing me from participating in it is foolish and shortsighted."

That would get him. Ben was *all* about business. Since he dealt with all the blog's advertisers, he would certainly want to keep them happy to keep the ad dollars flowing. Right? Surely he would be reasonable, now that he'd had some time to think things over rationally. Right?

Up ahead, Grace spotted the thick emerald green embankment that meant she was approaching Gulf Vista, their subdivision. A stately row of royal palms, underplanted with thick beds of asparagus ferns, lined both sides of the road, and a classic arched white stucco bridge crossed over a canal. A hundred yards ahead, she spotted the security gate and felt a sharp, unexpected wave of panic so strong that she had to clutch the steering wheel to keep from turning around and fleeing in the opposite direction.

Stop this! She told herself sternly. This is a business transaction. No need for emotion. Be strong.

She pulled the car alongside the electronic card reader and swiped her plastic key card through it, waiting patiently for the heavy iron gates to slide open.

Nothing. The gate didn't move. She wiped the card on the leg of her jeans, a trick she'd used many times when the finicky card reader refused to open sesame.

Grace tried three more times with the same results. Despite the fact that she had the Subaru's air-conditioner thermostat on the subarctic setting, she could already feel sweat beading up on her forehead. Her mouth was dry, but her hands as they gripped the key card were clammy.

The driver of the black Lexus behind her car tapped his horn impatiently, but Grace had no place to go. The gate wouldn't open, and there were two more cars behind the Lexus.

The driver tapped his horn again. Finally, near tears, Grace rolled the window down and leaned out to address the situation. "I'm sorry," she called, waving her key card. "It's not working. Can you back up so that I can back up?"

The driver, an older man with silver hair, gestured impatiently. Finally, all three cars backed up so that Grace could get out of the line. She parked her car on the shoulder of the road and went to the guard shack, whose dark tinted windows obscured those inside. She felt limp and defeated, and she hadn't even gotten to the house yet, a destination she was already dreading.

She tapped on the guard-shack window, and finally a uniformed security guard, a middle-aged guy with a graying military crew cut, opened the door. She was grateful for the cold blast of air-conditioning. The guard stepped outside and Grace recognized him at once.

"Oh, hi, Sheldon," she said, favoring him with a smile. "I'm so glad you're on duty." She held up her key card. "I'm

Grace Stanton. My key card won't work. Can you fix it for me?"

He frowned slightly, taking the card, turning it over and over to examine it closer. "Looks okay."

"I know, but it won't work," Grace said.

"Hang on a minute," Sheldon said. He stepped back into the guard booth and closed the door. A mosquito buzzed around her face, and she swatted it away. The sun beat down on her head, and she was sure she was about to melt.

The door opened, but only an inch or two. The security guard's friendly smile had vanished. Now he glowered at her. "Sorry. I can't help you."

"What?" Grace said, startled. "Why not?"

"I can't discuss it," Sheldon said, and he started to close the door again, but before he could, Grace grabbed the doorknob.

"Wait a minute," she said, feeling her face growing redder by the moment. "What's going on here? Why won't you fix my key card?"

He glanced around, to make sure he couldn't be overheard. As if!

"I can't help you because your card has been deactivated."

"That's ridiculous!" Grace said. "Is this because of . . . my marital situation? Did my husband call up here and tell you people to keep me out? He has no right! I live here. At 27 Sand Dollar Lane."

"I don't make the rules, ma'am," Sheldon said. "All's I know is, according to the computer, you are no longer listed as a resident of Gulf Vista."

"He can't do that," Grace said, her teeth gritted. "Please! Look, I don't want to make a scene . . ."

"Then don't," Sheldon said. He held up a walkie-talkie. "My supervisor told me to tell you that if you have a problem with the card situation, you should contact an attorney.

Until we have some kind of a legal document stating otherwise, I can't let you in." He reached around and gently removed Grace's hand from the doorknob. "Sorry."

Grace heard a light beep of a car horn. A white Lincoln rolled up beside her and the passenger-side window slid down. Anita McKenna, an older woman she knew slightly from the country club, gave her a friendly smile. "Hi! It's Grace, right? Are you having car problems? Anything I can do to help?"

"Anita! Hello," Grace said eagerly, stepping closer to the car. "Actually, I am having a little issue . . ."

There was a tap on her shoulder. She turned to find Sheldon standing directly beside her. "Mrs. Stanton? My supervisor thinks it would be a good idea if you would just move along now." He held up his walkie-talkie again.

Grace felt her spine stiffen. "I was just . . ."

Anita McKenna looked from Sheldon to Grace. "Oh," she said. "My goodness. I didn't realize." The window slid up again, and the Lincoln breezed through the gate.

She called Dickie Murphree's office twice more on her way to back to Cortez. Finally, his receptionist allowed her to leave a voice mail message.

"Dickie," she said, fighting back tears. "It's Grace Davenport. I've been calling and calling. I really need to talk to you. I've left Ben. Maybe you saw it on the news? Now he's frozen our bank accounts, cut off my credit cards— he's even fixed it so I can't get back to our house to pick up my clothes and things. Please, Dickie. Please call me."

Grace was pulling into the crushed-shell parking lot at the Sandbox when her cell phone rang. She saw that the caller was Murphree-Baggett-Hopkins.

"Hello?"

"Hiya, Gracie," Dickie said. "I just got your message. Sorry it took me so long to call you back. I'm in trial this week, and the damned judge just now cut us loose for a lunch break. How's your Uncle Dennis?"

"He's fine," Grace said. "He sends his best. Look, Dickie, if you listened to my message, you know I'm in big trouble. When can I come see you? To talk about my situation?"

"Welllll," Dickie drawled. "I'm not sure that's a good idea."

"Why not?" Grace asked, stunned. "Uncle Dennis said you're the best divorce lawyer in town."

"Hell of a guy, your uncle," Dickie said, chuckling. "He sure gets himself in some damned interesting jams, doesn't he?"

"Why isn't it a good idea for me to come see you?"

"Awwww, Grace," Dickie drawled. "You know I think the world of you, don't you? We had some good times, way back there in high school, didn't we? You broke my heart when you threw me over for that basketball player, sophomore year. What was that guy's name? He went on to play college ball at FSU, didn't he? It was years before I got over you."

"That's sweet, Dickie," she said impatiently. "His name was Calvin Becker. Could we discuss current affairs? Like my divorce?"

"The thing is, we can't talk, Grace," Dickie said. "It ain't even really proper for me to be talking to you right now, but I figured I owe you an explanation."

"What are you explaining?" Grace asked.

"That I can't represent you. Because I already agreed to represent Ben."

Grace put the phone down in her lap. She closed her eyes and rested her head against the steering wheel, utterly defeated.

"Grace?" Dickie's voice rose faintly from the phone. "Grace? Are you there?"

She pushed the disconnect button.

5.

"I take it things didn't go well with the asshole," Rochelle said, pouring her a large glass of iced tea and pushing it across the bar. "Drink that. It's sweetened. You're losing weight so fast it's starting to scare me."

Grace took a sip of the tea and sucked on an ice cube. "I never got to see Ben. I couldn't get through the security gate. He had my key card deactivated."

"Bastard," Rochelle said, pouring her own glass of iced tea. The lunchtime rush hour was over, and only two people remained at opposite ends of the bar, one watching the Rays game on the TV, the other staring intently down at his smartphone.

"Did your uncle's lawyer ever call you back?" Rochelle asked.

Grace stirred her tea with a straw. "Dickie Murphree. Yeah, he called. But I can't hire him."

"Why not? Just because you dated years ago?"

"I can't hire him because Ben beat me to it," Grace said, lifting her eyes to meet her mother's. "Yeah. Ben has already hired the best divorce lawyer in town. Face it, Mom. I'm screwed."

"No, you're not," Rochelle said. "The Yellow Pages are full of divorce lawyers. You can't swing a dead cat in this town without hitting a lawyer. We just need to find you the right one." She drummed her fingers on the bar's scarred wooden surface. A minute later, she disappeared into the kitchen.

When she reemerged, she handed her daughter a well-worn business card.

"Mitzi Stillwell, Attorney at Law?" Grace asked, lifting one eyebrow. "Who's she?"

"A lawyer I know," Rochelle said. "Give her a call."

Mitzi Stillwell didn't waste much time with niceties. She'd been practicing domestic law for a dozen years, and she generally believed her clients needed the truth more than they needed coddling.

She listened for fifteen minutes while Grace recounted her tale of what she now thought of as the meltdown, nodding and occasionally jotting some words onto a legal yellow pad.

"So," Grace said, when she'd finished. "What do you think? Can you help me?"

Mitzi tapped the pen against the legal pad. "You walked away from your own home—even though your husband was the one screwing around on you?"

"Yes," Grace said.

Mitzi cocked her head and a strand of gray-flecked dark hair fell across one eye. She was in her early fifties now, but when her hair started graying twenty years earlier, she'd chosen not to color it—just to give herself the look of an older, more experienced jurist. At home, she favored bright colors and clothes designed to show off the figure she worked hard at maintaining, but in the courtroom, Mitzi mostly chose expensively tailored business suits in neutral colors, with just enough feminine detailing to remind her clients—and prospective jurors—that she was a woman in charge.

"You know, Grace, it's supposed to work the other way around. You're supposed to kick his butt out of the house."

"Sorry," Grace said. "I'm new at all this. It never occurred to me to ask him to leave. Anyway, after I sank his car, I'd pretty much made the statement I needed to."

Mitzi laughed. "I've handled hundreds of divorces over the years, but you're my first client to drown a car." She half stood and bowed in Grace's direction. "Awesome. Although probably not prudent."

She sat down again and looked at her notes. "How are you for money?"

"I'm broke," Grace admitted. "Ben froze our bank accounts. He canceled my credit cards. I had to borrow money from my mom to buy gas to drive over here today."

The lawyer nodded. "Nothing unusual about that. We'll have to try to get the court to order your husband to come to a temporary financial agreement between the two of you."

Mitzi doodled something on her legal pad, then considered whether or not to share some unhappy news with her client. She hesitated to pile more bad news on Grace Stanton, whose life had taken an ugly turn for the worse ever since she'd drowned her husband's sports car two weeks earlier.

Grace caught the meaning of her lawyer's pitying glance.

"What?" Grace said, tucking a lock of hair behind one ear. "You're giving me that look."

"What look?" Mitzi asked.

"It's the look doctors give their patients before they tell them they've got an incurable disease. The look my college professor gave me right before he announced I'd pulled a D in statistics. The look that Ben gave me right before he admitted that night with J'Aimee wasn't the first. Come on, Mitzi. Spit it out."

Mitzi sighed. "Your divorce case has been assigned a judge, and we've got a date for an initial hearing."

"But that's good news, right? The faster we get things settled, the faster I can get my life back on track."

"It would be good news," Mitzi agreed. "Except that you drew Stackpole."

"Who's he? One of Ben's old drinking buddies?"

"If only," Mitzi said. "If we could prove he had some kind of association with your ex, that would be grounds for recusal, which would be great. But I doubt Ben and Cedric Stackpole have ever met."

"Then, why is he bad news?"

"Because," Mitzi said, "Cedric N. Stackpole Jr. is un-official head of the He-Man Woman Hater Club."

"Why?"

"Nobody knows. Stackpole just hates women in general and women plaintiffs specifically."

"But, he's a judge. I mean, judges are impartial, right?"

"Supposed to be," Mitzi said. "Only Stackpole never got that memo. He's a notorious misogynist. I've been lucky. I've only had one other divorce in front of him in the past."

"How did that go?"

Mitzi's eyes strayed to the row of framed diplomas on the wall opposite her desk. "Hmm? Don't ask. My client got shafted. Her husband abandoned her and her two small children, left them basically penniless while he lived it up, funneling their marital assets into a dummy corporation. We had clear proof that he'd hidden assets, but Stackpole refused to hear a word of it. But because she finally had to go out and get a job to support herself and the children and eventually hooked up with a decent guy and allowed him to move in with her and the kids before the divorce was final, Stackpole decided she was an unfit mother. Gave the ex custody of the kids, forced her to move out of the house and sell it and split the proceeds with the ex, who was already a millionaire several times over."

Mitzi shook her head at the memory. "The ex didn't even want the kids. He just didn't want to pay her child support. It was brutal."

"How can a judge get away with that kind of thing?" Grace asked, horrified. "Can't you report him or something?"

"That's not how it works, unfortunately," Mitzi said. "We're just going to have to hope for the best. We'll lay out the facts; Gracenotes is your business, carries your name, and is written and photographed solely by you. By locking you out of your own Web site, Ben has essentially hijacked your name, which is trademarked, right?"

Grace shook her head. "I was *going* to trademark it, but I just never got around to it. I guess I assumed Ben would take care of that."

"Unfortunate," Mitzi said. She scribbled a note to herself. "All right, the good news is, at least we know what we're dealing with."

"If that's the good news, I don't want to hear the bad stuff," Grace said. She gathered her papers and went home to figure out her next move.

6.

They'd gotten there early. The courtroom was half-full, and another hearing was still under way. Mitzi Stillwell led her up the right-side aisle and gestured at a vacant seat toward the front third of the room.

Grace studied the judge, who sat erect in his high-backed chair, listening intently. He looked to be in his late forties, with receding strawberry-blond hair combed straight back from a high forehead, steel-rimmed glasses, and a long, narrow, unsmiling face. "Is that our judge?"

"That's Stackpole, in the flesh," Mitzi said.

"I thought he'd be older," Grace said.

"He was two years behind me in law school at UF," Mitzi said. "And he was a pain in the ass, even then. But a politically connected pain. He was appointed to the bench at forty."

A uniformed bailiff, a young black woman with startling platinum marcelled hair who was standing at the side door to the courtroom, caught Mitzi's eye and gave her a very slight shake of the head.

"We gotta keep quiet," Mitzi murmured. "Or he'll have that bailiff toss us out."

* * *

A lawyer standing at the table on the left front side of the room stood and spoke into a microphone. "Judge, we'd like the court to view this video my client shot of her husband, while he was terrorizing my client." Grace couldn't see the lawyer's face, just the back of his balding head, and his neat, dark suit.

An older woman sitting at the opposite table stood. "Your honor, we have not seen that video, so we're going to oppose that being introduced into evidence."

The judge gave her a mirthless smile. "We'll all see it together right now, shall we, Ms. Entwhistle?"

"My client was deliberately goaded into an altercation by Mrs. Keeler's boyfriend. For months now, she and Luke Grigsby have repeatedly violated the terms of their custody agreement by either delivering Bo hours late, or not at all, at times when my client was scheduled to have Bo."

"Well, Ms. Entwhistle, I don't see where you've notified the court about that," Stackpole said evenly.

"No sir," Ms. Entwhistle said. "My client was trying to keep things amicable and civil, for the sake of the child. On the day that video was shot, Bo was to have been dropped off at his father's house before lunch. Mrs. Keeler was aware that Bo had a T-ball game at four that afternoon. My client even sent her a text message reminding her of that fact. But she was a no-show. She never notified my client of Bo's whereabouts, instead dropping him off at the park half an hour after the start of the game, and without his team uniform or his glove. The child was distraught, in fact, in tears, because he thought he'd let his team down."

The opposing lawyer stood up. "Judge, if you watch our video, you'll see that if there were indeed any tears, which my client states there weren't, it was probably only because Bo was afraid that Wyatt Keeler, who also happens to be his coach, and who obviously has a volatile temper, might be angry at *him*."

The man who'd been sitting at the table beside the female lawyer shot to his feet. He was coatless, but dressed in a pale yellow long-sleeved dress shirt and a blue necktie. He looked to be in his late thirties or early forties. His clean-shaven head was deeply tanned and gleamed in the glow of the courtroom lights. "That's not true," Wyatt Keeler called out, his voice cracking with emotion. "My son has never been afraid of me. He was crying because it was a big game, and Callie and Luke couldn't be bothered to get him there in time to play."

"That's enough, Mr. Keeler," the judge snapped. "Anything else, and I'll have the bailiff remove you from this courtroom." He closed his eyes for a moment and pinched the bridge of his nose. "All right," he said, gesturing to the same bailiff who'd already shushed Grace and Mitzi. "We're about to be running late. I want to see this video right now."

A moment later, a projection screen had been set up at the front of the room and the overhead lights dimmed. The video, grainy and depicting jerky movements, obviously shot from a cell phone.

As Grace and the other observers in the court watched, they saw Wyatt Keeler, dressed in a bright turquoise T-shirt with MARASOTA MAULERS in script lettering across the front, come storming toward the camera, his eyes narrowed, jaw set angrily, fists clenched.

"Hey, man," he called. "I'm not done with you."

Now the camera showed a second man, with dark, slicked-back hair, wearing khaki slacks and a red polo shirt, walking hurriedly toward the camera. He wore dark sunglasses. *"Make sure you get all this, Callie,"* he called, glancing over his shoulder. An unseen female voice said. *"I got it."*

Now Wyatt Keeler charged toward the other man, grabbing him from behind by the shoulders and spinning him around. It looked like he was saying something, but their voices were muffled.

The woman's voice rang out. *"Get your hands off him, Wyatt."*

Sunglasses man easily shook himself free of Wyatt Keeler's grasp and went jogging away with Wyatt Keeler following at a steady clip.

"Back away, Wyatt," the woman's voice called. *"If you put your hands on Luke one more time, I am calling the cops. I mean it, too."*

Wyatt Keeler looked right at the camera, stricken. His pace slowed and his facial expression softened, slightly. The camera moved back a little, now showing a gleaming white Trans-Am in the foreground.

"Don't do this, Callie," Keeler pleaded. *"Bo needs me. You can't just take him away like this. I won't let you. This is his home."*

"Not anymore it ain't," Luke Grigsby taunted. He was almost at the driver's side of the Trans-Am. *"You call living in a double-wide trailer a home? The kid doesn't even have his own room. He's coming with us to Birmingham, and there's nothing you can do to stop us."*

"Fuck you, Luke," Wyatt Keeler's voice rang out crystal clear. He was advancing again, his face menacing.

"Get in the car, Callie," Luke said loudly. *"Come on, before this maniac hurts somebody."*

Luke opened the driver-side door and started to slide onto the seat. The camera was moving now, so the footage was even jerkier and out of focus. Even with that, Grace watched, appalled. Grigsby's head popped up above the car door. *"See you later, alligator,"* he said, smirking, just before he closed the door.

Wyatt Keeler lunged toward the car. *"The hell you say,"* he bellowed, smashing his fist into the rolled-up car window.

"*Stop it, Wyatt,*" the woman yelled. Her shrill scream pierced the cool courthouse air. The video stopped abruptly, and a moment later, the lights in the courtroom were turned on again.

Grace stared, wide-eyed with horror at the now-white screen.

"Ms. Entwhistle?" Judge Stackpole's face was deadpan. "I can see why you didn't want the court to view that video." He turned toward Wyatt Keeler. "You, sir, are lucky that gentleman did not file assault charges against you. Frankly, what I've just seen here turns my stomach."

Wyatt Keeler bowed his head and buried his face in his hands.

His wife's lawyer saw an opening and dove right in. "Judge, as you can see, Wyatt Keeler is not a fit father or role model for a young child. We'd ask the court to grant my client's application to go ahead with her planned move to Alabama with her fiancé, Mr. Grigsby, and of course, we want to have the previously agreed-to custody settlement amended to reflect that. Mrs. Keeler would be willing to allow Bo to visit his father for monthly supervised weekend visits, and she'd also be open to discussions about alternating holidays and, possibly, summer visits of up to a week. Again, to be supervised by a neutral party."

Wyatt Keeler raised his head. "One weekend a month? This is my son we're talking about."

"Quiet, Mr. Keeler!" Stackpole boomed.

Betsy Entwhistle stood and placed a warning hand on her client's shoulder. "I apologize for my client's outburst. He won't do it again. And I'll add that he is not proud of his behavior that day. But judge, that video was choreographed and shot by Mrs. Keeler and Mr. Grigsby. It's just as important to note what you don't see as what you do. For instance, that video doesn't show Mr. Grigsby deliberately baiting my client . . ."

"I saw all I needed to see," Stackpole interrupted, waving his hand dismissively. "Mr. Keeler?"

Betsy Entwhistle gave a brief nod and her client stood.

Stackpole's eyes drilled into the hapless Wyatt Keeler. "Regardless of what that video did or did not show, I find the actions shown there to be alarming, bordering on criminal." He looked over at the opposing lawyer. "When do Mrs. Keeler and Mr. Grigsby intend to relocate to Birmingham?"

After a brief whispered conference, the other lawyer cleared his throat. "Early August, Judge. Although Mr. Grigsby will move there immediately, Mrs. Keeler needs time to settle things here. But we'd ask that your custody order become effective immediately."

Stackpole thought it over. "I don't see any need for a rush. I'm going to take this under advisement. I have some thoughts, and I'll issue a ruling, probably by the end of business today." He glared at Wyatt Keeler. "And you, sir, are to stay away from Mr. Grigsby. If this court hears of even a hint of any more aggression from you, I'll issue a temporary restraining order. Is that understood?"

"Understood," Betsy Entwhistle said.

"Understood," her client echoed.

Stackpole flicked his eyes over at Callie Keeler, who was dressed in a demure pale-blue, long-sleeved dress. "Mrs. Keeler, if there are any more incidents, you're free to take that back up with the court again."

"Oh, I will Judge," Callie said, her high-pitched voice sounding defiant. "You better believe I will."

Stackpole jerked his head at the bailiff. "Ten-minute recess. Then I'll hear my next case."

Mitzi touched Grace's arm. "Let's make a bathroom run before they call us." Grace followed her lawyer out of the courtroom and down a long, narrow hallway.

As they walked, Grace spotted Wyatt Keeler. He was sitting on a wooden bench, focused on conversation with his lawyer. He was deeply tanned, and from here Grace could see that his dress shirt was ill-fitting, the collar too big, the sleeves too long. The shirt had obviously just come from a package, as the factory fold marks were still visible.

The other lawyer looked up just as they were passing. "Hey, Betsy," Mitzi murmured, nodding. "Looks like Stackpole is in rare form today."

Betsy Entwhistle rolled her eyes. Her client turned, noticing the two women who'd been in the courtroom earlier, and blushed, then looked down at his hands. For the first time, Grace noticed that his right hand was heavily bandaged.

"He's a peach, isn't he?" Betsy said. "I saw you sitting in the courtroom. Are you on his docket today?"

"Unfortunately," Mitzi said. She gestured toward Grace. "This is my client, Grace Stanton."

"And this is my nephew, Wyatt Keeler," Betsy said.

Wyatt Keeler offered them a solemn smile, revealing choirboy dimples. His eyes were a deep chocolate brown, framed with stubby dark lashes. He was seated, but he had the lean, lanky look of somebody who spent a lot of time outdoors. "I hope you fare better with that guy than I did," he said quietly.

Up close, Grace thought, he didn't look quite as much like the deranged goon he seemed in the video shot by his wife. Up close, he looked sad. Defeated.

"I was just telling Wyatt he's lucky Stackpole didn't order him to be castrated," Betsy said.

"He did seem pretty worked up today," Mitzi agreed. "I was kind of surprised, since it's usually the wives he's antagonistic toward."

"That damned video didn't help us any," Betsy said bluntly.

Mitzi glanced down at her watch. "Whoops. Sorry, but we've got to make a pit stop before Stackpole readjourns."

"Good luck in there," Wyatt said.

They slid into their seats at the front of the courtroom just as the bailiff at the rear of the room was closing the doors.

Mitzi Stillwell shot Grace a sideways glance. "You okay?"

Grace nodded. "As good as I'm gonna get." She turned halfway in her chair and looked around the courtroom. There was no sign yet of Ben and his lawyer. She didn't know whether to be glad or mad.

"What happens now?" she asked, turning back to her attorney.

"It should be pretty cut-and-dried," Mitzi said. "We've asked the judge to order Ben to mediation for a financial settlement, since he's so far resisted all our efforts in that direction. We've produced plenty of documentation that the business is yours and that he's put you in an untenable situation. Even Stackpole should agree that you are arguably the rainmaker for Gracenotes."

"And then?"

"Then we figure out a way to divide up the marital assets, seek a final decree for you, and Stackpole pronounces you unmarried."

"You make it sound easy," Grace said.

Mitzi shrugged. "Not easy. The statutes don't want to make it too easy to get a divorce. But if Stackpole makes Ben play by the rules and divvy up the goods, this shouldn't be too terribly complicated from here on out."

Grace heard footsteps coming up the center aisle of the courtroom and turned slightly before swiveling violently back toward Mitzi. "He's here," she whispered. "Oh, God. I don't think I can breathe."

She still hadn't laid eyes on Ben since the night she'd driven his Audi into the pool on Sand Dollar Lane. He strode past her, eyes front, and sat at a table directly to the right of the one where she sat. He was dressed in a conservative charcoal suit, sharply pressed white dress shirt, and a purple silk tie. His glossy hair looked freshly cut, his black Gucci loafers were polished to perfection. He was carrying a briefcase Grace hadn't seen in years, and he busied himself now, snapping it open and sorting through file folders.

Grace felt something tighten in her chest. "Breathe," Mitzi instructed quietly. "In. Out. You can do this, Grace. Don't let the bastard get you rattled."

"I *am* rattled," Grace said, feeling her face flush. She felt a hand clasp her shoulder and looked up.

Dickie Murphree smiled down at her. "Gracie," he said, his hand lingering on her shoulder. "It's great to see you."

Dickie looked much as he had the last time she'd seen him, at an expensive restaurant on St. Armand's Circle, not long after she and Ben had moved back to town. Had it been three years ago? His thinning brown hair was a little too long in the back and he had a rakish mustache and that same impish smile he'd used so effectively to get his way all through high school.

"No hard feelings, right, Grace? This is just one of these things. You'll get past this, and you'll be fine. Right?"

No hard feelings? Grace felt her jaw drop. With Dickie's help, Ben had effectively impoverished her. Right this very minute, she was wearing the dressiest clothing she possessed, a pair of her mother's cast-off sandals, and an ill-fitting rayon knit dress she'd picked up for $3.60 at a thrift shop near the hospital. No hard feelings? Not long ago, Grace wouldn't have used this dress as a dishrag. Dickie didn't wait for her reply. He nodded now at Mitzi, flashing his easy smile. "Hey there, Ms. Stillwell."

"Dickie." Mitzi gave him a curt, dismissive nod.

He finally removed his grasp of her shoulder and slid onto the chair next to Ben's.

Ben was still busily sorting file folders, avoiding meeting her eyes.

"Exhale," Mitzi said quietly. "Think about a happy place. Picture yourself there."

"I don't have a happy place anymore," Grace whispered. "Ben got custody of it."

"Then try this. Picture your ex with his dick caught in a rattrap."

Implausibly, Grace began to smile. As the image formed in her mind, she began to giggle. Horrified, she clamped her hands over her mouth, but not before the giggle became a guffaw. Ben's head turned sharply. His eyes narrowed and he looked, briefly, disgusted. He glanced at the back of the courtroom and gave an almost imperceptible shrug before returning to his paper shuffling.

"Feel better?" Mitzi asked, a smile playing at the edge of her lips.

"Much," Grace said. Her eyes followed Ben's gaze toward the back of the room. Sitting in the last row, wearing a form-fitting chartreuse dress and dark sunglasses, a raven-haired woman was staring down at her cell phone, her fingertips racing over the keyboard. Probably sexting Ben, Grace thought.

"I don't believe it," Grace said, her mirth short-lived. "She's here. Right in this courtroom. She's wearing sunglasses, and I think she's dyed her hair, but that's definitely J'Aimee. I can't believe he had the nerve to bring her here."

Mitzi turned all the way around in her chair to have a look, not bothering to hide what she was doing. "Oh. The green dress, right? What is she, about thirteen? Did he have to sign her out of homeroom?"

Just then, the blond-haired bailiff strode past them to the front of the room. "All rise for the Honorable Cedric N. Stackpole," she intoned.

7.

Mitzi laid out the case neatly before the judge, letting him know that Ben had locked Grace out of their home, canceled her credit cards, and denied her access to their joint checking and savings accounts.

"Your Honor," Mitzi said, gesturing toward Grace, who was sitting straight in her chair, eyes forward, like an obedient schoolgirl on her first day of class, "Mr. Stanton has effectively impoverished my client. She has no funds, no home, and no way to make a living, thanks to him."

"No way to work?" Stackpole looked startled. "Now how is that possible? Didn't you tell me Ms. Stanton was some kind of professional writer?"

"Yes sir," Mitzi said. "Ms. Stanton is—or she was before all this happened—one of the most successful lifestyle bloggers in the country."

"A blogger?" Stackpole's high forehead wrinkled and his lips thinned in distaste. He waved his hands in the direction of the neat printouts Grace had made of six months' worth of Gracenotes. "Do you mean to tell me Ms. Stanton here makes a living writing this material?" He picked up one of the sheets and skimmed its contents.

"Recipes? Pictures of sofas? Directions for painting an old table? This looks like some kind of hobby to me, Ms. Stillwell."

Grace's heart sank. Mitzi had warned her that Stackpole might not take her work seriously.

"No sir," Mitzi said sharply. "Not a hobby in any way. Ms. Stanton's blog has 450,000 followers. That's just people who have subscribed to her RSS feed. Her blog receives 1.3 million unique visits each month. Since Gracenotes was monetized, which means Ms. Stanton started accepting paid advertisers, the site has consistently generated twenty thousand dollars a month in revenues."

"Impressive," the judge admitted.

Mitzi beamed. "We think so. Judge, Gracenotes is named for Grace Stanton. It was conceived by her and it is written and photographed solely by her. There are no other outside contributors. In other words, this blog is intellectual property, and, as such, it belongs to her. But Ms. Stanton's estranged husband, Ben Stanton, is deliberately blocking her from access to her blog."

"I see," Stackpole said. He swung his head to the left, smiling at Dickie Murphree.

"What do you say to that, Mr. Murphree?"

Dickie thrust his hands in his pockets and gave an exaggerated shrug. "Obviously, Judge, we'd refute just about everything Ms. Stillwell has just said. Grace Stanton is free to write whatever she wants, whenever she wants, and, as far as I know, there's nobody stopping her from doing that. The Internet is a big ol' marketplace, and there's plenty of room in it for everybody, last I heard."

"Mm-hmm," Stackpole said. "And what do you have to say about the dire financial situation of your client's estranged wife? Ms. Stillwell makes a convincing case that your client has effectively cut off her access to all the couple's marital assets."

Dickie's face registered what passed for genuine shock. Grace wondered if Dickie had ever done anything in his life that was genuine.

"Judge, I would just point out to you that Ms. Stanton is the one who initiated all the turmoil in this marriage. It was she who abandoned my client, moving out of their home, of her own accord, after a violent outburst. And, I would add, she did so in a manner that was calculated to humiliate and embarrass my client—not just in front of this couple's immediate neighbors, but in front of everybody in this community, and across the country, for that matter. If her business has been damaged, that is Ms. Stanton's own doing."

"He went there," Mitzi muttered under his breath. "I should have known."

"I'm afraid I don't understand," Stackpole said.

The lawyer clapped a reassuring hand on Ben's shoulder. "Your Honor, I deeply regret having to trot this out again. My client certainly didn't want me to drag all this out in the open again, but sometimes, sir, you have to get these things out in the open."

"What things?" Stackpole asked, leaning back in his chair.

Dickie let out a long, anguished sigh. "Well, ahhh, it's a long story, Judge."

Mitzi stood up. "Your Honor? If Mr. Murphree is referring to the matter I think he is, that matter has no direct bearing on the issue of my client's right to her share of this couple's marital assets. And I strongly object to his trying to introduce it here today."

"What matter?" Stackpole asked, looking peevish.

Dickie shrugged. "The matter of Ms. Stanton intentionally driving my client's 175,000 dollar Audi convertible into the swimming pool of their home on Sand Dollar

Lane, thus destroying it. The matter of her assaulting and slandering my client's employee."

"What?" Stackpole's eyebrows shot up. "When was this?"

"The night of May eighth," Dickie said. "Ms. Stanton misunderstood some communication between my client and his employee and flew into a rage. My client eventually began to fear for his life and locked himself into his home and called the police, who, unfortunately, arrived on the scene after Ms. Stanton destroyed the Audi."

Stackpole gave Grace a stern look. "Is this true?"

Grace's voice came out in a squeak. "It's true that I drove the car into the pool, yes sir. But it's not true that I assaulted J'Aimee. I would have, but I couldn't catch her. And anyway, she was my assistant, not Ben's. And it's a joke to think that Ben would be afraid of me. But Your Honor, you haven't heard the whole story."

"That's right, Judge," Dickie said quickly. "You haven't heard how Ms. Stanton raised such a ruckus that their entire neighborhood could listen in on this private marital spat. And I'm assuming you didn't see the network news footage of the aftermath — including footage showing Mr. Stanton's personal vehicle sitting at the bottom of his pool?"

Stackpole's eyebrows shot up. "It was on the news?"

"I had nothing to do with that," Grace offered.

"Enough!" Stackpole glared over the top of his glasses at her.

Dickie held up a small plastic rectangle. "I have the news footage right here on a flash drive, if Your Honor would like to see it."

"I don't intend to do any such thing," Stackpole said. "Let's get back to the matter of finances. Mr. Murphree, I want your client to come to some kind of equitable agreement with Ms. Stanton." He flipped through the files before him.

"Ms. Stanton? Your attorney has asked for what seems like an exorbitant amount of money to pay your monthly expenses. I find it hard to believe a resourceful woman like yourself can't live on $2,000 a month. My own wife manages quite nicely on that amount."

"But Judge," Mitzi sputtered. "Ms. Stanton is entitled to much more than that. She has business expenses involved in writing and producing her blog. And she'll need to find a place to live. She can't continue to live in her mother's very small quarters. And furnishings . . . Besides, it's really immaterial how much allowance you give your wife. Ms. Stanton was the primary breadwinner in this marriage . . ."

Dickie shot to his feet. "That's not true! Mr. Stanton incorporated Gracenotes. He managed the business, sold advertising, dealt with every aspect of the business, and built it up from a small-potatoes hobby to the entity it is today. He, in fact, is the CEO of Gracenotes, Inc., and the owner of the domain name, among other things. It was Ms. Stanton's choice to be paid a weekly salary on a work-for-hire agreement, because she did not want to be troubled with the business of running a business."

"What?" Grace shrieked, then quickly covered her mouth with her hands. She tugged urgently on Mitzi's hand. "I never agreed to any kind of a weekly salary," she whispered. "Ben just drew money out of the corporate account and put it in our personal checking account. I left all of that up to him and the accountant."

"Judge," Mitzi began, but Stackpole wasn't listening.

"Two thousand a month," he said firmly. "It was apparently Ms. Stanton's decision to leave this marriage, so I'm afraid she'll have to deal with the repercussions of that."

"Thank you, Judge," Dickie said quickly.

"That's not all," Stackpole said. He took his glasses off and rubbed the bridge of his nose. "Ms. Stanton, I find myself at a loss for words as far as your behavior in this matter goes. This is the second instance today of parties to a divorce acting in dangerous, violent, even criminal behavior. I'm troubled by that. Deeply troubled."

"Judge, if you'd just listen to what provoked my client," Mitzi began, but Stackpole held up a hand to stop her.

"There can be no justification for the wanton destruction of property or for harassment or assault on a third party. This is just the kind of thing that escalates, until we have domestic violence, armed stand-offs, and God knows what."

"It won't happen again," Grace said in her meekest voice.

"It certainly won't," Stackpole agreed. "We'll see how you do with this new financial settlement, while the two of you work out the other details of your divorce settlement. But in the meantime, Ms. Stanton, I want you to begin seeing a therapist who is an expert in divorce, uh, counseling. Immediately. Dr. Talbott-Sinclair does excellent work, as you'll see." He glanced down at his calendar. "I believe she has a group meeting on Wednesday. If she can fit you into her group meeting tomorrow night, that will give you six weeks.

Mitzi stared at the judge. "Your Honor, are you also ordering *Mr.* Stanton to attend these group sessions?"

"No," he snapped. "Mr. Stanton seems to have his anger issues under control. Now, Ms. Stanton, if Dr. Talbott-Sinclair signs off on your rehabilitation, then I'll take that into consideration when I see you later this summer. Understood?"

Grace could do nothing but nod. Inside was another story. Inside she was screaming.

But Mitzi wasn't done. "Judge, we still need you to rule on the matter of ownership of Ms. Stanton's business. As it stands right now, Ms. Stanton has been deprived of access to her blog, which in effect deprives her of making a living."

"Why can't she just start another blog?" Stackpole asked, gathering up his papers and shutting the file in front of him. "Nobody's keeping her from writing, are they?"

"Mr. Stanton is keeping her from writing," Mitzi said, sounding weary and out of patience. "He is in effect hijacking her intellectual property."

"Talk to me in six weeks after your counseling," Stackpole said. He jerked his head in the bailiff's direction. "I can feel my blood sugar getting low. Let's break for lunch."

Mitzi was stuffing papers into her briefcase. Ben stood and began to stride past, but Grace reached out and grabbed his sleeve.

Ben looked down at her with a blank expression. "Don't do this," he said, his voice chilly.

She jumped up. "Do what? Ask you to answer my lawyer's phone calls? Ask you to treat me with some kind of fairness, some kind of decency, even if our marriage is over? Why are you doing this? If I can't write my blog, neither of us makes any money. You realize that, right?"

Dickie was at Ben's side now. "Now, Gracie. This is very inappropriate. You heard what Judge Stackpole just told you. You need to get your issues under control. If you have something to say to Ben, you need to have your lawyer bring it up with me."

Ben looked her in the eye. "That means no more phone calls. No more showing up at the gates at Gulf Vista, embarrassing the security guards. You wanted it over, Grace, so that's what you've got. It's over. You get on with your life, and I'll get on with mine."

He carefully pried her fingers from the fine fabric of his suit coat, then picked up his briefcase and strolled toward the door, where J'Aimee was already standing, waiting for him. She grasped his arm and, just before walking out, turned and shot Grace a triumphant smile.

8.

It was four o'clock on a steamy Tuesday afternoon and Jungle Jerry's Olde Florida Family Fun Park was nearly deserted. There were no families present, and not much fun in evidence.

A quartet of blue-haired tourists from Michigan were taking advantage of the "buy one, get one" coupon they'd found in that day's newspaper. They were having a nice enough time, wandering the crushed-shell footpaths, admiring the unusual flora and fauna, especially the wading pool full of preening pink flamingos.

If they noticed that the temperatures were in the high nineties, and the humidity at 2,000 percent, they didn't remark upon it. Instead, they fanned themselves with the yellowing cardboard Jungle Jerry's Fan Club fans they'd bought for $1.99 in the gift shop and inhaled the heady fragrance of frangipani and ginger lily.

The four paused in their leisurely tour to stare up at the gnarled crimson boughs of a particularly eye-catching tree. "What the heck is this?" asked the only man in the group, a spry seventy-six-year-old who was actually the youngster of the crowd.

Wyatt Keeler happened to be nearby, trimming dead branches from an oleander bush that seemed particularly stressed by the summer's dry spell.

He was dressed as he always was at the park, in a khaki shirt bristling with epaulets and with flap pockets and embroidered Jungle Jerry patches, matching khaki cargo shorts, lace-up work boots, and, of course, his ever-present safari hat.

Wyatt walked up to the group and gave them a welcoming smile, flashing his dimples. Old ladies were crazy for the dimples. He gave the tree trunk a loving pat, as though it were a beloved family pet, which, to Wyatt, it essentially was.

"This is a gumbo-limbo tree," he volunteered. "It's one of the more unusual species we have in the park. It's Latin name is *Bursera simaruba*, and it's a native of tropical regions like Florida, of course, as well as Mexico, the Caribbean, Brazil, and Venezuela. Some people call it the 'tourist tree,' because the bark is red and peeling—like a lot of tourists we see down here in the wintertime."

The Michiganders laughed at this and themselves by association.

"Interesting," murmured one of the women, a sturdily built eighty-five-year-old widow in a pink sun visor.

Wyatt felt himself suddenly cheered by his own speech, and by the interested comments from these tourists.

The very oldest member of the group, a spindly legged ninety-year-old in a thin cotton housedress, stepped closer and peered at Wyatt's Jungle Jerry's name patch, which had faded into obscurity from years of laundering.

"You're not Jungle Jerry," she said sharply. "You'd be too young."

"No ma'am. I'm Wyatt Keeler," he offered her his hand. "Jungle Jerry was my grandfather. He bought this place in 1961, when it was still a commercial orange grove."

One of the women did a little full-circle turn. "You don't see a lot of orange trees here now."

"That's right," Wyatt said. "My grandfather, Jerry Brennan, bought six hundred acres here on County Line Road, back in the day when this was considered way out in the boonies, and he thought he'd become the orange king of Manatee County. And he might have done it, too, except that this area experienced a record-breaking frost in 1963. Temperatures dipped into the low teens and stayed there for three days. My granddad didn't know enough about citrus growing back then to know that he needed to fire up the smudge pots. He lost most of his orange trees in that freeze, and most of the family money, too."

"Too bad," the man muttered.

"Fortunately," Wyatt went on, "he met my grandmother, Winnie, not long after that. And *her* family still had some money. Granddad's family had once owned a little amusement park back home in Tulsa, and, since tourism was going great guns in Florida then, he decided maybe he could take the old orange grove and convert it into what he called a kiddie park."

Wyatt gestured to a rusty jungle gym partially obscured by a hedge of orange-flowering shrubs. "He put in all kinds of rides and playground equipment, and because my grandmother Winnie loved flowers, the two of them also started planting new trees and shrubs as they took out the dead orange trees."

"It's lovely now," the ninety-year-old said. "We used to bring our grandchildren here when we all came down every spring. Whatever happened to all your wild animals? I was just telling my friends, there used to be lions and a tiger, and do I remember a zebra?"

"Yes ma'am," Wyatt said with a laugh. "We had all that and more. My granddad watched a lot of those old Tarzan movies in his younger days. He bought the animals from

a traveling circus that had gone bust. A lot of circus outfits used to winter down in this area, you know. He'd always loved animals anyway. So he named himself Jungle
Jerry, and he got a retired lion tamer to teach him a few
tricks of the trade."

"I thought I remembered a lion show," the woman
crowed. "So that was the real Jungle Jerry?"

"The one and only," Wyatt said. "We had the big cats,
plus Zoey, that was the zebra, and an elephant, and even a
Florida black bear, right up until the late seventies. After
my granddad retired, my dad took over, and he phased out
most of the large animals."

The woman in the sun visor glared at Wyatt. "They
didn't . . . kill them. Tell me they didn't."

"Not at all," Wyatt assured her. "Those animals were
like my grandfather's own kids. Boo-Boo, he was the bear,
he died of natural causes the same year granddad retired.
Monty, the lion, and Tonga, that was the tiger, they retired
to an exotic animal shelter in Ocala. Daphne, our elephant,
was donated to the Lowry Park Zoo over in Tampa."

The four tourists all seemed relieved. "I love all the
tropical birds you have around here," said the woman in
the baggy shorts.

Wyatt put his fingers to his lips and gave a long, shrill
whistle. They heard a flapping, and suddenly a huge gray
parrot flew down from the top of a nearby poinciana tree
and perched on Wyatt's shoulder.

"Oh!" one of the women said, clapping her hands in
glee.

The bird nuzzled Wyatt's ear, then dipped her neck and
poked her head into the right breast pocket for a treat.

"This is Cookie," Wyatt said. "She's an African gray, a
total diva, and the star of the parrot show. I can't take any
credit for her, though. The birds were my mom's idea."

"Weren't there monkeys, too?" the ninety-year-old inquired.

"You've got a good memory," Wyatt said. "The monkeys were here when I was a little kid. But when this neighborhood started going residential, with all the subdivisions closing in, we were getting a lot of complaints, especially since the little boogers were too clever and kept getting out of their pens and frightening the neighbors. Eventually, all of them were adopted out."

Cookie found a parrot pellet in Wyatt's pocket and began chewing contentedly.

"That was certainly interesting," the old man said, pumping Wyatt's hand again. "This is a grand place you've got here. We're a little surprised to have it all to ourselves today."

Wyatt was not surprised. But he made a valiant effort to keep up a good front.

"You just happened to catch us on our slow day," he lied. "But you come back later in the week, and the crowds will be here, I guarantee."

That was a lie, too. They hadn't had what you could call a real "crowd" at Jungle Jerry's in months and years. Okay, decades, if you wanted to be brutally honest. In this post-Disney era, families got their kicks in air-conditioned comfort, with audio-animatronics and movie-quality special effects. Animal rights advocates didn't approve of exotic birds performing quaint tricks like riding a tiny bicycle on a high wire, and kids were bored silly just looking at a bunch of plants and trees.

Jungle Jerry's had shrunken significantly over the years. Right now, they were at around a hundred acres, since Jungle Jerry's son-in-law, Wyatt's father, Nelson, had been forced to sell off a chunk of land to pay inheritance taxes after Jerry's death.

Wyatt had never intended to work in the family business. He'd been a horticulture major in college and had gone to graduate school at Clemson for a degree in landscape architecture, which was where he'd met Callie Parker, a twenty-two-year-old graphic arts major from Orangeburg, South Carolina. He and Callie had been in a fever to get married, such a fever that he'd canned the idea of getting his master's and dropped out of grad school to get a job working for a mail-order nursery in Greenville.

He'd worked there for four years when his mother called to beg him to come home to run Jungle Jerry's. Nelson had suffered his first heart attack, and Peggy, his mother, had just been diagnosed with breast cancer, although she didn't tell him that until after he and Callie moved back to Bradenton.

Peggy lived just long enough to hold Bo, christened Nelson William Keeler II, before succumbing to the cancer.

The first few years at the park, Wyatt had worked furiously to try to turn the tide at Jungle Jerry's. He'd advertised, joined civic associations, networked like crazy. He'd phased out the old kiddie rides, which were rusting safety hazards anyway, and had begun emphasizing ecology and the botanical aspect of the park. And at first, things seemed to be working. Attendance crept up. Callie came to work at the park, designing posters and ads. Bo took his first steps chasing after Beezus, a gold-capped conure. They weren't getting rich, but they were young and happy. And dumb, Wyatt reflected now. At least, he was.

They'd bought their first house in one of the newer subdivisions nearby and enrolled Bo in the neighborhood school, one of the best in the school district. Wyatt was working crazy long hours at Jungle Jerry's, and Callie was doing some sporadic freelance work. Most of the other families on their block were like them, young marrieds with one or two kids. They cooked out together, took the kids en masse to Holmes Beach—all the things you did when you were young with not much money.

The one bachelor on the block, Luke Grigsby, was a salesman with a chemical company. Luke was the neighborhood fun guy. He wore cool clothes and drove a sharp white Trans-Am. His home was the biggest, newest house on the block, and since he had a pool, he entertained frequently.

Every year Luke threw a big, crazy Halloween party. Everybody competed to come up with the most outrageous costume. Wyatt wasn't a big one for parties, but Callie loved dressing up. That year, she decided they should go as Aladdin and Jasmine, the characters from the Disney movie.

Wyatt reluctantly allowed himself to be talked into wearing a turban, idiotic-looking billowy pants, and, worst of all, a short embroidered vest over his bare chest. For her own costume, Callie outdid herself. She took one of her old bikinis and covered the top and bottom with hot-glued gold sequins, then attached some kind of filmy fabric to the bottoms to make harem pants. She bought a felt fez, cut a hole in the top, and pulled her blond ponytail through, then made herself a veil with more of the filmy fabric.

Callie refused to let Wyatt see her in her costume until the night of the party. When she stepped out of the bedroom, he couldn't believe this was his wife.

She'd swept glittering blue eye shadow on her eyelids and outlined them in black liner. Her breasts jutted out of the skimpy sequined bikini top, and her harem pants skimmed right above her pubic bone. She wore half a dozen jangly gold bracelets on each arm, huge earrings, and little gold sandals. As a final touch, she'd somehow attached a huge plastic rhinestone in her belly button.

Callie's eyes danced from above the veil obscuring the

lower half of her face. She did a little pirouette followed by a suggestive hip grind that sent her bracelets jingling.

"What do you think?"

"Where's the rest of it?" Wyatt asked.

She pouted. "What's that supposed to mean? You don't like it?"

He looked over his shoulder, toward the kitchen, where the teenage babysitter was trying to con Bo into eating his dinner. "I like it just fine if we're staying home tonight—just the two of us," he said in a low voice, running a finger down her bare arm. "But don't you think it's a little, uh, I don't know, risqué for a neighborhood party?"

"No, I do not," Callie snapped. "I've been working on this costume for weeks. Yours, too. And that's all you can say? I look risqué?"

He shrugged. "You asked."

"Well I don't care what you think. I think I look hot. And cute." She grabbed a gold beaded clutch purse and opened the front door. "Are you coming?"

He went to the party, had a couple beers, talked football with a couple of the guys, and watched glumly from across the room while his wife knocked back half a dozen wine coolers and then proceeded to strut and shimmy and flirt with every guy in the room.

Callie was doing a tipsy but highly suggestive belly dance with Luke out on the patio when Wyatt tapped her on the shoulder. She whirled around, then frowned when she saw it was her husband. "What?"

"It's eleven thirty," he said pointedly. "We promised we'd get Melanie home by midnight."

"It's Friday night. There's no school tomorrow! Just call her and tell her we're going to stay later," Callie said. "It's no big deal."

"It actually is a big deal," Wyatt replied. "She's got to get up early because she's taking the SATs tomorrow."

"Oh, for God's sake," Callie said. "Just when the party is starting to crank up." She looked over at Luke and gestured at Wyatt. "Meet Aladdin—he traded his magic carpet for a wet blanket."

"You don't have to leave," Wyatt said stiffly. "I'll go, since she drove herself over to the house."

"You mean it?" Callie's face lit up, her pout forgotten. "I won't stay that much longer. I just want to hang around long enough to see who wins the costume contest."

Luke laughed and wrapped an arm around Callie's shoulder. "You already know who won—lady." He gave Wyatt a wink. "Don't worry about her. I'll walk her home myself. Okay?"

What could Wyatt say? Callie planted a perfunctory kiss on his forehead. He walked the two blocks home, paid the babysitter, and walked her out to her car. He looked in on Bo, who was fast asleep, then went to bed. Alone. He woke up at 3:30 A.M., glanced at the clock, and then back at Callie's side of the bed. She wasn't there.

He couldn't sleep. Finally, Wyatt got up. He peered out the front window, just in time to see Luke and Callie stroll slowly up the sidewalk. The window was open, and the curtains billowed in a faint breeze. Callie's giggle floated on the night air, and Luke said something in a low voice. She leaned heavily on the arm Luke had around her waist. As Wyatt watched, they stopped just short of the driveway. Luke pulled her from the sidewalk into the shadow of their neighbor's Florida holly tree. Wyatt's heart stopped. His hand clutched the curtain fabric as he watched his wife wrap her arms around Luke's neck, press herself up against his chest, and pull the neighborhood fun guy into a long, deep kiss.

As he walked back to their bedroom, Wyatt checked the dial on the clock radio on his side of their bed. He made a note of the time. 3:47 A.M. It was the moment time stopped in what he thought had been a perfectly happy marriage.

9.

Callie never did come to bed that night. She was asleep on the living room sofa in the morning. Her fez was on the floor, her hair mussed and spilling over the sofa cushion. The blue eye shadow and black liner were smeared into raccoon circles under her eyes. One breast peeked all the way out of the bikini top.

"What happened to Mommy?" He hadn't heard their barefoot son pad into the room. Bo stood looking down in horror at Callie.

Wyatt pulled an afghan over Callie's shoulders and scooped Bo up into his arms. "She didn't feel so good last night when she came home from the party, so she slept out here. Come on, sport, let's get you some breakfast."

Months later, after the trial separation, after the tears and accusations and denials, Wyatt knew, in retrospect, he should have said something the night of the Halloween party. Maybe if he'd let Callie know what he'd seen, told her he loved her and didn't want to lose her, maybe things would have turned out differently. Or maybe he might have admitted he didn't love her enough. Not enough to fight Luke for her.

But things didn't turn out that way. Eventually, Callie admitted that she and Luke were in love. Eventually, she told him the marriage had been in trouble for a long time. And so Wyatt did the decent thing. They agreed it was important for Bo's life to retain some degree of normalcy. Callie would keep the house so that Bo could stay in his school. Wyatt was thirty-eight years old, with a failed marriage and an ailing business.

Wyatt moved out of their little house and into a battered double-wide trailer at Jungle Jerry's that had once been the living quarters for a security guard — from back in the day when they actually had the funds and the need for a security guard.

When it came time to start divorce proceedings, his Aunt Betsy offered to handle his side, pro bono. They somehow worked out a time-sharing agreement, with Bo splitting his time between the two of them. Wyatt's dad, Nelson, moved into the second bedroom of the double-wide to help out with childcare for Bo on the weekends and after school on the days Bo stayed with Wyatt.

Wyatt was shocked at how fast his marriage unraveled and dumbfounded at the changes in Callie once she and Luke moved in together.

Or had she been somebody else all along? Wyatt would never be sure.

Their temporary custody-sharing arrangement got off to a rocky start. On the first weekend Bo was to spend with Wyatt, he got a tearful call from his son on Friday night, hours after Callie was to have dropped him off at Jungle Jerry's.

"Daddy?"

"Hey, Bo," Wyatt said, relieved to hear his son's voice. "Grandpa and I are waiting on you. We're having your favorite, mac 'n' cheese."

Bo sniffed, and then, in a thin, wobbly voice, "Mom says if you want me, you gotta come pick me up."

Wyatt frowned. That had not been the agreement.

"Sure thing," he said. "I'll be right over."

Now Bo was crying. "But, I'm not at Mom's house. I'm at Luke's friend's house, and it's way far away."

He heard Callie's voice in the background. "Just tell him you'll see him in the morning. Your dad will understand."

"But I wanna see Daddy," he heard Bo wailing, and his heart sank.

"Oh, for Pete's sake," he heard Callie say.

And then she was on the phone, her voice crisp and un-apologetic.

"Look, Wy, we've had a little change of plans. We went over to St. Pete Beach with Luke for a work thing, and with Friday traffic and everything, we're just not gonna make it back in time tonight. You understand, right? I'll drop him off first thing in the morning."

"This is crap, Callie," Wyatt protested. "You were sup-posed to bring Bo here as soon as school was out, four hours ago. Now you call me and tell me you took him all the way to St. Pete? And I'm supposed to be okay with that?"

"You're supposed to be okay with doing what's good for your son," Callie snapped. "Luke's friends live right on the beach here, and they have a pool, and Bo was having a blast until he all of a sudden decided he needed to talk to you. The next thing I know, he's blubbering and saying he wants to leave. And if we leave now, with traffic and every-thing, he'll be asleep by the time we get him there any-way. So what's the difference if you get him tonight or tomorrow morning?"

"The difference is, I haven't seen him in three days," Wyatt said, feeling his chest tighten with anger. "I made plans for tonight, with Dad and Bo."

"Whoop-dee-shit," she said. "Fine. Whatever. I'll pack his ass up now, and we'll get in the car and drive him all the way back over there so you can see him. Asleep."

Wyatt took a deep breath. "I wish you wouldn't cuss in front of him. But all right, he can stay. As long as you have him here first thing in the morning. And since you've got him tonight, I want him to spend Sunday night with me."

"Great." She hung up without another word.

10

Gracenotes

Despite what you might think, I am definitely not a neat freak. My desk is frequently a disaster area, and dust bunnies are not an endangered species at my house. But truthfully, I get deep personal satisfaction out of making my surroundings beautiful— and comfortable.

I've learned a few tricks that make housekeeping less drudgery and more delight. For one thing, I try and tidy up every night before bedtime. Dishes always get put in the dishwasher—is there anything more depressing in the morning than a sinkful of greasy crockery? I spritz the sink and kitchen counters with my favorite all-purpose organic cleanser, watered-down white vinegar.

In the morning, after I've showered, I use more of my diluted vinegar-water spray to freshen up the tub and shower surfaces, and I keep a special "squeegee" under my bathroom sink to allow me to

wipe down the glass shower door before it gets any
annoying water spots or streaks.

On the Wednesday after her court appearance, Grace
flipped the last of the heavy wooden chairs onto the tabletop. She dipped the mop in the bucketful of scalding soapy
water, then, with rubber gloved hands, wrung out the ex-
cess soap. She swished the mop back and forth across the
Sandbox's gritty linoleum floor, halfheartedly listening to
the morning news roundup of traffic accidents, taxpayer
revolts, and local political skullduggery.

The smell of coffee somehow managed to waft through
the biting aroma of Pine-Sol. Her mother was standing
at the bar, holding out a freshly brewed pot.

"Come on, hon," Rochelle urged. "It's early. You can
stop for one cup. That floor ain't going nowhere."

It was barely eight o'clock. Grace had been up since six,
taking a run along the quiet predawn streets of Cortez
while it was still relatively cool, then starting in on her
new ritual of swabbing down the restaurant, from floor to
ceiling.

Out of boredom and desperation, in the weeks since
she'd moved in, Grace had been waging a one-woman war
on the Sandbox's decades-old accumulation of grease,
grime, and clutter.

She'd started in the storeroom, clearing out an entire
Dumpster's worth of antiquated equipment, a deep fryer
her father had always meant to fix, an ice machine that had
stopped working ten years earlier, boxes and crates of old
business records, food service catalogs, and broken chairs
and tables.

From there she'd moved on to the kitchen, ruthlessly
tossing anything and everything that wasn't essential to
their food-service operation. She'd inspected every glass,

dish, and piece of cutlery, consigning anything chipped, bent, or discolored to a crate she'd allocated for the local homeless shelter's soup kitchen.

Along the way, she'd had to abandon all her old, genteel ideas about housecleaning. Diluted vinegar and baking soda were useless in her dust-busting efforts here. Now, her weapons of choice included every industrial-strength, commercial-grade cleaner she could find at the local janitorial supply house.

Grace set her mop aside, peeled off the rubber gloves, and sipped her coffee. She gestured around the room. "I feel like I'm finally making some headway, don't you?"

Her mother shrugged. "Place doesn't even smell like a bar anymore. You've scrubbed away every last trace of the Sandbox ambiance."

"Mom, that wasn't ambiance, it was crud. Years' and years' worth of baked-on, smoked-in, ground-down crud. This place was gross. Can't you just admit you like it better clean?"

Rochelle rested a hand on the old mahogany bar. "I liked it the way it was," she said pointedly. "We were shabby before shabby got cool. Now it's like a hospital operating room, for God's sake. Who wants to grab a beer and a burger in a hospital?"

"There's a difference between shabby gentility and run-down and decrepit, and it's really not so fine a line," Grace said. "Our regulars may grouse at first, but you wait, they're gonna appreciate pouring beer from a pitcher without a busted spout or eating with a fork without bent tines."

"*My* regulars don't know what a fork tine is," Rochelle said.

Maybe, Grace wanted to tell her, if we clean this place up, change the menu, and raise our standards a little, maybe we'll attract a clientele that actually will pay $15 for a decent dinner entrée.

But before she could lob another useless argument into Rochelle's court, she happened to glance up at the television and stopped, midsentence.

Rochelle followed her gaze. "Aw shit. Here we go again."

The morning news hour had segued into *Sunrise Sarasota,* one of those chatty, morning-magazine-format shows. The cohosts, an unbearably perky husband-and-wife team named Charley and Joe, were doing an "In the Kitchen" segment that had the wife, Charley, attempting to crack a Florida lobster shell while the husband, Joe, was being tutored in the finer points of crafting a table setting.

When Grace heard an all-too-familiar voice, a high-pitched nasal twang, she turned around to stare at the wall-mounted television above the bar.

The guest coaching Charley and Joe through their cooking segment was none other than J'Aimee. Her J'Aimee, or rather, Ben's J'Aimee.

Rochelle grabbed for the remote to change the channel, but Grace was faster, snatching it up from beneath her mother's fingers, then staring, dumbfounded, at the television.

"Don't go away!" Charley was saying. "We'll be right back with Gracenotes-style blogger J'Aimee."

"What?" Grace shrieked. "Gracenotes-style blogger? Seriously?"

"Just turn it off," Rochelle said soothingly. "Tune it out. This means nothing. You're just going to get yourself all worked up for nothing."

"It's not for nothing," Grace said, still staring up at the television. "This is all Ben's doing." She scrabbled around on the bar, looking for her phone.

"I'm calling my lawyer," Grace said, scrolling through the numbers on her contact list. "He can't do this. He can't promote her as a Gracenotes blogger. He can't turn her into me!"

"Looks like he already did," Rochelle said, under her breath.

Grace got Mitzi Stillwell's voice mail. "Mitzi! This is Grace. Turn on *Sunrise Sarasota* right now! Ben has J'Aimee on there, promoting herself as the Gracenotes-style blogger. You've got to do something, Mitzi. Call the judge, get an injunction or something. Call me back, okay?"

The commercial break was over, and Charley and Joe were back with their guest.

"Look at that whore!" Grace ranted. "See how good she looks? I swear, Ben's gotten her a makeover. She looks almost classy."

J'Aimee was wearing a sleeveless hot-pink dress, her newly dyed dark locks worn in a simple upsweep.

"They must have put some kind of concealer on that barbed-wire tattoo she has on her right bicep," Grace muttered. "And I think maybe she got Botox on her lips. You see how full they are now?"

Rochelle shrugged. "I never paid that much attention to the girl, to tell you the truth."

J'Aimee was now openly flirting with Joe, batting her artificial lashes at him, giggling and playfully flicking a dinner napkin at him . . .

"Hey! That's my damned napkin." Grace scrambled up on one of the barstools to get a closer look at the television. She pointed at the screen. "Those are my hand-blown Mexican wineglasses." She felt tears welling up in her eyes. "I carried those all the way back from Puerto Vallarta on my lap.

"And look. She's using that fugly damned pottery from my Gracenotes sponsor. That's strictly a Ben move."

She sank back down on the barstool, unable to take her eyes off the television. Now J'Aimee was placing a centerpiece in the middle of the table. It was a large, shallow glass bowl, heaped with shiny green Hass avocados.

"I always like to use fresh local fruits and vegetables in my table settings," she told Charley, adjusting one of the avocados. "It gives a party a sense of authenticity, don't you think?"

"Authenticity?" Grace howled. "She didn't know an avocado from an orange before I hired her."

Rochelle quietly removed the remote control from Grace's clutch. She aimed it at the television and clicked.

"You're getting yourself all worked up for nothing," she said. "So what if she's on television? So what if Ben has her writing a blog with your name on it? She's not you. She's just a cheap little floozie. You are the real thing. You're butter and she's . . . she's not even Parkay. Ben will figure that out soon enough. Your readers will figure it out. Everything will work itself out."

"No, it won't," Grace said tearfully. "She's stolen everything from me. My house, my husband, my napkins. That was my wedding silver she was setting the table with. My Repoussé silver, Mom."

Rochelle sighed and folded her weeping daughter into her arms. "It'll be okay, Grace. Really it will. I know it hurts right now, but you'll get through this. You will. I'll help you."

Grace looked up at her. Tears streamed down her face. Her eyes were red-rimmed and her nose was snotty. She sniffed loudly. "How, Mom?"

"I just will," Rochelle vowed. She grabbed the bottle of spray cleaner Grace had left behind the bar. "Look. I'll let you clean the office next, okay? You can throw out whatever you want, and I won't say a word."

After the judge refused to give her back her blog, Grace promised herself she would *not* look at Gracenotes. But that afternoon, once she'd filled the Sandbox's Dumpster with dusty files and years' and years' worth of old *Sports*

Illustrated and *Florida Sportsman* magazines, Grace
opened her laptop and clicked on the icon for her blog.

"Oh no she didn't," she murmured, looking at the home
page. Everything had changed. Including the name. It was
now Gracenotes for Living, with J'Aimee! The new banner was in a nearly unreadable font, in a garish orange and
teal color combination. The rails on both sides of the page
were filled with tiny, one-inch squares advertising everything from *New Unbelievable Anti-Aging Serum!* to bank
credit cards to cruise ship vacations to *Pet Meds by Mail!*

"Horrible," Grace said, shaking her head. "Heinous."
She counted three dozen ads on the home page. Ben must
have been having a field day, she decided, maximizing and
monetizing to his greedy heart's content.

She read the previous day's post. It was titled "How to
Buy Furniture."

"Hmm. Scintillating," Grace said. As she read, she
felt sick. The entire blog was really a thinly veiled adver-
torial for Room in a Box, a wholesale furniture company
with franchise operations all over central Florida. The
same furniture company whose banner ad now took up
the entire top of the home page.

Room in a Box's marketing people had been pestering
Grace for more than a year to write about their furniture.
They'd even had the nerve to ship a faux-leather recliner
chair to the house—as an inducement/bribery for Grace
to write testimonials about their product line.

"No way," Grace had said, as Ben cut the cardboard
crate away from the chair—which actually came with a
remote control allowing it to recline, vibrate, and even play
music. "Pack that thing up and tell UPS to come back and
get it. I don't even want it to stay here overnight."

Ben knew it was useless to argue with her. Obviously
he'd waited until he no longer had to argue with her.

Grace was gone, and with her had gone any hint of editorial standards.

She couldn't read any more of this drivel. She closed out the blog, opened a file, and began to type, her fingers flying over the keyboard.

By four that afternoon, she'd registered a new domain name for herself, TrueGrace. Maybe not the most original name, she admitted, but it would serve its purpose, hopefully letting her readers know this blog was the real thing.

This time around, she promised herself, the blog would be all hers. And for her first post, she decided to go public with what had happened in her life and to her old world.

No more prettying things up, Grace decided. She was still writing, deleting, revising, when she looked down at her watch and realized it was nearly 7:00 P.M. She hit the SAVE button, closed her laptop, and reluctantly went downstairs.

Rochelle was behind the bar, pouring a beer for an older woman Grace didn't recognize. She looked up in time to see Grace heading for the Sandbox's front door.

"Where are you headed?" Rochelle called.

Grace grimaced. "To my so-called therapy group."

"Looking like that?"

Grace looked down at herself. She was wearing a faded lime-green Sandbox T-shirt, white shorts, and flip-flops, the same outfit she'd changed into after her morning run. Her hair was knotted in a limp ponytail and she wore no makeup.

"The judge said I had to go," she said, her chin jutting out defiantly. "He didn't say I had to dress to impress."

Rochelle handed the beer to her customer and hurried around the bar to her daughter's side. "Honey, you don't want to go in there with an attitude," she said, her voice low. "Maybe these sessions will actually be helpful. Maybe you should keep an open mind. Or at least do something about your hair."

Grace sighed. She reached into the glass display case where they kept the Sandbox-branded merchandise, the koozies, tees, bumper stickers, and key chains. She grabbed a baseball cap with the Sandbox logo embroidered on the bill, jammed it on her head, and looped her ponytail through the opening in the back of the hatband.

"Better?" She didn't wait to hear Rochelle's answer.

11.

Grace had to check the street address on the therapist's door to make sure she'd arrived at the right place. This was a shrink's office? It was a drab one-story stucco storefront occupying the end slot in a strip shopping center that also boasted a Vietnamese nail salon, a hearing aid salesroom, a business called the Diaper Depot, and a tattoo parlor. The dusty plate-glass window was boldly lettered in gilt-edged black letters; PAULA TALBOTT-SINCLAIR, L.S.W. FAMILY AND MARITAL COACHING, DIVORCE DIVERSION, EMOTIONAL HEALING.

"Emotional healing," she muttered to herself, taking a last sip of lukewarm coffee before getting out of her car. "Right. Like that's going to happen." There were four other cars in the otherwise empty parking lot. One of them, a shiny black VW bug, boasted a yellow smiley-face bumper sticker with the motto "Change Happens." Had to be the therapist's car, she decided, hating her on the spot.

Paula Talbott-Sinclair's reception area wasn't much more impressive than her storefront. Worn and faded brown indoor-outdoor carpet, a low-slung olive-green pleather sofa, and a couple of armless chairs. There was a receptionist's desk, with a computer terminal and telephone, but no sign of a receptionist. Only a clipboard with a hand-lettered sign on the desktop: DIVORCE RECOVERY GROUP MEMBERS, PLEASE SIGN IN HERE. There were three other names on the sign-in sheet, all women, Grace noted.

The door on the wall opposite the front door was slightly ajar, and Grace heard the low hum of voices. She wrote her name on the sign-in sheet, hesitating a moment, before jotting down Grace Davenport.

"Hello?" she said softly, approaching the door. A woman popped her head out. Grace guessed she must be in her midforties. Her heart-shaped face was framed with a cascade of sandy-blond curls, and she had startlingly blue eyes behind wire-rimmed glasses. She was dressed in a figure-hugging sleeveless black tank top and tight black yoga pants, with a gauzy black shawl draped around her bony shoulders. And she was barefoot.

"Oh hi," she said brightly, looking Grace up and down. She grasped both of Grace's hands in hers and squeezed. "I'm Dr. Talbott-Sinclair, although in group, we all just use first names. So I'm Paula. And you must be Grace Stanton?"

"Actually, it's Davenport," Grace said. "If you don't mind."

"I see," Paula said, pursing her lips. "Well, that's something we're going to want to talk about, isn't it?"

"Taking back my maiden name?" Grace asked. "Does the judge have a problem with that?"

Paula cocked her head and blinked. "The question is, Grace, do you have a problem with it? Is this something you're doing out of anger? Because we can't have a healing when our hearts and minds are full of bitterness. You'll come to see that, I think, eventually, in group."

"It's *my* name," Grace said, feeling unusually obstinate. "I was a Davenport for way longer than I was a Stanton."

"All right," Paula said, pushing the door open. "Let's hold that thought. For now, come on in and meet the other members of group."

The inner office consisted of a large glass-topped desk and a swivel chair, in the corner of the room. It had the same brown carpet as the outer office and a pair of small-ish windows that were covered with a set of shiny bronze drapes in a cheesy sheer fabric. Five folding chairs were arranged in a semicircle around a high-backed brown leather chair. A row of framed diplomas was stretched across the wall above the desk, and three women, all of them looking ill at ease, were clustered around a small wooden table that held a coffeepot and a stack of Styrofoam cups, talking in subdued voices.

"Ladies," Paula said, her voice rising to let them know she had an important announcement. "Ladies!"

The women turned their attention to the newcomer. If Grace had any expectations about what her divorce recovery group would look like, this wasn't it.

"Don't I know you?" A tall, elegantly dressed black woman approached Grace, hands on her hips, studying the newcomer intently. She wore her hair in a sleek bobbed cut, and the first thing Grace noticed about her were her almond-shaped eyes and her luxuriously thick fringe of eyelashes. Fakes?

"I, I'm not sure," Grace said, stuttering a little. Wasn't group therapy supposed to be anonymous? Wasn't Paula Talbott-Sinclair supposed to protect her identity?

"Wait, I've got it," the woman snapped her fingers. "Gracenotes! Am I right? You're the lifestyle blogger who drowned her husband's 175,000-dollar ride. Damn! I covered that story, and it got picked up by all the networks." She patted Grace's shoulder. "Nice goin', girlfriend."

Grace felt her face flame with embarrassment. So much for anonymity.

"You! You're that reporter! Camryn. Camryn . . . something. You snuck into our subdivision, trespassed, talked to all my neighbors." She lowered her voice. "Did you follow me here today? Don't you people have any sense of decency?" She looked around for the therapist, ready to chew her out.

"Relax," Camryn said, chuckling. "Me, follow you here? Don't flatter yourself. I'm here for the same reason you are."

Grace narrowed her eyes. "You drove your husband's car into a pool?"

"Not quite," Camryn said. "Let's just say what I did do didn't set well with some parties."

Another woman walked up to join them. She was younger than Camryn Nobles but older than Grace, petite and slender, with sun-streaked shoulder-length blond hair pushed back from her forehead by a pair of designer sunglasses. Her skin was flawless, and she was dressed casually, in white capris and a flowery pink and orange tunic top and gold sandals. She wore a fine gold chain around her neck, and dangling from it was a whopper of a diamond, three carats, at least, Grace estimated.

"Hey, y'all," she said, in a honey-dipped drawl. She glanced over her shoulder at Paula Talbott-Sinclair, who had seated herself in the swivel chair and was looking expectantly at the door. "Are you thinkin' what I'm thinkin'?"

"What's that?" Camryn said.

"Well, I'm just wondering what kind of dog-and-pony show we've lucked into here. I mean, did you get a look at this shopping center? I've been living in Sarasota all my life, and I have never, and I mean ever, stepped foot in a place like this. What kind of a therapist has her offices between a tattoo artist and a diaper store?"

"The kind who charges three hundred dollars a session," Camryn said. "Obviously she's not spending what she makes on overhead."

"For real," the blonde said. "And the thing is, my lawyer says I probably can't make my ex pay for these sessions. Even though I'm not the one who was fuckin' around on the side. I'll tell you, that damned Stackpole has my lawyer runnin' scared."

"Stackpole!" Camryn said with a snort. "He's the judge hearing your divorce?"

"That's the one," the blonde said. "You too?"

"Unfortunately," Camryn said. She looked at Grace. "How about you?"

"Afraid so," Grace said. "My lawyer says he hates women. Especially women lawyers."

"My lawyer's a man, and I still got the shaft," Camryn pointed out.

"Me too," the blonde said. "Well, I guess we're in this together, huh? By the way, I'm Ashleigh. Hartounian."

"I don't think we're supposed to tell our last names," Grace said.

"Why not?" Camryn shot. "I got nuthin' to hide. Anyway, y'all both know my name, so why shouldn't I know yours?"

Grace sighed. "Whatever. I'm Grace Davenport."

"I thought your name was Stanton," Camryn said.

"It was. I'm taking back my maiden name."

Camryn rolled her eyes. "I'll bet the judge is gonna love that." She turned toward Ashleigh. "So, is your ex Boyce Hartounian? The plastic surgeon?"

"You know him?"

"Only his reputation," Camryn said. "He did an eye lift for one of my girlfriends at the station. I swear, she looks ten years younger."

"Boyce is good, all right," Ashleigh admitted.

Camryn took a step closer and examined the younger

woman's face. "How 'bout you? Did he do some work on you?"

"Some," Ashleigh admitted. She lifted her shoulders. "He gave me these boobs, not long after we started dating. And for our first anniversary, he gave me Reese Witherspoon's nose."

"Damn," Camryn said. "Those boobs are fine."

The fourth woman in the room wandered up, looking distinctly uneasy. She was older than all of them, in her early fifties. Her dark brown hair was streaked with gray, and a thin network of crow's-feet radiated out from her eyes. She was neatly dressed in a pale gray linen blouse and gray slacks.

"Hello," she said quietly. "I guess I should introduce myself? I'm Suzanne."

"Ashleigh."

"Grace."

"I'm Camryn. Look here, is the judge hearing your divorce named Stackpole?"

Suzanne looked startled. "As a matter of fact, yes."

"Uh-huh," Camryn said, nudging Grace. "And did you do something ugly to your ex? Maybe act out a little bit, something like that?"

Suzanne's face paled. "I can't . . . I don't . . . I won't . . ."

"Never mind," Grace said. "Whatever you did, I'm sure your husband deserved it."

Suzanne bit her lip. "I still can't believe I went through with it. And I can't believe I'm here, tonight. It all seems so surreal."

"What's surreal is the fact that this group is all women," Camryn said. "This isn't group therapy. It's ladies' night."

"A really, really, expensive ladies' night," Grace put in.

"Ladies . . ." Paula called from her seat at the front of the room. "Let's get started, shall we? I'm expecting one more member to join us, but I think we'll go ahead and get started. So take a seat, if you will."

Grace sat down on one of the folding chairs and crossed her legs. The other three women did the same.

"Well," Paula said, giving them a bright smile. "I take it you've all introduced yourselves to each other. Ashleigh, Grace, Camryn, and Suzanne. Tonight is an important night for all of you. Right? It's the night you all start the healing. And the forgiving."

"No way," Camryn muttered under her breath.

"Excuse me?" Paula said sharply.

"I said, no way," Camryn said defiantly. "That judge can order me to come to these bullshit counseling sessions. And he can order me to pay through the nose for the privilege of coming here. But he cannot make me forgive what Dexter Nobles did to me."

She crossed her arms over her chest. "And neither can you."

"I see," Paula said. She nodded at Ashleigh. "What about you, Ashleigh? Did you come here with an open mind tonight?"

"I came with an open checkbook," Ashleigh said. "That's the best I can do right now."

Camryn guffawed and Grace managed to stifle her own laugh.

"Grace?" Paula's look was expectant.

"My husband has locked me out of my own home," Grace said, feeling her throat constrict. "He's frozen my bank accounts. Canceled my credit cards. I have no way to support myself. I'm living with my mother, tending bar to pay for gas money. He's living in a two-million-dollar home, shacking up with my twenty-six-year-old former assistant. So no, right now, I'm really not ready for what you call a healing."

Paula frowned. "All this negativity. I find it very sad. Very disappointing."

Too damn bad, Grace thought. She glanced over at Camryn Nobles, and then at Ashleigh Hartounian. Their faces were impassive. Suzanne's face was scrunched in concentration.

"We've got a lot of work ahead of us," Paula said after a moment. She went over to her desk, picked up a stack of old-fashioned black-and-white-spattered composition books, and handed one to each of the women.

"This," she said. "Is your divorce journal. I want all of you to get in the habit of writing in it, at least once a day, although several times a day would be most helpful."

"Write what?" Ashleigh demanded.

"Everything. Anything. We're going to be doing some visualization exercises that I think will be helpful. And I'd like you to search, really search your souls, for the truthful answers to some questions I'm going to pose to all of you. Because, in here, honesty is everything."

Paula waved toward the windows. "Out there, with your family and friends, you can hide your pain. You can cover it up, sanitize it, deny it. But in here—with group—I expect nothing less than absolute honesty."

She opened the bottom drawer of her desk and brought out a boxy Polaroid camera. She walked briskly to the semicircle of chairs and snapped a photo of Grace, before Grace had time to object. When the photo ejected from the camera, the therapist handed it to Grace and moved on, taking pictures of Camryn and Suzanne, then Ashleigh, handing each woman her photo.

Grace stared down at the Polaroid, watching as the pale gray of the film disappeared and a grainy image of herself came into focus. She was shocked at what she saw. Her formerly full, round face looked gaunt. Her hair hung limply from a center part that emphasized her dark roots.

She hadn't bothered with makeup that day, hadn't actually bothered with it at all since the day she'd been turned away from the security gate at Gulf Vista. There were dark circles under her eyes and deeply etched grooves at the corners of her mouth. It struck Grace that she couldn't remember smiling, not in days. She looked sad. Sad and old, and defeated.

She glanced at the other women. Camryn and Ashleigh didn't look any more pleased with their photos. In fact, Ashleigh had pulled a compact from her Louis Vuitton satchel and was busily applying more lipstick. Suzanne stared at her photograph as though she'd never seen a picture of herself before.

Now Paula handed Grace a stapler. "I want you to staple the Polaroid to page one of your divorce journal. This is your before picture. Now, turn the page and describe what you see in yourself in this photo. Tell me where you are, today. What you're feeling about the place you're in, right now, emotionally. If you like, you can write about this experience you're having, your first night in group. Be honest. I know you all resent me, resent being here. I expect that." She looked down at her watch. "I'm going to give you fifteen minutes to write. And when I come back, I want you all to be ready to share what you wrote with the rest of the group."

"What if I don't feel like sharing?" Ashleigh asked, tossing her hair behind her shoulder. "What if I don't feel like writing anything?"

Paula's smile was tight. "Oh, Ashleigh. You know Judge Stackpole made your attendance at group mandatory as a condition for granting your divorce, right?"

"How could I forget?" Ashleigh asked.

"It's not as simple as just showing up," Paula said. "Judge Stackpole knows some people will just go through the motions, simply so they can get that divorce decree.

Despite what you all think, I must tell you, Cedric Stack-pole is really a very wise man. So he's asked me to be very clear about his expectations for all of you." She smiled.

"Each week, I'll be reporting in to Judge Stackpole about your progress in group. And if I feel that you're only coasting, just giving group therapy lip service, I won't be able to sign off on your attendance report."

"Attendance report?" Ashleigh asked. "Like in kinder-garten? Are you serious?"

"Very serious," Paula said. "You have fifteen minutes to write. Starting now."

She walked out into the reception area, closing the door firmly behind.

Grace began scribbling on the second page of the journal.

I can't believe I have been "sentenced" to group therapy. I have nothing in common with these other women. I don't see how hearing their pathetic sto-ries is going to help me get over what was done to me. I don't need therapy. I need a divorce. I was be-trayed by my lying, cheating, dirtbag husband. You want to know how I feel? I feel different ways, dif-ferent days. Most nights, I can't sleep. I don't know what's happening with my life. How will I make a living for myself? Where will I live? I can't keep liv-ing with my mother, but right now I don't have a choice. I have no choices at all. That's what I think I resent the most about all this. The feeling of power-lessness, of being helpless. It's so damned unfair. And I'm supposed to get over all of this? I'm supposed to reach a point where I don't feel this rage, bubbling up inside me, threatening to boil over at any mo-ment? Most of the time, I am CONSUMED with an-ger. And when I'm not, I'm just sad. So damned sad. And lonely. Everything I had is gone. I'm thirty-eight. And alone.

"This is bullshit," Camryn Nobles was saying, as she made bold, looping lines of script on the open page of her journal. "My lawyer didn't tell me anything about having to write in a journal, or having to report to therapy, like a high school kid to study hall. I'm calling him tonight, just as soon as I get out of here. That bullshit judge can't make us do this shit."

"Shh," Ashleigh whispered, jerking her head in the direction of the door. "She'll hear you and tell the judge what you called him."

"I don't care what she tells that damned judge," Camryn said fiercely. "I'm not in his courtroom now. This is America. Not some damned banana republic, where he gets to lay down the law and make us salute every time he farts."

Grace laughed despite herself. "Maybe you could do an exposé of the judge for your television station."

"Maybe I will," Camryn shot back. "Just as soon as I get my divorce from Dexter Nobles, I might just do that."

The room was quiet then, with only the scratching sounds of their pens as they scrawled their thoughts across the cheap notebooks.

After she'd filled two pages of her journal, Grace looked at her watch. "It's been thirty minutes. Where do you think Paula went?"

"Who cares?" Camryn said. "This whole thing is a charade."

"I'm gonna go check on her," Grace said. "I've had a long day. I just want to get out of here."

She walked across the room, opened the door, and peeked out into the reception area. Paula Talbott-Sinclair was slumped down in the chair behind the reception desk, her chin resting on her chest. She was snoring softly.

Grace stood there for a moment, uncertain what her next move should be. Then she heard the front door behind her open.

A man stepped inside the reception area, looking uncertainly around the room.

He was tall and lanky, and sunburned. He was about Grace's age, she guessed, and at first she thought he was completely bald, until a closer look revealed a fine dark stubble of hair covering his scalp. He was dressed like a workman, in baggy khaki cargo shorts, a grimy-looking faded khaki safari hat, and high-topped lace-up work boots. His eyes were dark, nearly black, with an astonishing fringe of thick, luxuriant lashes. And dimples. It was the dimples that reminded Grace that she'd seen this guy before, and recently.

"Hey," Wyatt Keller said, scowling at her. "I'm looking for Dr. Talbott-Sinclair?"

Grace nodded in the direction of the slumbering therapist. "You just found her."

12.

"Is this a joke?" Wyatt asked, narrowing his eyes. He pulled a slip of paper from his pocket and reread the card the judge had forced him to take. Then he took a closer look at Grace.

"Didn't we meet . . ." he hesitated. "In court?"

"That's right," Grace said.

"I'm supposed to be here for the, uh, divorce recovery group," he said.

"Well, you're late," Grace snapped. "It started thirty minutes ago. Not that you missed much."

"Damn," Wyatt said. "The bridge was up. I've got a sick bird, and I had to run her to the vet's office, and the asshole vet tech wouldn't wait for me to get there, and the office was closed by the time I got there, and I had to stop at a drugstore and buy some meds . . ."

"Really?" Grace sniffed. "That's the best you can do? The dog ate your homework?"

Wyatt bridled. "It's true. Anyway, what do you care?"

Grace shrugged. "I don't. I just care about getting out of here. Right now. I've had enough 'sharing.'"

Wyatt nodded in the direction of Paula, who hadn't stirred despite their odd conversation.

"What's wrong with her?"

"Don't know, don't care," Grace said. "It's eight o'clock. My time's up."

She marched over to the desk and shook the therapist's shoulder. "Paula," she said loudly. "Hey, Paula. Wake up."

Nothing.

"Is she sick or something?" Wyatt asked, taking a step closer. He reached out and touched the side of her neck, looking for a pulse.

"Who's that?" Paula's eyes flew open and she swatted his hand away. She looked wildly around the room. "What's happening?"

"You told us to write for fifteen minutes, but it's now been more than thirty minutes," Grace said. "I came out here to check on you, and found you dead asleep. Or passed out."

"Ridiculous!" Paula said. She stood, fluffed her hair, and straightened her clothing, looking like Stevie Nicks after an epic bender. "I was meditating, waiting on the group to complete their visualization exercise."

"Who are you?" she asked, looking Wyatt up and down.

"I'm Wyatt," he said. "Judge Stackpole said I had to come see you. For divorce recovery group."

He said the words with such distaste, that Grace almost laughed out loud.

"Didn't the judge tell you our sessions start promptly at seven?"

"He told me," Wyatt said. "But I had a family emergency. And the bridge was up. But I'm here. I've been here for . . ." he looked down at his watch, and then at Grace, his dark eyes pleading.

"Twenty minutes," Grace volunteered. "We weren't sure whether or not to wake you."

Paula studied Grace's face carefully. "Really?"

"It's true," Grace said, with a shrug. "You can ask the others. We were all waiting for you to come back and take a look at our journals, to see if we did what you asked."

Paula waved her hand distractedly. "Never mind that. It's late. I'll read them next week."

"So . . . we can go now?" Grace asked. "All of us?"

"Didn't I just say that?" Paula asked.

She went into the inner office and clapped her hands for attention. "All right. That's the session for tonight. I'll see everybody next Wednesday, at seven o'clock. Remember to bring your journals."

She turned and handed Wyatt a notebook. "And next week, please be on time."

Camryn and Ashleigh stood quickly and headed for the door, while Suzanne was still jotting in her notebook. "Ladies," Paula said, gesturing toward the newcomer. "Before you go? This is Wyatt. He'll be a part of group for the next few weeks. I'd like you to welcome him to our little circle of healing. Wyatt, this is Ashleigh, Camryn, and Suzanne. And you already met Grace."

Suzanne looked distressed. "Uh, Paula, no offense to him, but I thought this was just a women's group? Nobody said anything about men being part of it."

"We welcome anybody with an open, willing heart to group, Suzanne," Paula said.

"Hey," Wyatt mumbled, blushing slightly as the women carefully looked him over.

"Hmm," Ashleigh purred.

"What's your story?" Camryn wanted to know. "Did Stackpole sentence you, too? I thought he only hated women."

"Never mind that," Paula said. She grabbed her camera and snapped a picture of the startled Wyatt. When the photo had developed, she handed it to him.

"What's this?" he asked, gazing down at the picture. It was not what you'd call a flattering image. The harsh overhead lights cast his face in deep shadows. He needed a shave, he noted, and there was a distinct sweat ring around the collar of his shirt. Also? There was a telltale white dribble on the shoulder of the shirt. Parrot poop, from Cookie, who'd insisted on riding on his shoulder the whole way to the vet's office.

"That's your before picture," Paula told him. "Staple it in the book. And the journal is your homework assignment. I want you to write in it at least once a day, every day, more often if you can. Tonight's assignment is to write about how you feel about where you are in your emotional journey."

"Ohh-kay," Wyatt said slowly.

"And Wyatt? As the ladies can tell you, the one thing I insist upon in group, besides punctuality, is absolute honesty. No whitewashing. No lies. Understand?"

Camryn snorted. "He's a man. They're genetically programmed to lie."

"Telling a man not to lie is like asking him to pee sitting down," Ashleigh agreed.

"Ladies?" Paula said wearily.

Wyatt had had more than enough. He could feel the hostility radiating out of every woman in this room. Man-hating ballbusters, every one of them.

"Also?" Paula held out her hand. "Your counseling fees must be paid in full, in advance of each session. Did your attorney explain my fee structure? You understand I don't accept personal checks? Credit cards, although no American Express, or a cashier's check."

"She told me," Wyatt said. He reached into the pocket of his shorts and pulled out a tightly rolled bundle of money. The bills were faded and creased, and as he counted off each of the six fifty-dollar bills he thought of what that money should be going to. Groceries. New tennis shoes for Bo, and, now, payment on his ever-growing vet bill.

He pressed the money into Paula's hand.

"Cash?" She looked down at the bills as though he'd just handed her one of Cookie's bird turds.

"Yeah," he said. "Can I get a receipt for that? My lawyer told me to make sure and get one. To prove to the judge that I was here."

When he finally got outside the therapist's office, he took a deep breath of the hot, humid night air. May, and it was already sweltering. Well, that was Florida. Anyway, it felt good to be outside. It had been freezing in that damned office. And all those women, staring at him, like he was some kind of spawn of Satan.

Just because he was a man. Betsy had warned him it would probably be like this. "It's a divorce recovery group, honey," she'd said. "A bunch of sad, mad, depressed, repressed women. All of 'em blaming all their problems on some man who done them wrong. Just sit there and take it, and with any luck, six weeks from now, Judge Stackpole will sign off on your divorce and you and Bo can get back to living your lives."

He'd parked at the far end of the parking lot, mostly because he didn't want anybody riding by to know he was going to see a shrink. As he approached the truck now, he saw a woman standing beside it, bending down, looking in the open window.

It was that woman from group. What was her name? Grace, yeah. Grace.

He quickened his step until he was right beside her.

"Is there a problem?" he asked gruffly.

She looked up, puzzled. She had nice eyes, Wyatt thought, when she wasn't pissed off.

"You really do have a bird in your truck," she said, wonderingly.

"That's what I tried to tell you," Wyatt said. "What? You think every man is a liar?"

She ignored that, concentrating on Cookie, who was roosting on the steering wheel, her head tucked under her wing, eyes closed.

"It's a parrot, right? What kind?"

"African gray."

"Aren't you afraid he'll fly away, leaving the window open like that?"

Wyatt laughed. "Cookie? Nah."

"You said he's sick? What's wrong with him?"

"She. Same old thing," Wyatt said. "Cookie will eat any damned thing she can get her beak around. One of the kids at the park fed her something today. A gummy worm, probably. It, uh, didn't agree with her digestive system."

Grace looked closer at the slumbering bird. "Looks like she pooped all over your steering wheel."

"Yeah," Wyatt said with a sigh. "She's bad to do that."

She turned and pointed at his right shoulder. "I think she got your shirt, too."

"I would make a joke about getting shit on by everybody, but I wouldn't want you to think I'm bitter," Wyatt said.

Grace straightened. "Are you?"

"Oh yeah," he said easily. "Isn't everybody bitter about something?"

She thought about it. "I'd hate to think so, but yeah, it seems that way to me these days. Although maybe my mom isn't. God knows why, but I really think she doesn't have a bitter bone in her body."

"I've got enough bitter for both of us," Wyatt said.

Grace was looking at Cookie again. "You said something about a park. Do you work for the city or the county?"

"Hell, no," he said emphatically. "I work for myself. At Jungle Jerry's."

Her face lit up. "Jungle Jerry's," she said delightedly. "I remember that place! We used to go there every year on field trips for school. I used to love the parrots and the little Key deer. They were so adorable. Do you still have the parrot show? Where they ride the little toy bike on the high wire?"

"Yeah," Wyatt said, feeling himself thaw a little. "Cookie here is the star of the show. When she isn't eating Popsicle sticks and Happy Meal toys."

"Jungle Jerry's," Grace said wistfully. "I haven't been there in years and years. In fact, I didn't even know it was still there."

"You and everybody else in Florida," Wyatt said. "But we are definitely still there, right where we've always been.

He hesitated, then reached in the pocket of his shorts and pulled out a bright orange card. "That's a free pass. If you're not doing anything some day, you get in free with that. Bring your kids, if you want. It's good for the whole family."

"No kids," Grace said lightly. "Just me."

"Guess that's just as well," Wyatt said. "Since you're getting a divorce, right?"

"Yeah," Grace said. "Just as well. Since he turned out to be a scumbag."

Her mouth hardened and her eyes narrowed, and she looked like she had earlier in the evening, when he'd first walked into the therapist's office. Wyatt found himself missing her smile already, and wishing he could do something to bring it back.

"Guess I'd better go," he said, unlocking the truck.

"Me too," Grace said. "Gotta go home and write in my divorce journal."

"Yeah." Wyatt opened the driver's door and slid onto the seat. "Hey, uh, thanks," he said.

"For what?"

"Covering for me with the therapist," Wyatt said. "I can't afford to get crossways with her, or that damned judge."

"It's okay," Grace said. "Sounds like we're all in the same boat. Divorce-wise," she added.

"Yeah, divorce-wise."

She gestured at Cookie, who was awake now, and hopping up and down on the steering wheel.

"Will your parrot be okay?"

"She'll be fine," Wyatt said. "I'm gonna pick up some Pepto-Bismol at the Seven-Eleven, and see if that settles her down any."

"Hey. Does she talk?"

He laughed. "When she wants. If she likes you."

Grace leaned into the car, and Wyatt caught the scent of her, faintly soft and sweet, like the flowers in the park after a spring rain. She held her hand out, and Cookie happily stepped onto her outstretched index finger.

"Ohhh," Grace breathed. "Is this okay? She won't bite, will she?"

"Not usually," he said.

"Hi, Cookie," she said.

The bird cocked her head and blinked. "Wassup?"

Grace giggled just like one of the kids at Jungle Jerry's. "Cookie want a cookie?" She looked over at Wyatt. "Dumb, right?"

The parrot inched her way up Grace's forearm, until she was perched on the crook of her elbow.

Now Grace was getting nervous. "She won't try to fly away, will she?"

"No such luck," Wyatt said. "She knows where her bread is buttered. Literally."

"Gimme a beer," Cookie demanded. "Gimme a shot of whiskey. Gimme some peanuts."

"You don't really give her beer and whiskey, do you?"

"Nah," Wyatt said. "She just says that for the shock value. But she really does love peanuts."

Grace smiled again, and Wyatt found himself smiling back. "I better get going. It's trivia night."

"You play trivia?"

"Not really. I'm terrible at it. Actually, it's trivia night at the bar where I work, and it gets pretty busy about this time."

"You work at a bar?"

She bristled. "Anything wrong with that?"

"No," he said hastily. "Not at all. Which bar?"

"It's just a hole in the wall. Over in Cortez. You never heard of it."

"Try me."

"The Sandbox."

He grinned. "I know that place. My whole softball team used to go there after games. So it's still there? I heard the owner died a while back. What was his name? Butch?"

"Butch Davenport," Grace said. "Yeah, he's been gone a couple years now."

"You knew him?"

"He was my dad," Grace said. "My mom runs the place now. I moved in with her, after the split with my ex." She held her arm out straight and laughed as the bird waddled down her forearm and back into the truck.

"Good night, Cookie." She looked in at the bird's owner and was surprised to see him smiling at her, flashing those choirboy dimples.

"Good night, Wyatt."

"See you next week," he said.

13.

Wyatt found his father asleep in the battered leather recliner in the tiny living room, the remote control still clutched in his hand, the television turned to the Cooking Channel.

"Pop." He shook the older man gently. "Hey, Pop. C'mon. Why don't you go on to bed now?"

Nelson yawned and stretched. "I'm waitin' for Rachael Ray to come on. I like those quickie recipes of hers."

"You like that cute ass of hers," Wyatt retorted. "Anyway, her show just went off. Go on to bed, okay?"

Nelson pulled himself out of the chair with effort. He was only seventy-four, but a lifetime of physical labor around the park had left him feeling every ache and pain this time of night. "I gotta make Bo's lunch and put a load of clothes in the dryer."

"I'll do it," Wyatt said, giving his father a gentle push in the direction of his room. "Everything go okay around here tonight?"

"Sure thing," Nelson said. "Bo and me, we had some hot dogs and coleslaw for dinner. He ate up every scrap I fed him. That kid's got a hollow leg for sure."

"Don't I know it," Wyatt said ruefully. "He's already

outgrown the pants I bought him at Easter. And his toes are coming out of the top of his sneakers."

"How's Cookie?" Nelson asked. "The vet fix her up?"

"The damned vet tech closed up before I got there," Wyatt said. "Anyway, I think she'll be all right. I just put her up for the night. Anything else going on in the park?"

"Slow," Nelson said. "Like all week. No sense in staying open when there's nobody around. I locked up the gates around seven thirty." He brightened. "We got that Brownie troop coming tomorrow. Fourteen little girls, and the troop leaders and some mamas. I put some sodas in the snack-bar fridge, and I thought I'd go pick up some candy to sell in the morning."

"Skip the candy," Wyatt advised. "Just get some fruit—maybe some grapes and apples and stuff. These scout leaders don't let the kids eat the kind of junk we used to eat."

"It never killed you," Nelson pointed out. He started toward his room, then turned around.

"Callie called."

Wyatt sighed. "What now?"

"I don't know," Nelson admitted. "She wouldn't talk to me. Just ordered me to put Bo on the phone. I did, and when he hung up the phone from talking to her, he burst out crying. I should've told her he was outside playing and couldn't come to the phone. That's what I get for being honest. And stupid."

"Did he say why he was so upset?" Wyatt asked, his heart sinking. Callie knew damned well he'd be out of the house tonight, at his so-called divorce recovery group. She'd been sitting right there in the courtroom when the judge ordered him to attend.

"Oh yeah," Nelson said. "Callie told Bo she and the ass-hole are picking him up right after school on Friday, because they're going to Birmingham this weekend, to look for a new place to live."

"Dammit," Wyatt said. "I told her it's Scout's birthday party Friday. Anna's taking all the kids to that new water park, and then they're going out for pizza afterwards. Bo's been talking about it for two weeks now, ever since he got the invitation in the mail."

"Remind me who Scout is?"

"She's Bo's best friend, and she's our shortstop on the T-ball team. Anna is her mom."

"That's right," Nelson said. "Bo's had his bathing suit laid out on his dresser since Saturday. Poor kid. Now he'll have to miss it. All because Callie can't stand to see him have a good time unless it's something she engineered. Isn't there anything you can do?"

"I doubt it," Wyatt said, his jaw tensing. "It's her weekend. Technically, it starts as soon as he gets out of school on Friday. Never mind that most Fridays she calls me at the last minute and has me pick him up because 'something's come up'—like she wants to get her nails done, or she and the asshole are slugging down margaritas at The Salty Dog."

"Damned shame," Nelson muttered.

"And I can't call her anyway," Wyatt said. "Since she got the judge to forbid me to contact her, unless it's in writing."

"I know she's a woman, but she oughtta be horse-whipped," Nelson said angrily. "And that's my opinion on the subject."

Wyatt opened the bedroom door and undressed in the dark. He heard the soft rustle of sheets.

"Dad?"

He went over to the narrow twin bed and sat on the edge. He ruffled his son's light brown hair. "Hey, buddy," he said. "What are you doing awake?"

"I tried to wait up for you, but I fell asleep," Bo said.

"You're supposed to be asleep," Wyatt chided. "You're a little kid. You need a lot of sleep so's you can grow another six inches before tomorrow morning."

"I'm really mad at Mom," Bo said. "She says we have to go to dumb old Birmingham this weekend, and I have to miss Scout's birthday party."

"I know," Wyatt said. "Granddad told me, and I'm so sorry. I know how much you wanted to go to that water park."

The little boy sniffed. "Cory went there for his cousin's birthday. He says they have a killer wave machine that'll make you pee your pants just looking at it. And water cannons. They have water cannons so strong you could knock a kid down with 'em. I told Mom I didn't want to go to Birmingham. I told her I don't want to move there, and I don't want to live with you know who."

"Oh, Bo-Bo," Wyatt said. He rubbed his son's back, feeling the warmth of his skin through the thin fabric of his Lightning McQueen pajama top.

"Dad?"

"What, buddy?"

"I got so mad at Mom, I called her a bad name. Did Granddad tell you that?"

Wyatt had to stifle a laugh. "He didn't mention it. What kind of bad name did you call your mom?"

The child hesitated. "Granddad told me if I said it again, he might have to wash my mouth out with soap like he did when you were a kid."

Now Wyatt did laugh. "I'll tell you a secret on your granddad, Bo. He's all hat and no cattle."

"Huh?"

"That means he just talks a good game. He never washed my mouth out with soap. Not ever. Now, what kind of name did you call your mom? Just between us guys?"

Bo dropped his voice to a whisper. "I called her a shit."

Wyatt was glad for the cover of darkness, because his grin split his face in two. Then he forced himself to sound stern.

"Well, son, that's not a very nice thing to call your own mother."

"I was very, very, very mad at her."

"I know you were. But you can't go around calling people a shit, just because they made you mad."

"She called me a shit first," Bo said.

"When was this?" Wyatt asked, surprised.

"Right after I told her I wanted to stay with you this weekend and go to Scout's birthday party. She said, 'listen, you little shit. I am picking you up Friday right after school and that's final.'"

Wyatt tried to choose his words carefully. Betsy had warned him that he was on thin ice with Callie, now more than ever.

"I don't think your mom should have called you that, Bo," he said finally. "But that doesn't make it right for you to use bad words. Right now, your mom is really mad at me, too, because I don't want her to take you so far away from me. So, she might say some stuff to you that she doesn't really mean, because she's actually just mad at me. But, Bo, even if she says mean things sometimes, your mom really loves you. We both do. Right?"

"I guess so. But I still don't want to go to stinkin' Birmingham."

Wyatt leaned over and kissed his son's cheek. "Sleep now."

He climbed into the matching twin bed and pulled the worn sheet over his chest. The old walls in the mobile home were paper-thin, and he could hear his father snoring in the room right next door. A moment later, he heard the soft in and out of his son's drowsy breathing. For once, he was glad of the cramped quarters in their makeshift house. He reached out his hand and let it rest lightly on Bo's wrist. For tonight, anyway, Callie could not pull them apart.

14.

On only their second night of what she'd begun to think of as divorce camp, their counselor, Paula Talbott-Sinclair, looked, Grace decided, a hot mess. Her eyes were red-rimmed, her thick black mascara smeared. She seemed not to notice that her haphazard topknot of blond curls was coming undone or that a fine sprinkling of crumbs adorned one strap of her turquoise tank top.

She'd lit a stick of incense, and the pungent white smoke drifting through the room made Grace's eyes water and her nose itch.

"Everybody here?" Paula asked, looking around the room. She gave Wyatt Keeler a droopy-eyed wink. "Wyatt, I see you made it on time this week. That's good. Verrrry good."

She was slurring her words, Grace thought. Was she drunk, stoned? She looked around the therapist's office. Nobody else seemed to notice Paula's condition. Maybe it was just her imagination.

"Now," Paula said, giving her hands a clap that sent her half dozen bracelets a-jingle. "Who wants to read from their recovery journal?"

Silence.

"Nobody?" Paula frowned. "Friends, we have to share here. It's part of our healing process. So who will break the ice? Am I going to have to call on somebody, or will you volunteer?"

"I'll go," Camryn said. She was dressed in gym clothes tonight, a snug-fitting fuchsia Nike shirt, black bike shorts, hot-pink running shoes. She'd wrapped a hot-pink scarf around her hair and had ditched the false eyelashes.

Camryn opened her black-and-white notebook and cleared her throat. "Okay," she said hesitantly. "Here goes."

She traced a line of writing with her fingertip, took a deep breath, and began reading.

"I feel like a victim. It's my job as a journalist to interview people, to tell their stories, convey their experiences. So here is my experience, and I am going to tell you exactly how it happened and how it makes me feel, and the hell with anybody who wants me to say I am sorry, because I am not sorry.

"My husband, Dexter Nobles, is scum. He lied to me, he lied to our daughter, he lied to all our friends. Bad enough he cheated on me, but no, he had to do it with our daughter's best friend. A twenty-year-old! So how do you think that makes me feel when I look in the mirror? When I look at this picture of myself, I'm reminded of the victims I interview at a crime scene. Like the old lady who gets pistol-whipped by a thug on a street corner, or the guy whose car is jacked at a gas station. I used to wonder, what was that old lady doing out that time of night? Or why did that guy drive through that part of town in a new Mercedes? Were they that clueless? But now I know, a victim isn't asking to be jacked or pistol-whipped, or cheated on by somebody they used to love. I know it because I'm a victim. I'm somehow less than I used to be. And I don't like it worth a damn."

Camryn paused and looked up at the others, and then at Dr. Paula Talbott-Sinclair. "There's a lot more, but you get the idea."

Paula's eyelids drooped, then fluttered. "Very . . . revealing." She was quiet for a moment, her blond topknot resting against the leather armchair's headrest, her eyes closed.

"Are we supposed to talk about what Camryn wrote?" This from Ashleigh, who was leaning forward, her hands clamped on her knees.

Paula's eyes remained closed. She waved her hand. "Go ahead."

"Your ex actually did that? Screwed your daughter's best friend? Like, even in your house?"

"Repeatedly," Camryn said. "In my house, my bed, my living room. In motels, and in the apartment she shared with my daughter. Did I mention this girl is our daughter's roommate?"

"Ooh," Ashleigh said, wide-eyed. "That is cold."

"Stone cold," Camryn agreed, her smile evil. "But I dealt with the bitch."

"What? More talk of revenge?" Paula's eyes flew open and she seemed to rally for a moment. "None of that," she warned. "No revenge talk. That's regressive behavior."

Ashleigh rolled her eyes.

"Whoosh next?" Paula asked, blinking rapidly. "Audrey?"

"It's Ashleigh. And yes, I can share."

Paula tilted her swivel chair backward, then around, so that her back was facing the group.

What the hell? Grace looked wordlessly at Camryn, then at Wyatt, who shrugged.

Ashleigh opened her notebook with a flourish and began reading, her voice breathy, dramatic.

"I look good. I mean, why should I let the fact that

Boyce mistakenly believes he is in love with somebody else give me an excuse to let myself go? Working for a plastic surgeon, I see all kinds of women. I see middle-aged women who are trying too hard, desperately trying to stay young, and I see young girls who think a smaller nose or higher cheekbones or a tighter ass will change their lives, make them something they're not. But I'm not like that. Boyce fell in love with me—the real me. I am the same person he fell in love with, just a few years older. That whore he's with now? I know where she lives. I watch her come home—sometimes he's with her. I want to call her up, laugh in her face, tell her, 'just you wait. You think he's in love? Think he'll stay with you? Hah! What you don't know is this: you're just like a carton of yogurt at Publix. You've got an expiration date, only you can't see it, cuz it's stamped on your ass. You won't even know it, until one morning Boyce Hartounian locks you out of your condo and stops payment on your new Benz.' "

Ashleigh closed her notebook, looking expectantly at the others. "Well?"

Suzanne Beamon cleared her throat, and all heads turned to stare at her. She'd barely said a word since the group started, hadn't even looked any of them in the eye yet.

"That's an interesting metaphor for marriage, the thing about the expiration date," Suzanne said. "I'm an English teacher," she added apologetically.

"You're really watching your husband's new girl-friend?" Grace asked Ashleigh. "Isn't that a little creepy?"

"Isn't it actually stalking?" Camryn put in. "The judge finds out about that, he's not gonna like it."

"He won't find out," Ashleigh said. "What goes on in group, stays in group, right, Paula? Everything we say here is confidential, that's what you told us."

No answer.

Camryn got up and gently swiveled the therapist's chair around so that it was now facing the group. Paula's head rested at an awkward angle on her shoulder, her mouth was slack-jawed with a tiny thread of spittle trailing down her chin, but her eyes were closed.

"Passed out cold again!" Camryn stepped back so the others could see for themselves.

Suzanne knelt on the floor beside Paula Talbott-Sinclair and pressed two fingers lightly to the pulse point on her throat, relieved to find an even, steady beat. Her dark brown eyes were intent behind the tortoiseshell frames of her glasses.

"She's not dead, thank heavens. So, what do we do now?" she asked, looking to the others for guidance. "Should we call somebody, make sure she gets home okay?"

"Who would we call?" Grace asked, looking around the office. "We don't even know if she's married. Or where she lives or anything else."

Camryn walked to the desk in the corner, sat down, and boldly began searching through the desk drawers, a journalist to the last.

"Here's her purse," she said, drawing a small multicolored crocheted handbag from the bottom desk drawer.

Suzanne frowned. "Is that really necessary? It's such an invasion of privacy." She shuddered. "I'd hate for a bunch of strangers to go pawing through my purse."

"We're not strangers. We're her 'friends,'" Camryn said, making air quote marks. She unknotted the drawstring closure and pulled out a small leather billfold. She flipped it open to the driver's license.

"According to this, she lives over on Anna Maria Island," Camryn said, lifting one eyebrow. "Obviously, she spends her money on a mortgage, not on the rent on this dump." She dumped the rest of the pocketbook's contents on the desktop, taking inventory as she examined each object.

"Lipstick, just some cheap drugstore crap. Hand sanitizer. Car keys." Camryn held up the key. "Big surprise, granola girl drives that VW Bug out front." She put the key back in the bag. "Cell phone."

She tapped the phone's screen, looking, in vain, for a call history. "Cheap-ass phone, too," she complained.

"Hello!" she said brightly, holding up a small brown plastic pill bottle. "Here's something interesting."

She squinted down at the tiny print on the bottle's label. "Why do they make the writing so small? Melasophenol?"

Ashleigh snatched the bottle away. "Here, let me. I was married to a doctor."

Camryn calmly reclaimed the pill bottle. "And I was married to a lawyer, but that doesn't make me Perry Mason." She opened the bottle and spilled two different colored capsules into the palm of her hand. "These are all that's left. Sleeping pills, I bet."

Ashleigh picked up one of the capsules. "Believe me, honey, they haven't made a sleeping pill I haven't sampled. Well, the label says melasophenol, which is a fairly mild tranquilizer, but this blue one here"—she held it up—"isn't melasophenol, which is actually a pale yellow tablet." She held up the other pill, which was pale yellow. "She's mixing tranqs with something else. Which might be the reason she's so out of it."

She leaned over and lightly ran a finger down the sleeping therapist's cheek. "Paula? Yoo-hoo. Anybody home?"

The woman didn't stir, didn't flinch.

"Clinically speaking, I'd say she's out for the night," Ashleigh concluded. "I say we blow this place. It's so depressing, I'm tempted to borrow one of these babies. And I would, but I've got plenty better stuff at home."

Grace wanted to leave as badly as anybody else. But. "You really think we should just leave her like this? I mean, what if she has like, respiratory failure or something? Or chokes on her vomit or something? You read about that with celebrities."

"You want to take her home with you, be my guest," Ashleigh said, heading for the door. "But I bet she won't be happy when she wakes up and figures out you people went through her purse and dragged her out of her office, unconscious."

Camryn hurriedly stuffed the pill bottle and the bill-fold back in the pocketbook. "She's got a point, you guys," she said. "Right now, I do not need to piss Paula off and get the judge pissed off at me." She placed the purse back in the desk drawer and quietly closed it.

"I say we leave her like she is and just go. And I don't know about you guys, but I could definitely use a drink. Who's in?"

"A drink sounds fabulous," Ashleigh said, nodding vigorously. "Grace? Wyatt?" At the last minute, she included the quietest member of the group. "Suzanne?"

"I wouldn't mind a drink," Grace admitted. "But let's at least put her on the sofa in the reception area, make her comfortable. If she stays like this much longer, she's going to have a hell of a headache when she finally wakes up."

Without saying a word, Wyatt leaned down, scooped Paula into his arms, and carried her to the outer office. He set her carefully down on the sofa cushions, placing a pillow beneath her head. She snored loudly.

Ashleigh followed him out to the reception area, watching Wyatt with an appreciative eye. "Good work," she purred. She sat down on the edge of the sofa and unceremoniously lifted one of Paula's eyelids. The therapist did not stir.

"Out like a trout," Ashleigh proclaimed. "Wyatt? What about that drink?"

"I don't know," he said uneasily. "My day starts pretty early. And I've got my son tonight."

"It's just barely eight," Camryn said, coming up behind him. She turned to Grace. "What about you?"

Grace did not intend to spend any more time with these people than necessary. Still, a long night stretched before her. And she was getting sick of her own company.

"Tell you what," she said, wondering if she'd lost her mind. "We can go to my mom's bar. The Sandbox? Do you know it? Over in Cortez?"

"Cortez?" Ashleigh wrinkled her pretty little nose. "Isn't that kind of a dive bar?"

"Exactly," Grace said.

"Perfect," Camryn said. "I love a dive bar. Let's roll." She turned to Suzanne. "Are you coming?"

"Well . . ." she said, her brow furrowed. "I told my daughter, Darby, I wouldn't be late."

"You won't be," Camryn said. "One drink. Think of it as group therapy."

"I guess one wouldn't hurt," Suzanne said finally. "I don't think I've ever been to Cortez. Is it very far?"

"Ten minutes," Camryn said. "I did a story over there a couple months ago. You can follow me. I'm in the white BMW sedan."

"What do we do about locking up?" Grace asked, glancing around the room.

"Nothing," Ashleigh declared. "What self-respecting thief would want any of this crap? Look, Paula will probably wake up in a couple hours and either sleep it off here or take herself on home. Either way, it's her problem, not ours."

15.

It was a slow night at the Sandbox. Rochelle was seated on her stool behind the bar, halfheartedly watching *Dancing with the Stars*, when Grace walked in, followed by three women she'd never seen before.

Grace gestured toward a table in a darkened corner of the bar, and they all slid into the booth and gave her their drink orders.

"Margarita for me," Ashleigh said. "On the rocks. No salt."

"Vodka tonic, double lime," Camryn said. "I don't suppose you have Grey Goose?"

"Nope," Grace said calmly.

"Stoli?"

"Nope. We've got any kind of vodka you want, as long as you want Smirnoff." It was one of Butch's favorite lame jokes, and Grace was surprised to hear herself using it.

"Suzanne?" Grace was also surprised that Suzanne Beamon had actually come along. She was seated at the far edge of the booth, anxiously checking out her surroundings, as though she'd never been in a bar before.

"Oh. Uh, just club soda, if you don't mind."

"Club soda?" Ashleigh gave Suzanne a playful tap on the shoulder. "Come on, Suzanne, chill out a little."

Suzanne's nose turned pink. "I have to drive home tonight, and I live over in Bradenton. I don't dare risk giving my ex any more ammunition with which to torture me."

"Good point," Grace agreed. "Be right back."

Rochelle raised an eyebrow as Grace approached where she was seated.

"My divorce recovery group. Paula passed out again, halfway through the session, so we decided to come over here for a drink."

"Interesting," Rochelle said, looking over her daughter's head at the group arrayed around the table. "Didn't you tell me there's a guy in your group? Where's he?"

"At home with his little boy," Grace said. "Just us girls tonight."

The drinks came. Ashleigh took a long sip of her margarita. "So . . . who's going to go first?"

"First with what?" Grace asked.

"You know. The dish. What really happened with all of y'all's marriages. How everybody ended up in 'divorce recovery' with all of us outlaws."

"It's not that interesting," Suzanne said, her voice low. "We were betrayed. End of story."

"Oh, I disagree," Camryn said quickly. "Grace, for example, has a fascinating story."

"You should know," Grace put in. "Anyway, everybody already knows what I did and how I ended up as one of Paula's people. Everybody in Florida knows, thanks to you, 'girlfriend.'"

"Not me," Suzanne said. When the others voiced their disbelief, she added. "I don't watch much television. Anyway . . . I guess I've been caught up in my own drama."

"Come on, tell it," Ashleigh urged Grace. "We want to hear your side of the story."

Grace gave a condensed version of the swimming pool story. "Afterwards, when I was driving over here, thinking about it, I couldn't believe that was me. Grace Stanton? Well, Davenport, now. I didn't plan to do it. I'm not a person who acts out like that. But I guess you never know what you're capable of until you're put in a situation like that."

Camryn snorted. "It was just a car. And you know he had insurance on the damned thing. As for planning something? Oh, hell yeah, I'm big on planning. Especially when it comes to that kind of thing. You know that quote, 'revenge is a dish best served cold'? I am all about that."

Suzanne leaned across the table. The small candle lit her face, giving it a greenish glow. "Did you catch your husband and that girl?"

Camryn's expression changed, hardened. "No. And that's what makes this whole thing so nasty. Our daughter, Jana, caught her daddy, in bed, with her best friend and roommate."

"Oh no." Suzanne looked sickened.

The other women at the table were silent.

"Awful," Suzanne mumbled.

Grace blotted the tabletop with a paper napkin. "Did you confront him?"

"Oh yes."

"Did he admit it?"

Camryn shrugged. "What was he gonna do, call his baby girl a liar? And then I found that little DVD of his."

She turned to Grace, rattling the ice cubes in her now-drained glass. "You think I could get another one of these?"

Grace turned toward the bar, caught her mother's eye and held up Camryn's glass. Rochelle nodded and a moment later arrived at the table. She didn't seem in a hurry to leave, either. So Grace introduced her to the other women, Rochelle went to refill everybody's glass, and before Grace knew it, Rochelle had pulled a chair up to the edge of the booth.

"You mentioned a DVD?" Ashleigh asked, after the introductions had been completed.

"Uh-huh. The fool hid it inside the family Bible. I guess he thought Jesus loves a liar and was counting on forgiveness. But not from me." Camryn shook her head. "Not after what I saw."

"Porn?" Suzanne's nose wrinkled in distaste.

"You could say that," Camryn said. "Dexter had been a busy little boy, filming his very own self. Getting ready for his 'dates.' And yeah, he lied about that, too, Treena wasn't his only 'Forever Your Girl.' Uh-huh, yes. That was the theme song for his date nights. Paula Abdul's 'Forever Your Girl' was his turn-on tune. But what really turned him on was the sight of himself in the mirror, prancing around in his red satin thong."

"Eeewww," Grace said. She shuddered. "Just . . . eewwww."

"I used to really like that song," Ashleigh said sadly.

"You'll have a whole new appreciation for it if you see that video," Camryn said tartly. "You got a smartphone?" She held out her hand. "Give it here and I'll show you how to find it on YouTube."

"No thanks."

"So . . ." Rochelle interrupted. "How did the video get on YouTube?"

"I put it there," Camryn said. "Oh, yes I did. Dexter Nobles, in the flesh—a whole lotta flesh! Getting dressed in his lil panties, getting ready for business meetings, lunches. County Commission meetings. Oh, he loved the feel of that satin under his suit when he was doing county business."

"You really did that?" Ashleigh asked, glancing down at her phone.

"Sure did. And it's gotten over twelve thousand hits," Camryn said.

"And that's what got Judge Stackpole on your case," Grace said. "Right?"

"His lawyer got the video taken down, but as soon as he did, other people put it right back up there. It's gone viral."

"Does your daughter know you put it on YouTube?" Suzanne asked.

Camryn sighed. "I didn't tell her. But she found out. She's furious. Not speaking to me." She looked around the group. "Does that seem fair to you? Dexter's the one who cheated, the dirty pervert. But she's mad at *me*—for outing him."

"Kids don't want to know bad stuff about their parents," Rochelle said.

"Dexter and I? We'd been living separate lives for a long time now," Camryn admitted. "I guess we stayed together for Jana. I don't miss his sorry ass. Not a bit. But I miss my little girl."

"She'll just have to get over herself," Ashleigh said. "Like you said, he's the pervert. The cheater. I bet she'll come around."

Camryn managed a wry smile. "Hope so. Now what about you, Miss Ashleigh? What did you do to earn yourself a spot in divorce recovery?"

"It's really not that big a deal," Ashleigh protested. "Nothing like what you guys did. I mean, it's a paint job, okay? The whole thing got blown way out of proportion."

"Why don't you just go ahead and tell us everything that happened?" Grace asked. "After all, you heard what happened with us."

Ashleigh pulled her compact from her satchel, checked

her makeup, fixed her lipstick, and flipped her hair behind her shoulders.

"So . . . you already know who my husband is. Boyce Hartounian. We met when I was working as an insurance billing clerk in his office." She looked over at Rochelle. "Boyce is one of the top plastic surgeons in Florida. He is *the* man for boobs, in case you're ever interested. And, of course, he was married at the time, but honestly, Beverly, that *cow,* was totally a joke. So that happened."

"Wait," Grace interrupted. "What happened? Did we miss something?"

"They split up," Ashleigh said. "She hired this weasel of an investigator, and there were some unfortunate photographs, and what with that, well, Beverly did very, very well for herself in the settlement."

Suzanne interrupted. "I'm sorry, but I'm going to have to go." She opened her pocketbook and placed a five-dollar bill on the table. "Will this be enough?"

"More than enough," Grace assured her. "Are you sure you can't stay?"

"I really can't," Suzanne said, looking flustered. "My daughter, Darby, still isn't used to the idea of her father being gone. She gets anxious if she's alone at night."

"How old is she?" Camryn asked.

"She'll be eighteen in October," Suzanne said. "A senior this fall. This split-up has been very hard on her."

She looked around the table. "Good night, everybody. Thanks for including me."

Camryn watched Suzanne leave the bar. She turned to Grace. "There's something very odd about that woman. Afraid to leave an eighteen-year-old at home alone? And she still hasn't told us a thing about herself."

"I think she's probably just very shy," Grace said. "An introvert."

"I don't know about you guys, but I am *dying* to know

what she did to her ex," Ashleigh said. "It's those quiet ones who always surprise you with something outrageous."

"Speaking of outrageous," Camryn said pointedly.

"Okay, sooooo. Boyce and I have been married, what, four years now? And it was amazing."

"And then?" Grace asked.

"My biggest mistake was quitting my job. Boyce told me he didn't want me working so hard." She shook her head ruefully. "I never even saw it coming."

"Hello?" A man's voice bellowed. "Rochelle? Where the hell are you?"

Their heads swiveled. A grizzled, shirtless old man wearing baggy shorts that hung below his kneecaps stood at the bar, banging the wooden surface with his glass.

"Pipe down, Milo," Rochelle hollered back. She stood. "Hang on. I want to hear this. I'll be right back."

Rochelle scurried behind the bar, scolding her regular as she drew him a beer.

"Your mom seems nice," Ashleigh told Grace. "Did you say you're living together? Where?"

Grace pointed her index finger upward.

"Here? You live above a bar?"

"I grew up here," Grace told her. "There's an apartment upstairs, two bedrooms, living room, dining room, kitchen. It's not fancy, but I guess you get used to it. At least it's close to the beach."

"I'm back," Rochelle slid back onto her chair. "You were saying?"

"Long story short, Boyce wanted me out of the office because he was having a fling with this slutty little drug rep named Suchita." Ashleigh laughed bitterly. "He even took her to the same suite at the Ritz where he used to take me, back when he was married to Beverly."

"That's just plain tacky," Rochelle said. "But how'd you find out?"

Ashleigh flipped her hair over her shoulder. "One of the girls in the office spilled the beans that he was getting friendly with the Juvenesse rep. I knew it was this Suchita chick right away. I parked across the street from his office and followed them to the Ritz."

Tears welled up in her eyes. "That was *our* place! Afterwards, I followed her back to her house, and when I saw the neighborhood she was living in, I knew it was true. No drug rep can afford to live in Newtown. So I decided to fix her little red wagon. Teach her a lesson."

"There was a Home Depot a couple miles away," Ashleigh continued. "I went home and changed into my guerrilla warfare outfit: black T-shirt, black Theory slacks, black Tory Burch flats. Then I went back after midnight. I painted HE'S MARRIED in these big, scary red letters all across the front of her house. Oh yeah, and on the front of her Beemer."

"You wore Tory Burch on a covert mission?" Camryn looked offended.

"They were last season, and I'd worn them to death," Ashleigh said. "So that's it. See?" She glanced around the table. "The whole thing just got blown way out of proportion."

"I'll bet," Rochelle said, helping herself to a sip of Grace's pinot.

"I know, right?' She turned to Grace. "Apparently in this state it's considered some kind of capital offense or something if you paint all over your husband's mistress's house. And then there was some crap about defacing private property . . . I let my lawyer deal with all that. I paid some fine. But then!" She paused for effect. "Stackpole found out. And he literally blew his stack!"

"And that's how you ended up at Ladies' Night," Rochelle said. She picked up Ashleigh's empty glass. "Anybody ready for another?"

Camryn frowned. "Better not. The station put me on 'probation' after they found out about the YouTube video. My lawyer says the only reason they didn't fire me is because I'm a community institution. I'm not but forty-two. And they act like I'm friggin' Betty White or something. Plus, I have 26,345 Facebook fans."

"You're only forty-two?" Ashleigh leaned way across the table to study Camryn's face. "Have you ever thought of Botox?" She traced a finger over Camryn's forehead, and down to her upper lip. "Because I could totally hook you up. Boyce showed me how to inject myself. It's really easy-peasy."

Camryn drew back. "Uh, thanks just the same. I don't think I'm up for any DIY Botox sessions at this time."

Ashleigh sighed and looked at her watch. "Guess I'd better get on home, too." She fumbled around in her bill-fold, finally finding a twenty-dollar bill, which she laid on the tabletop. "Thanks, ladies. It's been fun."

Grace hung around downstairs, long enough to help count out the cash register, wash the last of the dirty glasses and dishes, and turn off the neon WE'RE OPEN sign on the front door.

"That's a fascinating group of women you've got going there," Rochelle said, as she trudged up the stairs to the apartment.

"I don't know that I'd call them fascinating," Grace said, three steps ahead. "Bat-shit crazy is more the word that comes to my mind. I was a little worried about Ashleigh. She was slamming those margaritas pretty seriously."

"No worries," Rochelle said. "They were actually fakearitas. I just barely passed the tequila bottle over 'em."

"Good thinking," Grace said. "And I will admit it's just a little bit comforting to put things in perspective and find out there are people who've done worse things than me."

"Yeah . . ." Rochelle agreed. "I might need you to show me how to look at that YouTube video that Camryn was talking about. You know," she added hastily, "just to help you put things in perspective."

"I keep thinking about Paula, the therapist," Grace said, when they got up to the living room. "She was really zonked. I don't feel so good about leaving her all alone like that."

"What else could you do?"

"I could have made sure she got home okay," Grace said finally. She turned around and headed for the door.

"You're going back to check on her?" Rochelle asked.

"Yup."

16.

The strip shopping center looked even gloomier after midnight. Empty beer bottles and discarded fast-food wrappers littered the asphalt pavement. Blue lights flickered from behind the tattoo parlor storefront, and she could see a burly, bare-chested man inside, reading something on a computer screen. There were only three vehicles left in the parking lot, and none of them was the shiny yellow VW. But one was a pickup truck.

Grace pulled along beside it and rolled her window down. "I thought you had to get home to your little boy."

"I did," Wyatt said. "He's asleep. My dad's there, so it's cool."

"You came back to check on her too, right?"

Wyatt Keeler got out of the truck and walked over. "Paula's gone," he said sheepishly. "I looked in the windows of the office, and I could see the sofa, so she's definitely not there. I checked around back, too, just to make sure her car wasn't there."

Grace let out a long breath. "That's a relief."

"Yeah," Wyatt said. He thumped the roof of her car. "Guess I'll head back home. See ya."

Grace didn't start her car just then. "You're not such a bad guy after all, are you?"

He raised an eyebrow. "Who said I was?"

"I was in the courtroom the day your ex's lawyer showed that video, remember? You put a fist through that guy's car window. It looked pretty scary from where I was sitting."

He sighed. "If I had it to do over again, I'd have turned around and walked away. Next time I will. What if I told you my side of the story?"

"What? Here?" Grace looked at the clock on her dashboard and considered. "Can we go someplace else? This place gives me the creeps. Gus's is just down the road."

She followed him in her own car to a brightly lit doughnut shop a few miles away. Seated at the counter, just a few stools away from a couple of goth-looking teenagers, Wyatt ordered coffee and two apple crullers while Grace ordered an iced tea—and a chocolate-iced cake doughnut.

He looked surprised.

"I usually don't eat a lot of sweets," she explained. "But I've been losing weight, since, you know, and anyway, their chocolate doughnuts are the best. Ever."

"You know this place?" He looked around. The dull green linoleum floor tiles were chipped and cracked, the red leather booths were held together with duct tape, and the white tiled walls were lined with yellowing framed newspaper clippings and faded family photos.

"Yeah, we used to come to Gus's all the time when I was a kid," Grace said. "It was a big treat."

"So, you really grew up here? Living above the Sandbox?"

She nodded. "How about you?"

"Sarasota. Kinda like you. We didn't exactly live above the company store, but we did have a house right around the corner from Jungle Jerry's."

"Right," Grace said. "I almost forgot."

The waitress brought their food, and Wyatt took a huge bite of his cruller. "Sorry," he said, in between chews. "I missed dinner tonight. I'm starved."

He washed down the first doughnut with coffee. "You've lived here, always? Never moved away?"

"I went to college at Florida State, which is where I got my interior design degree, and after college, I moved down to Miami. We moved back here a few years ago."

"Miami. Is that where you met your husband?"

"Afraid so. What about you? Where did you meet . . . what's her name?"

"Callie. We met while I was in grad school at Clemson. But for some reason, I thought it was more important to get married than finish my master's. I was working for a seed company in South Carolina, and Callie was pregnant with Bo. Jungle Jerry's was in rough shape, and my dad really wanted to retire, and my mom was begging me to come back down here to run it. She'd been diagnosed with cancer then, but she didn't want that to influence my decision. Anyway, we came back, Bo was born, and my mom died just a few months later."

"I'm sorry," Grace said.

"She got to hold him right after he was born, babysit him a few times, before she got really sick," Wyatt said. "And we named him after her father, which really tickled her."

"How old is Bo?"

"Six," Wyatt said. "Just finished first grade." He reached for his cell phone, scrolled through his photos, and held it out for her to see.

A sturdy freckle-faced boy with soft brown bangs and his father's dimples grinned into the camera, showing off two missing front teeth. He wore a baseball cap set back on his head and had an aluminum bat resting on his right shoulder.

Wyatt touched the screen with his fingertip. "Kid lives

and breathes baseball. He's as crazy about it as I was at that age."

"Very cute," Grace said, taking the phone to study the little boy better. "What position does he play?"

"He's a catcher. Like I was. I tried to get him to play shortstop, told him he didn't want to be crawling in the dirt like I did the whole time I played ball, but he was determined to catch. He's not bad, either, even if I am his dad. And his coach."

She handed his phone back.

"So. I know you said you don't have kids. Ever want them?"

Her face colored, and he instantly knew he'd made a misstep.

"Sorry," he said. "That's a pretty personal question. Forget I asked."

Grace picked at the chocolate frosting with her fingernail. "That's okay," she said finally. "I do want kids. Well, I did. I'd started seeing a fertility specialist . . ." She blushed again. "I guess it's a good thing it never got that far." She gave him a sideways glance. "I don't know that I'm cut out to be a single parent."

"Sometimes, you don't have a choice," Wyatt said grimly. "I never thought I'd be a single dad, that's for sure. But I'm not sorry we had Bo. He's the best thing that's ever happened to me."

She broke off a piece of the doughnut and chewed. "You asked me if I wanted to hear your side of the story. About why you busted out that car window. I would like to hear it, if it's not too painful."

Wyatt held up his hand. The bruises were still a vivid greenish-black. "Pain? Me? Nah."

"Callie and Luke were gaming me, for months. That day at the ball park was the last straw. I coach Bo's T-ball team.

Callie had the game schedule. I gave it to her myself. But all spring, she'd drop him off late for the games half the time, without his glove or his shoes, or even his uniform shirt. It got so I bought extras of everything and kept 'em with me. But I'd sent him home with the spares the week before. That day? They didn't bring him until the second inning—and again, with no equipment. Poor Bo was so upset, he was in tears. Luke acted like it was nothing, just blew me off. Told me if I didn't like it, too damn bad."

Wyatt flexed his right hand and winced. "You saw how I reacted. Not my finest moment."

He'd finished his doughnuts and his coffee. Grace broke off half her doughnut and placed it on his empty plate.

"Really?"

"Yeah, I think I just wanted a taste. To remind me of old times here. You know how that is?"

He gobbled the doughnut. "I'll tell you a secret. I feel the same way about Krystal's sliders."

"Ick," Grace said. "Not the same thing at all."

"Krystal was where my granddad would take me on Saturdays, for lunch, when I was a kid," Wyatt said. "Just the two of us. He'd order me two sliders, and he'd eat four. Right out of the paper sack, in the front seat of his old tan Buick Regal. Every once in a while, not that often, but sometimes, if I have Bo on a Saturday, we ride through the Krystal, get ourselves a bag of sliders, take 'em out to Holmes Beach, sit on the sand, and scarf 'em down."

"Sweet sentiment, but still, ick," Grace said. "Does your ex know you do that?"

"If she did, she'd probably sic the Department of Child Welfare on me."

"Not to mention Judge Stackpole," she added.

"You saw how he treated me," Wyatt said, leaning back on his stool, "How did you do?"

"Let's put it this way," Grace said. "Not great. Mitzi—

she's my lawyer—is trying her best, but we still can't get
his lawyer to respond to us, and I'm still essentially locked
out of my business. He's supposed to be 'giving' me two
thousand dollars a month, but I haven't seen a dime yet.
And, oh yes, that money he's 'giving' me? It's mine anyway. All this while he transforms his new girlfriend into
Grace 2.0." She fluttered her eyelashes. "Does that make
me sound bitter?"

"Kind of," Wyatt said. "But then, I'm on a first-name
basis with bitter these days. Right now, it looks like Bo's
going to be moving to Birmingham by the end of summer,
and so far, there's not a damned thing I can do about it.
Yeah, technically I can see him weekends, but how do I
pull that off when he's living nine hours away? I can't afford to buy a plane ticket every weekend, and anyway I've
got a business to run. Or what's left of a business."

"That's really rotten," Grace said. "I can't believe any
mother would deliberately deny a child the chance to see
his father. It's just cruel."

"Callie's into cruel these days," Wyatt said. "She'll do
anything she can to punish me. And the weird thing is, I
can't figure out what I did to make her hate me like this.
She wanted out of the marriage, I let her out. She wanted
the house, I gave it to her." He shook his head and yawned.

"Yeah," Grace said, standing up and stretching. "It's
pretty late for me, too."

"Thanks for listening to me vent," Wyatt said. He hesitated. "I got the feeling, back there at Paula's office, all of
y'all were ready to tar and feather me. Just for being a guy."

Grace shrugged. "Everybody in that room is there
because a man dumped on her."

"Hey, a guy dumped on me, too," Wyatt said. "Remember?"

"Right."

They paid at the cash register and walked out to their

cars. Wyatt looked back at the old-timey neon GUS'S DO-
NUTS sign. "I gotta remember this place. Bo would love it."

"If you feed that child Krystal sliders and Gus's for the
same meal, I'll report you to Stackpole myself," Grace
threatened.

"Hey," Wyatt said. "Thanks for listening to me tonight."

"You're welcome," Grace said, meaning it. "See you
next week."

"If Paula's conscious. Do you think she's really on
drugs?"

"She's definitely on something," Grace said. "My mom
would say she's one ant short of a picnic."

Wyatt laughed. "One brick shy of a load. I can't believe
I have to come up with three hundred dollars a session
for this crap, on top of all the child support I'm paying
Callie."

"Do you think it would do any good to report her?"
Grace asked, fumbling for her car keys.

"Report to who?" Wyatt asked. "Stackpole? I'll mention what's going on to Betsy, but I already know what
she'll say. 'Shut up and turn up.'"

17

Grace sat cross-legged on her bed, her laptop balanced on her lap, tapping away at the keyboard.

Lately, I've gotten interested in the farm-to-table movement. Here on Florida's Gulf Coast, where I live, there's the tendency to think farms are all in the Midwest, or up north. But that's not true. We have amazing small farms all around us. Citrus growers, of course, and small avocado groves, but once I started looking around, I was surprised to find honey producers, organic chicken and egg farmers, and even small family "row-crop" farms producing gorgeous lettuces, tomatoes, peppers, cucumbers, corn, and, of course, strawberries. In addition, we're lucky here to have local seafood brought to port by fishermen who keep us supplied with fish, crabs, and shrimp caught right in the gulf and bay, and beef from the cattle farms that have been in the interior parts of this area since I was a little girl.

My mother's generous friend Felipe brought us a bushel of white corn on Sunday. Picked that morning, it had the sweetest taste you can imagine. We feasted on it for dinner, but then I started thinking of new ways to combine it with other locally produced goodness, and I came up with this corn-crab chowder recipe. It utilizes the corn, plus sweet blue crabs, which are being harvested here right now, not to mention red bell peppers and jalapeño peppers, readily available anywhere. I hope you'll try this at home, and let me know what you think.

She glanced over at the notes she'd scrawled in the kitchen earlier in the day. The corn-crab chowder really had been a triumph. She'd diced sweet yellow onions, jalapeños and red peppers, and some garlic, then sautéed them in bacon drippings in the cast-iron Dutch oven. Rochelle had grumbled about what a pain in the ass it was to cut all the corn off the cobs, but once she'd dumped them in the bacon drippings, along with diced tiny new potatoes and added chicken broth, the aroma wafting through the Sandbox kitchen had been irresistible. After the corn had simmered for twenty minutes or so, Grace had dumped in the crab. It was just back-fin crab, because Rochelle insisted you really didn't need lump claw meat for a soup, and, although crab was in season, her supplier still charged her $6.99 a pound.

Half-and-half was carefully added to the corn and crab mixture, along with a generous sprinkling of Old Bay seasoning—at Rochelle's insistence. As that simmered another five minutes, Grace diced up the crisp bacon she'd set aside from the pan drippings.

She'd gone outside to snip chives from the pots of herbs she'd started growing by the Sandbox front entrance, and when she reentered the kitchen, she caught her mother, standing over the stove, the Old Bay tin poised over the pot of chowder.

"Hey!" Grace protested, snatching the can from Rochelle's hand.

"I was just adjusting the seasoning." Rochelle dropped a wooden spoon into the big stainless steel sink.

"It doesn't *need* any more adjustment," Grace said, through gritted teeth. "Do you know how much salt is in that stuff? Not to mention the sodium in the bacon?"

"I don't need to know. I just know you can't make soup—especially soup with corn and crab, without a good douse of Old Bay," Rochelle retorted. "I've been making soup for way longer than you've been alive, young lady, so don't go lecturing me on salt. Or on cooking."

Grace bit her lip. She wanted to remind her mother that she was already on medication for high blood pressure and that her doctor had been urging her to cut back on sodium. Instead, she began snipping the chives into a milk-glass custard cup. "If you want more Old Bay in your soup, you can keep the shaker by your bowl. But please don't add it to the pot. Please?"

"Hmmph." Rochelle began tossing dirty dishes into the sink, a sure sign that she was miffed.

Ignoring her mother's tantrum, Grace found two old ice cream sundae glasses and placed each on a white plate. She started for the bar, to grab the sherry bottle, then, quietly, picked up the Old Bay can and took it with her. Just in case.

She turned the burner down to low and added a splash of sherry to the soup. Tasted, then added another splash.

A few minutes later, she made diagonal slices in the loaf of Cuban bread that had been delivered to the restaurant that morning, dribbled olive oil over the slices, and ran them under the broiler just long enough to toast them a light brown.

She placed a slice of bread on each plate, then dipped a ladle into the Dutch oven, carefully spooning the chowder into each sundae glass. A sprinkling of chives and diced bacon topped each glass.

Grace grabbed her camera and began snapping photos.

"Who serves crab chowder in a sundae glass?" Rochelle asked.

"I just like the way it looks," Grace said, snapping away. "Eccentric."

"Weird," Rochelle muttered, watching from the sink. "Are we eating or shooting?"

"Eating," Grace said, setting the camera down. "But if the finished product tastes as good as it looks, I think this will make a terrific blog post."

She grabbed two blue and white striped dish towels from the stack on the stainless steel prep counter and draped them over her arm before picking up the soup dishes and pushing her way through the swinging door into the bar.

Grace unfolded the dish towels and spread them out as a placemat on the bar. She grabbed a couple of wine-glasses, poured in some white wine, and stood back to look. Finally, she added a paper-thin slice of lemon to the side of each plate for a shot of color. Pleased with the effect, she went back for her camera and took a couple more exposures. "Let's eat," she called, over her shoulder.

Rochelle eyed the place settings at the bar. "Pretty fancy, just for Saturday lunch for the two of us."

"You eat with your eyes, as well as your tastebuds, you know," Grace said, refusing to let her mother bait her.

"Hmmph," Rochelle said. But she dipped her spoon into the soup, tasted, and closed her eyes.

"Well?"

Rochelle took another bite of the soup. "Not bad. Not bad at all." With a fingertip, she fished a small limp green fragment from her soup and held it up for Grace to see.

"What's this?"

"Sorry," Grace said. "It's just a sprig of tarragon. I was supposed to remove it before I served the soup, but I got distracted. So . . . you really like it?"

"I do," Rochelle said. She dipped a piece of toasted bread into the soup and chewed.

Grace ate slowly, pausing to make notes on her ever-present yellow legal pad. Next time, she thought, she might do cheese toasts to go along with the soup, maybe adding slivers of goat cheese to the bread before broiling. She pondered the soup's consistency, finally deciding she'd need to add an immersion mixer to the kitchen equipment at the Sandbox, so that in the future she could puree part of the soup. Her own immersion mixer was back in the kitchen at the house on Sand Dollar Lane. Ben's house.

When Rochelle finished her soup, she got up from her seat, found a piece of chalk, and began writing on the blackboard on the wall by the cash register.

Today's SPECIAL—CORN CRAB CHOWDER
à la GRACE. $10.

"You really think the customers will like it?" Grace asked, secretly pleased. She'd been living with Rochelle for nearly two months, and it seemed like the first time she'd done something in the kitchen or the bar that Rochelle approved of. "And more importantly, that they'll pay ten dollars for a bowl of soup?"

"They'll lap it up," Rochelle predicted. "We just won't tell 'em how healthy it is. And if anybody gripes about the price, I'll show 'em my bill from the seafood wholesale house."

They'd had a busy evening. One of the local softball leagues was having a tournament, and word had apparently gone out that the Sandbox was the place to meet after the games.

The first batch of soup was gone by 7:00 P.M., and Grace made another gallon, using up all the crab in the big walk-in cooler. At 9:30, she had to tell Rochelle to "eighty-six" that night's special.

A loud groan rose up in the bar as Rochelle crossed the special off on the blackboard.

They were both exhausted by the time Rochelle's late-night shift, consisting of Almina, a young Latin woman, and her husband, Carlos, showed up to take over at 10:00.

While Rochelle showered in the apartment's only bathroom, Grace settled down to write her blog post, referring to her notes and editing and refining the photos she'd shot earlier before uploading to her blog, accompanied by a list of local farms, complete with their links.

It was after midnight when she tapped the PUBLISH button. She viewed the blog in its final form and smiled. "Take that, J'Aimee," she muttered, right before padding off to take her own shower.

Sunday morning, Grace was still sleeping when she heard the cell phone on her nightstand ding softly, signaling an incoming message.

She sat up and yawned, looking out the window. It was barely daylight. But the message on her phone woke her in a hurry.

HAVE U SEEN YR OLD BLOG TODAY?

The text message on her phone was from ShadeeLadee, one of her earliest Gracenotes followers and another life-style blogger based in Miami. Over the years they'd met at various blogger meet-ups and gotten friendly, and, although ShadeeLadee had a real name, which was Claire King, Grace always just called her Shadee.

Grace clicked over to what she thought of as Faux Grace-notes, and swore. Loudly.

The photo was the exact one Grace had posted on her own blog, but with the headline Grab Some Crab.

Beneath it was Grace's corn-crab chowder, which J'Aimee (or more likely Ben, Grace decided) had re-christened Crab-Corn Bisque. She'd cleverly changed the recipe in the slightest ways, calling for a sprig of rosemary instead of tarragon and decreasing the amount of half-and-half. But otherwise, it was Grace's recipe. And it was definitely Grace's photo.

"Oh, hell no!" Grace exclaimed. She scrolled down to see the number of comments J'Aimee's post had garnered. There were seventy-six, and it was barely 7:30 A.M. on a Sunday, usually her slowest day for blog traffic.

She quickly typed in a comment of her own. "THIS RECIPE AND PHOTO WERE HIJACKED FROM TrueGrace.com. To see the original, much better, recipe, click over to here." And she added a link to her own blog.

Most likely, Ben, whom she assumed was the blog's administrator, would delete Grace's comment and block her from trying to comment again, but Grace didn't care.

She opened her own blog. Nothing. Her new banner was there, but the only thing beneath it was a vaguely worded link. She instinctively clicked on it, and immediately regretted it. The link took her to the vilest, most sickening display of pornography she could have imagined.

Grace stared at the screen in stunned silence. How? She didn't have to ask who had done this, who'd not just erased her blog post, but sabotaged her entire blog. It was Ben, that she knew. She just didn't know how.

How could he have infiltrated her blog? She had a new protected password; he couldn't have accessed it, or could he?

Fuming, she left the blog and went to check her e-mail. Her in-box showed she had eighty-eight new messages.

She read the first one, from another lifestyle blogger, Shana, of Design or Die, and cringed.

Grace, what's going on with you? Your blog has been hacked, and it's not only got a porn link, it's infecting anybody who opens it with a virus. Love ya, girl, but for the sake of my readers, I'm removing you from my blog roll until you get your act together.

The next e-mail was from Nathan Woods, an influential interior design blogger with nearly half a million followers. Grace had been on cloud nine the day Nate had e-mailed to tell her how much he loved her post "Window Treatments That Ought to be Outlawed," which he'd privately called "Swags for Hags." He'd done two cross-promotions with Grace that had gained her a slew of new followers, and had even given her invaluable business advice about which advertisers to avoid on her own blog.

Nathan's e-mail was terse and to the point.

What the fuck is this??? It was followed by a link, which took her to an infamous online forum called SnarkSauce, where contributers posted venomous items about Internet celebrities.

I HATE NATE was the post's headline.

Closet queen Nathan Woods's tenuous hold on the title of "Biggest Boozer" has never been challenged, but recently the Manhattan-based designer and blogger was knocked down a rung when textile giant F. Schumacher & Company ended their five-year contract with Woods, whose lame-ass line of botanical-based fabrics never quite lived up to its

*early promise. Apparently the only person in the
tightly knit New York design community who was
surprised by the move was Woods himself. Insiders
tell me Woods is also about to be asked to leave
his post as contributing editor at Architectural
Digest. Also? We hear Woods's love interest, boy-
about-town Marc Klein has moved out of Nate's East
Village love nest. Stay tuned y'all!*

Although the posts on SnarkSauce were usually anonymous, the Nate item was signed. *Grace from Gracenotes.*

Her fingers flew over the keypad. "I never wrote any
such thing. This is all Ben, my soon-to-be ex. You have to
believe me, Nathan, I would never, ever write anything like
this. Ben has hijacked my blog, and he's sabotaging me
every way he can. I don't know why he's decided to do this,
but I'm going to get this post taken down, and make Snark-
Sauce print a retraction. I swear."

A moment later, she saw that Nathan had replied. His
message was succinct. "You are dead to me."

Grace was devastated. She closed the laptop and put it
on the floor, like a diseased thing, best avoided.

18.

Grace stormed downstairs to find Rochelle sipping coffee at the bar. "I'm going to kill Ben, so help me. Right after I tear that little bitch J'Aimee limb from limb."

"What've they done now?"

She poured a mug of coffee for herself and plopped onto the barstool next to her mother's. "I spent hours yesterday making that crab soup, photographing it, editing, then writing and posting my blog. Hours!"

"So? If you're still fishing for compliments, I'll say it again. The soup was damned good."

"The soup was amazing," Grace cried. "And the photos were amazing. So amazing that Ben lifted the recipe, nearly word for word, and the photos, my photos, and put them on J'Aimee's blog. And, somehow, he managed to erase my blog post. In its place, he put a link to the foulest, most degrading porn site on the planet. A site that, if you were to click the link, would give your computer a virus."

"You're sure it was Ben?" Rochelle asked.

"Who else? It had to be him. I can't figure out how it's possible, how he could figure out the password to the new blog, but somehow he did."

Rochelle rolled her eyes. "What a slimy bastard. It's a damned shame Ben wasn't locked in the trunk of that car when you drove it into the pool."

"And that's not all he did," Grace said. "When he was done hijacking my blog post, he hopped all around the Internet, poisoning people against me. He left nasty comments on my friends' blogs signed with my name, and he wrote this incredibly bitchy piece on SnarkSauce about Nathan Woods and signed my name to that, too."

"Who's Nathan Woods? And what's SnarkSauce?" Rochelle asked. She could never keep all this Internet stuff straight.

"Oh, Mom, you've seen his show on Saturday mornings. He's probably the best-known interior design blogger in the country. His blog has like, I don't know, probably seven hundred thousand followers. He did a cross-promotion with me back in February, and my analytics took a crazy jump, just because of my exposure on his blog."

"You still haven't explained SnarkSauce," Rochelle reminded her daughter.

"I don't know if anybody can explain SnarkSauce. I guess you'd say it's hater central for lifestyle bloggers. People post these vicious remarks about well-known bloggers. I never read it, but Ben always did. He thought it was hilarious. That's how I know it must have been Ben that wrote that crap. Now Nathan is furious with me. He says I'm dead to him. And all my other blog buddies hate me, too, all because of Ben."

Grace banged her head on the bar top. "Why me? Why?"

"Did you let these people know it wasn't you that wrote the stuff? That it was Ben, trying to get even with you?"

"Of course! But I don't think anybody believes me. People are dropping me from their blog rolls and defriending me on Facebook. At this rate, I won't have a single friend in the business." Grace jumped up and paced back and forth in front of the bar, close to tears.

"Grace?" Rochelle's voice was stern. "Sit down and listen to me." She caught her daughter by the elbow. "Sit."

"What?" Grace knew she sounded like a spoiled brat, but she couldn't help herself.

"Anybody who thinks that you would be capable of doing something like that doesn't really know you. And if you tell them you didn't do this stuff, and they still don't believe you, well, screw 'em. They were never your real friends at all."

"But they were," Grace insisted. "You don't know what the blog world is like. We read each other's blogs and comment and cross-post and guest blog. And we see each other at meet-ups, once or twice a year. I care about these people, and they care about me."

Rochelle shook her head. "No, they don't. Did any of these so-called friends call you after your big breakup with Ben was all over the news? Did any of them drive over here, take you out to lunch, or just give you a shoulder to cry on when you needed it most?"

"That's not how it works in my world," Grace said stubbornly.

"Then your world is seriously screwed up. You've gone through a lot in the past two months, but as far as I can tell, not a single friend has stepped up. And not just these so-called blogger buddies of yours. Where are your old girlfriends? The couples who used to come to all those dinner parties you used to throw all the time?"

Grace clutched her coffee mug so tightly she thought it might crush. "I don't know," she whispered. "A couple left me messages on my phone. But I was just too embarrassed to call them back. After a while . . ."

"They quit calling," Rochelle finished her sentence. "Fair-weather friends, every last one of 'em."

"I guess Ben got custody of all our old friends." Grace blinked back tears, and wondered if her tear ducts would ever dry up. "And that hurts, too. I try to keep busy, to keep from dwelling on everything, but everyday, it's like something else happens, another slap in the face. My blog? I know it seems silly to you, but, Mom, this is my work. If I don't have a marriage, and I don't have any friends, and then, somehow, I can't even make a living, what the hell else do I have? What kind of life is this?"

Rochelle handed her a paper towel. "Dry your eyes, honey. This is the life you've got, so put on your big-girl panties and make it what you want it to be. All your old friends are gone? Find some new ones. Ben's attacking you. Counterattack. Stay on the offensive. The best way to do that, from where I'm sitting, is to figure out a way to do what only you can do, and then get on with it. Everything else will take care of itself."

"How?" Grace's voice quivered with emotion.

Rochelle threw up her hands in surrender. "I don't know, Grace. I'm not Dr. Phil. But you can't just give up and sit around and whine. That's not how we raised you."

She leaned closer to Grace, rested her forehead against her daughter's. "Figure out what you want. And then go get it."

She hadn't had all that much contact with the Gracenotes advertisers. That had been Ben's department. But she'd had some correspondence with the bigger, most important ones: Home Depot, Levolor, Benjamin Moore, Viking, a big carpet manufacturer, and DeWalt, a power tool manufacturer.

Now Grace scrolled through the contacts on her laptop, searching them out, mentally composing the message she'd send.

*Dear Sir: Just wanted to take the time to thank you
for your past support of Gracenotes. Unfortunately, a
situation has arisen that I wanted to make you
aware of. I am currently in the middle of an unpleasant split from my husband, Ben. The result is
that although Gracenotes.com is still online, I am no
longer authoring or associated with those posts.
I've started a new blog, TrueGrace.com, and I
hope you'll take a look at it. In the meantime, you
should know that Ben is actually lifting my intellectual property—my writing, my recipes, and my
photographs—and publishing them on Gracenotes,
representing them as original. I also believe he's
actually engaging in sabotaging my career as a blogger, by posting potentially libelous, scurrilous, negative comments and material on other lifestyle blogs
and signing my name to them. I know your company
values your brand and identity too much to under-
write these kinds of activities, and I hope you will
take the appropriate steps to ensure that your company is not associated with individuals who rely on
devious, underhanded, negative activities. All best,
Grace Davenport (formerly Stanton), the True Grace.*

She pushed the SEND button and, for the first time in
weeks, felt like herself. The real Grace.

19.

Grace had never been what you would call athletic. She'd been a book nerd as a kid, always happier inside with a book than outside with a racket or a club or playing a sport that made her sweaty.

It was only after her sophomore year of college, when she'd gained not just the freshman fifteen but a whole twenty pounds, that she'd reluctantly taken up running. She'd kept it up, off and on, since then. Running to keep her weight down or the stress of daily life at bay.

Lately, she'd started running for sanity. Since the split with Ben and moving into the apartment above the Sandbox, she'd taken to waking before dawn. Sometimes she read; sometimes she worked on her blog; sometimes she laced up her running shoes and hit the road.

Reading again through all the e-mails in her in-box left her feeling infuriated and helpless, even a day later. Ben—or somebody—had done a thorough job of poisoning her Internet presence. Using her name, he'd posted inflammatory blog comments on every single blog from her old blog roll. She knew this because nearly all of the bloggers had e-mailed to tell her that she was dead to them, too.

She had to get away. It was still dark when she slipped down the stairs and let herself out the Sandbox's side door.

Grace wasn't fast, and her running form left much to be desired. She popped her earbuds in, pressed the PLAY button on her iPod, and loped down the street. The route she'd developed took her along the winding roads that paralleled the Gulf of Mexico. If she looked to her left, she could see blue skies, sometimes catch patches of blue-green surf through the tree line of shaggy Australian pines and palm trees.

After crossing the bridge from Cortez, she ran through Bradenton Beach, on to Holmes, and Anna Maria. After an hour, her nylon tank top was drenched with sweat, her gym shorts plastered to her butt. Even her ponytail dripped sweat onto her shoulders.

The last mile of her run was actually more of a cool-down walk. She did a run-walk on the beach for a half mile or so, keeping her eyes on the surf line, scanning for any shells, watching the seagulls and sandpipers. At one point, she stopped and stared at a huge gray heron, poised, motionless at water's edge. The bird never flinched as Grace approached and stood, marveling at its elegant blue-gray plumage. Eventually, she moved on, but the heron did not.

It was early Monday morning, so the streets of Anna Maria were quiet. She loped up one sandy, narrow street after another, walking, fuming. Every once in a while, she felt a faint breeze coming through the tree line. The houses on these streets were cottages, many of them bearing real estate signs indicating they were vacation rentals.

This was a new neighborhood to Grace. She slowed to a stroll, appreciating the modest concrete block or frame structures, so unlike the rambling, overblown megamansions on Gulf Vista. She wished she had her camera to capture the early morning sun, the tropical gardens of palms, bromeliads, crotons, bougainvillea, and hibiscus.

Grass was sparse here. Instead, the small yards seemed to consist of dense plantings of vines and ferns and flowers. Lizards darted across the narrow sand-strewn road, and she saw hummingbirds hovering over the thick hedges of ixora with their star-shaped coral blossoms.

It seemed the whole world was still slumbering, until she came across a house that stood out like a sore thumb on this block of neatly maintained homes. The curb was heaped high with trash, the yard weedy and strewn with dead palm fronds and fallen limbs. Barely visible, behind an overgrown hedge of ficus, she could see a glimpse of faded white siding.

Also blocking her view was the mountain of refuse. Two big city-issued receptacles were spilling over with plastic bags of garbage. Alongside these were sodden cardboard boxes overflowing with old clothes and shoes and more. A stained king-sized mattress leaned against the receptacles and was propped up by two cheap fiberboard nightstands.

Grace heard a screen door slam, and, as she watched, an old man muscled a long rattan couch through the doorway and into the yard. He cursed softly as he pushed and shoved the sofa to the curb.

"Hey," he said, barely noticing Grace. He dumped the sofa, wheeled, and went back into the house.

Something about that sofa caught her eye. She glanced at the house, to see if the man was watching, but he'd disappeared.

The rest of the discards at the curb were junk, cheap, soiled, ruined junk. But this sofa . . . Grace squatted to get a better look.

The rattan arms formed huge pretzel-like shapes. It was a three-seater, and it looked, she thought, like it could be

by Paul McCobb. The rattan wrappings were in surprisingly good shape, and all the seat supports looked intact.

A moment later, the screen door slammed and the man
reappeared, this time with a wheelbarrow heaped with
thick cushions covered in a hideous orange and rust synthetic plaid fabric. He dumped the cushions without comment and wheeled back inside.

Grace was intrigued. She walked across the street,
down the block, and then doubled back again. It was like
a floor show whose second act she couldn't bring herself
to miss.

By now, an armchair had joined its matching sofa. And
the man with the wheelbarrow was back, this time bringing a low-slung, boomerang-shaped rattan coffee table
with a yellow pine top, which he unceremoniously dumped
on end. The table's top, Grace saw, was marred with cigarette burns and water rings, but the legs and the rattan
wrappings were in fairly decent condition.

The man looked annoyed at having a spectator. He was
tall and thin, with a high forehead and thinning gray hair
and a lit cigarette dangling from one corner of his mouth.
He wore a pair of loose-fitting khaki slacks and a shapeless gray T-shirt.

"Can I help you?" he asked.

Grace blushed. "Did somebody die?" she blurted out.

"I wish," he said. His voice was gravelly. He set the
wheelbarrow down, took a wrinkled handkerchief from his
back pocket, and mopped his face.

"My damned tenants moved out and left me with this
mess," he said, removing his eyeglasses and wiping them
down.

"That's awful," Grace sympathized.

"You don't even know," he agreed. "Three months back
rent owing, not to mention they trashed the house so bad,

I don't know how long it'll take me to get it into shape to rent again."

He was gazing at her, taking in her sweaty, disheveled appearance. "Don't I know you?" He gestured at her ball cap, with the Sandbox logo. "Maybe from the bar?"

Now that he mentioned it, she did think he looked familiar. "Maybe. I'm Grace Davenport. Rochelle's daughter."

"Riiight," he said, wiping his hands on his pants and shaking her hand. "And I'm Arthur Cater. I knew your daddy. Took him fishing a couple times. Butch was a great guy. How's your mama gettin' along?"

"She's good," Grace said. "We miss him, but if you know Rochelle, you know she's a tough old bird."

"She is that," he said with a laugh.

Now he gestured toward the mountain of trash. "Should have trusted my gut instinct. But they were a young couple, and my wife felt sorry for 'em. Famous last words."

Grace gestured toward the mound of trash. "You're throwing all of this out? Not even calling Goodwill to come pick it up?"

He snorted. "Goodwill wouldn't take this mess. Would you? Mildewed, pee-stained. They had dogs, even though the lease specifically forbids pets, and they swore they didn't have any. So everything is crawling with fleas."

Grace shuddered and took a tiny step backward.

He flicked his handkerchief at the rattan sofa. "This was my grandmother's. She left me the house, and this was always in it, as long as I could remember. We've been renting this house, furnished, with no problems for fifteen years, and then these bums move in, and now it's not fit for the dump."

He was mopping his neck. "You see anything here you want, be my guest."

"The rattan furniture is actually very pretty," Grace

ventured. "Probably from the forties. You're sure you don't want to keep it? Maybe have the cushions redone?"

"Nah," he said dismissively. "We got a house full of furniture. And my wife doesn't like this old grandma stuff." He studied her. "There's an end table and another armchair inside, that goes with this set, if you think you might want it. Course, you'd have to haul it off yourself."

"I just might want it," Grace said, surprising herself. And then she had an idea.

"Would it be all right if I came inside, took a look at the furniture?"

"You got a clothespin for your nose? And if you get bit up by fleas, don't blame me."

The walkway to the front door was brick, but it was barely visible beneath the tendrils of vines and weeds that grew up in the sandy yard. The house was raised up from ground level on concrete block piers. It had a steep gabled roof with slatted wooden air vents near the V-shaped peak and a half-shed tin-roofed porch with large wooden brackets supporting the overhanging porch eaves. The siding was aluminum, and it was pulling away from the house in several spots.

Arthur Cater yanked open the screened door, and she followed him inside.

It took a moment for her eyes to adjust to the dim light. She was on a screened porch, or what was left of it. Most of the rusty screens were torn, and in some cases, they were missing entirely. Two cheap plastic armchairs were overturned, and the painted wooden floor was littered by overflowing trash bags.

Her new friend pushed open the front door. "After you," he said with a flourish. She was greeted with a pungent smell—a mixture of urine, mildew, and stale cigarette smoke.

"Oh my," she gasped, forcing herself to breathe through her mouth.

"Now you see what I'm dealing with," he said.

The front of the cottage was basically one room. They were standing in the living room. Its windows were cloudy and smeared with dirt. Venetian blinds hung crazily from one hook on a long window that looked out on the porch. The rattan armchair was pushed up against the wall, heaped with an old sleeping bag and pillow, and a matching end table rested, upside down, atop it.

"That's it, right there," the man said. "And I warn you, it's heavier than it looks."

Grace upended the table, setting it on the filthy avocado-green shag carpeting. Its top had more water rings and cigarette burns, but she loved its rounded-off triangular shape. She gingerly removed the bedding from the armchair and concluded that it, too, was in sound shape, although the cushion was ruined.

"You really don't want these?" she asked Arthur, who'd walked to the other end of the room. Which was a dining room, from the looks of it. The only furniture here was a flimsy card table and a pair of old-timey folding aluminum beach chairs with rotting plastic webbing. A cheap brass chandelier dangled over the table, but only one of its candle arms was lit.

"What?" He turned around. "Nah. But I would have liked the dining room furniture that used to be here."

Grace went over to join him. "They stole your furniture?"

"Yup," he said. "Mahogany table and chairs, and a buffet kind of thing. Those were my mama's. I thought about taking 'em out of here, but we didn't have room at the house, and I thought they'd get ruined if I left them in the garage." He shrugged. "I'd love to know how they got that heavy stuff out of here. They didn't have but one car, and that was a crappy little Kia."

"Mm-hmm." Grace wasn't really listening. She was taking a good look at the house itself now.

It was a typical Florida cracker house, she thought. These walls were board and batten, probably old pine under the multiple layers of paint and dirt. The ceilings were quite tall, also board and batten, although they'd never been painted. Through a tall doorway, she could see into the tiny galley kitchen.

"Okay if I look around, Arthur?" she asked.

"Just watch your step," he advised, heading back toward the porch with another load of trash.

A single grungy window over the kitchen sink let in feeble light. Grace found a light switch, and as the ceiling fixture flickered on, half a dozen cockroaches skittered for the shadows. She shuddered, but was not surprised. Roaches were as much a part of living in Florida as palm trees and sunshine. Her least favorite part.

The kitchen was something of a time warp. The countertops were speckled gray formica. The cabinets were wooden, with gummy-looking chipped white enamel paint. There were two wooden upper cabinets, one on either side of the sink, and two lower ones, each topped by a drawer. The cabinet doors were all ajar, and she could see a sad assortment of mismatched pots and pans, some cloudy glasses, chipped plates. An old avocado-green stove sat at the far end of the counter, its surface spattered with grease and food particles. A small saucepan with an unspeakable layer of burnt . . . something . . . sat on the front burner. The oven door was open, and when Grace closed it she saw another scattering of roaches.

Turning around, she saw the refrigerator. It was a somewhat newer model than the stove, but its white surface was freckled with rust. To the left of the fridge was another counter, with a pair of wall-mounted upper cabinets. Beneath the counter there was nothing but an open space, where an evil-smelling plastic trash can was tipped on its side.

Through a second doorway was a short hall. An open door showed the bathroom. The black-and-white penny-tile floor was now a grimy gray. The sink, commode, and bathtub were pale pink, which meant, Grace knew, that they probably dated from the early fifties.

There were two more doors, both closed. Grace was about to open one when she heard a faint scratching sound coming from inside the room.

She took a step back. Rats? She took another step back.

Arthur poked his head inside the hall. "I wouldn't open that door unless you wanna get attacked," he warned.

Grace decided she'd seen enough of the house.

"Bad enough those lowlifes trashed the house like this," he said. "They went off and left their damned dog behind. I ask you, who moves out and leaves a dog behind?"

"No," Grace said, appalled. "There's a dog in that bedroom? Can I see it?"

"Look all you want," Arthur said. "I penned her up in there because with me coming and going outside, I was afraid she'd run out and get hit by a car. I'm no dog lover, but even I couldn't stand that."

20.

As she and Arthur talked, the scratching grew more intense, and now it was accompanied by a series of high-pitched yips.

She put her hand on the doorknob. "Don't say I didn't warn you," Arthur said.

Grace pushed the door open and stepped inside the bedroom, where a small brown bundle of fur began leaping at her knees in a frenzy of barking and yipping.

"Heyyyy," Grace said softly, bending down to get a closer look. The dog leapt into her arms and began lavishing her chin with a soft pink tongue.

"Oh my God," Grace said, holding the reeking animal at arm's length. "You poor thing."

Her best guess was that she was some kind of poodle mix. But it was hard to tell because the dog's fur was filthy and matted. Its liquid brown eyes were cloudy and tinged with some milky substance, and there were speckles of dried blood on its muzzle.

She set the dog down gingerly and wiped her hands on the seat of her shorts. The dog sat back on its haunches and looked at her expectantly.

"Pathetic, ain't it?" Arthur asked, standing behind her in the hallway. "She'd been locked up in this room, I don't know how long, when I got over here this morning." He jerked his head in the direction of the bedroom. "You can see the mess she's made. Not that you could blame her."

The room was, as Arthur said, a disaster. Even mouth-breathing could not contain the stench.

Grace picked the dog up again and stepped into the hallway, closing the door to the horrors within.

"What will you do with her?" Grace asked, still holding her at arm's length.

Arthur reached into the bathroom and found a threadbare bath towel. "Here. Wrap her in this. She's got fleas pretty bad."

As Grace wrapped the towel around the dog, she felt it shivering violently.

"I think she's sick, too," she said, looking up at Arthur.

"Gotta be," he agreed "I give her a bowl of water when I found her this morning, and what was left of the sausage biscuit I had out in my truck, but there's no telling how long it had been since she'd been fed."

"Those people should be tracked down and put in jail for something like this," Grace said fiercely. She swallowed hard, feeling nauseous.

"I've filed a report with the sheriff's department, but there's no telling how long they've been gone. I know the wife, well, I guess she was his wife, I don't really know, but she did mention at one point that they had family in Alabama."

He looked down at the shivering bundle of fur in Grace's arms. "I was gonna take her to the animal shelter. Later on. But if you'd take her, that'd be a whole lot better." He reached out and scratched under the dog's chin, and she wriggled in delight. "She's kinda cute, in a homely sort of way."

Grace looked down at the dog and sighed. "She seems like a sweetheart. But I'm living with my mom, above the bar. And if you know Rochelle, you know she doesn't believe in having inside pets."

"And my wife has got three big ol' tomcats, and they don't like dogs any more than I do," Arthur said. He took the dog from Grace's arms, opened the bedroom door, and set her back inside before firmly closing the door.

The dog's plaintive whines tore at Grace's heart.

Arthur knew how to deal with such a thing. He stalked out to the living room and began loading his wheelbarrow with more trash.

Grace wanted not to hear the dog's cries. "How long do you think it'll take to get this place cleaned up?" she asked.

"Who knows? However much time it takes, it's more than I can spare," Arthur said. "We usually spend the summer up in North Carolina. Fixing to leave next week, until this happened."

"I have an idea," Grace said slowly. "It's kind of crazy."

"Crazier than me letting these folks do me out of three months' back rent?" Arthur asked.

She took a deep breath. "What would you think of letting me fix the place up for you?"

"Why would you want to do something like that?" Arthur asked, his eyes narrow with suspicion.

"I'm an interior designer, and I write a blog about home design and home improvement," Grace said. She gestured at the dank room they were standing in. "This little house actually has good bones. It's small, but it could be terrific. I could make it terrific. And I could photograph it and write about the process. If you'd let me."

She was already writing the blog posts in her mind, picturing the rooms, stripped of their filth, the cottage returned to its old Florida vernacular architecture. Let J'Aimee try to copy that!

Arthur shook another cigarette out of the pack in his breast pocket. "I don't know . . ."

"Okay," Grace said easily. "As I said, it was just an idea."

He lit the cigarette and inhaled. The smoke smell was actually an improvement. "What would you charge for something like that?"

"Uh, nothing," Grace said. And then she hurriedly backed up. "That is, you'd need to pay for the materials." She did a 360-degree turn around the room. "Paint, new light fixtures."

"Carpet, for sure," he added.

Grace stubbed her toe into the shag carpet. "What's under here, do you know?"

"Wood floors, best I remember," he said. "God knows what kinda shape they're in. We've had carpet down, ever since I can remember."

"Best-case scenario, rip up this carpet and refinish the wood floors," Grace said. "It's way cheaper than buying new carpet, and if you put down a good finish, your next tenants shouldn't be able to ruin it."

She walked out to the kitchen. "I'm thinking you'll need new appliances in here." She knelt down and peeled at an edge of the vinyl-roll flooring. "This stuff would have to come up, too. So either refinish if there's wood or put down new vinyl."

He nodded. "I was gonna have the stove and fridge hauled off, probably tomorrow."

"How much were *you* thinking it would cost to get it ready to rent again?" Grace asked.

Arthur pursed his lips and flicked his cigarette ash onto the carpet. "With appliances—there's a washer and dryer on the back porch, and they're ruined, too, I'm thinking a couple thousand."

"With appliances? I'm thinking at least five thousand,"

Grace shot back. She'd walked out to the porch and was staring out at the overgrown yard. "The screens out here are all shot and you've got rotten framing, too."

She turned around. "How about the air-conditioning? Does it work?"

"Window units," he said, pointing to a rusting brown hulk that stuck out of the front living room window. "Couple of smaller ones in the bedrooms. They do the job. Or they did, up until now."

Grace put her hands on her hips. "What do you charge for rent? If you don't mind my asking?"

"Four-fifty a month," he said. "And we pay utilities."

"Oh, Arthur," she said with a knowing smile. "This house has such potential. And you're only, what? A block from the bay? If we fixed this place up—I mean, really fixed it up, cleaned up the yard, got it landscaped, maybe put in a little central air unit . . ."

"No central air," he growled. "Think I'm made of money?"

"It couldn't cost that much," Grace said. "How many square feet here?"

"A little under a thousand," he said.

"If you're paying for the electric, you're spending way more money now with three old window units," Grace said. "I bet if you put in a new efficient central unit, you'd save enough to pay for it after just a couple years. Plus, once I've got it fixed up and looking great, you're gonna get more rent anyway, and definitely attract a better-quality tenant."

"You make it sound so easy," Arthur said. "You have any experience fixing up houses? Or handling investment properties, for that matter?"

"I've fixed up three old houses," Grace said. "And my ex-husband and I had a little two-bedroom, two-bath in Bradenton that I did this very same thing with. That one,

I gutted to the studs. By the time we sold it, a year ago, we were getting $1,200 a month. Unfurnished."

"Ex-husband?"

"About to be," Grace said casually. "We split a couple months ago. That's why I'm living with my mom right now."

"Sorry to hear it," Arthur said.

"I'm not," Grace said, lifting her chin. "So? What do you think?"

"Have to run it by my wife," he said. "Five thousand. You're talking about a lot of money."

She decided to push her luck. "Five thousand, more or less. I haven't even seen those bedrooms. And we don't know what shape the floors are in."

He chewed on that for a minute or two. "All right. Assuming my wife doesn't hate the idea, you've got a deal."

"Great!" Grace beamed. "What about the rattan furniture? It's really good stuff, Arthur. I love it, but I don't actually have a place I can use it right now. Once I get this house cleaned up, it'll be perfect in the living room. Is there a place we can store it until then?"

He yanked his head in the direction of the back of the house. "There's a garage out back. Guess I could lock it up out there for now."

She couldn't believe what she'd just done. Gone out for a run, found a set of cool old furniture, and ended up with a new decorating gig and several months' worth of potentially fabulous, totally original blog posts. This was a non-paying gig, sure, but she couldn't wait to dig in, turning this toxic-waste dump into a treasure.

"When can I get started?" she asked, trying not to sound too anxious.

"As soon as you like," Arthur said. "I'll get the worst of this crap hauled off tomorrow. Meet me over here then, and I'll give you a key."

"How will we work out paying for the materials?" Grace asked. "I'm, uh, kind of tight on funds while I wait for my divorce to play out."

"I'll set up a draw for you at the hardware store," Arthur said. "Just keep the receipts. Oh, and there's just one more thing. Part of the deal, you might say."

"Yesss?" Grace felt her throat tighten. She knew it was too good to be true.

He walked toward the hallway. A moment later, he thrust the stinking, shivering bundle of fur into her arms. "You keep the dog."

21.

She didn't dare tell her mother what she was up to. It was nearly 9:00 A.M. by the time she'd walked home with her bundle tucked under her arm. She thanked every holy force she could think of that it was Monday, and Rochelle had gone out do the week's grocery shopping.

Grace dragged a washtub from the carport and filled it with water from the garden hose.

"It's okay, sweetie," she cooed, keeping one hand on the dog's back for reassurance. "We're gonna get you cleaned up a little. This won't hurt, and you'll feel a lot better afterward." She squeezed a little of her own shampoo into her hand and gently rubbed it into the dog's fur.

The animal whimpered a little, but Grace rubbed and cooed and breathed through her mouth as a vile stream of brown water surged off the quivering animal.

When finally the water had turned clear, and she could see no more crust in the dog's fur, Grace wrapped her in a beach towel. Upstairs in her bedroom, she set the beach towel on her bed and turned her blow-dryer to cool, running it back and forth over the little dog's damp fur.

Even though she was now semiclean, the poor little thing still looked so pitiful, Grace could have wept.

"Okay, sweetie," she said, ruffling the dog's ears. "There's a vet over on Anna Maria. I think we'll just run over there to see if they'll take a look at you."

It was Grace's first time in a vet's office. The receptionist looked up at her with a blank expression.

"So . . . you don't know anything about this dog?"

"No. Basically, she'd been abandoned, in a house. Locked in a bedroom, and I don't know for how long. When I got her, she was kind of bloody. I think she'd tried to scratch her way out. I gave her a bath, but I think there's probably something else wrong with her. Because she keeps shivering."

Grace looked down at the little brown dog, huddled under the swaddling of beach towel. "But you're a good girl, aren't you, sweetie?"

The girl had been typing on the computer. She looked up. "That's her name, Sweetie?"

"Uh, sure," Grace agreed. It was as good a name as any.

"It's slow right now," the girl said, clicking over to another page of her computer. "I think Dr. Katz can see her pretty soon. Can you wait?"

"The vet's name is Dr. Katz?" Grace suppressed a giggle. "Really?"

The girl rolled her eyes. She'd heard it all before. "Really. How did you want to pay today?"

Grace hesitated. "Cash, I guess."

"You can sit over there," the receptionist said, pointing to a chair. She held out her arms and Grace handed the dog over, towel and all. "It's okay now, Sweetie," the girl said softly. She reached into a glass jar on the counter and gave the dog a biscuit, which she eagerly snapped up. Then she disappeared behind a swinging door.

Grace sat in a hard vinyl chair and read a magazine about schnauzers. She hadn't realized there was so much to say about schnauzers, but apparently there was. On the opposite side of the waiting room, an elderly lady cradled a pet carrier in her lap. A huge tabby cat nearly filled the thing, its tail sticking out through the wire-mesh door.

Thirty minutes later, the receptionist was back at the desk. "Sweetie Davenport?" she called.

Grace suppressed a giggle. It was as though she'd acquired a new baby sister. "Yes?" she said, standing.

"Dr. Katz is back with Sweetie, in examining room one," she said. "You can go back and talk to her."

The veterinarian was a compact blond woman, in her late forties. She wore a short white lab coat that had silk-screened cartoon images of dogs and cats on it.

Sweetie was lying on a stainless steel examining table, and the vet held one hand on her back, slowly stroking her fur. When the dog spotted Grace, her stubby brown tail beat a tattoo on the table.

"Hi there," the vet said, nodding at Grace. "You've got a very good little girl here. She let me examine her, and she didn't make as much as a squeak."

"Is she okay?" Grace asked.

"A little dehydrated," Dr. Katz said. "And she's got an intestinal parasite, and some wounds on her paws, which are infected."

Grace felt her throat tighten with anger. "The people who owned her, they just left her, locked in a bedroom of the house they'd been renting, and took off. She'd apparently been trying to dig her way out. We don't know how long she'd been there when the landlord found her today."

"It happens," Dr. Katz said, ruffling Sweetie's fur. "I'm sorry to tell you we see all kinds of cruelty to animals. It's upsetting, but not unusual."

"What can you do for her?"

"I'd like to keep her overnight. Put her on some IV fluids and get her started on antibiotics," the vet said. "We don't have any idea of her medical history, but given the fact that she was abandoned in this condition, I think we should assume she's never had any shots. We'll give her parvo and rabies shots, and start her on worm meds. And," she added, "give her a good flea dip."

"Right," Grace said. She hesitated. "Look," she said, her cheeks flaming with shame. "I'm in the middle of a divorce, and right now I just don't have a lot of money. I'm living with my mother, and getting a dog was the last thing I'd planned. How much will all this cost?"

Dr. Katz put a hand on her sleeve. "Don't worry too much about that. Let us work on Sweetie a couple days. We'll call you Wednesday and let you know what time you can pick her up. We do have a special rate for people rescuing strays, and we can always work out a payment plan, if need be. Does that sound all right?"

"Yes," Grace said. "Thank you! I'll be honest with you. I've never owned a dog, and wasn't looking for one. But I couldn't just leave her there and let her be dropped off at the dog pound."

"Good for you," Dr. Katz said.

"Can you tell me anything about her?" Grace asked. "Like what breed she is, or how old?"

Dr. Katz continued to stroke Sweetie's head. "She's no puppy. Judging by her teeth, I'd say she's probably at least four years old. It's hard to tell without doing DNA testing, but I feel confident that she's got a good bit of toy poodle in her, maybe some cocker spaniel, too. Considering what she's been through, she's surprisingly calm and docile. Once we get her feeling better, she'll make you a loyal, adoring little buddy."

Grace's eyes rested on Sweetie's big brown ones. She could have sworn the dog was grinning at her.

"And Grace?"

"Yes?"

"I think she's housebroken! I was examining her, and she started to whimper, so we took her out to the dog run, and she did her business right away."

Now Grace returned Sweetie's smile. "Thanks, Dr. Katz. That's the first good news I've heard today."

22.

She spent Tuesday working in the bar and fuming over Ben's sabotage of her blog. But early Wednesday morning, Grace bounded down the stairs to the bar, her camera bag in hand.

Rochelle had the blender going, whipping up an evil-looking green concoction. She shut it off, poured the sludge in a glass, and sipped, all the while taking in Grace's work ensemble, which consisted of a pair of thrift-store jeans, oversized T-shirt, and cheap tennis shoes. "No run this morning?"

"Nope," Grace said, unable to suppress a grin. "I've got an actual job." She poured herself a mug of coffee and snagged a banana from the fruit bowl on the bar back.

"Is that so?"

"Yup."

"How'd you get this job? Where is it? What's it pay?"

Grace couldn't remember when she'd been this excited at the prospect of working for free.

"You won't believe it, Mom," she said. "When I was out for my run Monday I passed this really rundown house over on Anna Maria. There was a huge pile of junk at the curb. Obviously, somebody was doing a clean out. I stopped to look, because this guy had just dumped a great old mid-century rattan sofa. And then he added more pieces, and I kind of struck up a conversation with him. The house had been a rental, but the tenants trashed the place and skipped out on the rent, and the guy I met was the landlord. The rattan was really good stuff. Very collectible, so I asked him if I could have it, although God knows where I'd put it. He invited me inside the house—which was a disaster area, but it could be really wonderful."

"Slow down," Rochelle ordered. "You went into a house with a strange man? Are you nuts? What if he'd been some kind of deviant or something?"

"He wasn't a deviant; he actually knew Dad," Grace said. "So he was complaining about how long it was going to take him to get the place fixed up to rent again, and I asked him if he'd let me do it. You know, as a before-and-after story for the blog. And he said yes!" Grace was practically jumping up and down.

"How much?" Rochelle asked.

"I finally got him to agree to a minimum budget of five thousand dollars, although I think it'll probably run more than that," she said.

"He's paying you five thousand? Honey, that's great," Rochelle said. "I'm so proud of you."

Grace shook her head. "No. He's not paying me anything. The budget to fix up the house is five thousand. Or more. I'm doing the work for free. So I can do a before-and-after series for my blog. Wait 'til you see this place, Mom. It's over on Mandevilla, on Anna Maria, about a block from the bay. It's a real old-timey Florida cracker house, with the pitched roof and the screened porch. All the inside walls are the original pine. Right now, there's some skanky carpet on the floors, but I'm sure there's hardwood under there. It's got a tiny little galley kitchen, again with the original cabinets. I'm thinking I'll take the doors off the upper cabinets . . ."

"Wait," Rochelle said. "You're going to do all this work? Without getting paid? How is this a good thing?"

"Because it's design work," Grace said. "I'll be rehabbing a historic old cottage. It's what I love to do! And I can photograph it from every stage and blog about it. And that is something that not even Ben and J'Aimee can rip off."

She dug into her camera bag and brought out some Benjamin Moore paint chips, rifling through the colored cards until she found the one she wanted. "Here. Dove White. I'm thinking of using it for all the interior walls. The house is kind of dark inside, because of the porch overhang, so I want to brighten it up, make it look crisp and clean. Have you ever seen a prettier white?"

"You know all white paint looks the same to me," Rochelle said. "But if you say it's the best white ever, I believe it."

"I might do the kitchen another color, maybe a soft aqua, something like that," Grace mused. "But I want to get it all defunked, have a clean slate, before I make too many design decisions."

"What's the owner going to say about all those design decisions? And who is it? You said it's somebody who knew Butch?"

"He doesn't care what I do, as long as I get it presentable and ready to rent again," Grace said. "He'll be the perfect client—especially since he's leaving soon to spend the summer in North Carolina. I won't have him breathing down my neck, second-guessing everything I do. Oh yeah. His name is Arthur Cater. He said he used to take Dad fishing on his boat."

"Arthur Cater? He's your client?" Rochelle rolled her eyes.

"What's that supposed to mean? No, never mind. I don't

want to hear it. I am not going to let you rain on my parade. Whatever you know about him, keep it to yourself."

"I wasn't gonna rain on your parade," Rochelle said. "Arthur's an okay guy. He used to come in here a lot, when they lived on the island, back before he got fancy and moved over to Longboat Key. There's just one thing I want you to know about him."

"Whatever," Grace said, packing up her paint chips impatient to get started on her new project. "Can I have the key to the shed? Thank God I didn't get around to cleaning out Dad's tools. All my stuff is still back at Sand Dollar Lane. I don't even have a hammer or a pair of pliers to my own name now. And I want to get that nasty carpet pulled up this morning. First thing."

Rochelle went into the kitchen and came back with a key ring, which she handed to her daughter. "Just know this about Arthur. He is the world's biggest cheapskate. He's got tons of money, but he didn't get that way throwing it around. He will nickel and dime you to death. Your dad used to say Arthur was so tight he squeaked when he walked."

"I don't care," Grace said, cramming her sweat-stained Sandbox ball cap on her head. "I've dealt with cheap and I've dealt with difficult. I'm just happy to have a job again."

Arthur Cater was standing in the driveway of the house on Mandevilla, directing two Hispanic day laborers as they loaded the avocado-green stove into the back of an ancient rust bucket of a pickup truck.

"Hey, Arthur," Grace greeted him.

"So you didn't have a change of heart, huh?" He took in her work clothes and toolbox.

"No way," Grace said. "Did your wife give us the thumbs-up?"

Arthur mopped his face with his handkerchief. "She

says you're a big-deal interior designer. She's all excited now. Says she reads your blog and she can't believe I could trick you into working for nothin'."

Grace laughed. "She doesn't know I'm the one who tricked you, does she?"

He gestured toward the house. "I got over here right at sunup this morning and set off a couple of flea bombs in there. I just opened up all the windows, so you should be all right to go in now." He reached in the pocket of his own faded blue jeans. "Here's the keys. Front and back doors, and the garage." He nodded at his workers, who were bringing the washing machine out on a furniture dolly. "I had the fellas put all that furniture in the garage, and put a tarp over it. There's some other odds and ends out there you can maybe use."

"All right," Grace said. She took her camera from around her neck and stepped into the street, clicking off a few frames.

"Stand right there by the mailbox, will you Arthur," she called. "I like to document everything, right from the beginning."

Arthur stood awkwardly by the curb, his hands thrust in his pockets. "You don't want pictures of this ugly old mug," he growled. "It'll break your camera."

"Let me be the judge of that," Grace said, stepping backward to shoot. "Arthur, do you have any idea when this house was built?"

"Let me see. Well, I'm seventy-three, and we've got old family pictures of my grandma, standing out front of this house with me in her arms. I know my grandpa bought the house, probably sometime in the thirties. It looked a lot different back then. There was no front porch, no real trees, just some scrub palmettos and sand, and where the kitchen is now, was a porch they used to cook on. There was an old wood cookstove out there. My grandpa used to fry mullet on it Friday nights. Hard to believe they raised seven kids in this little bitty place, isn't it?"

It was just a little after nine, but the sun was already high in the sky, the summer heat relentless. Grace walked all the way around the house, photographing it from every conceivable angle, swatting at mosquitoes and stopping to pick off the sandspurs clinging to her ankles. She prayed no snakes were lurking in the thick underbrush. Despite that, the more she saw of the house, the more she liked. Virtually nothing had been done to change the house in the years since the porch had been added. In a way, she decided, it was a very good thing that Arthur Cater was a cheapskate.

When she got back to the front of the house, Arthur was standing by the truck, waiting on her. He handed her a slip of paper. "Here's my phone number. You call me if there's a problem, hear? I set up a draw for you at the hardware store. And my wife said I should tell you she'd like it if you'd e-mail us some pictures as you go. She's all jazzed up about this project of yours. Good thing we're leaving town, or she'd be over here all the time, sidewalk super-intending."

Grace stood on her tiptoes and planted a kiss on Arthur's grizzled cheek. He looked surprised, but not displeased. "All right then, get to work," he ordered. He drove off with the two laborers in the back of the truck, wedged in among the rusted appliances. A moment later, he was backing down the street toward where she stood at the curb.

He hung his head out the open window. "Meant to ask you about that little dog," he said, failing miserably at pretending he didn't care. "How's she doing? Did you find somebody to take her in?"

"Sweetie is going to be just fine," Grace said. "They kept her overnight at the vet's office, giving her some IV fluids and some antibiotics. I'm going to pick her up this afternoon. And I'm going to keep her myself, until I figure out something else."

"Sweetie, huh? Dumb name for a dog."

Grace paced every inch of the cottage interior, snapping photos and making notes. She found an old broom in a tiny utility closet off the kitchen and swept up an entire village of dead insects. Then she cranked up the music she'd downloaded onto her iPod, adjusted the tiny little speakers, pulled on her work gloves, and got down to business.

A veteran of the remodeling wars, Grace donned a paper face mask before tackling the carpet. It was a hot, filthy job. The carpet was so old and brittle, hunks of it tore apart in her hands as she pried it from the nail strips along the baseboards. But when she pulled up the thin foam padding and got the first glimpse of the intact oak floors, she got a new burst of energy. By noon, when she took her lunch break with a sandwich and a bottle of water she'd brought from home, she'd pulled up all the carpet in the bedrooms, rolled it up, and dragged it out to the curb.

She was buzzed with adrenaline, dancing around the smaller of the two bedrooms doing a creditable accompaniment to Adele's "Rolling in the Deep," using the broom as a makeshift microphone. The music echoed in the high-ceilinged empty rooms, and she whipped her sweat-dampened hair from side to side as she cataloged the all-too-familiar misery of a lover done wrong.

Grace didn't hear the front door open. Didn't hear anything except the music, until she happened to turn around and see Ben, standing in the doorway, arms folded over his chest, watching her performance with no trace of amusement.

Her face flamed. She grabbed for the iPod and shut it off.

For a moment, she couldn't think of anything to say. Her throat went dry, and all she could think of was how idiotic she must have looked to him, dancing around a filthy house, in her filthy clothes, playing air guitar with a broom.

Then she got mad and found her voice again. "What are you doing here?" she asked, clutching the broom, because she needed to clutch something. It was the first time she'd seen him since their day in court.

He was dressed for golf, in a spotless white polo shirt, crisp black shorts, golf shoes, his aviator sunglasses pushed back off his forehead.

"I came to see the floor show," Ben said. "Good thing it's free."

"How'd you know where to find me?" Was he following her?

"Your mother told me you were working at a house over on Mandevilla. You're not that hard to find. She really, really doesn't like me, you know."

"That makes two of us," Grace snapped. "I'm surprised she actually spoke to you at all. But then, probably you lied to her. Lying seems to be your good thing."

He smiled. His orthodontics were a thing of beauty. "I told Rochelle I had something to give you. I guess she assumed it was money."

"But it's not."

"No," Ben said. And his smile dissolved, like Alice in Wonderland's Cheshire cat. "No money. Just some advice."

He took a step into the room. "I got a call this morning, from Anna Stribling, at Home Depot. It seems she had some 'concerns,' as she called them, about the originality of our material on Gracenotes."

"Oh?" Grace wondered if he could see her hands shaking as she clutched the broom.

"Yes. She was specifically wondering if J'Aimee's corn-crab chowder recipe was original. Because, she said, she'd had a disturbing e-mail from you, accusing us of stealing your material."

"Which you did. A blatant rip-off," Grace said. "My photos, my recipe, my everything. And that's what I told her."

"But you don't have any proof of that, do you?" Ben raised one eyebrow, amused.

"Because you hacked into my Web site and erased it. And put that filthy porn link on there," Grace fairly spat the words at him.

"And you don't have any proof of that, either."

Ben took a step closer. She could smell his elegant cologne. The Clive Christian 1872 that sold for $310 a bottle at Saks. Everything about Ben was elegant. "What I told Anna during our chat today is this. I told her that you're delusional. That you're bitter and jealous and emotionally fragile. I mentioned that you're in court-ordered counseling. I think she felt a lot better after our conversation. In fact, I know she felt better, because Home Depot just agreed to take a bigger Gracenotes banner ad starting next month."

Grace clamped her lips together to keep her jaw from dropping. She hoped Ben wasn't close enough to detect the sense of defeat that swept over her, threatened to knock her off her feet and destroy her hard-won equilibrium.

Ben towered over her—intimidation through proximity was his motto. "Don't fuck with me, Grace," he said, his voice light and even. "You'll get mowed down every time. Know this. If you send out any more of those incendiary e-mails, I'll haul your ass back to court in a New York second. And that judge will be only too happy to shut you down for good."

She took two steps backward, nearly tripping over the damned broom. "Get out," she said, recovering quickly.

She poked the broom at his spotless two-toned golf shoes. "OUT!"

He stood his ground. She jabbed at his ankles. "I said out!" He chuckled, shook his head, and strolled for the door, with Grace right on his heels. He'd left the door open, and now she saw an unfamiliar car in the driveway, a gleaming ebony Porsche Pantera.

"Nice car," she spat.

He gave her a mock bow. "Glad you like it, since I have you to thank for it. And you know? I actually like this one much better. It handles so much smoother."

She finished ripping out the rest of the carpet, without the music, now that Ben had managed to poison that source of joy. Slowly, she swept the living room and dining room floors, taking grim satisfaction from the cockroach body count.

Grace retrieved her cleaning supplies—bucket, mop, sponge, and spray cleaners—from her car and attacked the filthy windows, using an entire roll of paper towels on the front room. Logistically, it made no sense to spend so much time cleaning a house that still had so far to go in the rehab process, but she did it anyway, inhaling the scent of the strong pine cleaner as she filled her bucket with hot water.

When she found herself humming as she mopped, she got her iPod and turned it on again. The music filled her head and helped erase, temporarily, the image of Ben, smug, self-important, all-powerful Ben. "Gonna wash that man right out of my hair," she muttered, dumping the gray mop water down the toilet and flushing it with a flourish.

Finally, satisfied that the surface layers of crud had been eradicated, along with Ben's overpowering cologne, she set down her mop and picked up her camera again.

She photographed the front rooms, pleased with the way the afternoon sunlight slanted in, leaving atmospheric shadows on the old oak floors. She was so absorbed in her work she was startled at the sudden rattle of rain on the tin roof of the porch.

Time to go, she thought. She had to pick up Sweetie at the vet's office, get cleaned up before her Wednesday-night "therapy" session, and, in the meantime, figure out how to hide a dog from her mother.

23.

Wyatt Keeler stood in front of the tiny closet he shared with Bo, barefoot and dressed only in his cotton boxers, and felt gloom. He walked over to the closet, opened the door, and his mood did not improve. He hadn't thought about clothes in months, not since the breakup with Callie. Okay, maybe even before that. His style guidelines in adulthood had gotten simple; he liked clean, and he liked cool. As in temperature, not trendiness.

At one time, he'd prided himself on being a sharp dresser. Just the right label jeans, good-quality classic shirts, ties and jackets. Nothing too flashy or outrageous. He'd learned a lot from his fraternity brothers in college. He'd been, like the ZZ Top song, a sharp-dressed man.

No more. Now, he idly plucked at the meager assortment of shirts and pants hanging limply on the wire hangers. "Dude," he muttered under his breath, "you are really, really lame." Finally, he found a pair of presentable navy blue Dockers and a short-sleeved plaid dress shirt that had been a Father's Day gift from Callie. The J.C. Penney price tag still hung from the sleeve.

The pants fit reasonably well, but they were wrinkled.

He put on the shirt, then padded out to the living area, where Nelson was eating a chicken potpie at the dinette and reading the sports section. "Dad, do we own an iron?"

"Dunno," Nelson mumbled, his fingers poised over the box scores. "Your mother always handled that." He glanced up, looked surprised. "Since when do you iron?"

"Since now," Wyatt said. He checked under the kitchen sink, then on the top shelf of the hall closet, to no avail. "Screw it," he said, tossing the pants into the dryer.

While he was waiting for his pants, Wyatt went back to the bathroom. Feeling foolish, but somehow lighthearted, he brushed his teeth, again, and flossed. Back in the bedroom, with the door closed, he checked himself out in the cloudy mirror on the back of the closet door.

He wasn't a bad-looking guy. His teeth were straight, he was clean-shaven. After that crack Callie had made about his baldness he'd thought about letting his hair grow out again, just to prove he had plenty, but later he'd changed his mind. Screw Callie. He worked outside in the blazing Florida sun all day, and it was just much cooler without hair. Obviously, she liked a guy with hair. Luke wore his hair deliberately shaggy, like a surfer dude, although the guy had clearly never been anywhere near a surfboard. And Wyatt had always secretly suspected Luke of being a bottle blond.

Luke, Wyatt thought, had a body like the Pillsbury Doughboy. Big, pillowy hips, blobby butt. He was a desk jockey and looked it. But a successful desk jockey.

Now Wyatt turned and surveyed his own body, sucking in his gut—okay, just a little. He had wide shoulders, and all those years of hard labor at the park left him with the pecs and abs to prove it. He was just a shade over six feet tall.

Callie'd always claimed his eyes were what made her start flirting with him at that bar back in Clemson, all those years ago. That and the dimples. His eyes were a mud color, he'd always thought, but he had his mother's eyelashes, thick, black, Bambi lashes, as she called them.

A lot of good they'd done him lately.

What the hell. He fetched the pants, got dressed, put on his grandfather's gold watch. For maybe the millionth time, he looked at the plain gold wedding band on the ring finger of his left hand. He'd taken it off dozens of times, put it back on again the same number of times. He couldn't say why. Callie had replaced her wedding rings with the flashy diamond "engagement" ring Luke had bought her. Was it technically possible to be engaged while you were still married? Maybe he'd remove his own ring once the divorce was final. He only knew it wasn't time. Yet. Probably this made him a double loser. He took a deep breath and picked up the truck keys from the dresser.

"You goin' to church?" Nelson asked. He'd moved to the recliner in front of the television and found the Braves game. He was dressed in an old T-shirt and a pair of faded pajama bottoms. *Geezus H.*, Wyatt thought. *Save me from ever wearing pajama bottoms.*

"Church? No. Remember, Dad? I told you. I've got to go to that divorce therapy session."

"Oh, right," Nelson said vaguely. "And Bo's at his mom's?"

"Yes," Wyatt said patiently. "Bo is with Callie tonight. I'll pick him up Thursday. Remember?"

Every night he replayed this same scene. Nelson would ask where Bo was, and Wyatt would tell him. Most of the time, his father seemed perfectly with it, lucid, same old Nelson. But in the evenings, he got . . . vague. Wyatt told himself his father was fine. He was still physically fit, strong as an ox. He ran the concession stand in the park, took tickets, helped out with the never-ending landscaping and maintenance. But in the past year, Nelson had begun a slow, almost indefinable slide. Sometimes, he needed help with the bank deposits. He got aggravated if there was even the slightest deviation in his carefully mapped daily routine.

Wyatt worried. But hell, he worried about everything. Like now. He doubled back to the bedroom, hung up the dress pants and the plaid shirt. He rolled up the sleeves of the white dress shirt he'd worn to court and put on his nicest pair of shorts. And what he thought of as his dress shoes, a pair of leather flip-flops. At least he felt like some version of himself.

Paula Talbott-Sinclair greeted them all in the reception area. Her usually flyaway hair had been tamed and twisted into a sleek, artful chignon. She wore a long wispy yellow and green flowered dress with bell sleeves that made her look like a butterfly, bright coral lipstick, and her usual dozen or so bracelets. She wore gold gladiator-style sandals, and tonight she seemed lucid and bright-eyed. She was, Grace thought, a woman transformed. Which made Grace immediately suspicious.

"Hello, friends," she said, grasping the hand of each group member as they arrived at the office. She made a show of having them all sign in, inviting them to have coffee, asking them how their week had gone.

Grace was surprised when the first person she saw was Wyatt. He'd obviously taken pains with his appearance tonight. "Hey," she said, sidling over to him at the coffee machine. "You look nice tonight."

"No parrot poop, right?" He looked embarrassed. "You look nice, too. But unlike me, you always look good."

"You wouldn't say that if you'd seen me a couple hours ago," Grace assured him. But she was glad he'd noticed. On her last thrifting excursion, she'd found a pair of nearly new black DKNY capris at the Junior League for three dollars and a simple acid-green polished cotton wrap blouse, which set her back ninety-nine cents at the hospice shop. The blouse was sleeveless, and she thought it was flattering to the new tan she'd acquired from all that running. With the black ballet flats from Target and a wide gold bangle bracelet she'd borrowed from Rochelle, this was the nicest outfit she owned, and she'd spent less buying it than she had a tube of lipstick in her old life.

Wyatt nodded his head in Paula's direction. "Obviously, she found her way home last week."

"Look. She's even wearing shoes. Maybe she's got a hot date afterward," Grace murmured.

At the stroke of 7:00 P.M., Paula began herding them to their seats. "Please be seated," she said, clapping her hands. Paula looked around the room, taking a silent body count. Grace prayed she would overlook the oversized tote bag she'd stowed under her folding chair.

"So," Paula began, her voice in a slightly higher-than-normal pitch. "We've completed two weeks of recovery therapy. At this stage of your process, I hope you're beginning to feel a little more comfortable in your own skin. We've talked a little bit about how you see yourselves, following the breakup of your marriage. And I'd like to continue that discussion this week, with having you share from your journals."

Paula's cell phone was in her lap, and while she spoke, her eyes continually watched it.

She gazed around the room. "Who haven't we heard from?"

Wyatt and Suzanne slumped down in their chairs, ducked their heads, hoping they wouldn't be noticed. It was painfully clear the therapist had no memory of what had transpired in their previous session.

"I don't think Suzanne has shared with us yet," Ashleigh volunteered.

"I'll just bet you were that kid in elementary school who always reminded the teacher she hadn't assigned homework, just before the bell rang," Camyrn said, giving Ashleigh the evil eye.

Suzanne's olive skin flushed.

"That's right," Paula said. "Thank you, Ashleigh. Suzanne?"

Grace felt a sharp pang of sympathy for Suzanne, hunched down in her chair, eyes glued to her journal. Her face was pale, with two bright spots of pink on her cheeks, but her face was beaded with a fine sheen of perspiration.

Suzanne was dressed in a dull, unflattering beige dress and scuffed brown leather sandals. It was as if she was wearing her own brand of camouflage, to blend into the surroundings.

"Uh, well," Suzanne stuttered and blinked rapidly. Grace noticed that the damp palms of her hands had begun to make the ink on Suzanne's journal run.

Suzanne's voice was low.

"Once, I was a wife," she began, reading in a stilted monotone.

"I was a lover, a mother, a teacher, a mentor. I had value, to others as well as myself. And then I discovered my husband's treachery. He was cheating on me, with one of my coworkers. I didn't confront him. I kept telling myself it might not be true. I became obsessed with checking on him, on her, confirming my worst suspicions. I figured out where they were having their trysts. I followed him. I checked into the same cheap motel room after they'd left, and I told myself I would take some pills and kill myself, in that same bed, and it would be the perfect, poetic justice. Just another Shakespearean tragedy. But I couldn't even do that. Even after I knew, I did nothing. I was para-

lyzed. He loved someone else. She was younger, prettier, cleverer, sexier. How could I compete with her? I was a failure, at everything, especially marriage. If I couldn't keep Eric, how could I be a success at my job? How could I be a good mother to my daughter Darby? So I have stopped trying, because if I don't try, I can't fail. Every day I shrink a little more. Soon I'll be invisible. Will anybody notice? Will Eric?"

Suzanne closed her notebook, but didn't look up.

"Oh, wow," Ashleigh breathed, breaking the silence. "You actually slept in the same motel room they'd just screwed in? That is all kinds of crazy."

"Ashleigh!" Camryn's eyes blazed. "Will you please shut the *fuck* up?"

Paula didn't appear to have heard Ashleigh's comment. She was staring down at her cell phone, reading something on the screen.

Now, she looked up, realized the group was expecting some comment from their therapist.

"That was very powerful, Suzanne," she said, beaming, and then looking around at the others. "Any comments? Thoughts?"

Wyatt twisted his wedding band. "I've been there," he said, finally. "I couldn't put it in words like you just did, Suzanne. But yeah, every day, when I think about it, letting some other guy just take my wife, just stepping aside and letting her leave? What a loser I am. So who could blame her for leaving me for him?"

"You're not a loser," Grace said fiercely. "None of us are losers. Just because my husband didn't value me—all the things I am? That doesn't change who I am. But it changes who he is. Somebody who lies. Somebody who cheats." She sat up. "My ex came to see me today. And I finally saw him for what he is."

"Oooh, girl," Camryn said. "Was he begging you to take him back?"

"No." Grace thought about it for a moment. "He just wanted to grind his heel in my face. Punish me some more, make me feel like crap. Let me know he'll always have power over me."

Suddenly, Paula stood up. "Very nice, Wyatt and Grace. Excellent work, sharing with our friends. Let's take a little ten-minute break, and then we'll come back and, um, I have a surprise for all of you. Also? Who haven't we heard from yet?"

"Me," Wyatt said reluctantly.

The others shot out of the room like first graders at recess. All except Suzanne, who sat demurely in her chair, ankles crossed, hands in her lap.

Grace slid into the chair beside hers. "Suzanne? That was really wonderful, what you wrote. I think all of us saw something of ourselves in what you've gone through."

Suzanne brightened, just a little. "So, you don't think I'm the queen of crazypants?"

"You? Nah. That title belongs to Ashleigh," Grace said. Out of the corner of her eye, she saw a small pink nose pop out of the top of her tote bag. "Oh, Lord," she breathed. "I've gotta go outside for a minute. So—will you come to the Sandbox tonight, after? Just for a little while? At least so we can discuss what's up with Paula?"

Suzanne brightened. "So, it's not just me? There is definitely something weird about her. Weirder than usual tonight, because she's actually acting normal! About the Sandbox, I'd come, but it's just such a long way there and then home again."

"If you like, you can leave your car here and ride over there with me," Grace offered. "I'm sure one of the others will give you a ride back afterward."

"Maybe," Suzanne said. "Let me think about it, okay?"

* * *

"Friends," Paula began, once their break was over, her face flushed with excitement. "I didn't want to announce this earlier, because, well, I wasn't sure it was going to happen. But I got a message just before our break, and it appears that we are going to have a guest joining us tonight. I, for one, am incredibly honored that he's taking time out from his very busy life to be with us." She glanced down at her watch and, then again, at her cell phone.

She took a deep breath. "I'm sure he'll be along shortly. In the meantime, I'd like us to think about options." She looked around the room. "From what you've told me, all of you feel you've been badly hurt by your spouses. Of course, since we don't have your partners here with us, I only have your version of events that led to your breakups."

Camryn snorted. "We're the ones who got ordered to be here, Paula. If you want Dexter Nobles's version of what happened, feel free to drag his ass in here."

"Camryn?" Paula frowned at her. "Sharing time is over. Now. All of you have spoken of your feelings of powerlessness and inferiority. Now, I'd like you to explore what options you have, going forward with your lives."

A man cleared his throat. All heads swung in the direction of the reception-room door. "Er, hello?"

Paula jumped up from her chair and clapped her hands in glee. "Judge Stackpole! Your Honor, we're so glad you could be here!"

24.

Judge Cedric N. Stackpole Jr. was dressed in his version of business casual and Grace's idea of what not to wear to divorce therapy. A black short-sleeved knit shirt with the top button fastened—although Grace saw the glimmer of a thick gold chain resting amidst a tuft of chest hair sticking out over the top button. Very shiny, very faux-distressed, very obviously brand-new jeans, belted and worn navel-high. Highly polished black slip-ons, no socks.

His thinning reddish hair was slicked back with some type of hair product that he'd obviously bought in bulk in the eighties.

He nodded curtly at the group, and cracked something similar to a smile at Paula.

"Hello, hello," he said briskly, his hands thrust awkwardly in his jeans pockets. "Uh, Dr. Talbott-Sinclair invited me to drop in tonight, just to see how everybody is doing. Er, uh, I hope you are all listening closely to her message. Because, uh, if more people like you all came to sessions with therapists like Dr. Talbott-Sinclair, there'd be lots less work for judges like me." He seemed to think this was a hysterically funny line. "Right?" he asked. "Judges might not have jobs. Right?"

Paula's laughter trilled up and down the musical scales. "That's right!" she said, clasping her hands. "Very intuitive, Your Honor."

Grace didn't dare cut her eyes sideways to the left to see Camryn's reaction to this. Instead, she pretended to study the journal on her lap. Through lowered eyelashes, she could see Wyatt, on her right, his arms folded across his chest, glaring directly at the judge, barely disguised hostility emanating from every pore.

"Well," Stackpole said, "please don't let me interrupt. I'll just sit here in the back of the room, and you all go on as though I weren't here."

Like that's gonna happen, Grace thought. She glanced nervously down at her tote bag, but for now it was very still.

Paula stood and faced the group. Her hair was neatly combed, and Grace noticed she'd reapplied her lipstick and powdered her nose during the break. And was the neckline of her dress tugged just a little lower? Showing just a hint of cleavage that hadn't been visible before?

"Most of you are here because in the heat of the moment or, perhaps, after some very deliberate but ill-thought-out reasoning, you decided to strike out—violently, publicly, even *criminally,* against your spouse. Probably, you reasoned, 'this person has hurt me, and my only option is to strike back.'" She nodded at Grace.

"Isn't that right, Grace?"

"No," Grace heard herself say. "That isn't what happened at all."

Paula gave her a patronizing smile. "We'll come back to that."

"What I'm trying to say," Paula went on, "is that whether

you know it or not, you had options at the time you acted out, and you have options now. Do you stay, or do you leave? Forgive? Forget? Neither?"

"Huh." Wyatt shook his head. "That ship has sailed, Paula."

"Yeah," Camryn put in. "I already left, or rather, I kicked his butt out the door. You want me to forget? How do I erase the image of him in bed with my twenty-two-year-old daughter's best friend? I wish I could forget it," she said, throwing up her hands in surrender. "What's that drug they used to give women during childbirth? Scopolamine, yeah, the twilight drug. You feel the labor pains, but after, you have no memory of the pain. You tell me how to find the equivalent of Scopolamine for what he did to me and my family."

Grace's mind flashed again to the scene of Ben and J'Aimee in the darkened garage. She closed her eyes and willed the scene to disappear, the same way she had nearly every night since it had occurred.

"That's right," Suzanne murmured, pressing her fingertips to her forehead.

"I don't have any drugs to give you," Paula said, her face flushing. She was looking past Camryn and the others, directly at the back of the room, where Stackpole sat.

Grace heard a little gasp at this, but then, at almost the same time, she felt the tote bag at her feet move. She dropped her journal to the floor as a cover, reached in, and scratched the warm furry head there, felt a tiny pink tongue rasp against the palm of her hand. She stole a backward glance at the judge, who was staring down at his watch, pointedly tapping the crystal. She sat back up again.

"I can tell you, though," Paula said, her voice rising, "that until you spend time figuring out what went wrong with your marriage, until you stop blaming yourself, your partner, the other lover, you will never move past those scenes like the one Camryn describes. Even if your marriage is irretrievably, undeniably finished now, there was a time when you had hope. You had love. Whatever your version of love is. Next session, I want you to try really hard to get past your bitterness and write down one quality, perhaps one anecdote, that might explain what drew you to your partner. What about that person made you happy?"

"That's easy. It was the big ol' honkin' ring he gave me," Ashleigh whispered, with a giggle, fingering the bauble she wore around her neck.

Paula hadn't heard, as usual. "I'll see you all next week."

Grace looked at her watch. It was barely 7:30 P.M. Why was Paula suddenly in such a hurry to end the session? When she looked up again, she saw Stackpole speeding toward the door with the look of a man with a mission.

25.

"Sandbox?" Camryn murmured, as the group drifted out to the parking lot.

"I'm in," Ashleigh nodded vigorously. She turned to Suzanne. "You coming?"

"Well, I guess I could. I did tell my daughter I might be a little late," Suzanne said.

Grace looked at Wyatt. "How about you?"

He hesitated. Camryn tugged at his arm. "Oh, come on. You can't hold out forever."

"I thought this was a girls-only thing," he said. "No boys in the tree fort?"

Ashleigh gave him a wink. "For you, we'll lower the rope ladder. Right, ladies?"

A hastily scribbled RESERVED sign was taped to the booth in the corner. Rochelle hurried over to the table when Grace pushed through the front door. "They're coming to-night, right?"

"Yeesss," Grace found herself slightly annoyed at her mother's eagerness, but she couldn't say why. While Rochelle returned to her post behind the bar, she slipped outside with the tote bag, and when she returned five minutes later, the rest of the group were arranged around the table, each with a drink in front of them. She slid into the booth beside Wyatt, who was sipping a beer.

"What was going on with Paula tonight?" Ashleigh asked.

"Here you go," Rochelle said, as she placed a glass of white wine in front of Grace and a big basket of freshly made popcorn in the center of the table. She plunked herself down beside Camryn at the opposite end of the booth.

"Why?" Rochelle wanted to know. "What was Paula doing?"

"She was, like, sober," Ashleigh said. "All dressed up. With shoes and everything. She actually kind of looked like what I pictured a professional therapist would look like. It was kind of crazy."

"Mm-hmm. Mama was definitely on some new meds tonight," Camryn agreed. "There were a couple times tonight she managed to almost sound coherent. Not that I agree with any of that forgiveness crap she was selling," she added hastily.

"I couldn't get over how changed she was. And when Judge Stackpole came in, I was really struck by the transformation," Suzanne said. "It was like she was hoping for his approval. Dying for it."

"The judge showed up?" Rochelle asked, her eyes widening.

"Asshole," Wyatt muttered, staring down at his beer.

All the women turned to look at him at once. "Can't help it," he said defensively. "He's gonna ruin my son's life, letting Callie drag him off to Birmingham. How often will I be able to get to Birmingham to see him? Every other month? Probably not even that. Even if I could forgive her, I'll never forgive him, if I lose my kid."

Ashleigh waved the straw from her half-empty margarita glass in the air. "I think Paula's got a big ol' schoolgirl crush on Stackhole."

"Stackhole, that's good!" Rochelle said. "What do you think, Grace?"

Grace had been surreptitiously slipping a handful of popcorn in the direction of the tote bag, which was between her feet. She was distracted by the soft snuffing sounds and hoped the din of the bar would drown them out.

"Well . . . I agree, Paula was definitely on her best behavior tonight. And I did wonder about Stackpole's appearance. Why was he there? Paula told us she reports to him on our progress. Doesn't he have anything better to do than sit in on our sad little sessions?" She turned to Suzanne. "Do you think maybe there's something going on between them?"

"Maybe," Suzanne said, her voice tentative.

"Eeew," Ashleigh said, wrinkling her nose. "Paula and that . . . old man? And isn't he married or something?"

"He's not all that old. My lawyer, Mitzi, was in law school with him. When he was appointed to the bench, he was the youngest judge in Florida. But, yes, he's definitely married," Grace said. "During our hearing he made a point of telling my lawyer that his own wife has no problems running his household with two thousand dollars a month."

"Which pays for what?" Rochelle asked. "I'll bet he doesn't expect her to pay a mortgage or utilities or insurance for that."

While they batted ideas around, Camryn was busily typing away on her iPhone. "I've got the Florida judiciary Web site here," she announced, thumbing down the page. "Gimme a minute. Okay, here it is. Cedric Norris Stackpole, age fifty-one. B.A., University of Florida, 1980. J.D., University of Florida, 1983. Appointed to the bar, 2000." She looked up. "Wow, a judge at forty. That's impressive, even if he isn't." She scrolled a little more. "Married, 1999, to the former Eileen Bolther of Kissimmee."

"Bolther? Why is that name familiar?" Suzanne asked.

"If she's a Bolther and she's from Kissimmee, she must be related to Sawyer Bolther. As in Bolther Groves and Bolther Beef. Two of the biggest cattle and citrus growers in Florida. Not to mention Bolther Bank and Trust," Camryn said.

"How do you know all this stuff?" Ashleigh asked.

"I'm a reporter. I don't know it off the top of my head, but I get paid to know how to find it out," Camryn said. "I covered the last three governor's races, and, as I recall, Sawyer Bolther was one of the biggest campaign contributors to that last joker we elected. So that gives you an idea how ol' Cedric got named a judge at the ripe old age of forty. His wife's family is politically connected."

"What about Paula?" Suzanne asked. "I'm a little curious about her, I have to admit. She's such an enigma. After those first two sessions, I'd written her off as a total fraud, or at least a deeply troubled person with some kind of substance-abuse issues. But tonight?" She looked around the table for consensus. "She actually said a couple things that I thought made sense."

"Like what?" Wyatt asked. "I mean, I'm not disagreeing."

"I can't quote her directly," Suzanne said, flustered. "It was something about taking the time to figure out what went wrong with our marriages, putting blame aside, and just, you know, taking a look at what the problems really were."

"Wasn't the fact that everybody's husband or wife cheated on them the big, overriding problem?" Rochelle asked.

"A problem? Or maybe a symptom?"

All heads turned toward Grace. She shrugged. "I don't know anything. I probably know the least about marriage of anybody here. I thought my marriage was just peachy, until it all went up in flames. I'm not saying I want Ben back. If I ever did before, the things he's done since I left have opened my eyes to the kind of person he is. I keep wondering how I didn't see the real him."

"Sometimes, maybe we do see the real person, but we convince ourselves that we can live with him, or somehow change him, just by loving him enough," Rochelle said.

Grace stared. Where had this come from? And why did Rochelle keep hanging around?

"Dexter changed, once he had a taste of success, once he got into politics," Camryn said. "In college, when he was at Morehouse, and I was at Spelman, he wrote poetry! Yes, he did. He was this shy, skinny, geeky mama's boy. Not anybody I ever would have taken a second look at. But one of my sorority sisters was dating his roommate, and she begged me to go out with him, as a favor so the two of them could get some privacy on a Friday night. I asked him to a mixer, and it turned out the guy could dance. I mean, dance! Later on, he admitted he'd been watching Michael Jackson videos for years, learning his moves. I thought that was so sweet. You know? That's the Dexter I fell in love with. He had ideals. He wanted to change the world."

Camryn sipped her drink. "I don't know him now. Obviously."

"Would any of you take your husbands—or wives—back, if they wanted to come back?" Ashleigh asked.

The table got very quiet. "I'd take Boyce back," Ashleigh volunteered. "But, I mean, there'd have to be some changes. For one thing, I'd go back to managing his practice. Some men you just have to keep on a short leash. I know he doesn't love that tramp he's seeing. She's not even his type! I've learned my lesson, I'll tell you that." She grinned mischievously and leaned forward. "I'll tell you something else, too. When he comes back—I'll be a lot more adventurous. In the bedroom, you know? Keep him guessing."

Grace felt herself blushing. She'd just met these people. There was no way she'd ever talk about her and Ben's love life—especially with her mother sitting right there!

Ashleigh pointed at Camryn. "How about you? If Dexter wanted you back—would you do it?"

"Oh, hell to the no," Camryn said. "How could I respect myself if I took him back? I know what a sleaze he is. Jana's sad about us breaking up, but I want her to know, as a black woman, she needs to have some standards. I don't want her settling for second-rate, or thinking it's okay for some brother to cheat on her and degrade her. Besides? He's been dipping his pen in a lot of ink. And I know Dexter. I know he wasn't wearing a condom for any of those close encounters. Who knows what kind of diseases he might be carrying around?" She shuddered. "We hadn't been sleeping together for months anyway, but just to be sure I got myself tested as soon as I saw that little DVD of his. Somehow, I got lucky. Everything tested negative."

"How about you, Wyatt?" Camryn asked pointedly. "You've been pretty quiet all these sessions."

"Yeah," Ashleigh agreed. "I'd just loooove to know how it feels when the shoe is on the other foot."

Wyatt's face colored. "You don't think women cheat on their husbands? Look, it's different with me."

"Because you've got a penis? And choices?" Camryn asked.

"Because I've got a six-year-old son to raise," Wyatt half stood, obviously roused. "I've got to put my kid first, and myself second."

"What if you didn't have a kid? Or what if she broke up with the other guy?" Ashleigh persisted.

Wyatt glared at her. "Can we just drop it?"

"No, we can't," Camryn snapped. "Can you quit being macho man long enough to answer an honest question?"

He eased back into his chair, some of the fight gone out

of him. With his thumb, he twisted his wedding band around and around. "You read all these statistics about the children of divorce. They don't do as well in school, have emotional problems. I don't want that for Bo."

"Listen, Wyatt," Rochelle said, reaching down the length of the table and grabbing his hand. "Shrinks can come up with all kinds of statistics to make people feel guilty. What kind of home will you be raising Bo in if he knows you and Callie hate each other? Kids aren't dumb. They can sense things. And what happens if you take her back and she decides to go off with some other guy?"

Wyatt's face contorted and Grace wished she could kick her mother under the table. Instead, she spirited some more popcorn into her tote bag.

"Suzanne?" Now Rochelle was concentrating on the least forthcoming member of the group.

"What about you? Would you take your husband back?"

Suzanne seemed to shrink into her chair. "Our situation . . . is unique," Suzanne said. "I'm sorry. You've all been so open and honest. I feel like a voyeur, sitting here, contributing nothing. I'm still . . . still trying to sort out my feelings." She took a deep breath and started again.

"Let me try to explain. I come from a very religious Catholic family. My father dragged us to Mass every Sunday. My mother was very pious. From the outside, we looked like the ideal family. Inside?" She shrugged. "He cheated on her. Always. Made her life miserable. She'd never worked outside the home, what was she going to do? Leave him? Besides, we Catholics don't divorce, right? So she stayed, a martyr to the end. Why did she put up with his crap? My two sisters and I swore a pact that we would never, ever fall into the same trap she did.

"Damned if we didn't. Tricia's husband is a closet drinker. Eileen? We think he abuses her, but we don't have any proof, and even if we did, she has kidney disease, and she needs his medical benefits. And me? Eric and I lived together off and on for eight years. When I was thirty, and still working on my Ph.D., I got pregnant with Darby." Suzanne's small, sad face suddenly lit up. "It was a huge surprise. I'd had ovarian cysts in my twenties, and my doctor told me I probably wouldn't have children."

Suzanne took several deep breaths, sucking in more oxygen to fuel her narrative. The others waited, willing her to continue. "Even then, I waited until Darby was two, just to be absolutely sure, before I agreed to marry Eric. I thought we had something good, you know? Not perfect, but a much better marriage than my parents'."

"You poor thing," Rochelle said. She stood quickly. "Don't say another word, okay? I need to see if everything's all right in the kitchen. Can I get anything for anybody?"

Ashleigh raised her nearly empty margarita glass. "I could use a freshie."

Grace could feel her jaw tightening. Did she dare suggest that Rochelle stick to bartending instead of marriage counseling? Probably not.

"Listen, Suzanne," Grace said gently, "don't feel like you have to talk, if you don't feel like it. We all understand."

"No!" Suzanne said, taking a gulp of her tea. "I think this is probably good for me. I've never discussed my family's . . . marriage issues, to anybody. Ever. Not even with my best friend. Not even with my sisters. So thanks, for listening. And not judging."

"Oh, you are just so welcome," Ashleigh said, looking around the table for consensus. "Isn't this awesome? I mean, I feel soooo much better, hearing what you guys have been through. If I didn't hate the whole idea of paying three hundred dollars an hour to Paula, I would think just being with you all was totally worth it."

Camryn had her chin propped on her hands. "Yeah. I can't believe Stackpole is making us pay Paula that much money for the privilege of watching her fall asleep and drool on herself once a week." She grimaced. "Speaking of sleep, I've got to be at the studio at six, to tape an interview with some exercise diva, and if I don't want to have king-sized bags under my eyes, I better get out of here right now." She stood, pulled money from her billfold, and placed it on the tabletop.

"Grace, tell Rochelle I said 'bye. See y'all next week!"

Ashleigh yawned widely. "I can't believe it's not even ten o'clock and I'm this sleepy. Guess I need to take off, too." She stood up and slapped her backside. "My new trainer is making me do this really intensive booty camp, starting tomorrow." She added some bills to the pile on the table. "I'll just run by and tell Rochelle never mind on the drink," she added. "I probably don't need the calories anyway."

"I hate to ask," Suzanne said, turning to Grace. "But is it too much trouble for somebody to give me a ride back to Paula's office?"

"I'd be happy to take you, but the front seat of the pickup is loaded with sacks of bird feed and crap for the park," Wyatt said apologetically. "Didn't want the chance of it getting rained on."

"I can take you," Grace said. She was painfully aware that the tote bag at her feet was starting to wriggle, and every once in a while a small brown muzzle would pop out. "Be back in a minute."

By the time she got back to the table, Suzanne and Rochelle were deep in conversation. Wyatt was standing, looking around, unsure of his next move.

"If you're going to take Suzanne back to Paula's office, why don't you let me ride with you?" He was trying to sound casual, cool even. "It's not that great a neighborhood."

26.

There were now a dozen cars in the shopping center parking lot. The lights were on in the tattoo parlor, heavy metal music blaring from within, and a trio of imposing black Harleys were parked on the sidewalk in front of it. Suzanne leaned over the front seat console. "Here's my car." She pointed to a silver Prius. "Thanks again, Grace. Wyatt. See you next week."

Grace pulled alongside Suzanne's car and waited until she'd started the car and eased out of her parking spot.

"Hey, look." Wyatt pointed at the very end of the parking lot, where a black Lexus had just pulled into the space nearest the end. As they watched, Paula emerged from the passenger's side of the sedan. She slammed the car door, and then, while they watched, she kicked the tires. Next, she ran around to the driver's side. She was screaming something, slapping at the car windows, pounding, but the driver never cut the engine, instead throwing the car into reverse. Its tires screeched and skidded as the driver slammed it into drive and sped out of the parking lot, turning left onto Manatee Avenue.

Paula stood, hands on hips, watching it go. Then, she walked back, unlocked her office door, and disappeared.

"Oh my God," Grace said. "Do you think that's Stackpole in the black car? Looks like they were having a knock-down, drag-out fight, huh?"

"Only one way to find out," Wyatt said, leaning forward to keep his eyes on the car.

"I'm on it," Grace said, pulling out of the shopping center. Traffic was light that time of night, and she could see the Lexus's red taillights only half a block ahead of them.

"Good of him to be such a safe driver," Grace said.

"If it's Stackpole, the last thing he wants is to get pulled over by a cop," Wyatt pointed out.

Grace followed the Lexus west on Manatee, for five blocks. It stopped at the light at West 75th and put on its blinker to turn left. Grace pulled behind the Lexus and did the same. "You think this is really a good idea? Following Stackpole—or whoever is in that car?"

"We're just two people out for a drive. No big deal. You're not speeding and you didn't even drink all your wine, right?"

"That's right."

"And I had a beer, over the course of two hours," he said. He glanced toward the backseat. "How's the dog?"

She grinned sheepishly. "How'd you know?"

Instead of answering, he reached around and pulled the wriggling dog out of the bag, setting her carefully on his lap.

"She popped her head out of there a couple times, back at group," Wyatt said. "It was all I could do to keep a straight face. Every time she heard your voice, the whole bag would move—she was wagging her tail so hard." The dog stretched its neck and rewarded Wyatt by licking his chin.

He held it at arm's length, checking its undercarriage.

"Hello, little girl," Wyatt said, rubbing the top of the dog's head, then scratching its belly. "What's your name?"

"Meet Sweetie," Grace said. "The new kid on the block."

Sweetie put her front paws on the passenger window, straining to see out the window.

"Where'd you get her?" Wyatt asked.

"Sweetie has kind of a sad story." While she recounted the tale of the dog's rescue, her adoptee climbed over the console, wriggling its way under Grace's arms. "But she's feeling better now. The vet fixed her up, gave her some IV meds, kept her overnight."

"And you got yourself a dog," Wyatt said. "What's Rochelle think about that?"

"She doesn't know," Grace admitted. "My mom is not really what you'd call a pet person. You can't really blame her, I mean, we live above a bar. So I'm guessing I'll try to keep her a secret, until I figure something out."

"Do you think you'll be getting your own place pretty soon?"

"I hope so," she said fervently. "I'm too old to be moving back in with the folks. You've seen what Rochelle's like. I love her, but she's . . . got an opinion about everything. If my asshole husband will start making the payments the judge has ordered him to make, and if I can get my blog up and generating income, I hope I can move out, sooner rather than later."

"What are you going to do with Sweetie until then?" Wyatt asked. "You can't keep hiding her in a purse."

"I know. She does seem pretty laid back. She's house-trained, so that's a big plus. The vet said she was amazingly calm while they treated her, and she's been so good all night tonight, not making a peep, just sleeping in my tote bag."

Grace scratched the dog's ears affectionately. "She's

really a very chill little girl. My plan is to keep her in my room with me at night and sneak her down the back steps first thing in the morning, for a potty break."

"What about during the days?"

"That house where I found Sweetie? It's on Anna Maria. I was out for a run and spotted this cool old rattan sofa in a pile of junk on the curb. I struck up a conversation with the landlord, this old guy named Arthur, who, it turns out, used to be kind of fishing buddies with my dad. He invited me in to see the house. It's a wreck right now, but it's got wonderful potential, and it's in a great location—a block from the bay. I'm going to be working on it, fixing it up, redecorating it for Arthur, getting it ready to rent again. I'll be photographing and writing about it for my blog. Sweetie can stay there with me during the day while I work on it. In fact, I'm thinking I'll write her into the story, too. It was her house, after all."

"Look, he's turning up ahead," Wyatt said, pointing at the Lexus. "He's headed back out to the beach. I bet he lives out there."

"Not at Cortez, for sure," Grace said. "We're not fancy enough. I bet he lives at Longboat Key."

"You're probably right," Wyatt said.

Grace stayed back a few car lengths but made the same turn. She kept on Cortez Drive, passing the turnoff for the Sandbox in the fishing village, crossing the bridge over the Intracoastal Waterway and into Bradenton Beach. At the light at Gulf Drive, the Lexus signaled to make a left turn.

"Well, he's definitely not going to Anna Maria," she said, following as the black car turned south.

The moon was nearly full, and as they followed the road paralleling the ocean, they could catch occasional glimpses of silvery water through the thick fringe of Australian pines and sea grapes lining the road in the intermittent patches of undeveloped land.

Grace smiled, as she always did when passing the sign for Coquina Beach. "That was our beach, growing up," she said. "How about you, which beach did your family go to?"

"Holmes Beach, mostly," Wyatt said. "Once I could drive, though, I was too cool for school. A bunch of us used to hang out at Siesta Key, where the rich girls were—or so we thought."

As they drove, the landscape changed from sparsely developed to the manicured civility of Longboat Key. High-rise condo complexes hugged the shores of the gulf on the right and the bay on the left, and imposing stucco homes painted in sherbet hues were set back behind hedges and gates. Grace slowed when she saw the Lexus's brake lights and then turn signal.

She waited until it made the left turn into a sprawling development called Lido Bay. "Should I keep following him, you think?" She glanced over at Wyatt. "If it's Stackpole, I really don't want him to notice us."

"Up to you," Wyatt said. "I don't want to get us in trouble either, but I'd like to know if it really is Stackpole."

He looked out the window at the homes lining the neatly landscaped street. All the homes were done in a similar hybrid Tuscan/Spanish-mission style, with stucco walls painted in pinks, peach, apricot, and buff, with red barrel-tile roofs. "Nice real estate," Wyatt said. "Wonder what these homes sell for?"

"Hmm, four or five years ago they were probably selling for seven hundred to eight hundred thousand dollars," Grace said. "The ones on canals or directly on the bay used to go for over a million. Now? You could probably move in here to a perfectly lovely home for under three hundred thousand."

"If I had three hundred thousand, I wouldn't want to live here," Wyatt said. "Too cookie cutter for my taste. Huge houses all jammed in here together on these little-bitty lots. Anyway, that's never gonna happen."

The Lexus made a wide left turn, and, as Grace started to follow, its brake lights went on. "Better slow down," Wyatt said. "Maybe turn off your lights. We don't want him to see us."

Grace pulled to the curb four houses down from the driveway where the Lexus turned in and, as suggested, cut her headlights.

"Come on, Cedric," Wyatt quietly urged. "Get out of the car and let us see your pretty face."

"Damn!"

As they watched, the garage door slowly, soundlessly rolled up, and the Lexus pulled in, with the garage door rolling down right behind it.

Grace burst out laughing, and after a moment Wyatt laughed, too. "Well, that was certainly anticlimactic," she said, turning around and driving out of the subdivision.

He was still sizing up the real estate. "Even with the real estate market in the toilet, that subdivision was pretty high cotton," he mused. "Wonder what kind of money a judge makes in Florida?"

"Don't know," Grace said. "But remember, Camryn said his wife's family is loaded. So maybe it's her money. Or maybe he does well in the stock market. Or he's cornered the market for black-market Oxycodone."

He gave her a startled look.

"Just kidding," she said. "Remember, we don't even know if that really was Stackpole. It could be anybody. It could even be Paula's husband, if she has one."

"Don't think so," Wyatt said. "Remember, we checked her driver's license. Paula lives on Anna Maria. Not Longboat."

"I'd love to know what that fight was about," Grace said, after a moment. "Paula seemed so different tonight, and then, wham, something really upset her apple cart."

She reached down and scratched Sweetie's silky brown ears. The dog hopped across the console to Wyatt's lap and scratched at his door, whining.

"Uh-oh," Grace said. "I think somebody needs a pit stop."

"Why don't you pull over up here at Coquina Beach," he suggested. "It's a nice night, and I haven't been to the beach since all this crap started with Callie. We can take her for a walk, if you want."

She raised an eyebrow. "You know dogs aren't allowed on the beach, right?"

"I won't tell if you won't," he said. "Besides, Sweetie's been such a good girl, she deserves a little treat, right, Sweetie?"

The dog's tail beat a tattoo on the window.

"I swear she knows her name already," Grace said.

She parked the car beneath one of the towering Australian pines and clipped a leash to Sweetie's new pink collar, extracting a plastic bag from her tote bag.

Grace slipped off her shoes and Wyatt did the same with his flip-flops, and they left them, side by side, in the soft white sand at the parking-lot edge. After Sweetie had taken care of business and Grace had disposed of the plastic bag, they took the boardwalk over the dunes, past gently waving fronds of sea oats.

The tide was out, and the moon bathed the beach with a silvered pearlescent sheen. The ocean surface was as calm as a puddle after a summer storm, lapping gently at the edge of the shore. Only the faint breeze rippled the water.

Sweetie paused and looked startled when her feet first

touched the damp sand, then sat on her rump and gave Grace a quizzical look.

"Come on, girl," Grace said, tugging gently at the leash. "Let's walk."

"I'll bet she's never been to the beach before," Wyatt said.

Grace tugged again, and finally the little dog stood and began trotting toward the water. She got all the way to the surf line, stopped, and looked back at her mistress.

"It's okay," Grace coaxed. "You can get your feet wet. Give it a try."

To demonstrate, Grace waded in, letting the warm ocean water lap against her ankles. "It's like bathwater," she told Wyatt, who followed her in.

The dog edged in and immediately scampered back onto the dryer sand, barking as the wavelets edged toward her.

"Okay," Grace agreed. "You walk on the sand; we'll walk in the water."

"Can I take her?" Wyatt asked. Grace handed over the leash.

"Come on, Sweetie," Wyatt called, veering onto the beach. "Let's run!"

He broke into a trot, and the dog obediently followed behind. After less than a hundred yards, though, Sweetie ran toward the shell line, where mounds of crushed seashells and seaweed marked the high-tide line.

Sweetie sat, barked, and began nosing in the shells, digging frantically and occasionally stopping to give an excited yip.

"What's she doing?" Grace asked, when she caught up to the pair.

"She smells something," Wyatt said. "I think she must have some terrier in her, the way she's going after it."

Suddenly, the little dog yelped. She backed away slightly

and gave a menacing growl, barked again, crouched, and growled again.

"It's a ghost crab," Grace laughed, as the pale creature scuttled away. She bent down and picked up the dog. "Stay away from crabs, Sweetie. Crabs are not your friend!"

They walked down the beach in companionable silence, with Sweetie meandering along, sniffing the air and occasionally stopping to growl at imagined threats to her security. After half a mile or so, by unspoken agreement, they turned and walked back toward where the car was parked.

A concrete picnic bench was perched under the shadows of one of the big old pines. "Let's sit for a little bit," Grace suggested. She sat on the tabletop and placed Sweetie in her lap. Wyatt sat beside her.

"We used to come out here and go 'parking' in high school," she said, with a sigh. "Seems like a long time ago."

"When I was in high school, we liked someplace a little more secluded," Wyatt said. "There was this dead-end street over on Holmes Beach. You could pull your car way up under the trees, and it was on a little bit of a rise, with a perfect view of the water. Although"—he laughed ruefully—"I don't remember being that interested in actually looking at the water back then. I was a horny little bastard, back in the day."

"And now?" Grace turned to look at him, her gray eyes teasing.

He hesitated, but stood abruptly, brushing sand from the seat of his pants. "I don't remember."

She felt her face aflame with embarrassment, jumping to her feet and startling the dog, who yipped her reaction. "We should probably go."

"Look. I'm not divorced yet. You're not divorced yet. I'm pretty sure this is against every divorce-recovery-group rule Paula ever thought of."

"This?"

He sighed. "You know. Us getting together. Gotta be against the rules."

Something inside her rebelled. Against rules, and best intentions and common sense. That mischievous smile of hers was back. "I won't tell if you won't." She tilted her face up, waiting to be kissed.

And then . . . he coughed politely. She opened her eyes and saw that he was putting on his shoes.

Ever since they'd pulled over to the Coquina Beach parking area, Grace had been anticipating this moment. Wondering what she would do if Wyatt tried to kiss her. Or even touch her.

Okay, maybe she'd been wondering all of the above since the minute he'd walked into Paula's office earlier in the evening. Not that he hadn't been kinda hot the other times, unshowered, dressed in his Jungle Jerry's safari work clothes. She didn't usually go for all that down-and-dirty muscley, manly type, but somehow, on Wyatt, it worked. Then, tonight, he'd obviously made an effort to look good. Was it for her? And had he noticed that she'd dressed up tonight, too? She hadn't anticipated how crazy all of this was making her feel.

It had never occurred to her that they would come this close—and he would so totally and completely shut her down. Dammit, she was no good at flirting after all this time.

But maybe Wyatt didn't know that.

Grace cursed all that stinking moonlight. She gathered her keys, her shoes, and her dog and stomped off toward the car.

"Jesus!" Wyatt's voice was hoarse. He grabbed her arm as she was unlocking the car. "Don't think I don't want this, Grace. I do. More than I can tell you, I want it. But where do we go from here? It makes no sense."

She spun around to face him. "I don't care. I don't want to make sense. I just want to be held, and be kissed." She raised her eyes. "By you. Does that make me a criminal? Or some kind of a slut?"

"No! Of course not. Don't call yourself that."

She felt her jaw clench. "That's how you're making me feel."

She placed Sweetie on the backseat, brushed the sand from her feet, and sat in the driver's seat, with the engine running. A moment later, he got into the car.

"Grace?"

She didn't answer, just pulled the car out of the lot and onto the beach road, keeping her eyes straight ahead. Sensing the tension in the air, Sweetie whined from the backseat, but Grace kept her back stiff.

"Look," he said, running his hand over his gleaming head. "I'm playing way out of my league here. You know?"

"No, I don't know."

He closed his hand over her shoulder, but she wrenched it away. He tried again. "You are incredibly beautiful, smart, and sane, and nice."

"Sane?" She raised one eyebrow. "Nice? What kind of left-handed compliment is that?"

"I don't know!" he shouted. "I don't know anything. I haven't been with another woman in eight years. Okay? I have no idea what I am saying or doing tonight. My instincts say go for it, but I'm afraid, all right? What happens if you and I . . . start something? Where does it go?" You say you'd never take your husband back, but maybe you'll change your mind. How do I know?"

"How do I know you won't take Callie back?" she retorted. "Right now? I just don't care. I really don't. I'm tired of worrying about what might happen. I've got no control over anything: your marriage, what's left of my marriage, that asshole judge, my career. From now on, I'm going to do just what everybody else in this world does. I'm going to do what feels good. And the *hell* with the what-ifs."

"I don't have that luxury," he said quietly.

27.

It was the most erotic sensation she could ever remember having. She was having smoking-hot, crazy sex—under a Hawaiian waterfall of all places. Or she guessed it was a Hawaiian waterfall, from the profusion of flowering orchids and waving palms surrounding them. She couldn't see her lover's face, but my God, his body was sleek and hard and muscled and tan all over, and he had magic hands that did the most amazing things, and it seemed to go on forever and ever, until he had her body humming like a concert violin. And then, just as she was about to climax, a gigantic parrot swooped in and landed on his shoulder. "Gimme shots, gimme beer," the parrot called. Her lover turned his head. It was the honorable Cedric N. Stackpole Jr.

The horror made Grace sit straight up in bed so abruptly that Sweetie, who'd been nuzzled on the pillow next to hers, yelped.

"Shhh!" Grace bundled the dog into her arms and hugged her close. "It was just a dream, Sweetie. No, not a dream, a terrible, terrible nightmare." She shuddered at the memory of it. Looked over at the nightstand to realize it was five in the morning. "Stupid men," she said, pounding the bed with her fist. "Stupid, stupid men!"

Sweetie hopped off the bed and made a beeline for the bedroom door. "Okay," Grace said wearily. "Let me put some shoes on."

The only good thing about waking up early from a nightmare was getting to work early, Grace decided. It was still dark outside when she unlocked the door of the house on Mandevilla and switched on the lights.

Dark outside, but sweltering inside. She set Sweetie down on the floor, then ran from room to room opening all the windows she'd closed the previous day. She sniffed the air. The house reeked of Pine-Sol, in a good way, but there were still strong undernotes of mildew and pet smells, not to mention more dead bugs.

It took two more trips to retrieve the rest of the day's supplies, which included a pair of old box fans she'd found in the shed back at the bar. She set one fan in the window of the living room and another in the back bedroom where Sweetie had been imprisoned and switched them both to the HIGH setting.

The little dog apparently hadn't been totally traumatized by her time living in the house. She trotted from room to room, her nails clicking on the wooden floors, and had a high old time in the kitchen, barking and growling at a cockroach in the death throes.

Her plan for the day had been to carefully assess the house and work out a list of priorities and a timetable. But her mood, following the previous evening's disastrous encounter with Wyatt, and the revolting sex dream that had followed, left her in no mood for assessments.

"Right," she said briskly. She wheeled in the huge plastic trash can she'd borrowed from the shed, lined it with a black contractor's bag, snapped on her rubber gloves, and began emptying the kitchen cabinets of their contents.

She'd considered trying to salvage the pots and pans and dishes left behind, but one glance at their cracked and battered status convinced her to discard them, too. When the house was done, she'd bully Arthur into letting her buy new cookware.

With the cabinets empty, Grace took another look. In a perfect world, she'd rip out all the upper and lower cupboards and fit the kitchen with inexpensive Ikea cabinets, ones with Shaker-style door panels, with matching drawers. She'd outfitted their little rental house in Bradenton with the exact same ones, spending less than seven thousand dollars for everything, including hardware and countertops. She didn't have that kind of budget here.

Instead, she got out her cordless electric screwdriver and removed all the upper-cabinet doors, setting them aside, just in case she found another use for them down the line. The kitchen immediately looked better.

The gray aluminum-edged Formica countertops were funky but age-appropriate for the house, and the deep porcelain-over-cast-iron sink was filthy, but she knew a good cleaning with Bar Keepers Friend would make it shine again.

Grace gazed out the kitchen window and saw the first orange streaks of daylight at the edge of the overgrown yard.

On an impulse, she clipped a leash to Sweetie's collar and walked out the kitchen door, drawn to the glorious glow. They walked the block to a sandy lot that overlooked the bay, and the two of them stood there, basking in a Technicolor Florida sunrise. Whoever ended up renting the little house on Mandevilla would have the privilege of watching that same sunrise whenever they liked. Maybe she would have to make it a habit to get over here every morning in time to do the same thing. It wasn't a bad way to start the day.

She turned to go back to the house, resolving to start ripping up that revolting vinyl kitchen floor. It would feel good to jab something inanimate with a knife, a pry-bar, a chisel, or anything sharp she could put her hands on.

For months now, Wyatt had been meaning to take down the sprawling thirty-foot-tall Brazilian pepper tree that had taken over the area near his grandmother's old orchid slat-house. As he set out on his golf cart with his weapons of battle—chain saw, ax, and ladder—he grimly decided that today, Wednesday, was as good a day as any.

The Florida Department of Agriculture had placed the Brazilian pepper, a nonnative invasive "shrub," on its hit list of noxious plants. It was definitely a pushy interloper— with its massive crown of branches, it shaded out anything else in its path, and it grew so rapidly he hadn't noticed it had sprung up and taken over the old orchid-house area.

Though it was a typical summer day, with temperatures promising to rise to the nineties, he knew enough about the Brazilian pepper's near-poisonous sap to take precautions, outfitting himself in long pants, a long-sleeved shirt, work gloves, and a blue bandanna on his head. He set up the ladder next to the trunk, fastened a rope to the chain-saw handle, and began climbing into the canopy. When he'd gone as high as he could, he steadied himself against the main trunk, hauled the chain saw up from below, and fired it up.

The roar and the whine of the saw as it chewed its way through the brittle wood made a huge din, and the gas fumes filled his nostrils.

For two hours, Wyatt hacked away at the tree, dropping

the limbs to the ground, steadily moving downward as he decimated the upper canopy.

Twenty feet aboveground, with a buzzing chain saw in hand, he was focused only on the tree, the chain saw, and avoiding falling out of the tree.

By noon, his clothes were sweat-soaked, his face was itchy from the pepper-tree fumes, and the tree itself was looking like a grotesque, defoliated skeleton. He considered going back to the house to shower, change clothes, and grab lunch but went back to work instead. The pepper tree, like Callie and Luke and their lawyer and Judge Stackpole, was his nemesis. And this one he intended to cut right down to the ground.

"Jesus, son!" Nelson recoiled at the sight of Wyatt when he came tramping into the house. "What the hell did you do to yourself?"

"To me? Nothing. It took me all day, but I cut down the pepper tree, sprayed the stump with the legal equivalent of napalm, then raked up every limb, leaf, and seedpod I could find and hauled it all off to the dump."

Wyatt collapsed onto one of the wooden kitchen chairs. "I'm whipped. What's for dinner?"

"Beanie-weenies, Tater Tots, cornbread, coleslaw. Doesn't your face hurt?"

Wyatt stripped off his gloves and put a finger to his cheek, which, come to think of it, did feel kind of hot and swollen to the touch. The backs of his hands were covered in a nasty red rash, too.

"Guess I better hit the shower," he said. "I might be having a slight reaction to the pepper-tree sap."

"If that's slight, I don't want to know severe," Nelson said.

The face of a monster stared back at Wyatt in the

bathroom mirror. His entire face was mottled red and swollen, his nose a puffy red blob, his eyes rimmed in pink. Dime-sized welts ran down his neck and to the V of where his shirt collar had been open.

When he took off his shirt he saw that his chest was also streaked with angry crimson slashes. He unzipped his pants and stepped out of them, as well as his boxers, and looked down.

Holy shit! His crotch was covered in blisters. *Everything* was red and inflamed—and not in a good way. He turned on the shower full force and jumped in, letting the cool water sluice over his head and chest. He grabbed a bar of soap, lathered up, but the first touch of the soap to his chest felt like a splash of acid.

Wyatt dropped the soap and looked down again. Not good. How the hell had this happened? He'd been so careful, with the long pants and shirt, high socks, work boots, gloves. And then he remembered and would have smacked himself in the face if that face hadn't felt like an open wound just then.

He'd had to pee. And who could unzip and do all the rest wearing work gloves? He must have gotten some of the sap on his hands, and then, well, his boys. Which were now itching like a son of a bitch.

He tried to think back to a college class he'd taken on noxious plants. They'd studied poison ivy, oak, sumac, and a few others, and, of course, over the years, working in landscaping and now running Jungle Jerry's, he'd run into all of the above. But he couldn't remember anything about the hazards of Brazilian pepper.

After gingerly toweling off the inflamed skin, he found a bottle of Calamine lotion in the medicine cabinet and slathered it all over himself. Within a few seconds, the thick pink goo had dried and started to cake and crack. And he itched, God how he itched.

Wrapped in nothing more than a towel, he carefully stepped over the clothes he'd just discarded. In his bedroom he donned the loosest pair of cotton shorts he could find and an old, threadbare cotton T-shirt.

Wyatt sat down at the kitchen table as his father was taking a pan of cornbread from the oven. "Does it feel as bad as it looks?" Nelson inquired, after he'd served his son a plate heaped high with food.

"Worse," Wyatt said, pointing toward his crotch. "It's . . . everywhere."

"Ow," Nelson grimaced and poured him a glass of iced tea. "I think we've got some Benadryl around here somewhere. That might help some."

"Maybe after dinner," Wyatt said. "I'll fall asleep with my head in the plate if I take it now, and I've got some stuff I need to do tonight."

They cleaned up the kitchen, and Nelson retired to his recliner to watch his nightly roundup; *Wheel of Fortune, Jeopardy,* and the Rays game.

Wyatt sank onto the old sofa and tried not to think of his inflamed privates while he leafed through the paper, but he was so acutely uncomfortable he gave in shortly after eight and went looking for the bottle of Benadryl.

"Okay, Dad," he said, poking his head out from the hallway. "I'm turning in."

"Hmm?"

"I'm going to bed," Wyatt repeated.

"Did you ever talk to your Aunt Betsy?" Nelson asked, his eyes glued to the television.

"No. Why would I?"

"She called here looking for you. Guess you must have had your phone turned off."

Wyatt came around and stood directly in front of the television, the only way he knew to get his father's attention this time of night. "Dad? What did Betsy say?"

"Hey! Come on now, it's the bottom of the inning, two outs, and we've got the bases loaded."

"What did Betsy say? Did she have news? Come on, Dad, this could be important."

Nelson waved his hand in irritation. "How'm I supposed to know what she wanted? She just said to call her. Not tonight, she had something goin' on. Now, can I watch my game?"

Wyatt called her anyway and left a message on his aunt's phone. The itching was driving him nuts, but he resisted taking the Benadryl. At 9:30 he called and left another message for her, and at ten, in desperation, he texted. *WHAT'S UP? DAD SAID YOU CALLED.*

Thirty minutes later, his phone dinged and he lunged for it. Betsy's message was clear as mud. *CAN'T TALK, CALL U IN A.M.*

Finally, sometime after ten, he popped some Benadryl and fell into an uneasy sleep, imagining all the bad news his attorney might be saving up for the next morning.

28.

Betsy Entwhistle was sitting at a table near the window of Eat Here, her favorite breakfast spot in Holmes Beach, when she spotted her nephew making his way through the parking lot, a baseball cap pulled down low over his face, sunglasses covering his eyes.

She sighed. She hated the bruising Callie was giving Wyatt. He'd been a good husband and a loving father, and the little idiot thought she could do better with that punk Luke? She'd known Callie was trouble from the start, and she'd told her sister, Wyatt's mom, that, in confidence. In confidence, Peggy had agreed wholeheartedly. But Wyatt was in love, and they both hoped things would work out.

"Hey," Wyatt was almost out of breath. He dropped into the chair opposite hers. "What's going on? What couldn't you tell me last night?"

"Good Lord, what have you done to your face?" Betsy reached over and tipped back the bill of his cap, removed the sunglasses. Wyatt's handsome face was a crimson, contorted mess. His eyes were nearly swollen shut, his nose and cheeks covered with red blisters that crawled down his neck to his chest. His hands were covered with a similar eruption.

"I took down a tree at the park yesterday, and I've had some kind of reaction to the sap," Wyatt said. "Just tell me what's going on, would you? Have you heard from the judge?"

"Honey, that's not just a reaction," Betsy said. "Your eyes are nearly swollen shut. Have you seen a doctor?"

"I don't need a doctor," he insisted. "It's like poison ivy. I put some Calamine on it and it's some better."

She pressed her lips in disapproval. "I'll tell you what's going on, but then I'm taking you to see my dermatologist. Wyatt, that stuff is in your eyes. What if you lose your eyesight?"

"Okay, whatever," he said. "Would you please talk to me now?"

Betsy took a sip of her coffee. "Don't you want some breakfast? I ordered you some pancakes and bacon."

"Betsy!"

"Okay. Here it is. I got a call from Stackpole's clerk yesterday. It seems Callie is claiming you've been interfering with her time with Bo. He wants to see you in his office this afternoon."

"Me?" Wyatt was incredulous. "I haven't done a damned thing. I don't even call Bo anymore when he's with her. Whatever she's telling the judge, it's total bullshit, Betsy."

"I know it is, but Stackpole doesn't," Betsy said.

"Did the clerk give you any details about this so-called interference?"

"Something about a birthday party Bo was supposed to go to this past weekend?"

"Yeah? What about it? Callie deliberately planned a trip to Birmingham with Fatso, supposedly to look at houses. She knew last weekend was his best friend Scout's birthday party at that new water park, but she planned the trip anyway and insisted Bo had to go. Bo was furious with her." He laughed. "He confessed to me that he called her a shit."

"It's not funny, Wyatt," Betsy said.

Wyatt slapped his hat on the table in disgust. "I didn't tell him to call her that. In fact, I told him it wasn't nice to call his mother names, although, privately, I can think of lots worse names to call her. And incidentally, he says Callie called him a shit first, and I happen to believe him. So that's what this is about? Some name-calling? Seriously?"

"It's worse than that," Betsy said. "When Callie went to pick him up at school on Friday, Bo wasn't there. She claims she called you, but you never answered her phone call."

"Wait? Are you telling me Bo went missing? And this is the first I'm hearing of it?"

"Calm down," Betsy said. "I did some checking. Apparently, Bo never had any intention of going on that trip to Birmingham. He told Scout's mom, Anna, his mom wanted him to spend the night with her and go to the party, and Anna, not knowing any better, took him home from school with her, and on to the party."

"That little con artist," Wyatt said. "I don't know whether I want to pat him on the back or whack him on his butt. But I still don't see how Callie can say any of this is my fault. It was her weekend to have Bo. I didn't call him, didn't pick him up, didn't hide him from his mom."

Betsy shrugged. "Don't kill the messenger, okay? Callie's made a serious charge, and Stackpole, in his totally random way, seems to find her story believable. So we're going to see the judge this afternoon." She looked over his shoulder and saw the waiter approaching with a tray of food. "Right after we get you your pancakes. And see my dermatologist."

* * *

"Sir, remove those sunglasses and that hat," the Honorable Cedric N. Stackpole said, as soon as Wyatt and Betsy were seated in his office.

Wyatt shrugged, took off the glasses and the baseball hat. Stackpole cringed. "Are you having some medical issues?" he asked brusquely.

"An allergic reaction to some underbrush he was clearing," Betsy said. "He's gotten a cortisone shot and he has some steroid cream. He'll be fine."

Callie was sitting in a chair on the judge's left side. She was dressed in a short pink skirt and a tight-fitting black tank top that displayed yet another tattoo, and glimpses of her abdomen whenever she moved. She leaned forward and grimaced. "You look like something out of a horror movie." She glanced over at her lawyer. "I don't want my son to see him like that. It's upsetting."

"I'm fine," Wyatt said, clenching and unclenching his fists. "The swelling has already started to go down. It's not contagious. Bo has seen me with poison ivy before."

"Let's stick to the subject at hand, shall we?" Stackpole said. He looked down at a file on his desk. "Mrs. Keeler, you're alleging that Mr. Keeler is interfering with your son's visits with you? Something about a birthday party?"

"Bo knew we'd been planning this trip to Birmingham, to look at houses," Callie said. "Wyatt knew it, too. We'd been planning the trip for weeks, and then suddenly, Bo was having a fit over going, because of some little party a friend was having. When I went to pick him up from school on Friday, he wasn't there!"

She leaned across her lawyer and glared at Wyatt. "You put him up to this. And I know it."

"Put him up to what?" Wyatt demanded. Betsy gave her client a small head shake, warning him not to be baited.

"Bo deliberately lied to his friend's mother, told her I

wanted him to spend the night with them that night, so he could go to the party! He even packed a bathing suit and pajamas and hid them in his school backpack," Callie said. "He never would have done that on his own, not without his father giving him the idea."

The judge eased back in his leather desk chair. "Mr. Keeler, did you suggest to your son that he disobey and lie to his mother?"

"Absolutely not," Wyatt said. "This is the first I'm hearing about any of this. Bo did tell me his mother had scheduled a trip out of town, and he was upset over having to miss his friend's party that he'd been looking forward to for weeks. He even admitted he called his mother a bad name. But when I told him that wasn't acceptable behavior, he told me his mother called him that name first."

Stackpole raised an eyebrow. "What kind of bad name?"

"Bo told me his mother called him a little shit," Wyatt said calmly.

"Ridiculous," Callie snapped.

Stackpole's head swung in her direction. "Do you deny calling your son that name?"

Her face reddened. "Bo's been hostile to me for the last few months. He acts out, talks back. Whenever he comes back from a visit with his father, he's belligerent and defiant. And he's openly disrespectful to my fiancé."

"Mrs. Keeler, did you call your six-year-old a 'little shit'? Yes or no?"

Callie burst into tears. "He's my little boy! How would you like it if your son told you he hated you? How would you like it if you went to pick up your son and he refused to get in the car? I may have called him that, in the heat of the moment, but I never meant it."

Wyatt folded his arms across his chest and looked away. Callie loved to turn on the waterworks whenever she was backed into a corner. It was her go-to tactic. He wondered if Stackpole would fall for it. Betsy claimed the judge hated women, but Callie seemed to be the exception to that rule.

Betsy saw an opening and went for it. "Judge, Mr. Keeler is also concerned about his son's behavior. If Bo is unhappy after returning from a visit with my client, it's because he is uncomfortable seeing his mother living with a man other than his father. Bo is upset over the breakup of his parents' marriage, which is totally understandable, and I want to address that in a minute. But in the meantime, Mr. Keeler would like to know more about this past weekend. If Bo wasn't at school when Callie went to pick him up, why didn't she notify my client?"

"I left him a voice mail!" Callie said. "He never returns my calls. I basically assumed Wyatt had Bo."

"But she didn't know that," Betsy said calmly. "Did she do anything else to check up on her son's whereabouts? Question the teachers at the school? Go over to my client's home to see if Bo was there? Did she call his friends' homes to see if he'd gone home with one of them?"

"I just told you, I figured Bo was with Wyatt." Callie glared at Betsy.

Stackpole frowned. "Mrs. Keeler, did you leave town for the weekend without knowing your son's exact location?"

"We had to get on the road," Callie said, her voice shriller by the minute. "We had dinner reservations. It's a long drive to Birmingham, and I was positive Bo was with his father. I never would have left Bo home alone. And it turned out fine! He was with Anna."

Betsy went in for the kill. "He could have been abducted, Judge. My client relied on Mrs. Keeler's representation that his son was in her custody for the weekend. He had no knowledge that Bo wasn't where he should have been. And we find that very disturbing."

"As do I," Stackpole agreed. He looked Wyatt up and

down. "Mr. Keeler, Dr. Talbott-Sinclair tells me you've been attending her divorce-recovery sessions, and I, ah, noted your presence there this week when I stopped by. She seems pleased with your progress."

He swung around in his chair and considered Callie, who was dabbing at her crocodile tears with a Kleenex in a valiant effort to look brave and vulnerable.

"Mrs. Keeler?"

"Yes?" she whispered, her lower lip trembling.

"If you and your son are having relationship issues, perhaps you'd better spend more time working on your relationship with him, and less on your fiancé."

Stackpole said the word "fiancé" as though it were some revolting sexual practice. Wyatt felt his spirits start to brighten.

"A young, impressionable boy needs a father in his life. Mr. Keeler had that regrettable episode at the baseball park, but he seems to be making some progress handling his anger and hostility. I'm starting to rethink the wisdom of allowing you to move your son so far away from his father."

Yes! Wyatt wanted to jump up, fist-bump Betsy, maybe even hug Stackpole. Nah, not that. But still.

"Now, Judge," began Callie's lawyer, who'd been noticeably silent until now. "Mrs. Keeler's fiancé has already accepted a job in Birmingham and put his home on the market. It's going to work a real hardship on them if you prevent them from moving . . ."

"I'm not preventing anybody from doing anything, yet," Stackpole interrupted. "I'm just saying I'm rethinking. I still want to wait a few more weeks to make sure that Mr. Keeler completes his therapy, and I want to hear reassurances from Dr. Talbott-Sinclair that there won't be any more episodes of violence before I rule on this custody issue."

"Thank you," Wyatt said fervently. "Thanks very much, Judge."

Stackpole was staring at Callie, eyes narrowed.

"And Mrs. Keeler?"

Callie blew her nose on the tissue. "Yes, Your Honor?"

"The next time you are in my presence, I do not want to be assaulted with the vision of your body piercings. Is that clear?"

Callie looked down and yanked her top over the diamond-studded navel ring winking from her abdomen.

Wyatt waited until they were in the elevator to gather his aunt into a bear hug. "You did it!" he exclaimed. "Finally, a win for our side."

"Not a win, necessarily, but at least a point for our team," Betsy conceded. "I can't believe that little . . ."

"Shit?" Wyatt grinned.

"Shit works, although I *was* going to call her an ignorant slut," Betsy said, returning her nephew's smile. "No offense."

"None taken," Wyatt said. "You were awesome in there, the way you kept on about how Callie just left town, not knowing where Bo was."

"I wasn't just grandstanding. It really is appalling that she was so focused on her little trip she didn't even care enough to make sure Bo was somewhere safe. In the past, I just thought Callie was a selfish, stupid, self-involved little twit. But now I'm starting to wonder how fit a mother she is."

Sobered, Wyatt nodded in agreement. "I keep telling myself she really does love Bo, but since she hooked up with Fatso, Callie's changed. It's like she's turned into this eighteen-year-old party animal overnight. She wasn't always like this. She was a good mom. She wouldn't even let Bo sleep in his nursery until he was, like, eigh-

teen months old, because she'd read all this crap about
Sudden Infant Death Syndrome. He slept in a bassinette
in our bedroom or in bed with us, until I finally convinced her he'd be okay in his own room. Maybe we got
married too young. Maybe she's just immature. Maybe
this, the tattoos, the piercings, the clothes, maybe it's all
just a phase."

"I hope you're not making excuses for her," Betsy said.
"She's thirty-six. It's a little late for her to be in a 'phase.'"

"Hell no, I'm not making excuses for her." Wyatt pulled
his baseball cap on again. "Maybe I'm making excuses for
me, for letting her go without putting up a fight."

"Don't beat yourself up," Betsy said. "Callie and her
lawyer are doing enough of that. You're a good guy. Remember that, okay? And don't go getting soft on me." She
made a fist and thrust it into his face. "And if you start
thinking about taking her back, I'll punch out *your* car
window."

"No worries there," Wyatt said.

"Listen," Betsy said suddenly. "Did I understand Stackpole right? Did he actually sit in on your therapy session
the other night?"

"Yep," Wyatt said.

"So weird. What was he doing there?"

"Paula said she invited him," Wyatt said. "But there's
something definitely . . . kinky going on between the two
of them."

"Kinky and Stackpole are not two words you necessarily think of together," Betsy said. "Kinky how?"

"There's a vibe between them. And everybody in the
group noticed it. Paula was positively giddy that he showed
up. In fact, she was stone-cold sober, which is a major
change."

"Your therapist? You mean she's not usually sober?
Wyatt, what's going on with this group?"

* * *

The elevator dinged, and the doors opened. They emerged into the courthouse lobby. Betsy pulled Wyatt by the arm, gesturing for him to sit on a bench.

"Talk," she ordered.

"Paula's stoned out of her gourd during most of our sessions," Wyatt said. "The first one, I got there a little late, and she was passed out cold. I had to wake her up to make sure she realized I was there. On a good night, she's just vague and glassy-eyed. During our second session, the light was getting dimmer, if you know what I mean, and then after we got back from break, she zoned out again. We actually left her on the sofa in the reception area. But before we left, just to make sure she hadn't overdosed or something, we checked her purse and figured out she's mixing tranquilizers and sleeping pills."

"Don't you think that's something you might have mentioned to your lawyer?" Betsy scolded.

"Wouldn't do any good," he said. "Like I was telling you, Stackpole showed up at our last session. Paula was on her best behavior, all dressed up and proper and professional. She actually ran the session."

"She doesn't usually?"

"Not really," Wyatt said. "But this week was different. She had her act together, and was so excited about him being there, it was kind of pathetic. He made a stupid little speech, about what a good thing it was we were all doing, blah, blah, blah. And it was going good, and all of a sudden Paula just ended the session. We're supposed to be there an hour, and it wasn't even thirty minutes."

Betsy was shaking her head. "How on earth did he find this woman? And if she's obviously on drugs, like you say, why would he refer people to her?"

Wyatt glanced around the lobby and lowered his voice.

"I'll tell you why, but you're not gonna believe it. Because he's in her pants."

"Shhh!" Betsy yanked him up by the arm and hustled him out of the courthouse.

"Oww," Wyatt winced and she loosened her clutch.

"In my car," she said, making a beeline for the parking lot.

When they were in Betsy's car, with the air conditioner blowing at full blast, he gave her the whole story. Or as much of it as his pride would allow.

"Wednesday night, after Paula let us leave early, we all went over to the Sandbox, like we always do."

She gave him a fishy look. "Tell me that's not a strip joint."

"All those women? You know I'm the only guy, right? The Sandbox is a bar. In Cortez."

"That dumpy little fishing village?"

"It's not all that dumpy," Wyatt said. "Anyway, the Sandbox is a classic dive bar. It's even got an original Ms. Pac-Man. One of the women in the group, Grace, her mother owns it, which is why we go there."

"Who's we?"

"Everybody in the group. Me, Grace, Camryn, Ashleigh, and Suzanne. Like I said, I'm the only guy. At first I thought they were gonna scratch my eyes out, because they've all been shafted by their husbands, and they all hate men, but we're cool now."

"You were telling me about Stackpole being, as you indelicately put it, in your therapist's pants? What makes you think that?"

"For one thing, you had to see them in the same room together. Paula was all giggly and flirty. And then, well, there was this other thing."

"Tell me." Betsy dug in her pocketbook, pulled out a stick of gum, offered it to her nephew, then took one for herself.

"Okay, but you're not gonna like it," he warned.

When he'd finished recounting his story, Betsy sighed. "You're right. I reallllly don't like what you guys did."

"Do you happen to know where Stackpole lives?" Wyatt asked eagerly.

"I have no idea. But I would imagine he probably lives somewhere over on Longboat."

"How about his car? Do you know what kind of car he drives? Like I said, this was a Lexus."

"Stackpole is as conservative as it comes, so whatever he drives, I'd be willing to bet it's a big American-made land yacht."

"Hey!" A light came into Wyatt's eyes. "Do judges have assigned parking spaces? Here at the courthouse?"

"Probably," Betsy said. "God forbid a judge might have to drive around and hunt for a parking spot like the average Joe."

She sighed. "I suppose you want me to swing through the county parking deck to check this out?"

Wyatt leaned over and pecked her on the cheek. "Did I ever mention that you're my favorite aunt?"

"I'm your only aunt," Betsy said. But she started the car and went on the prowl.

29

Transformations and Dirty Laundry

Dear Readers: If you've managed to follow me over here to my new blog, TrueGrace, from my former blog, you know that my personal life has been dealt some, uh, "challenges" lately. My marriage came off the rails in a fairly spectacular way, I've left my husband and lost my home, and now my former blog has been co-opted by my estranged husband and my former assistant. It sounds like it should be a funny story, but unfortunately there's no punch line.

Somebody—and I have a good guess who that is—has been sabotaging me professionally, wiping out my blog posts, leaving nasty comments falsely attributed to me on other blogs, and just generally smearing my good name in the blogosphere. I won't make any accusations, but I would like to assure all my readers, and other bloggers, that I have never and would never engage in such scurrilous behavior.

On a positive note, my life these days is a clean slate. And I have an exciting new project to share with you! Over these next few weeks and months I hope you'll follow along as I rehab, restore, and redecorate a wonderful original 1920s cottage.

Mandevilla Manor, as I call it, is a classic example of a vernacular Florida cracker cottage. Built of heart pine on a raised cinderblock foundation, it has the original pine board and batten walls, oak floors, and an airy screened porch.

I discovered this diamond in the rough when I was out for a morning run recently. I noticed a huge pile of trash sitting on a curb, which meant a house was being cleaned out. As I watched, a gentleman dragged a fabulous 1940s rattan sofa to the curb. When I struck up a conversation with Arthur, who turned out to be the landlord, I learned that his deadbeat tenants had vacated the house after thoroughly trashing it.

The house has been in Arthur's family for three generations, and he was disheartened by all the work it would take to make it habitable again.

At Arthur's invitation, I toured the house, and, although it was filthy and in terrible disrepair, I could easily see all the charm just waiting to be rediscovered. So Arthur and I worked out a deal. He has provided a tiny budget, and I will provide the vision—and the sweat—to bring Mandevilla Manor back to life.

This will be a true shoestring operation. I'll be shopping at discount centers, thrift stores, and yard sales, and, yes, I'll probably be doing some Dumpster diving and curb cruising. Since my budget is so small, I'll be providing most of the girl power myself. As you can see from this first batch of before and "in process" photos, I've already torn down all the yellowing venetian blinds and ripped *up all the nasty old carpet. The kitchen cabinet doors have been removed, and that ugly vinyl flooring is currently under attack. Watch this space for frequent updates!*

One other thing. Meet my new BFF, Sweetie. She is an adorable poodle mix who was cruelly locked in a bedroom at the cottage and abandoned by her former owners. Can you believe she is the first dog I have ever owned? Sweetie is an expert at watchdogging and cockroach wrangling, and she works cheap—just a little kibble and a lot of love. Life is full of twists and turns, dead ends and detours, isn't it? Lose a husband, gain a dog, take a run, find a house to transform.

I can't wait to see what the next chapter of my life will bring.

Grace uploaded all the before photos she'd taken of the little cottage, resizing and writing captions as she went. The last photo she posted was her favorite, Sweetie, posing on the front steps of the cottage, ears pricked up, tongue lolling, as though to say, "Hey, check me out!"

She held her breath and clicked the PUBLISH toggle on her new blog's dashboard.

"Just try and hack me now, Ben," she muttered to herself. She'd knocked off work on the cottage at noon, just so she could come home and re-create her blog. One more time. She'd chosen a new, easier platform, WordPress, and gone through every security move she could think of to foil any other attack on her blog, including running a malware program that would pinpoint and hopefully eliminate whatever method Ben had used to sabotage TrueGrace.com.

"Everything new" was her motto this time around. She didn't have the graphics knowledge Ben had, and she sure didn't have any of her former advertisers. But her new plat-form was clean and simple. The writing was brutally hon-est, and from the heart. The photos of Mandevilla Manor were clear, and Grace felt certain this project would reso-nate with all the homeowners, thrifters, and DIY-ers in the world, in a way her old blog never had. How many people, after all, could relate to a three-hundred-dollar Belgian linen tablecloth like the one that had adorned the dining room table at Sand Dollar Lane? Were there really all that many hostesses who wanted recipes calling for black truf-fle oil and imported pink sea salt?

After she published the blog post, she copied the URL and e-mailed it to every lifestyle blogger she'd ever read, explaining to them that Gracenotes had been taken over by Ben and apologizing, again, for any spurious negative comments they might have seen floating around on the Internet.

I've reinvented myself, and my blog. I'm TrueGrace now, and I would love it if you'd drop by and check out my new project. And since I'm starting from scratch, I'd be humbled if you saw fit to add me to your blog roll.

Grace lolled back on her bed pillows and closed her eyes. It was nearly six. She'd been hunched over her lap-top for hours. She was tired and sore from being down on her hands and knees hacking away at the kitchen floor. She told herself she was in no mood for divorce-recovery group. And she really dreaded seeing Wyatt Keeler again after her clumsy and humiliating encounter with him af-ter their last session.

She was surprised to find that she was looking forward to seeing the others. Camryn's wisecracks and brutal hon-esty never failed to entertain her. Suzanne, quiet, vulner-able Suzanne, seemed close to revealing whatever secrets were tormenting her, and even that gold-plated gold dig-ger Ashleigh was at least good for comic relief.

And yes, she was definitely curious about Paula after witnessing her encounter with the mystery Lexus driver. She got dressed and slipped Sweetie into her now-familiar tote bag, giving her a doggie treat to chew on and keep quiet.

A hastily scrawled note on the back of an envelope was taped to Dr. Paula Talbott-Sinclair's office door.

*DUE TO FAMILY EMERGENCY NO GROUP
SESSION TONIGHT—PTS*

"What's going on?" Ashleigh Hartounian stuck her head out the window of her red BMW and called to Camryn Nobles, who was standing in front of the office door, fuming.

"No session tonight," Camryn said.

"Whaaat?" Ashleigh scrambled out of her car and joined Camryn on the sidewalk in front of the office. She peered into the office window, but there was nothing to see.

"What are we looking at?" Grace asked, as she walked up to the two women.

"See for yourself." Camryn gestured toward the note taped to the door.

"Huhh," Grace said, frowning. "And there's no sign of life inside the office?"

"None that we could see," Ashleigh said. "So what do we do now?"

"We don't spend three hundred dollars on Paula's bullshit, at least tonight," Camryn said.

"Oooh, that's exactly how much the pair of shoes I've been stalking at Saks are," Ashleigh said, rubbing her hands together in glee. She bowed in the direction of the door. "Thanks, Paula."

Camryn adjusted the strap of her pocketbook on her

shoulder. "Since I had to clear my calendar anyway, should we go somewhere and grab dinner?"

"Absolutely! I know this adorable new bistro at Saint Armand's Key," Ashleigh said. "If we hurry, we can still get in on happy hour martinis."

Grace glanced at her watch. "What about Suzanne? Shouldn't we wait for her? I'd feel bad if she came all the way over here just to turn around and go home again. She's always so quiet, but I get the feeling we're the only ones she can really talk to."

"Although she hasn't really told us anything at all," Ashleigh pointed out. "I'm thinking whatever she did to get Stackpole to order her to therapy must have been really, really radical. And scary."

"Scarier than writing on her husband's mistress's house and car with blood?" Camryn asked.

"I told you, it wasn't blood. It was only red paint," Ashleigh said. "Although now I kind of wish it had been blood, which would wash off, because I was in such a hurry when I did it, I grabbed oil-based paint. And since my lawyer is making me pay to have the bitch's house and car repainted, it's costing me a fortune."

As they talked, a Prius rolled up to the office.

"Oh good, here's Suzanne now," Grace said. "Looks like the gang's all here."

"What about Wyatt?" Ashleigh asked. "We can't leave him behind."

"It's five after," Grace said. "Maybe he's ditching us tonight."

"Who's ditching us?" Suzanne asked as she joined the group. "And why are we all standing out here on the sidewalk?"

"Paula's got some kind of family emergency," Grace said, pointing at the note on the door.

"Allegedly," Camryn added. "We're just talking about

going out to dinner, since we're all here anyway. Care to join us?"

Suzanne hesitated. "Well, since I'm here anyway . . . but what about Wyatt?"

Grace made a show of checking her watch again. "He's probably not even coming tonight. Look, we better get going if we're going to Saint Armand's. You know how crowded it gets there."

"Saint Armand's?" Suzanne's face fell. "I, well, never mind. You all go on without me. I'll get something to eat on the way home."

"No, Suzanne," Grace protested. "We don't have to go to Saint Armand's, if you have a problem with that. We could go anywhere."

"What's your problem with Saint Armand's?" Ashleigh asked. She was promptly given a not-so-subtle elbow in the ribs from Camryn.

"Why don't we just go over to the Sandbox, like we usually do?" Camryn said. "I'm not really in the mood for a twelve-dollar martini tonight anyway. Your mom serves food, right, Grace?"

"Sure, anything you want, as long as it's fried."

"Then it's settled," Camryn said. "Suzanne, do you need a ride? I can drop you back here afterward."

As they headed for their cars, Grace took a quick look around, mentally crossing her fingers and hoping Wyatt would not drive up as they were leaving.

When she got home, she bounded up the outside stairs at the Sandbox, unlocked her bedroom door, and opened the top of the tote bag. Sweetie climbed out, yawned widely, then hopped onto the bed.

"Good girl," Grace laughed. "I'll be back in a couple hours or so, and we'll take a quick walk before bedtime." She scratched the dog's ears and earned a generous tail wag for her efforts.

* * *

"You're early," Rochelle said when Grace strolled into the bar. "But I already reserved your table. Where are the rest?"

"They'll be along," Grace said, moving toward the table. "Could you bring some menus when they get here? We're going to have dinner."

A few minutes later, Rochelle appeared with menus, a glass of wine for Grace, and a basket of popcorn for the middle of the table. "Did your therapist pass out on you again?"

"She wasn't there," Grace said, helping herself to a handful of popcorn. "There was a note on the door saying she'd had some kind of family emergency. Very cryptic. Very mysterious."

"Does anybody really believe Paula had an emergency tonight?" Ashleigh speared a french fry with the tip of her fork and chewed slowly. "I mean, I find it hard to believe Paula even has a family. She's just so . . . spacey. I mean, can you imagine having her for a mom? Or a wife?"

"It might not be something with a child or a husband," Suzanne said timidly. "Maybe she has elderly parents. A friend I teach with has to use up every day of her sick leave and vacation time caring for her mother and her aunt, who both have dementia."

Grace tore off a piece of her patty melt and chewed slowly. "I was thinking it could have something to do with Paula's behavior last Wednesday night. She was definitely on edge."

"Family emergency, my ass," Camryn said. She squirted ketchup on her burger. "I knew all along there was something odd about that woman . . ." She broke off her sentence.

"Oh, my precious baby Jesus! Will you look at that boy's poor face?"

They all turned to see what she was talking about. And that's when they spotted a familiar-looking figure, threading his way through the maze of tables and chairs in their direction.

He was still dressed in the neatly pressed navy slacks and dress shirt he'd worn to court earlier in the day, and the bill of the baseball cap was still tilted low over his eyes, but he'd removed the sunglasses.

"How'd he find us?" Grace muttered, but as he got closer to the table and she saw his face, she gasped aloud.

"Hey, ladies," Wyatt said. He pulled a chair from a nearby table and sat down. He nodded curtly at Grace. Before he could say anything else, Rochelle arrived with a pitcher of beer and two glasses. She poured one and handed it to him, then sat down and poured a glass for herself. Rochelle reached out and gently touched Wyatt's cheek. "Your face! Did you fall into a fire-ant hill?"

"Not exactly. I did something even stupider. I purposely cut down a Brazilian pepper tree."

"That's bad?" Camryn asked.

"It is if you're allergic to the sap, which I apparently am," Wyatt said. He tried to smile, but his stiff, swollen lips were nearly immobile. "I know it looks pretty gnarly, but this is actually an improvement. My aunt dragged me to a doctor, and he gave me a cortisone shot and some steroid cream, so I'm starting to feel semihuman again, even if my face does look like a piece of raw meat."

Ashleigh leaned her body across Suzanne's to get a closer examination, and to give her pseudo-professional opinion. "Hmm. It looks like the eruptions haven't scabbed over. That's a good thing. I'd hate for you to have scars all over that pretty face of yours."

Wyatt ducked his head, obviously embarrassed by all the attention.

"What can I get you to eat?" Rochelle asked. "Hamburger? Wings? Loaded potato skins?"

"Nothing, thanks," he said. "I had a late lunch after my date with Stackpole."

"Stackpole?" Grace stared, wondering what he'd been up to, halfway dreading the answer.

"Yeahhh," he said slowly. "It's kind of a long story." And then his face cracked painfully, but he smiled anyway.

"Well, since Paula called off our session, we've got all night," Camryn said. "So don't keep us in suspense."

He filled them in on Callie's efforts to get him into hot water with the judge, and how his lawyer had instead managed to turn the tables on her.

"Wyatt, that's huge!" Suzanne said, beaming. "I'm so happy for you." She looked at the other faces around the table. "We're all happy for you."

Grace saw Wyatt watching for her reaction. "It's great, really," she said. "For once, the good guy comes out ahead with that clown Stackpole."

"Thanks, Grace," he said. "Maybe he'll change his mind about you and Ben, too."

"I wouldn't count on that," Grace said. "I'm a woman, remember? I'm the gender he loves to hate."

"Did you, uh, tell everybody about last week?"

Grace blushed at the memory.

"What?" Ashleigh demanded. "Did something happen after we left here?"

"You might say that," Wyatt said. Had Grace imagined it, or had he actually winked at her? She'd hoped to avoid any mention of their late-night chase the previous week.

"We don't actually know for sure that the car was Stackpole's," she put in, when he was done.

"Although . . ." Wyatt was trying his best not to look

smug, but it was a hard-fought battle. "Today, while I was at the courthouse, my aunt and I took a drive through the county parking deck. Did you guys know judges get assigned parking spaces?"

"They probably don't even have to pay for 'em, either," Camryn said. And then she perked up. "Stackpole drives a Lexus?"

"A black one," Wyatt said, "with a little Florida gator decal in the lower left corner of his rear window."

Grace grinned despite herself. "So, it was Stackpole!"

"Maybe," Camryn cautioned. "Half the judges in this state probably have a UF Gator sticker on their car. And of those, there's probably a whole bunch of them who drive a black Lexus."

"But there's only one judge in Manatee County who drives a black Lexus with a UF sticker *and* who resides at 4462 Alcazar Trace, Longboat Key. And that is the Honorable Judge Cedric N. Stackpole Jr." Wyatt said.

"You're sure?" Grace asked.

"Yup. Betsy did an online search. It's him."

"Well, I'll be damned," Rochelle said. "What do you think that means?"

"I knew it!" Ashleigh said. "You can always tell with those straitlaced types. They're the biggest horndogs on the block. And, of course, they're *always* married."

"It might not mean anything," Grace cautioned, although she hoped against hope it did. "Maybe they were just having a professional meeting, and he told her he didn't like the way she was conducting our group session."

Camryn was drumming her long acrylic fingertips on the tabletop. "Okay, y'all, I'll tell you what I think it means. I think it means a hard-nosed piece of investigative journalism will unveil a web of intrigue and paybacks between a respected local circuit court judge and a disgraced therapist. And I think, maybe, just maybe, it might mean a daytime Emmy for a certain hard-hitting member of the News Four You I-Team."

She held up her iPhone. "I've been doing a little dirt digging on my own."

30.

"Paula Talbott-Sinclair," Camryn said, pausing for dramatic effect, "used to live in Oregon. But three years ago, the state revoked her professional license. She moved to Florida sometime after that and set up an office here, but she's not licensed by the state of Florida to be a clinical therapist. So how does she get away with charging three hundred dollars an hour for a group session? And more importantly, when the phone book is full of marriage counselors, why does Stackpole insist people like us attend counseling sessions with her?"

"Do we know why they revoked her license in Oregon?" Suzanne asked. "And does the state of Florida require her to be licensed in order to be a therapist here?"

"This is Florida, honey," Camryn told her. "Just like we attract every kind of poisonous reptile, bug, or plant, every whacked-out criminal, huckster, or con artist, we also get every loony-toon variety of self-appointed therapist on the planet. Even though Florida seems to have pretty strict licensing requirements for therapists, there's always a loophole. So you could still call yourself something else, hell, you could call yourself a divorce whisperer, and as long as you have a business license from the county, you're good to go. Paula does have that. I checked. As for why Oregon took away her professional accreditation, I'm working on it, but it's slowgoing. All these state licensing boards have layers and layers of confidentiality rules. I've got an intern at the station working on trying to dig up the particulars, but so far we're getting sandbagged."

"I wonder if her losing her license had anything to do with drugs?" The others at the table turned to look at Grace.

"She's obviously impaired, at least some of the time. And we did find those sleeping pills and tranquilizers in her purse," Grace reasoned. "Camryn, can your intern check to see if she's had any drug arrests, or something like that?"

"I can ask," Camryn said. "But this kid's no rocket scientist."

"I don't care what she's done or how she lost her license," Suzanne spoke up. "Paula is obviously troubled, but I honestly believe she cares about us. I don't know about you guys, but she's helped me. A lot. I feel sorry for her. Can't we help her, instead of making her part of an exposé?"

Ashleigh laughed. "You think she's helped you? I mean, no offense, Suzanne, but you've never said one thing in group about what happened in your marriage. All we know is that your husband's name is Eric and he cheated on you with another teacher at your school."

"Ashleigh!" Grace chided.

"I don't care," Ashleigh tossed her honey-colored tresses. "We've all opened up our innermost secrets, and she just sits there, every week, with her lips zipped."

"Something you might try once in a while," Camryn said.

"No, Ashleigh's right," Suzanne said. "I haven't been

open. And that's not fair to you or me. That's one reason I was so disappointed our session with Paula was canceled tonight. That question she asked us Wednesday night—the one about a moment with our spouse when we were happy?" She gave a sheepish smile and pulled her journal out of her pocketbook. "I wrote ten pages! Which is hard for me to believe right now, but I did."

"Well? Are you gonna read it?" Ashleigh asked, daring the others to shut her up.

Suzanne glanced at the table directly behind them, where two grizzled fishermen sporting three-day beards and sweat-stained T-shirts lolled backward in their chairs, obviously interested in their conversations. "It's sort of private," she whispered.

"Let me handle this," Rochelle said. She stood, hands on hips and faced the table. "Miller, Bud, you guys need to pay up and move on." She jerked her head in the direction of the door. The men scowled but pulled some rumpled bills from their pockets, threw them on the table, and ambled toward the bar.

"Nuh-uh," Rochelle called, following in their wake. "You two are done for the night. Unless you plan to actually buy a drink or some food."

"Oh no, Grace, make her stop," Suzanne blurted. "I don't want your mom to chase off paying customers for me, especially your regulars."

Grace rolled her eyes. "They're her regular deadbeats. That's not even their real names. She just calls them that because that's what they order. A Bud and a Miller. But only one. They eat a boatload of popcorn and generally annoy all our paying customers. Plus, they stink to high heaven. And they're crappy tippers. Believe me, they'll be back tomorrow. They're shameless barflies."

Rochelle shooed the men out the front door, then returned to the table. "What were you saying, Suzanne?"

Suzanne took another deep breath. "If you guys really want to hear it, I think I'm ready. Don't worry," she added hastily. "I won't read all ten pages. I'll give you the abridged version."

She took a gulp of wine and laughed nervously. "Liquid courage, right?"

"It was a Saturday night, and our daughter Darby was playing in an out-of-town soccer tournament. I guess I am the ultimate soccer mom. Usually Darby and I share a room during the tournaments, because Eric rarely goes, and I love giggling and gossiping with her. We are so much closer than most moms and daughters. But this time, Darby specifically asked me not to go because she wanted to room with her two best friends, so I stayed home.

"At first, Eric and I didn't know what to do with ourselves on a Saturday night alone! We talked about going out to a nice restaurant, but it was raining out, so instead we stayed home. Eric did something he hadn't done since the years when we first moved in together. He fixed me my favorite dish and cleaned up the kitchen, too. After dinner, we opened a good bottle of wine, and we sat on the sofa together and dialed up a movie on Netflix, a silly little chick flick. But it made us laugh, and parts of it were so romantic. I was stretched out on one end of the sofa, with my shoes off, and Eric was giving me a foot massage. And it was just . . . so sweet, and tender. I just, I don't know, got really turned on."

Suzanne stopped reading. "I can't . . . I can't believe I am reading this out loud. My heart is pounding so hard right now, it feels like it might jump out of my chest."

"You're doing great," Rochelle said, patting Suzanne's hand.

"Thanks," Suzanne said, her voice sounding wobbly. "I

think I'll be okay if I just don't look at your faces while I read. Dumb, huh?"

She stared down at the notebook. "Uh, I'm going to skip over this part." She blushed furiously, flipping the notebook pages. "And this. Nobody wants to hear this."

Ashleigh's hand shot up. "I do."

"Damn, Suzanne," Camryn drawled. "Ashleigh's right for once. Don't be such a scaredy-cat. You had relations with your husband? Why is that such a big deal? We're all grown folk here. You said you were going to read, so read already and quit making us beg for the good stuff."

"Sorry, sorry, sorry," Suzanne said, fanning her face with her hands. She turned back to her starting point and began to read again.

"Eric couldn't believe I was actually initiating sex with him. And I couldn't either. But I did. I undressed him, right there on the sofa, and he undressed me, and we . . ."

She bit her lip.

"We did it! We had sex in the family room, on the same sofa where Darby does her homework every night. Eric made me leave the lights on and everything. I don't know what came over me that night, but it was all different. I did all the things he's been begging me to do for years. Tried different positions. I talked dirty to him. He loved it."

Suzanne whispered, without looking up at the others. "I loved it."

"We were different people that night. We were who we used to be, before life reshaped us. Mutated us. I can't remember ever achieving that sense of intimacy before, even when we were dating. I thought maybe that night would change our marriage. I thought the next morning, I would get up and make us a late breakfast in bed, and we would make love again and everything would be different.

*But it wasn't. Still, that was the happiest I've ever been
with Eric. It made me remember how we used to be."*

Suzanne closed the notebook and folded her hands on the
cover.

"Wow," Grace breathed. "Just, wow. The next morning,
after your night of grand passion. What happened?"

"Nothing. I woke up, and Eric had gone for his ten-mile
run," Suzanne said, her shoulders slumped. "When he got
back, he disappeared into his office for the rest of the afternoon. Then, Darby got home from the tournament, and,
well, things went right back to the way they'd been."

"Did you ever talk about that night?" Wyatt asked. "Did
you tell Eric how much you enjoyed it? Or try doing the
same thing again?"

"No," Suzanne said, her voice small. "The time just never
seemed right. And not long afterward, I . . . discovered
he was cheating on me. So there wasn't any point to any
of this, was there?"

"You had fabulous sex! There's always a point to that,"
Ashleigh said.

After the laughter died down, Grace brought up something that had been on her mind since the first night she'd
met Suzanne.

"Suzanne, you say you and Darby are really, really
close. And it sounds like you're pretty wrapped up in her
life and her soccer and everything. I'm wondering if maybe
you're too involved."

"Yeah, maybe you're one of those helicopter parents I
hear about," Ashleigh said. "Why do they always call them
that, I wonder?"

"Because those are the parents who're always hovering
right over their kids' shoulders, doing their work for them,
or interfering with teachers or coaches, or whatever," Camryn said. "I did a story about it. It's a real problem."

"Helicopter parents? That's ridiculous," Rochelle scoffed. "You've never had kids, Grace or Ashleigh, so you don't understand. Suzanne is a great mom. Darby's a senior this year, right, Suzanne? So this will be her last year at home before going off to college. It's totally understandable that you want to be part of her life. When Grace was in school, I never missed a class play or one of her tennis matches."

"Maybe," Wyatt said, carefully choosing his words, "you got so wrapped up in your daughter's life, you forgot to pay enough attention to your husband. Maybe Eric felt, I don't know, neglected?"

"Spoken just like a man!" Rochelle snapped. "Honest to Pete, I am so tired of hearing men make excuses for their own bad behavior. If her husband was feeling neglected, maybe he should have gone to those soccer tournaments with them, instead of sleeping with any woman who caught his eye. Right, Suzanne?"

"Maybe," Suzanne said quietly. "Maybe if Eric was feeling abandoned, he could have told me that. Or maybe I should have made more of a point of including him. I just don't know anything."

"You knew enough to kick his cheating butt to the curb," Rochelle said. She glanced over her shoulder and saw a tall black man with a gleaming bald head standing pointedly in front of the cash register at the bar. She jumped up. "Oh, Lord. There's Garland, from the health department. Hold that thought," she told Suzanne. "I'll be right back."

Five minutes later, Rochelle returned to the table, grim-faced, with Sweetie clutched firmly under her arm.

She glared at Grace. "Of all the dumb luck. Garland drops in for a beer, and this little mutt comes scampering down the back staircase and into the kitchen." She thrust the dog at Grace. "You know anything about this?"

Grace sighed and held the wriggling dog against her chest. "This is Sweetie. She was left behind at Mandevilla Manor. I know you don't like dogs, but . . ."

"But you decided you'd bring her here to the Sandbox. Are you crazy? We can't have a dog in a restaurant. You want the health department on my ass? I could lose my license, if Garland decided to report this."

Grace glanced over her shoulder. Garland gave her a stern look and waggled a finger at her. "I'm really sorry. I thought I'd closed my door tight. I don't know how she got out. I'll take her back upstairs."

"And then find her a new home, tomorrow," Rochelle said firmly.

Grace carried Sweetie to her bedroom and examined the door where the dog had scratched and clawed to escape.

She carried Sweetie into the bathroom and set her down on the floor. Sweetie gave her a quizzical look. Grace sat on the edge of the bathtub, to lecture the dog at eye level.

"I know you don't like being penned up, but you just can't go downstairs, or you'll get me kicked out of my mom's house. And then we'll both be homeless." She pulled a treat from her pocket and tossed it to Sweetie, who caught it and retreated beneath the pedestal sink to savor it.

"Stay here for now, and we'll figure something out tomorrow," she promised, giving her a final, reassuring head scratch.

When Grace got back to the bar, the group was still having a spirited discussion and Rochelle was back behind the bar. She set a fresh basket of popcorn on the table and tried to avoid her mother's disapproving stare from across the room.

"What did I miss?" she asked.

"Just a lot more man bashing," Wyatt said, helping himself to a handful of popcorn. "The usual."

Camryn rolled her eyes. "It seems like Suzanne's husband was jealous of all the time she spent with their daughter, so that's his excuse for having an affair?"

"Affairs. Plural," Suzanne said quietly. "But I wouldn't really characterize them as affairs. More like one-night stands, from what I could find out."

"Oh, no." Grace blurted. "That's so awful."

"Like my asshole husband," Camryn said disgustedly. "Men really are such shits."

"Thanks," Wyatt said. He stood up and pulled some money from his pockets. "On that note, I think I'll just take my sorry, shitty man self on home and let you girls continue the vagina monologues." He did a little half bow. "Ladies?"

Camryn reached out and caught him by the elbow as he started to walk out. "Don't be such a wuss, Wyatt. You know I wasn't talking about you."

"Don't go!" Ashleigh pleaded. "We really don't hate all men. Well, I don't. I don't know about the others." She turned to Suzanne. "You tell him."

"Please stay," Suzanne echoed. "We want to hear a man's point of view. Right, Grace?"

She could feel Wyatt watching her, one eyebrow cocked expectantly.

"Right," she said finally, looking anywhere but directly at him.

Camryn tugged impatiently at his arm. "Come on, dude. Sit back down. Don't make us beg."

"It's getting late," Wyatt said, his resolve ebbing a little.

"It's not even nine o'clock yet," Ashleigh pointed out. "And didn't you tell us your little boy stays with your wife on weeknights?"

"We alternate days. I pick him up after school tomorrow," Wyatt admitted.

Camryn was steering him back toward the table. "What about you?" she asked, after he'd sat down again. "You've got a kid. Did you ever resent your wife spending more time with your son than with you?"

Wyatt took a sip of his beer. "Maybe when Bo was just a baby, yeah, I probably felt a little left out, especially when Callie was nursing him. Things got better after the pediatrician convinced her she could pump breast milk and let me take the early-morning feedings so she could get some sleep."

"You did that?" Grace turned to him in surprise.

"Sure," Wyatt said, shrugging. "It was kind of cool. I'd take Bo out to the living room, give him his bottle, and we'd watch cartoons until we both fell back asleep. I swear, he loved *Phineas and Ferb* when he was only six weeks old. He'd laugh his little ass off."

Camryn shook her head. "Dexter Nobles used to sleep right through those midnight feedings. And I don't remember him changing all that many diapers either."

"Eric changed a lot of diapers, and sometimes he'd sit up and read aloud to me while I nursed Darby," Suzanne said wistfully. "I kind of miss those days."

"He read to you? That's so sweet," Ashleigh said. "What did he read?"

"*Harry Potter,* actually," Suzanne said. "A college classmate who was living in the U.K. sent us the first book as a baby gift for Darby. Another nice memory I'd completely forgotten about."

"How about you all?" Suzanne asked, polling the others. "Did anybody else come up with any deeply repressed happy moments?"

Ashleigh wrinkled her nose. "I didn't really get that

question when Paula asked it. See, I was happy right up until Boyce started up with that Suchita chick."

"Any one particular memory?" Suzanne queried.

"Oh yeah," Ashleigh said, dreamy-eyed. "One of the drug companies had a 'seminar' for plastic surgeons in the Napa Valley back in the fall. They put us up in this fabulous old inn in the wine country. Boyce and I drove over to Calistoga and did a couples-only mud bath and massage . . ." She giggled. "We got pretty naughty. I ended up with mud in the most *interesting* places . . ."

"Spare us any more smutty details," Camryn said drily. "We get the picture."

"Your turn," Ashleigh said, pointing right back at her. "And don't try telling us you were never happy. You were married longer than any of us, right? There must be some reason you stayed with your husband all those years."

Camryn sighed. "The last really happy time? I'd have to say it was that first Christmas Jana was old enough to understand about Santa Claus. Dexter bought her this ridiculously expensive Victorian dollhouse with about a million itty-bitty pieces to it. That night, after we put her to bed, we put on my Johnny Mathis CD, and he popped a bottle of champagne he'd been saving for a special occasion. We stayed up drinking and laughing and dancing to Johnny Mathis. "I Saw Mommy Kissing Santa Claus" came on, and the next thing you know, we'd forgotten all about that dollhouse . . ." She blushed. "I sound like Ashleigh now, spilling about our sex life. Of course, that was fifteen years ago."

"You've really been that unhappy all this time?" Grace asked.

Camryn rested her elbows on the table and propped her chin on her hands while she thought about it.

"I guess I was going with the flow. At one point, when

Jana was about eight, I realized things weren't great. But then Dexter made partner at his law firm, and I finally got hired on at News Four. We bought the new house with the pool and we put Jana in private school at Saint Stephen's, which was not cheap. And I thought, why rock the boat? Things will get better. But they never did. I should've ended it a long time ago. Before things turned ugly like this."

"Graaaaccce?" Ashleigh tilted her nearly empty glass. "Is your mom coming back? 'Cause I could use another of her 'ritas."

"I'll get it," Grace stood.

"And then it's your turn to share," Camryn said, making quote marks with the fingertips of both hands. "So don't think we're going to forget."

Rochelle deliberately turned her back to Grace when she walked behind the bar. "I'm fixing Ashleigh another fake margarita," she told her mother. "Could you add it to our tab?"

"Is the dog locked up?" she asked pointedly.

"She's in the bathroom, taking a nap," Grace assured her. "It won't happen again."

"We're waiting," Wyatt said pointedly, when Grace returned to the table with Ashleigh's drink.

She stuck her tongue out at him. "I notice you haven't read from your journal tonight."

"But I shared. And it was honest and it was meaningful," he taunted. "Right, ladies?"

"Come on, Grace. Your turn." Ashleigh noisily sipped her fakearita.

"Okay, okay," Grace grumbled. She pulled her notebook from her bag and skimmed what she'd written.

"I'd never lived in a real house, until Ben and I bought our first little place in Bradenton. It was the worst house

on the street. Concrete-block and less than a thousand square feet. Two tiny bedrooms, one miserable bath that didn't even have a shower, a galley kitchen so narrow that when you opened the oven door it almost touched the cabinet on the opposite wall. The countertops were plywood covered with plastic tile."

"Sounds dreamy," Camryn said.

"I knew we could make it dreamy. But we had zero money to work with."

Ashleigh waved her hand in the air. "Excuse me, Grace, but when does the happy-memory part come in? Because, so far, this is all sounding pretty grim to me."

"That was just the setup. The prologue," Grace said. She flipped through the pages of her notebook and began reading.

"I was working for a big developer in Sarasota, designing their model-home interiors. This was before the economy tanked, when condos were selling as fast as they could put them up. Ben was an account executive with an advertising and marketing company. We'd work all day, then go straight to the house, change clothes, and work 'til one or two in the morning, go back to the condo we were renting, fall into bed, then get up and do the same thing the next day. For six months, we worked every weekend. Some nights we were too tired to even drive home, so we'd just crash on a mattress on the living room floor. Neither Ben nor I had any real do-it-yourself skills. So we taught ourselves. It was all a huge adventure, and we were in it together. We just figured if we messed up, we'd rip it out and start over. We were absolutely fearless. One night, I wanted to put up this ten-inch cove-ceiling molding in the living room. We had exactly enough to do that one room, and I knew it would be fabulous. Ben bet me I couldn't do it. And of course, I totally messed it up and ended up in tears. He took pity on me, took over, and

*somehow made it work. But it took hours. It was close to
midnight by the time we ate our dinner of Chinese take-
out and cheap jug wine, sitting on overturned plastic
joint-compound buckets. We got silly drunk and ended up
naked, hosing each other off in the backyard. And Ben
won the bet, so you can probably figure out what happened next. I can't remember a happier time in our life
together."*

Grace closed the notebook. She heard a soft exhalation
of breath from somewhere behind and turned just in time
to see Rochelle, scurrying back toward the kitchen.

"Good night," Grace said, walking out into the Sandbox
parking lot with the others. They'd discussed what to do
about Paula but hadn't come to any kind of consensus.
"Let's see what happens next Wednesday," Suzanne had
suggested, and short of any other brilliant ideas, they'd
agreed to do just that.

She'd turned to go back inside. "Hey, Grace?" She
turned and saw Wyatt, standing in the shadow of a clump
of palm trees.

"Hi," she said.

"Can I talk to you?"

"Okay." She leaned up against the bumper of his truck
and squinted to see his face in the flickering green and red
light cast by the bar's neon sign.

"Wow. That rash or whatever it is on your face really
looks painful," she said.

"The stuff on my face isn't the worst of it," Wyatt said,
grimacing and jerking his chin downward, toward his belt
line.

"Oh." She caught his meaning and grimaced, too.
"Sorry."

"I'll be okay. As soon as I get home, I'll, uh, apply the

cortisone cream. And take some Benadryl and drift off to la-la land."

"I hope you feel better," she said, sounding cold and insincere, even to herself.

"I hope you mean that," Wyatt said. "I know I screwed up at Coquina Beach."

Grace stepped sideways in order to escape the flash of the neon, to hide her confusion and embarrassment.

Wyatt cleared his throat. "Look. I'm not good at this crap. I wasn't good at it when I was a teenager, and I sure as hell haven't gained any momentum with age. I just wanted to tell you . . . don't write me off. Okay? I really, really like you. The other night? That was great. Really, really great. I wanted to kick myself in the ass afterward."

Grace just looked at him.

"Is any of this making any sense to you?"

"Not really."

He sighed. "Instead of divorce recovery, they should have dating-reentry therapy. For dweebs like me who never figured this stuff out."

She had to laugh then. "Dating reentry. Not a bad idea. Maybe you should suggest that to Paula. If we ever see her again."

"The point is, I think maybe I had a breakthrough when I was at Stackpole's office with Callie today."

"Oh?"

"She hates me. My wife, soon to be ex, hates me. I don't exactly know why, but she does. And to tell you the truth, I'm not so crazy about her, either. Maybe your mom is right. Maybe Bo is better off if we just split up and get on with our lives."

"And if Callie gets her way and moves to Birmingham and takes Bo with her?"

"Right now, Stackpole seems like he's switched sides.

But whatever he decides to do, I'm gonna fight that as hard as I can, to keep them from taking him away," he said, his jaw tightening. "Not just because I'd miss my son, but because I know those two aren't fit to raise him. He's an afterthought to them. A bargaining chip."

Grace did what she'd been wanting to do all evening. She reached out and brushed his face with the palm of her hand. He caught her hand in his and kissed the back of it.

"For a guy, you're not so bad," she said.

He pulled her closer, wrapping his arms around her waist. "And for a man-hating ballbuster, you're not so bad yourself."

She leaned in and closed her eyes.

The screened door from the kitchen flew open, and Rochelle stuck her head out. Her voice echoed in the still evening air. "Grace? Your goddamn dog was upstairs whining to get out."

Sweetie scampered out into the crushed-shell lot, looked up at Grace and Wyatt for only a moment, then discreetly trotted around the palm tree to complete her toilette in private.

31.

Grace scooped the little brown dog up into her arms. Sweetie squirmed in ecstasy, covering her chin and neck with kibble-flavored kisses. "Poor little girl," Grace said. She looked at Wyatt over the dog's ears. "Sweetie hates being locked up. I think she has the doggie version of post-traumatic stress disorder. So that's that. I've got to figure out something else."

"She really won't let you keep a dog? Not even after you explain the circumstances?"

"She's not a dog person. And anyway, it's against all kinds of health codes," Grace said. "Guess I'd better start looking for an apartment."

"Can you afford that?"

"Not really."

He hesitated. "Look, I was going to suggest this anyway. Why don't you let me keep Sweetie at my place?"

"Oh no," Grace interrupted. "I found her and adopted her. She's my responsibility."

"Just hear me out. You could keep Sweetie with you during the day while you're working at the house on Mandevilla, and she could stay with me over at Jungle

Jerry's, nights, and any other time you need her to. She'd love it there. The whole place is fenced in, so there's no way she could run off and get hurt. She can sleep in the house with us at night. I'll fix her a bed right beside Bo's. He'll be crazy for her. He's been bugging me to get him a dog, and I was going to, but then Callie started busting my chops about that, claiming I'd just be doing it to get back at her."

"I don't understand how your having a dog affects her," Grace said.

"Luke's allergic. Or so he claims. Funny, though. He has this huge Siamese cat, and that doesn't seem to bother his allergies. The cat hates Bo, scratches him every time it gets a chance."

"I don't know . . ." Grace hugged Sweetie to her chest. "It's crazy, but I'm already so attached to her. She sleeps on the pillow next to me. And she's such good company."

"It'd just be 'til you get your own place," Wyatt promised. "Think of it as temporary joint custody. But I swear, I won't pull any of Callie's custody crap."

Grace scratched Sweetie's chin. "No alienation of affection? No bribing her with special dog treats?"

He held up his hand in the Boy Scout pledge. "I'll never drop her off late for visitation or forget to bring her leash."

"Well . . ." Grace sighed. "I guess that will work. If you're really sure she won't be an imposition."

"She won't be. I can take her home right now, if you want."

"I'll just run upstairs and get her stuff," Grace said. Wyatt held out his arms, and she reluctantly handed Sweetie over.

Five minutes later she was back, having hauled an overflowing black trash bag down the outside stairway from her room.

"All of that? You haven't even had her a week and she

already has more stuff than I do." Wyatt took the bag and set it on the front seat of the truck.

Grace edged around him and began showing him Sweetie's belongings. "Her bed is in the bottom here. But, like I said, she likes to sleep with me."

"Who wouldn't?"

She frowned. "Is that a line? Somehow it doesn't sound right, coming from you."

"I got lines," Wyatt said. "I've got moves, too. I'm a little rusty from lack of practice, that's all."

She lifted two stainless steel bowls from the bag and set them on the seat. "Here's her water bowl, and here's her food bowl. I put the dog food in here, too. I give her a cup in the morning and a cup in late afternoon."

"Got it."

Grace handed him a pink leopard-print leash with lime-green banding. "Here's her leash. I let her out first thing in the morning. But she won't go right away. You have to walk her around a little bit, let her sniff things out before she picks her spot."

He handed the leash right back to Grace. "You keep this one. I'll get her one that's a little less, uh, girly."

"Nothing too butch," she warned him. "And no camo. Sweetie has standards." She went on unloading the bag.

"Here's her Greenies. I give her one last thing at night."

He wrinkled his nose. "Greenies?"

"They're supposed to promote healthy teeth and gums. And help with the whole doggie-breath thing."

"You're kidding."

She raised one eyebrow, which shut him up, then continued with her inventory. "Brush."

"Brush," he repeated.

"Pillowcase."

He held up the pink and white striped case with a questioning look.

"It's the one I usually sleep on," Grace admitted. "I read that dogs can get separation anxiety. This one smells like me. So she won't feel like she's in a strange place. Just put it in her bed, okay?"

"Okay."

She went back to unloading the bag. "Flea and tick medicine. She gets it once a month."

"Once a month."

"Heartworm meds. Again, once a month. I put it in the middle of a little peanut butter sandwich, so she won't figure out it's good for her."

"Peanut butter," he repeated dutifully, putting the meds back into the trash bag. "Is that it?"

"One last thing," she promised. "Chew toy." She reached in the bag and pulled out a nude Ken doll.

Wyatt held the doll up to the light and examined the teeth marks ringing Ken's overly tanned buttocks.

"Is this supposed to be symbolic?"

"Not at all," Grace said. "The first night I brought her home, Sweetie was rooting around in the closet in my bedroom and she found it in a box of my old toys and dolls. She loves Ken. It's the cutest thing, the way she carries him around in her mouth."

"You couldn't let her chew up a Barbie doll?" He handed the doll back to her.

"She likes Ken," Grace said, with a shrug.

He handed the doll back to her. "If it's just the same to you, I'll get her a ball or a squeaky cat or something else to chew on while she's at my place."

Grace looked down at the Ken doll. "I'll take this over to Mandevilla and keep it there for her."

"Good." Wyatt propped the little dog on his forearm. "Say good night, Sweetie."

Grace caressed the dog's ears and gave her one more head scratch, then looked up at Wyatt.

"Call me if you need me. Really. Like, if she won't sleep or she starts that scratching-at-the-door-and-whining thing, I could come over and calm her down."

Wyatt cupped Grace's chin in his hand. "She'll be fine. Stop worrying. I'll bring her over to you at Mandevilla first thing in the morning." He set the dog down gently on the passenger seat and closed the door.

"I'm there by eight," Grace said, following him around to the driver's side. "You won't forget to give her the pillowcase, right?"

He got into the truck and leaned out the open window. "Stop being such a helicopter parent."

She opened her mouth to protest, but she didn't have a chance, because suddenly he was kissing her. Both his hands were tangled in her hair, and he pulled her right up against the door and teased her lips open with his tongue. The kiss lasted another minute or so, and left Grace breathless and dazed. And hot. When a car pulled alongside the truck, she reluctantly pulled away.

"See?" Wyatt said, grinning as he put the truck into reverse. "Moves."

32.

The little cottage—okay, he could call it a cottage, but it was really a glorified double-wide—was ablaze with lights when he pulled the truck under the carport. Wyatt tucked Sweetie under one arm and carried her and her luggage inside.

"Home sweet trailer," he said, setting her down on the vinyl floor. She took a few tentative steps and sniffed one of Bo's discarded flip-flops before picking it up in her mouth and turning to him, as if asking permission.

"Knock yourself out," Wyatt said generously. "It's way better than a Ken doll, right?"

He could hear the television in the back room. "Dad?" He called loudly. All his conversations with Nelson had to be at top volume these days. He walked toward the tiny den and poked his head around the doorway. The recliner was facing the television, but there was no telltale tuft of white hair poking above the headrest. "Dad?"

The chair was empty, the television turned to a *Law & Order* rerun. A plate with the remains of a chicken potpie sat on the folding TV tray beside the recliner. Wyatt felt his pulse blip. He passed the open bathroom door, knocked softly on Nelson's closed bedroom door. "Hey old man," he called. "You sleeping?" When there was no answer, he opened the door to find the room empty and the bed still made, the worn quilt folded neatly at its foot. The room smelled like his father, like Old Spice and Bengay. But where the hell had the old man gotten to?

He opened the back door and peered out into the darkness. "Dad?" Nothing. He gave a soft whistle and Sweetie dropped her flip-flop and trotted over, her nails clicking on the harvest-gold vinyl flooring. "Come on girl, let's take a walk and find Granddad." Now he wished he'd taken that ridiculous pink leash.

"Stay here," he told the dog. He went out to the carport and rummaged around until he found a length of clothesline. Back in the house, he found a flashlight and fashioned a makeshift leash from the rope.

His heart was pounding as he stepped out of the cottage. It was nearly ten. His father was usually fast asleep by now, either in his recliner or his room. Nelson's car, a gas-guzzling Olds, was parked in the carport, its hood covered in a fine haze of cobwebs and pine needles. He seldom drove it anymore, claiming his night vision was fading, but Wyatt suspected his father probably realized his driving days were mostly over. Now he noticed that the golf cart was missing. He cursed softly.

Sweetie sat on her haunches and looked up at him expectantly. What was it Timmy used to tell Lassie in those old Nick at Nite reruns? "What's that girl? Granddad fell down the old well?" Only Sweetie was definitely not a collie, and as far as he knew, there were no abandoned wells at Jungle Jerry's Olde Florida Family Fun Park.

"Let's take a walk," he said in a surprisingly calm voice. Sweetie inched forward, testing the air with her nose, and then set off at a trot. For lack of a better idea, Wyatt let her take the lead, playing the flashlight over the curtains of green. It was a typical summer night in Florida, the air nearly dripping with humidity. Clouds of mosquitoes swarmed his already-inflamed face, and the smell of night-blooming jasmine blanketed the thick spongy air. Sweetie trotted on, heading past the huge old banyan tree with its sinister-looking tracery of roots draping from the elephant-gray lower limbs, and around the reflecting pool with its island rookery for herons and egrets nesting in the moss-draped cypress trees. The moon was nearly full and its reflection was a butter-yellow orb in the black water of the pool. Every hundred yards or so, the little brown dog stopped, sniffed, and then readjusted her course.

Sweetie, Wyatt thought, had a lot more hunting dog in her gene pool than he would have guessed.

They were just rounding the Nursery Rhyme Garden, with its two-story concrete Mother Hubbard shoe when a pair of sharp cracks pierced the still night air. Wyatt knew that sound. It was Nelson's double-gauge shotgun.

Sweetie pricked up her ears and took off at a surprisingly fast full run, with Wyatt following close behind, the flashlight's beam bouncing off the landscape. She was barking now, excited and on full alert. She made a sharp right turn at the stand of crimson-flowering royal poinciana trees, and Wyatt realized she was headed for the area they'd always called Birdland, because it was where all the tropical birdcages and the parrot-show amphitheater were located.

The little dog barked as she ran, and Wyatt's mind conjured up every conceivable tragedy as he sprinted through the thick tropical foliage. Maybe his father had gotten confused and wandered off into the darkness, on the golf cart, armed with his favorite old shotgun. Maybe he'd imagined an intruder and gone to investigate. None of the story lines flashing through his imagination had a happy ending.

Finally, Sweetie skidded to a stop. She sat on her haunches, her ears folded back, a deep, guttural growl rising in her throat, aimed at some unseen enemy lurking in the darkness.

Silvery moonlight revealed Nelson Keeler, sitting on one of the splintery green-painted benches ringing the amphitheater, his shotgun resting across his pajama-clad knees. In the round, chicken-wire-ringed aviary nearby, Cookie, the African gray parrot, hopped agitatedly from foot to foot. "Shots and beer, shots and beer," the bird muttered.

"Hey, son!" Nelson exclaimed, spying him. Sweetie stayed where she was, on full alert, growling menacingly.

"Dad?" Wyatt sank down onto the bench beside his father. "What's going on?" He was out of breath, bewildered. "What are you doing out here?"

Nelson pointed into a clump of ferns and bromeliads ringing the aviaries. "I got the sumbitch. One clean shot. The second for insurance."

Wyatt's heart sank. For months now, the park had been the target of petty criminals. Twice, they'd managed to break into the gift shop, stealing less than fifty dollars' worth of cash, some cases of coke, and some stale candy bars. Another time, they'd gone farther into the park and attempted to cut through the wire to steal the parrots, apparently thwarted by the hue and cry raised by Cookie and the others. Although Wyatt viewed the crimes as a nuisance, Nelson had been enraged at the idea of anybody breaching the admittedly lapsed security at Jungle Jerry's.

A dozen years earlier, they'd had the park wired for an alarm system and installed motion-detector cameras. Now, though, the technology was outdated and the cameras were inoperable. And they didn't have the money to install a new security system.

For a week or so, after the last break-in, Nelson had

taken to patrolling the grounds on the golf cart Wyatt used for landscaping, finally growing bored after encountering nothing more than a few errant fruit rats on his nocturnal rounds.

Had his father shot and killed some young punk? Wyatt took a deep breath. "Who'd you get, Dad? Where is he?"

"Over there," Nelson gestured. "He slunk off into the ferns. See the blood? He's dead, though. I guarantee you. I nailed the sumbitch."

Wyatt's stomach turned as he observed the fine spatter of bloodstains on the crushed-shell walkway. He stood, and Sweetie took that as a signal to advance. She crept forward, her round belly scraping the sand, her nose sweeping back and forth. Five yards from the clump of ferns, she sat straight up on her haunches and growled again.

He held his breath as he played his flashlight over the greenery. Sweetie stayed close to his side on high alert. Finally, he saw where the trail of crimson ended. At first he thought it was a clump of Spanish moss. But as he grew closer, he spied a muzzle in a ghostly shade of gray, and then what looked like the emaciated body of a dog. He turned and glanced back at his father, who'd risen on shaking legs to follow them to the spot.

"What the hell is that?" Even as he said it, he realized what the form was.

"Coyote," Nelson said grimly. He turned and pointed to an aviary at the edge of the amphitheater. The wire door was ajar and the tree-limb perch was vacant. Brilliant red and yellow scarlet macaw feathers littered the cage floor. "Sumbitch got Heckel and Jekyll. I'm sorry, son."

The two macaws were the park's most senior residents, having been bought by Wyatt's grandfather in the late sixties. At one time they'd been a featured attraction in the parrot show, but now the colorful birds were officially retired from active duty. Wyatt patted his father's shoulder. "Not your fault, Dad. I'd heard about coyote sightings in and around town, but for some reason it never occurred to me they might turn up here."

"The hell it wasn't my fault," Nelson said gruffly. "I'm the one who fed all the birds today. I guess I must have left the macaws' cage unlatched. They were so old and lazy, it probably never occurred to them to try to fly away. The damned coyote had already finished 'em both off by the time I heard Cookie screaming and got over here on the cart."

Wyatt went to Cookie's cage, unlocked it, and reached in. He extended his hand and the bird gingerly walked up his arm to his shoulder. "Hey, Cookie," he said. "You're one hell of an alarm system." The gray parrot cocked its head and seemed to wink at him. "Gimme a beer," she said. He fished in his pocket and brought out a bird treat instead. "Performance bonus," Wyatt said. When the parrot finished chewing, Wyatt placed her back in the aviary and locked and double-checked it. Then, he walked around and checked the other cages. Marilyn and Lana, the cockatoos, were huddled together in the far corner of their cage, and Elvis, the huge blue and gold macaw, improbably, seemed to be sleeping.

"Okay, everybody's safe and accounted for," he said finally. "C'mon, Dad, it's late. Let's go home. I'll come back in the morning and bury the coyote." Wyatt took the shotgun from his father and placed it in the cargo hold of the cart, then climbed behind the wheel. Sweetie hopped up onto the bench seat beside him.

Nelson lowered himself into the cart, looking down at the dog in surprise. "Who's this?"

"This is Sweetie," Wyatt said, backing the cart up and heading down the path toward the house. "She's gonna be staying with us for a while." He reached over and ruffled the dog's ears. "I think she'll fit in nicely around here, don't you?"

The old man regarded the dog with a practiced eye. "Got a lot of poodle in her. Maybe some schnauzer or cocker spaniel. Poodles used to be great hunting dogs, before they started being bred as silly show dogs. Did you know that?"

"I didn't," Wyatt said.

"Where'd you say you got her?"

"A woman in my divorce-recovery group found her in an abandoned house. She's living with her mom right now, over in Cortez, but the health regs don't allow a dog to live in a bar, so I said Sweetie could stay with us until Grace moves into her own place."

"Cortez?"

"Yeah. Her parents own the Sandbox. You remember that place?"

"Sure. Used to take you there when you were a little kid, after we'd been over at Holmes Beach. You used to love their cheeseburgers. This Grace, is she Butch Davenport's daughter?"

"Yeah. Did you know him?"

"Everybody in Manatee County knew Butch Davenport. He was quite a character. Is he still around?"

"No, he passed away a few years ago. Rochelle, Grace's mom, runs the Sandbox now."

"And what's your connection to this Grace person?" Nelson frowned. "You going out with her? Hanging out in dive bars like the Sandbox with her? Before your divorce is final? You better hope Callie and her lawyer don't get wind of that."

"Callie is living with her boyfriend, and has been for months now, so I don't think she has anything to say about my personal life. Anyway, like I just told you, Grace is in my divorce-recovery group. The whole group goes to the Sandbox after our meetings, just to sort of unwind. I have a beer or two and come home. End of story."

"But you like this girl."

"I do," Wyatt nodded. "She's a nice person. You'd like her, too."

"You sleeping with her?"

Wyatt felt his face burn. "Jesus, Dad! No. Where'd you get an idea like that?"

Nelson shrugged but said nothing else.

Wyatt pulled the golf cart under the carport and switched it off. Nelson unfolded himself from the seat, grunting with the effort, clutching the side of the cart for balance, swaying a little as he stood, trying to catch his breath.

And it struck Wyatt again: his father was aging before his eyes. The vagueness, forgetfulness, especially in the evenings, these had crept up and even accelerated since Wyatt had moved in with him. Nelson had always been strong—even into his sixties; he was fit and used to hard physical labor. Now, though, his gait had slowed and his energy level was diminished. It was all he could do to putter around the gift shop or the office a few hours in the morning before he returned to the cottage for a nap and endless hours of television.

He followed Nelson into the cottage, making sure the old man got safely into his bed before walking around the cramped cottage, switching off the lights and the television. The thin walls seemed to close in on him, choking him with claustrophobia. Sweetie followed close on his heels, seemingly sensing Wyatt's restlessness.

He held the back door open. "Come on then, let's go for a midnight ride."

As the cart jolted along the shell pathway, the headlight picked out the shaggy, overgrown landscape. Just like his father, Jungle Jerry's was aging, and not gracefully. Even the moonlight did not become it.

In his mind, Wyatt ticked off the unending items of maintenance that needed tending to. The gift shop's roof was leaking badly. He'd patched it so many times himself that the patches outnumbered the original asphalt roofing. The crushed-shell parking lot was pocked with potholes and washouts, and half the neon in the Jungle Jerry's sign had burned out.

In the park itself, dead or half-dead trees stood, waiting to be trimmed or cut down. The flower beds were choked with weeds and vines, and the abundant rain-forest plants swallowed whole sections of the pathways. His earlier visit to the amphitheater reminded him that half the benches there were rotted or splintered and all of them needed painting or replacing. The aviaries his grandfather had built decades ago for the tropical birds were rusting and were too small by current-day standards.

And that was just the physical plant, Wyatt mused. With only three employees—him; Joyce, his bookkeeper, ticket taker, and gift-shop manager; and Eduardo, who helped out with maintenance and landscaping—there were never enough bodies or hours or funds to get everything done.

Probably, Wyatt thought, he should have been smarter about all this. Six years earlier, not long before Bo's birth, a developer had offered to buy the park from the family for what seemed like a stunning amount of money—three million. His parents had considered taking the money and making the deal, but Wyatt, young and stupid and full of plans and dreams for the family business he intended to nurture for his unborn son—had urged them not to sell. How could they let a shopping center and yet another condo complex erupt on this gorgeous garden his grandparents had worked so hard to create?

Even then, Jungle Jerry's was struggling. They weren't

losing money, but they weren't making much money either. Wyatt was certain he could turn things around. He'd taken marketing classes in college, had all kinds of ideas to drag the park into the twenty-first century. Callie had been furious with him. How could he be so stupid? All that money would have set them up for life! She'd raged at him for weeks after his parents turned down all that delicious money.

And then, before he could even get a Web site designed for the park, the economy tanked. Their attendance figures plummeted, and developers quit calling. Every month, the aging park went deeper into debt.

Wyatt steered the golf cart through the empty parking lot, hanging onto Sweetie's collar to keep her from flying off as the cart jounced through the potholes.

He fought the urge to surrender to the melancholy mood of the evening. Not everything in his life was crap. Earlier in the day he'd won one tiny battle against Callie. Starting tomorrow, he would have Bo for the weekend. He glanced over at Sweetie, sitting erect on the golf cart beside him. And maybe, just maybe, he would find a way to convince the dog's real owner that he wasn't such a total jerk after all.

33.

She'd set her alarm for 6:00 A.M. Her to-do list for Mande-villa was long and getting longer, and she was eager to get to work. Grace opened her laptop and clicked on the comments section of TrueGrace.

This was her favorite part of blogging. Styling, photographing, writing, editing, and coming up with new ideas fed her creative soul, but hearing from readers was what kept her motivated. When she'd first started writing Grace-notes, she would stay up for hours after publishing a post, clicking and refreshing, anxious and nervous to see if anybody out there in the darkness was reading her work.

Now, she gasped. More than three dozen readers had left remarks about her last post. She clicked over to her dashboard and saw that over two hundred readers were now subscribing to the blog feed, meaning they would be automatically notified whenever Grace posted a new article.

A typical post on Gracenotes, where she had 239,000 subscribers, would have generated a couple hundred comments. But she was starting over now, from scratch, and each and every one of these readers and commenters were like gold for TrueGrace.

"Yay," she said, in a small voice. Then, louder. "Oh hell yeah, yay!"

Scanning the comments, her smile grew wider. "Go, Grace," said Justamom32. "Love your new blog. So much more approachable and attainable," commented Wild-4Style.

Of course the naysayers showed up for the party, too. "I liked your old blog better." Or, "Why don't you take some photography classes and get yourself a decent camera?" And, "Not much new or original here. All your ideas are tired and clichéd." All of the negative comments, not to her surprise, were anonymous. Her finger hovered over the delete button for a moment, but then she read a note left by Rinquedink. "Hey, Grace, don't let those bitches get you down. Haters gonna hate, taters gonna tate."

Ben had always monitored the comments on Gracenotes, deleting anything that even smacked of criticism. No, Grace decided, she would only delete comments that were obscene, libelous, or obvious spam. She'd let her readers make up their minds themselves on what was spurious.

The final comment made her laugh out loud. "I've deleted that fraud, faux Gracenotes, from my feed. You really are the one, true Grace. Wishing blessings for you and the ex-husband genital herpes." It was signed Cindy-LouWhoo.

When she got out of the shower, Grace checked her e-mail and saw that she had responses from six of the bloggers she'd contacted to request a place on their blog roll. The first message she clicked on was from a lifestyle blogger who called herself Eleganza.

Eleganza's real name, as everybody in the blogosphere

knew, was Kennedy Moore. She'd been a contributing editor at several of Grace's favorite, now-defunct shelter magazines, including *House and Garden* and *Southern Accents*.

Grace knew Kennedy's backstory by heart. She'd been an interior designer, like Grace, and then, in the late eighties, after her children were off to college, had gone to work in the magazine world. Along the way, she'd weathered a divorce, remarried, and, within the past five years, lost her adored second husband and then her job at *Southern Accents*.

Kennedy had reinvented herself as one of the first professional lifestyle bloggers, writing witty, original posts; posing question-and-answer sessions with big-name designers; and sharing photos of the transformation of Hedgehog Cottage, her own small farmhouse in rural Connecticut. Eleganza, which featured her very personal take on interior design, cooking, entertaining, and affordable luxury, was hugely influential in Grace's world.

Grace held her breath as she clicked on the e-mail.

Congratulations, Grace, for landing on your feet again. The little house on Mandevilla is a gem, and I can't wait to see what clever tricks you'll come up with to make it shine. I was sorry to hear of the end of your marriage, but as I know all too well from past experience, endings are really all about beginnings. I'll be happy to add you to my blog roll. As soon as you get one of your rooms furnished, please send me pics and we'll discuss you doing a guest post for Eleganza. All best, K.

If the room had been larger Grace would have turned a backflip. A guest post on Eleganza was at the top of her blogger bucket list. Kennedy Moore's blog was the biggest-drawing lifestyle blog in existence, with more than three million subscribers. Her advertisers ranged from Home Depot to Tiffany to Coke. And now, TrueGrace would be on the very short, very select Eleganza blog roll. She flopped back on her bed, kicking her legs in celebration.

Quickly, she read the other responses. All but one were warm welcomes from bloggers who'd formerly included Gracenotes on their blog rolls.

The sixth e-mail contained a sobering message.

Dear Grace. I'd be only too happy to add TrueGrace to my blog roll, but I just can't. I think you should know that certain people are out there making veiled threats to anybody who gives you a hand. Since my husband was laid off his job last year, my little blog and the money it generates is our family's sole income. Unfortunately, I can't afford to make any enemies right now. Wishing you all the best, PeanutButter&Jedi.

Grace blinked. Was Ben actually contacting other bloggers and threatening anybody who helped her? Obviously, the others who'd agreed to add her name to their rolls either hadn't been contacted by him or just didn't feel threatened.

PeanutButter&Jedi was an emerging mommy blogger from Denver whose blog had been one of the first Grace added after establishing Gracenotes. Susan, its author, was the mother of four young boys, including a set of triplets, and Grace loved reading her wry accounts of decorating their home on a budget, thrifting, and her inventive recipes.

She felt a tiny stab of fear. What, exactly, was Ben threatening? His contacts with their advertisers were extensive. Maybe he'd casually dropped a hint to those same advertisers that anybody associated with Grace was poison?

Whatever he'd done, it was enough to scare off Susan at PeanutButter&Jedi. And how many others?

It didn't matter, she decided. Ben would do whatever he could do. J'Aimee could preen and poach off her blog, but she would never be anything more than a poser.

Suddenly, Grace's path seemed very clear. She thought back to that first house she and Ben had restored together. They'd had nothing but sweat and perseverance. It was a cliché, but they'd made lemons out of lemonade back then. She would do it again, she vowed. Without Ben, without his connections, without money. And without fear.

34.

Grace stood in the paint aisle at the hardware store on Friday morning, staring at the huge display and its thousands of one-inch color chips. What she wouldn't do for her trusted paint fan-decks, with all the notes she'd scrawled on the backs of the cards and the yellow Post-it notes reminding her what paint strength and finish she favored for all her favorites. But the fan-deck, along with all her old files and design library, in fact, all her old life, were back at Sand Dollar Lane.

She knew she wanted the equivalent of either Farrow & Ball's White Tie or Pointing, two very specific whites for the walls at Mandevilla. Farrow & Ball itself was out of the question. Imported from England, it was just too expensive. She liked Benjamin Moore, too, which was what she'd used at Sand Dollar Lane, mostly because the Benjamin Moore paint store in Sarasota was one of her blog sponsors. She had shelves and shelves of BM paint at her old house. Now, however, neither paint would work for her tiny budget on Mandevilla. She sighed. Cheap paint always just looked shoddy to her eye, and using it would require at least three coats, which would take up too much of her precious time.

She walked around to the clearance endcap and scanned the assorted cans of "oops" paint cramming the shelves.

There was a logical reason these cans were marked down; they were mistints, custom colors that had been rejected by the original customer. Most of the gallon cans were in shades she deemed either truly heinous—a neon bubble-gum pink, a muddy-looking taupe, a sickly green that reminded her of gangrene—or they were just unsuitable for a simple vernacular cottage like Mandevilla.

She did, however, find six gallons of an innocuous white in Benjamin Moore's low-VOC paint, marked down to ten dollars a can. That she could afford. Grace pulled a can from the shelf and studied the dab of paint on the tin lid. This paint had been custom-tinted, so it didn't have a color name or a formula. The shade was what she'd always thought of as a "dead white." But maybe if she had it tinted?

The clerk at the paint counter was a middle-aged man in a red apron. Grace set the oops can on the counter. "Help you?" he asked.

She gave him her sweetest smile. "Hi there. I'm wondering if you can add a little something to this paint to brighten it up a bit?"

He looked puzzled. "Like what?"

"Well, I was thinking you could add a little black to tint it, to see if I like it better."

The clerk took a closer look at the paint can. "Sorry. This is an oops paint. See, the sign says all paint is "as-is." That means we don't remix or add tint."

Grace sighed dramatically. "Look, it just needs the teeniest amount of black paint. I'm trying to match it to Farrow and Ball's Pointing shade. It wouldn't take very much time, and I would be soooo grateful?"

This approach had always worked for her in the past—at

furniture showrooms, fabric houses, plumbing-fixture showrooms. A sweet smile and a plea for mercy, especially with men, had always been a winning formula in the past.

The hardware store clerk, though, seemed immune to her charms. "Sorry. Store policy. Can't help you." He went back to working on a display of weed killer.

And Grace went back to the clearance counter, where she loaded up all six gallons of the dead white, along with a pint of black latex paint. She would just have to experiment with mixing her own paint. She added in two gallons of white latex enamel for the trim, a paint tray, a five-gallon plastic bucket, canvas drop cloth, and rollers and brushes, sighing, again, at the thought of her workshop back at Sand Dollar, where all of her painting equipment and tools were lined up neatly, ready for her next project. At the last minute she plucked six Benjamin Moore paint cards from the display, to give herself an idea of the shades she was trying to achieve.

When the cashier added up all her purchases and applied them to the account Arthur Cater had set up for her, she was shocked that she'd already managed to make a four-hundred-dollar dent in her five-thousand-dollar budget.

It was nearly nine by the time she pulled up to the new cottage. Wyatt's pickup was parked out front, but he and Sweetie were walking around the yard, inspecting the property.

Grace's heart skipped a little beat. She told herself it was because she was happy to see her dog. But maybe Wyatt Keeler had a little to do with it, too.

He was dressed in his khaki Jungle Jerry's safari shirt, cargo shorts, and work boots, and he was bare-headed, stooped over, examining some kind of weedy shrub near the right edge of the porch. He had, Grace reflected, a fine-looking butt, tanned, muscular calves and thighs, and an admirable set of shoulders across a nice, broad chest.

"Sweetie!" Grace called. The dog turned and looked at her and, after a moment, came bounding over. She gave an excited little yip and jumped up into Grace's outstretched arms.

Wyatt followed in her wake, but he did not jump into her arms. "I was just checking out the yard. Hope you don't mind."

"It's a disaster," Grace said, "like the inside of the house. If you've got any landscaping advice, I'd love to hear it. How'd Sweetie do last night? I hope she wasn't too much trouble."

"No trouble at all. I would have been here sooner this morning, but I had to bury a coyote."

She raised an eyebrow. "A coyote? Around here?"

"In the park. My dad heard the parrots raising a ruckus last night. Turned out to be a coyote. By the time he got to the old amphitheater, where we have the aviaries, the damned thing had already finished off two of our parrots."

"Oh no! Not Cookie. Please tell me the coyote didn't get Cookie," Grace said.

"Fortunately, no. Cookie's cage was locked up tight. But our macaws, Heckel and Jekyll, weren't so lucky," Wyatt said, his expression grim. "Dad shot the varmint before he could do any more damage."

"That's awful," Grace said, feeling a chill go down her spine. She hugged Sweetie closer and shivered, despite the ninety-degree heat. "Could a coyote attack a dog?"

"Maybe," Wyatt said. "But after what happened with the macaws, I won't let her roam around off a leash at night. She doesn't seem inclined to go very far from me anyway, which is probably a good thing."

"You're not kidding." Grace breathed. She set Sweetie

down carefully in the yard. "So. What do you think of my little project?"

"Great house," Wyatt said. "I love these old Florida cracker places. Not too many of them left around here."

"I know," Grace said, warming to her subject. "Do you want to see the inside?"

He glanced at his watch. "Can I have a rain check? Dad's a little worn out from his big adventure last night. I need to stick pretty close to the park today."

"Sure," Grace said, feeling a little let down.

"This yard could be really pretty with some work," Wyatt said, gesturing at the shrub he'd just been examining. "You've got some nice specimen palms in the front here, and that hedge of gardenias by the porch is in pretty good shape. Might want to spray it for aphids and trim it a little."

"What about this pathetic yard?" Grace asked, stubbing the toe of her sneaker into what was left of the crabgrass-and sandspur-infested patch of sand. "What could I do with it that won't eat up my fix-up money?"

Instead of answering, Wyatt walked away, pacing it off. He bent down, kicked at something in a patch of crabgrass, stood, and grinned. "You've got an old sprinkler system here, did you know that?"

"No!" Grace said, bending down to look. "You think it works?"

"I'd have to take a closer look," Wyatt said. "But if the lines are intact and the system is in place, that's half the battle. You can replace the old sprinkler heads and even buy new timers if necessary, but with those in place, you'd be able to replace the lawn with something hardier and keep it watered until it's established."

"A new lawn would do wonders for the curb appeal," Grace said. "But that'd cost thousands and thousands. And

I don't even have hundreds and hundreds. Maybe that's something Arthur would be interested in doing down the line."

"Arthur?"

"Arthur Cater. He's the owner. He's kind of a tightwad, but my big hope is that once he sees what I've done here, he'll loosen up and give me a little more money to work with."

"This yard isn't that big," Wyatt said. "I was walking around before you got here, just kind of brainstorming. You've got a lot of planting beds and borders that are all overgrown with weeds right now, but if you weeded and mulched them and put an edging around them, you're left with just a nice little swath of green up front here and one in the back. The sides of the house are mostly shaded by those oaks, and they're underplanted with some beat-up old hostas and leather-leaf ferns and begonias, but again, get that cleaned out, separate the hostas and give them some breathing room, and it'll be fine."

"What about the backyard?" Grace asked. "Pretty disgusting, huh?"

"It needs work, yeah. But it's not impossible. I'd get rid of that old tin storage shed first thing. It's falling apart and you don't need it anyway with that big garage. You've got the start of a nice fruit grove back there."

"Really? I just thought they were a bunch of old half-dead bushes. They're all overgrown with moss and half the branches look dead."

"They need some help, for sure," Wyatt said. "But you've got a couple of tangerine trees, a ponderosa lemon, a lime, a grapefruit, and a kumquat." He laughed. "You could set up your own fruit stand."

"I might if it were my house," Grace said. "But it's Arthur's. And it's a rental house."

"Have you thought about asking him if he'd rent to you?" Wyatt asked.

"Only since the first minute I saw it," Grace said wistfully. "I could do so much with this place, if it were mine . . ."

"But?" He crossed his arms over his chest.

"I told him when I've finished with it, it should rent for at least $1,500 a month, this close to the beach and being on Anna Maria. That's more than I could afford."

"But you're doing all this work, essentially for free, right?"

"So that I can photograph and write about it for TrueGrace," she said. "It's that kind of trade-off. Essentially to get material for my new blog."

"Maybe you could work out some kind of arrangement with the guy," Wyatt said. "You don't know until you ask."

"Maybe . . ." Grace said hesitantly.

He glanced at his watch again. "Okay, gotta go. What time should I pick her up this afternoon?"

"Her?" Grace was lost in thought.

"Sweetie. Remember?"

"Oh, right." She laughed. "Just come whenever it's convenient. I'm gonna try to finish ripping up the kitchen floor today, and then I hope to get started painting. It'll be a late night. So come whenever you like. I'll be here."

35.

The music boomed through the empty rooms of the old house, echoing off the wooden floors and high ceilings. Grace poured a gallon of white paint into the five-gallon bucket. Yup, too dead white. She pried the lid from the can of black paint and dipped in a plastic measuring spoon. A quarter of a teaspoon to start. It wasn't scientific, but it was the best she could do. She took the wooden paint paddle and started to swirl the black into the white. Hmm. Not bad.

She dipped her index finger into the paint and smeared a bit of it on her Benjamin Moore paint chip. Not quite enough oomph, for lack of a better word, but not a bad start either. She added another eighth of a teaspoon and repeated her test.

Better. Grace slipped one of her father's old T-shirts over the tank top she'd worn to the hardware store. Its hem touched the top of her thighs and nearly reached the ragged hem of the faded blue cutoffs she'd picked up at the animal-rescue thrift shop in Bradenton. She hesitated for a moment, then stripped off her bra. It was kinky, she knew, but for some reason, she'd never been able to paint in a bra. She knotted her hair in a ponytail and tied a bandanna over the finished coiffure. She was good to go.

She'd already taped off one wall of the living room and spread out her canvas drop cloth. Now, she dipped a trim brush in the bucket and brushed it onto the wall in a two-foot-wide square. She stood back and checked the effect. It did not suck. She moved her equipment to the long wall opposite the front door and painted a swatch there. Maybe?

She fired up the box fan she'd placed in one of the dining room windows and pried open all the rest of the windows that hadn't been painted shut. It was still hot in the house, but she was pleasantly surprised when the cross-ventilation at least kept the warm air moving. Grace still wasn't convinced that the ancient window-air-conditioning units actually worked, and, anyway, the house still needed airing out.

While her test paint swatches dried, Grace went back into the kitchen. She'd managed to pry up most of the harvest-gold vinyl flooring, but what she'd found underneath was a nasty surprise. Plywood sheeting. No heart pine, like the rest of the floors, just plywood. And it was speckled with bits of mastic that had been used to glue down the vinyl. Whatever she did with these floors, she'd have to get rid of all those gobs of goo. It made her back ache just thinking of it.

The first day she'd set up her laptop in the house, she'd been thrilled to discover she could piggyback off a neighbor's wireless Internet. Now she clicked over to her blog again and read another handful of comments, all positive, except for one from someone calling herself Freebird.

Wow, what happened to that showplace mansion you used to live in? Oh that's right, your hubsand kicked you out for a real woman. This place is a pigsty and a waist of time. Save the paint and buy a box of matches and a can of gas instead.

She was positive Freebird was really J'Aimee, who couldn't spell to save her life.

Leaving TrueGrace, she clicked over to Craigslist. She'd done some preliminary shopping and discovered that even the cheapest stoves and refrigerators at the big-box chain stores would put a worrisome dent in her budget. Maybe, she thought, she could find a bargain on Craigslist. Stainless steel would be nice, but she'd be happy with nearly-new good quality white appliances if the price was right.

She typed stoves into the search bar and came up with a list of nearly two hundred possibilities, ranging from the ridiculous—"Free stove, only one burner works, door has to be duct-taped. Must pick up today." To the sublime: "Viking 48-inch stainless steel pro series dual fuel, six burners, 12-inch steel griddle, simmer plate, convection/gas oven, electric broiler, Like new, $6,000."

"This is more like it," she muttered, reading a listing for a, "Like-new GE Profile refrigerator, and electric range, removed from model home, still in warranty, $200 must pick up." She e-mailed the owner, asking about availability, and then logged off.

Grace walked back and forth between the paint swatches, debating whether or not the white would work. Was it too cold? Too gray? She held the Benjamin Moore paint chips up against the walls for comparison. It wasn't Farrow & Ball, that was for sure. She would never be able to duplicate the depth of color or matte finish of the English paint, but this color? Yeah. She nodded. It was a happy, clean white, and a huge improvement over the current dirty taupey-pink walls.

She finished taping off all the trim, cranked up the tunes on her iPod, and went to work. Grace had always secretly enjoyed painting and had done a lot of it in her early days as a single career girl and then in the first few houses she and Ben rehabbed.

But at Sand Dollar Lane, she'd happily relinquished the job to the contractor. All those soaring cathedral ceilings and huge window walls and stairwells, not to mention the miles and miles of moldings and the window frames themselves, were too intimidating. Besides, Ben insisted it was time to have everything in the new house "first-class."

"You're going to be photographing the house all the time, and we're gonna shoot videos here, so how will it look to your readers and followers if they see streaky or chipped paint?" he'd said.

Now, she worked quickly, rolling the paint to the beat of the music. Unlike most people, she loved the smell of wet paint, especially mixed with the leftover fumes from all the Pine-Sol she'd used to get rid of the funky white-trash odors the house had absorbed.

She didn't stop for lunch until after she'd finished the living room and the dining room. Then, she took her sandwich, a bottle of water, and a ripe peach out to the front porch, where she sat in an old aluminum-and-plastic-webbed lawn chair she'd found in the toolshed. Sweetie sat at her feet while she ate, gobbling up whatever crumbs Grace tossed her, then curling up in a sunny spot near the screened door for a nap.

Grace stood up and stretched. She'd considered starting on the paint in the kitchen, but since she still didn't have a solution for the kitchen floors—and because she dreaded the thought of painting the old cabinet boxes and drawers, she decided to move on to the bedrooms.

It was no good trying not to play the "if I lived here game." She'd been trying to repress the urge since day one. So while she rolled faux Farrow & Ball on the larger of the two bedrooms, she allowed herself to daydream.

The room had two decent-sized windows that looked out to that big, deep backyard.

If I lived here, I'd replace those windows with a pair of French doors and build a big, wide stoop that ended in a little patio made of old mellow bricks. Maybe I'd have some kind of trellis partially enclosing it for privacy. I'd plant a pink climbing rose on the trellis, and I'd have a pair of lounge chairs out here. Or maybe I'd even have a fabulous outdoor shower, with one of those giant rain-shower heads.

The closet in the bedroom was nowhere near big enough to be a real master-bedroom-sized closet. The closet in the house on Sand Dollar Lane was bigger than this bedroom.

But if I lived here, I wouldn't need a huge closet. I don't need a lot of clothes anymore, so that's a blessing in disguise. Maybe I'd look for a big old armoire or a chifforobe, or even one of those oversized entertainment cupboards that are a dime a dozen now that everybody has a flat-screen. I'd paint it a dusty, weathered gray-blue, and I could look for old leather suitcases at estate sales and thrift shops, and I could store my extra clothes there and stack them on top of the armoire. And I'd find a great bed, maybe use a pair of twin headboards, something rattan or tropical? This house seems to scream for that Old Florida/British Colonial look.

Grace dragged the drop cloth over to a new section of wall. She didn't really know why she even bothered using one. The wood floors were already spattered with old paint and pockmarked with nail and tack holes from the wall-to-wall carpet she'd ripped up. She'd meant to check on the price of renting a floor sander at the hardware store, but she'd been distracted by figuring out the paint situation.

If I lived here, I'd stain the floors two shades darker,

*and I'd use a matte-finish poly. With the soft white walls
and the sunlight coming in through the French doors,
they'd have a deep, natural glow. No carpets underfoot,
just maybe a striped cotton runner, or possibly a worn old
Oriental in pale, faded greens, blues, and browns.*

Planning it all out in her head, listening to the music,
Grace found her painting groove again. She was dripping
with sweat and spattered head to toe with paint, but it didn't
matter. She was doing just what she wanted to do, how she
wanted to do it, with no interference from anyone. It was
a very good day.

She was just starting to move into the second bedroom
when she heard the screen door open. "Hellllooo?" A male
voice echoed.

"Wyatt?" She stripped the bandanna off her head and
ducked into the bathroom to survey her appearance. Disastrous. Epic, Titanic-level disastrous. Her face was flecked
with white paint, her arms and legs were flecked with white
paint, and she had a giant smear of dirt on her right boob.

"Grace?" His footsteps echoed in the living room. "Are
you in here?"

"Be right out," she called, pulling the bathroom door
shut. She found an old washcloth in the linen closet, ran
the water in the bathroom sink until all traces of rust were
gone, and scrubbed her face and arms with it. She sighed.
It was the best she could do. Anyway, who was she trying
to impress?

When she got out to the living room, Wyatt was walking
around, checking her handiwork. And there was a little
freckle-faced boy rolling around on the floor with Sweetie,
who was engaged in a spirited tug-of-war over what looked
like a rag of some sort. Until she got a closer look, and realized they were actually using her discarded bra.

"Sweetie," Grace called, her face in flames. The dog

looked up, with a bra strap clenched between her teeth. Grace scooped her up, disengaged the bra, and stuffed it into the back pocket of her cutoffs.

She cut her eyes over to Wyatt, whose chest was heaving with barely suppressed laughter. He was studiously avoiding meeting her eyes.

"Well, hello," Grace said, sitting down on the floor next to the child. Sweetie jumped out of her arms and began sniffing the little boy's shoes. "I bet you're Bo."

The child ducked his head. "Yes ma'am." Sweetie put her front paws on the child's chest and sniffed his neck, wedging her head under his hand until he was forced to scratch the dog's head.

"My name's Grace," she said, extending her hand. "I hear you're going to be helping take care of Sweetie."

"Yes, ma'am," the boy said. "Does she do any tricks?"

"I don't know, Bo. I've only had her a few days. But I think she's a pretty smart little thing. Maybe you could teach her some tricks?"

Bo flopped onto his back and Sweetie dutifully stepped onto his chest and began licking his neck and face, which prompted a huge fit of giggles from the child.

Finally, he sat back up and cradled the dog in his arms. "My dad taught Cookie to ride a bike and talk. Maybe we could teach Sweetie to do that."

Wyatt laughed. "Thanks for that vote of confidence, son, but even though Sweetie is really, really smart and cool, I think bike riding and talking are probably not in her future. How about if we just work on teaching her how to fetch a stick and sit up and bark on command?"

"Cool," Bo said, tickling Sweetie's belly. "Can we start tonight?"

"In the morning, maybe," Wyatt said. He touched a fingertip to one of the newly painted walls. "Man, you work fast. I can't believe you got this whole place painted in one day."

"Not all of it," Grace said. "I was just starting on the second bedroom when you guys showed up. I've still got the bathroom and the kitchen to do, not to mention the screened porch. Those are the rooms that are going to take the most work."

"Still," Wyatt said, walking into the abbreviated hall and then into the bedroom. "When you said this morning that the place was a mess, I was picturing something much, much worse."

"You should have seen it the first day I got here," Grace said, wrinkling her nose. "If my camera had smell-a-vision, I could have totally grossed out everybody on the Internet. It was so, so, nasty. Rotting wall-to-wall carpet, skanky old appliances. Everything was filthy. And that bedroom, where they'd locked Sweetie . . ." She shuddered.

"Are you ready to knock off for the day?" Wyatt asked.

"I don't even know how late it is. I kind of lost track of time."

"It's nearly six," Wyatt said. "Bo and I are going for pizza. We were wondering if you'd like to join us?"

"Pizza?"

"There's a place just over on Holmes Beach," he said. "Arturo's. Nothing fancy, but it's good and it's cheap, and if we get there reasonably early, we can get a table on the beach and watch the sunset."

Grace glanced at Sweetie. "What about her?"

"It's pet-friendly," Wyatt promised. "As long as we get a table outside."

She glanced down at her paint-spattered, braless self. "I can't go like this."

"Sure you can," Wyatt said. "Bo and I don't care. And neither does Sweetie."

"But I do," she said gently. "Certain standards must be maintained. I'll tell you what. Why don't you guys go ahead to Arturo's. I'll get cleaned up and meet you over there in thirty minutes."

"Thirty minutes?" he scoffed. "I've never known a woman yet who could shower and change and show up someplace in that little time."

"Thirty minutes," Grace swore. "If I'm one minute late, the pizza's on me."

At precisely 6:30, Grace hurried through the door at Arturo's. She was dressed in a pair of white capris, a black tank top, and a pair of gold metallic sandals from Pay-Less. Her hair was still wet from the shower and the only makeup she wore was a bit of coral lipstick. A pair of simple gold-hoop earrings sparkled at her ears, and around her neck she wore a necklace made from a tiny nautilus shell she'd found on the beach, hanging from a long thin gold chain. She walked through the main dining room and through a set of doors onto an expansive veranda, where she spied Wyatt and Bo sitting at a table close to the beach.

Wyatt's eyes swept over her appreciatively. He scrambled to his feet and gently pulled his son to a standing position, too.

"You clean up pretty good," he told her, pulling out a chair for her.

"And fast," she reminded him. "Thirty minutes. That might be a new land record for me."

"I guess that means dinner's on me," he said.

They ordered the Arturo's special, which meant a huge pie with everything, including pepperoni, Italian sausage, onions, peppers, olives, and anchovies; a glass of milk for Bo; and a pitcher of beer for the adults.

"Anchovies?" Grace asked, glancing over at Bo, who'd

devoured two slices of pizza in the time it took Grace to work her way through one. "Your kid likes anchovies?"

The boy looked up, his face smeared with enough tomato sauce to fashion another whole pie. "I love anchovies!" he exclaimed, his broad smile revealing two missing front teeth.

"I haven't found anything he doesn't love," Wyatt said ruefully. "He's eating me out of house and home. I swear, every week he's grown another two inches."

"I'm the third tallest boy in first grade," Bo reported. "Cory Benton was the second tallest, but he's not going to our school next year, so I'll be the second tallest. Unless I grow some more, and then I'd be the first tallest." He took a gulp of milk and stood up, whispering in his father's ear.

Wyatt nodded. "It's inside, near the bar. Don't forget to wash your hands, and come right back here, okay?"

When he was gone, Grace took a sip of beer. "What a nice boy. I love that he's figured out he's the third tallest."

"He's fascinated with numbers and statistics," Wyatt said, shaking his head. "I do not know where he gets it. There are no bean counters in my family, and certainly none in his mother's. I haven't had the heart to point out to him that if Callie gets her way, he won't get to be the second tallest boy in the second grade at his school, because he'll be going to a new school. In Birmingham."

"Maybe it won't come to that," Grace said.

36.

Bo came bounding back to the table. "Guess what, Dad? Scout's here! She and Coach Anna and her dad are eating dinner. Can I go sit with them for a while?"

Wyatt half stood, craned his neck, and spotted Anna and her family in the dining room. Anna nodded and pointed to an empty chair at the table and Wyatt gave her the thumbs-up sign. "Okay, but are you all done with your pizza?"

He eyed the last remaining piece on the tray. His father scooped it up into a napkin and handed it to him, and Bo ran off to join his friend.

"Anna's assistant coach on Bo's T-ball team," Wyatt said casually. "Scout's our pitcher, and Bo's best friend—on days he doesn't think girls are icky."

"What about Bo's father? Does he still think girls are icky?" Grace kept her tone playful.

"No, I'm a reformed girl hater." He reached across the table and tucked a strand of her damp hair behind her ear. "Especially where present company is concerned."

"Good to know," Grace said. "I've been meaning to ask you, how's your dad doing? You said he was pretty worn out today?"

"He's okay," Wyatt said. "I'm just going to have to get used to the idea that he's not getting any younger. All my life, he was this rugged, can-do guy. He literally did everything and anything at Jungle Jerry's: he built buildings, including the gift shop; paved the parking lot; dug the reflecting pond for the bird rookery. It was nothing for him to work a twelve- or fourteen-hour day, come home and play ball with me, and then get up and do it all over again the next day. I think my mom's death kind of took the wind out of his sails. He's only seventy-four, but some days, you'd think he was twenty years older."

"Your dad's seventy-four? Wow. Rochelle is only fifty-eight. How old are you?"

"I'm thirty-eight," Wyatt said. "You wanna see my ID?"

"I trust you," Grace said.

"Dad was thirty-two when they had me, same age I was when we had Bo. Dad went in the navy when he was just eighteen and got out in the late sixties. He and my mom met at an Allman Brothers concert in St. Pete, at the old National Guard Armory there. Crazy, huh? To think about your parents grooving to the Allman Brothers back in the day? My mom was six years younger than him, so she wasn't that old when she had me."

"Rochelle always says she was just a baby when she had her baby. She was only twenty when she got pregnant with me. Of course, my dad was a good bit older, too. He was already thirty, and he'd just bought the Sandbox when she came to work as a waitress. Dad claimed he threatened to fire her if she didn't marry him."

Wyatt thought for a moment. "It still bugs me, you know? That my parents had this long, happy marriage, and I had a happy childhood, and, with all that, I'm still ending up divorced. And you're in the same boat, right?"

"I guess." Grace took a sip of her beer. "I mean, I always assumed they were happy. Lately, I'm not so sure.

Little things Rochelle's says. Maybe she wasn't as happy as I always thought. Certainly, I didn't have what you'd call the average childhood, growing up in a bar, but I don't think there was any lasting psychological damage."

"You grew up in a bar; I grew up in a tourist trap, playing with monkeys and parrots. And I always thought that was totally normal. I thought all kids had to shovel zebra poop when they got home from school every day," Wyatt said. His voice turned wistful. "I always just assumed Bo would have that life, too. He really loves hanging out at the park."

Grace's eyes widened. "You mean he won't, because Callie's taking him to Birmingham?"

"Not just that," Wyatt said. "I'm really not sure how much longer we'll be able to hang on at Jungle Jerry's. People don't want to spend half a day wandering around a park where the big attraction is a bird riding a bike. Nobody cares about a tree that's two hundred years old or an orchid that doesn't grow anywhere else in the world. We're an anachronism. And we're bleeding money."

"It's that bad?" Grace asked.

He shrugged. "This is too depressing. Let's discuss something else. Like your new project."

"It's not depressing," Grace insisted. "It's just reality. Isn't there anything you can do to turn things around?"

"I've tried everything I can think of. Billboards, social media, Groupon offers, coupons in the mail. It helps a little, just never enough. Did you know that up until nineteen seventy, there were at least a dozen roadside tourist attractions, right here in this area?" He ticked them off on his fingers, "Sunken Gardens, Sarasota Jungle Gardens, Weeki Wachee, Silver Springs, Rainbow Springs, the Aquatarium, Tiki Gardens, Six Gun Territory, and that's just the ones I can think of off the top of my head. Lots of them are long gone, but others are still limping along, like

Cypress Gardens. The last I heard, most of it had been turned into Legoland."

"I remember some of those places from when I was a little girl," Grace smiled at the memory. "I guess Disney coming to Florida in the seventies probably was the kiss of death."

"That and the interstates bypassing them," Wyatt said. "And people's tastes change. So, Jungle Jerry's is a dinosaur. A really expensive, dying dinosaur."

"What'll happen to it?" Grace asked.

"I'm not sure. We had a hot offer from a developer, right before Bo was born. They wanted to build one of those new urban centers, shopping and office and multifamily housing. My mom was sick; she had cancer—although we didn't know then that it was terminal—and she wanted us to keep the place running. Her father started it. He was the original Jungle Jerry. And like the fool I was, I thought maybe I could make it work." He shook his head. "Callie never let me hear the end of it afterwards. 'We could have been rich. You should have sold out.'"

"And then the economy tanked," Grace said. "How well I know. Since nobody could sell a new house or condo, they sure didn't need a decorator to design a fabulous model home. And developers and builders probably couldn't afford to break ground on yet another new project with all that unsold inventory sitting around."

"Six months after we turned down the deal, we heard the developer defaulted on all his bank loans," Wyatt said. "So probably, even if we had made the deal, we never would have gotten paid."

"I know housing starts are starting to inch up again. Do you think it's possible that another developer would be interested?" she asked.

"Right now, there's only one interested buyer," Wyatt

said, lowering his voice, as the waitress came by their table to ask if they wanted another pitcher of beer.

"Who?"

"The state of Florida," Wyatt said.

"Really? But that's good news, right? What would they do with the park? Keep it?"

"I don't know," he said, sounding irritated. "Dealing with bureaucrats is a major pain. They say they'd turn it into a state park. They say if the state legislature approves their next budget, the money's there, if Manatee County can kick in some money, too. There's a lot of 'ifs' flying around."

"What does your dad think?"

"He says he's okay with the idea," Wyatt said. "But I'm not sure he really understands all it involves. He just knows I'm worried all the time, and that worries him."

"Hey Dad!" Bo ran toward their table with a little girl with blond braids close on his heels. "Anna says we can have ice cream for dessert if you say it's okay."

"Hi Scout," Wyatt said, reaching out and tugging one of the girl's pigtails. "How was your pizza?"

"She *hates* pizza," Bo announced. "She had 'pasketti. And I had some, too."

From the looks of it, Grace thought, Both Bo and Scout had applied as much spaghetti sauce to their faces as they had to their bellies.

"It was dee-lish!" Scout announced. She was kneeling on the patio, and Sweetie was jumping up to lick her face.

"This is Sweetie," Bo told his friend. "We get to keep her at our house at night."

"Cool!" Scout said. "Does she go to your mom's house, too?"

Bo's shoulders sagged. "No. You know who is allergic. But I get to keep her at Dad's, and he's going to teach her how to fetch and stuff."

Wyatt took a napkin and wiped the outer layer of sauce from Bo's face. "Tell Scout's mom I said it was okay for you to have ice cream." He reached in his pocket and took out two dollar bills and handed it to the little boy. "That's to pay for your dessert. Don't spend it all in one place. Right?"

"Okeydoke." The two ran back inside.

"He's the real reason I hesitate to pursue this thing with the state," Wyatt said, nodding in his son's direction. "Dad and I will be okay. Theoretically, we'd come out of the deal with a little money. Enough to pay our bills and keep a roof over our heads. But Jungle Jerry's is Bo's legacy. He's grown up with the park. He thinks Cookie is his little sister. How can I sell that out from under my son?"

Grace met his eyes. "You're asking me?"

He clasped his hand over hers. "I'm asking you."

"It seems to me that Bo's legacy is you. And his grandfather. Times change. You know that as well as I do. I think we have to be flexible to survive. Look at me. When my work as an interior designer dried up—I mean, in this economy how many people need a twelve-thousand-dollar hand-knotted silk rug or eighteen thousand dollars' worth of window treatments? I had to reinvent myself. I had to go back to my roots, making do with what I had, doing most of it myself, with a lot of creativity and not much money. You do what you have to do, right?"

"Yeah." Wyatt sighed. "I just keep thinking, if I could hold on a little longer . . ."

He laughed. "Like I did with my marriage. And you see how well that turned out."

"It was different for me," Grace admitted. "These months, since I walked out on Ben, I've been blaming him for everything. And he's responsible for a lot of it, truly. But I think in the last few years I changed. My belief system and my values changed. It became more about status, having the best, the most expensive everything. Even though I started out writing DIY on Gracenotes, that changed, too. We monetized, got advertisers, and I needed to make them happy in order to survive. Or so I thought."

She took a sip of her beer. "I guess I sold out. And it wasn't entirely Ben's fault. I liked all that free stuff, giving big parties, living in the big house in the gated subdivision. And I loved having what seemed like unlimited resources available for any project I dreamed up. Ultimately, along the way, that's when our marriage started to go south." She gave a wry smile. "Rochelle would tell you I got too big for my britches."

Wyatt scooted his chair over toward her and leaned down to give her an unconvincing leer. "Your britches look just fine to me."

"Wyatt?"

He turned around to see Anna Burdette standing there, with Scout and Bo holding on to her hands. Anna gave Grace a friendly, if curious smile. "Hi there."

Wyatt stood. "Anna Burdette, this is my friend Grace . . ."

"Davenport," Grace finished for him, not wanting to be introduced by her married name. She shook Anna's hand. "I hear Scout's the Babe Ruth of T-ball."

Anna's nose crinkled as she laughed. "To hear Wyatt tell it, you might think so." She was studying Grace's face. "I don't mean to keep staring at you, but I keep thinking I know you from someplace."

"She's a famous blogger," Wyatt said.

Anna snapped her fingers. "Gracenotes, right? Your blog is my guilty pleasure. I read it in the middle of the night when I can't get to sleep."

"Thanks," Grace said. "Actually, I've changed the name. My old blog got, er, co-opted by my soon-to-be ex. Check out TrueGrace, if you will."

"I definitely will," Anna said. "In the meantime, the

kids have been telling me about this spectacular little dog named Sweetie. I hear she's going to learn all kinds of tricks over there at Jungle Jerry's."

"She's actually Grace's dog, but she can't keep her where she's living right now, so we're sort of sharing custody. Bo has big plans for her," Wyatt said.

"Anyway," Anna said, "the reason I came by . . . Jack had to go on to work, but I told the kids I'd take them to play putt-putt for an hour or so, if that works for you. I can drop him off back at your place around eight."

"Please, Dad, please, please, please?" Bo was hopping up and down.

"I guess that would be okay," Wyatt said. "But not too much later, right, buddy? We've got a big game tomorrow, and your granddad is making you pancakes in the morning."

"Don't worry, the assistant coach is not gonna risk letting her star catcher suffer from sleep deprivation," Anna said.

"Let me give you some money to pay for Bo's golf," Wyatt said, half standing to get to his wallet.

"Not necessary. I've got buy-one, get-one coupons," Anna said. "Grace, it was nice to meet you."

"My pleasure," Grace said.

Anna leaned over and put her head next to Wyatt's. "She's cute, dude," she said in a stage whisper. "Classy, too. Don't screw this up, 'kay?"

37.

"Sorry about that," Wyatt said, when they were alone again. "Anna's worried about my love life. She keeps trying to get me 'back in the game,' as she calls it. But she's about as subtle as a slap in the face."

"You haven't dated at all since your split?" Grace asked.

"Me? The only other woman in my life besides Anna right now is Joyce Barrett."

"Who's she?"

"Our eighty-year-old bookkeeper slash office manager. I love Miss Joyce to pieces, but I seriously doubt she's interested in starting a new relationship."

As the waitress passed by, he gestured to her to bring the check. "It's still another hour 'til sunset, and Bo won't be back from putt-putt 'til after eight. Would you like to go someplace else for a drink? Or just take a walk on the beach?"

"Sweetie would probably love a stroll on the beach. And so would I," she said.

Grace stepped out of her sandals and stuck them in the back pocket of her pants, and after a moment of hesitation,

Wyatt tied the laces of his Top-Siders together and slung them over his shoulder. They walked through the powdery white sand to the shoreline, and Grace stood and let the mild breeze blow through her hair. They walked for a while, close, but not touching.

The bright blue sky gradually darkened to deeper layers of dark blue, violet, silver, and then ochre and pink. The wind began to whip whitecaps on the incoming waves. Families lingered on beach blankets with coolers of drinks, radios playing softly. Closer to the dunes, at every pathway from the road, knots of people stood beneath the clumps of Australian pines, sea oats, and beach myrtle, waiting for the sundown ritual to begin.

The county had an ordinance against dogs on the beach, but Sweetie stayed close to Grace's side, and, as if by tacit agreement, other law-breaking dog walkers passed by and nodded in a conspiracy of silence.

The sun dipped lower, glowing gold, and when they came to a dune walkover with an empty bench, they sat down to watch the show. Sweetie hopped up onto Grace's lap, and Wyatt stretched his arm across the back of the bench; when his hand brushed the bare skin of her shoulder, she smiled to herself.

She leaned back, resting her head against his arm, and the warmth of his skin on hers felt familiar and exciting at the same time.

"Look," Wyatt said, pointing with his free arm. Out in the waves, the graceful gray backs of a pod of dolphins curved through the water. There were four or five larger ones and three or four smaller ones. "Some moms and some calves," he said.

"I've been watching dolphins in the gulf and the bay my whole life," Grace said. "But it never gets old. I used to love it when we'd go out on my dad's boat and they'd follow us, waiting for us to throw in some bait or a too-small fish."

"Yeah," Wyatt said with a sigh. "Kind of reminds you why you live here, doesn't it?"

"Mm-hmm."

The sun was sinking lower and the clouds above growing purple and midnight blue. "You ever see the green flash?" he asked, his hand grazing her shoulder.

"You mean the thing that happens the moment the sun slips below the horizon? Yes. We used to make a big ceremony out of it when I was growing up. My dad had a cowbell he'd ring at that exact moment."

But there was no green flash tonight, just another bright yellow glow, and then striations of deepening colors.

"This is nice," Grace said, snuggling back against his arm as the air grew cooler. She leaned against his chest, inhaling his clean, woodsy scent, feeling his warmth seep into her bare shoulders.

"You cold?" He wrapped both arms around her. "We could go back to the car."

Grace shook her head. She wondered if he would ever get up the nerve to kiss her again. Or if she would have to be the one to initiate things. In the meantime, she closed her eyes and told herself to enjoy the moment.

At some point, she must have enjoyed the moment so long that she dozed off. When her eyes fluttered open, it was dark.

She sat up with a start.

"What?" Wyatt asked. "You finished your nap?"

She yawned and laughed. "I'm sorry. I've been working so hard every night, I fall asleep as soon as the sun goes down." She glanced at her watch and jumped to her feet, grabbing Wyatt's hand and pulling him up, too. "Come on, Cinderfella. I regret to remind you that at eight o'clock, you turn into a dad again."

He groaned. "I'll text Anna, tell her to play another round of putt-putt. On me. That'll give us another hour, at least."

"No way. She'll think I'm seducing you."

"Anna's a hopeless romantic. She'd probably offer to get us a room."

Grace sighed. "Bo's expecting you to be home when Anna drops him off. I don't want to be the one who causes you to break promises to your son."

"I hate it when you talk sense," Wyatt grumbled.

They walked hand in hand back down the beach, with Sweetie staying close at their heels. Wyatt stood awkwardly beside her car as she unlocked the door. She sensed his nervousness, and found it touching.

She leaned over and kissed him lightly on the cheek. "About that dating-reentry counseling you mentioned—maybe we could take a class together."

38.

At exactly 8:15 A.M. Wyatt hopped out of his truck and dashed into the house on Mandevilla. He found Grace sitting on the floor in the back bedroom, taping off baseboards.

"Gotta run," he said, setting Sweetie down beside her. "I promised Bo I'd throw him some extra batting practice before the game."

"Okay," she said. "How about if I just drop Sweetie off to you at the park later? Say six?"

He was halfway out the door, but he turned around, came back, and pulled her to her feet. "I thought about what you said last night. Just before you left. You're killing me. You know that, right?"

She smiled. "In a good way, right?"

"Absolutely. See you at six." And then he was off again. A minute later, she ran out to the porch, hollered at him as he was getting into the truck. "I'll bring dinner. What do you like?"

"If you bring it, I'll like it." He threw the truck into reverse and headed down the road.

* * *

She was still on the floor, barefoot, dressed in her messy, paint-spattered T-shirt and cutoffs, a bandanna tied over her hair, scooching along on her butt, painting the baseboards, when she heard footsteps in the living room. Maybe Bo's T-ball game was over early? She turned expectantly.

J'Aimee stood in the doorway, looking down at her, eyes blazing with hostility.

Grace scrambled to her feet, dusting off her butt with both hands. "What do you want?" she asked, her voice cool.

J'Aimee was dressed in all black, a sheer, sleeveless black chiffon midriff-baring top worn over a black bra, black skinny jeans, and high-heeled silver-studded black sandals with gladiator-wrapped ankles. With her jet-black dyed hair she looked like a refugee from a bondage flick.

Although J'Aimee was actually about Grace's height, today, in the heels, she glared menacingly down at Grace.

"You think you're pretty damn smart, don't you," J'Aimee said, poking Grace in the chest with her forefinger. "With those bullshit e-mails you sent my advertisers. Me, steal your content? Who the fuck do you think you are?"

J'Aimee's breath was hot on her face. Grace was tempted to take a step backward, but instead stood her ground.

"Me? I'm the person who started Gracenotes. I'm the actual Grace. I'm the person who developed, cooked, photographed, and wrote that corn-crab chowder recipe you so blatantly lifted off my blog to pass off as your own work."

"There are a million recipes for that soup floating around on the Internet," J'Aimee said with a shrug.

"Ben managed to wipe out that post on my page, so I can't prove it, of course," Grace said calmly. "But I've got a new blogging platform for TrueGrace and a new protected password, and I've installed malware now, so tell him not to bother to try to mess with it. Also? I've started watermarking my photos with my TrueGrace logo, so you won't be able to poach my photos anymore either."

"Me? Poach your shit?" J'Aimee's throaty laughter was harsh. "Who are you kidding?"

She took a step backward, her eyes sweeping disdainfully over the room. "So this is your exciting new project? This *shack*?" Abruptly, she turned and walked out of the room, her high heels clacking sharply on the wood floors.

J'Aimee walked into the kitchen, took in the beat-up, doorless cupboards; the gaping spaces where appliances should have stood; the bare, glue-spattered plywood floors. She sniffed and wrinkled her nose in disgust. Just as quickly, she walked into the hallway, peered into the bedroom and then the single bathroom with its outdated tile and filthy tub and toilet.

"You're pathetic, Grace," J'Aimee said, her eyes glittering with malice. "You are desperate and pathetic, like this house. You put yourself out there to all the world on the Internet as this all-knowing authority. Miss Know-It-All: the perfect designer, entertainer, gourmet cook . . ."

J'Aimee admired her own reflection in the bathroom mirror and then stomped out of the bathroom and into the living room. "But you're not even woman enough to keep your husband interested in you. You want to know how long it took Ben to jump my bones after you hired me? A week."

She laughed at the look of shock on Grace's face. "And don't be telling yourself that I'm the little tramp that went after him. He came on to me. Uh-huh. That's right. The first time? Oh, that was while you were out giving a speech to some fancy society women's fund-raising luncheon. I even remember the title of your talk, because I had to type it and print it out for you. 'A House Is Not a Home.' And while you were giving your lame talk, I was back at your house, fucking your husband's brains out." She paused and laughed again. "In your bed."

Grace wanted to knock J'Aimee down, shove a fist in her throat, anything to shut up the torrent of bile spewing from her mouth. But she was paralyzed, speechless.

J'Aimee's smile was mirthless. "TrueGrace? That's what you're calling yourself now? Who are you kidding? Ben was the brains behind Gracenotes. He and I did all the scut work, making it look pretty and effortless, while you took all the credit."

She took another step closer to Grace again, until she was directly in her face. "Look at you now, Grace *Davenport*. Living with Mommy above a shitty bar, hiring yourself out as nothing more than a glorified housepainter." She whipped a cell phone out of the pocket of her formfitting jeans, and before Grace could stop her, she'd snapped a picture of Grace, standing there, covered in paint, her mouth gaping. "This'll give Ben a good laugh."

The click of the camera lens suddenly snapped Grace back to consciousness.

"Just what is it you want here, J'Aimee? You want more material to leave some more snarky, barely literate comments on TrueGrace? Don't bother to deny it either. I know you're Freebird. Since you're living in Ben's pants these days, you might want to get him to explain ISP numbers to you."

Now it was Grace's turn to fight. She put her paint-spattered hand squarely in the middle of J'Aimee's chest, leaving a perfect white handprint on the black chiffon.

"Hey," J'Aimee cried angrily, swatting Grace's hand away.

"You're a fraud, *J'Aimee*," Grace said, rolling the name out with the exaggerated French pronunciation. "Oh. Wait. Even your name's a fake, *Jamie*. You've never had an original idea in your life. You're the kind of bottom-feeding parasite who has to be content with whatever crap sinks to the bottom of the cesspool. But hey, you want my old blog, take it! My house and that bed you seem to love? Help yourself. It means nothing to me now. Oh, and how about my husband?"

"He's mine now," J'Aimee purred.

"And you're welcome to him," Grace said. Suddenly, she remembered something Ashleigh Hartounian had said during their first session of divorce-recovery group, something about her husband's new mistress.

"You are more than welcome to Ben Stanton, that lying, cheating piece of garbage. But here's something you need to know, J'Aimee. You are just like a cup of Publix yogurt."

"Huh? You're crazy."

"Nope," Grace said, starting to enjoy herself. "You, J'Aimee, are just like any other garden-variety skank. You've got an expiration date stamped on your bony little ass. But you won't even know when it's past—until Ben throws you out for something sweeter and newer."

Clearly, J'Aimee had no clever response. "Screw you," she said, her teeth clenched. "Leave my advertisers alone. Quit making trouble for Ben and me, or you will live to regret it." She turned to stalk away.

"No, screw you," Grace said. "Now get out of my house." On an impulse, she managed to land a kick, leaving a perfect impression of her bare foot in faux Farrow & Ball white on J'Aimee's black-clad butt.

For the rest of the morning, Grace fumed. What, she wondered, had prompted J'Aimee to seek her out here? She was obviously worried about her advertisers. Had one of the companies she'd e-mailed dropped their support for Gracenotes? Wouldn't that be poetic justice! When she fin-

ished with all the trim in the bedroom she struggled to
her feet and went to check the time.

It was nearly twelve thirty. There was a peanut butter
and jelly sandwich out in the kitchen, calling her name.
But as she was about to put her phone down, the screen lit
up with an incoming text from a number she didn't recognize, with a Bradenton prefix.

*Got some news about Paula. Meet me for lunch at
Rod & Reel Pier, 1 pm?*

Who is this? Grace texted.

Camryn. R we good?

She looked down at her messy clothes. She'd have time
to wash her hands and face, but not much more time than
that. Fortunately, the Rod and Reel was an open-air restaurant at the end of the fishing pier on Anna Maria. She could
go dressed as she was.

OK!

She almost didn't recognize the woman sitting at one of
the tables by the window. Most of the tables were full of
families, tourists, and anglers who'd spent the morning trying their luck fishing for trout or redfish on the pier. Finally, a lone woman in a floppy straw hat and sunglasses
waved her down.

"Camryn? Is that you?"

"You see any other black women loitering around here?"
Camryn snapped. She fanned herself with her hands.
"Lord, Jesus, I'd forgotten how hot it is out on this pier."

Grace shrugged and sat down. "You picked this place,
so don't blame me."

"I'm just sayin'," Camryn said. "I come here once a year
for the fried grouper sandwich. Best thing I ever put in my
mouth, but I try not to eat fried food, so I generally stay
away."

"Why the disguise?" Grace asked.

"I'm what they call a minor celebrity in this town," Camryn said. "When I first got in the business, I got a big kick out of having people come up to me at Dillard's or a restaurant. 'Ooh, you're the lady on TV.' Uh-huh. Then I gotta have my picture taken with 'em, maybe autograph something. And I swear, every time I step foot out of my house without makeup or my hair all looking nappy, that's when somebody spots me. You think I don't see them snapping pictures of me with their cell phones, telling their friends at work, 'I saw that Camryn Nobles on channel four at the gym, and girl! Without her TV makeup, she is looking old in the face.'"

"So on Saturdays, you leave off the makeup and wear a hat and sunglasses. Makes sense."

Camryn studied her. "If I went somewhere in this town, looking like you look right now, people would be tweeting and Facebooking my picture all over the Internet."

"I was painting a house when I got your text," Grace said, deciding not to be insulted. "There wasn't time to go home and change. So what did you find out about Paula?"

"Let's order first," Camryn said. The waitress took their orders: fried grouper sandwich for Camryn, mahimahi for Grace, unsweetened iced teas for both.

When their drinks came, Camryn sucked down half her tea. "First off, don't you think it's funny that a supposed marriage counselor is divorced?"

"Maybe not," Grace said. "After all, she's not counseling us on how to hang on to our marriages. She's helping us deal with breakups. So I guess it's not all that surprising that she's in the same boat. How'd you find out she was divorced?"

"I got tired of waiting for our silly little intern to do her job, so I made some phone calls myself. Did some googling, a little investigative journalism. To tell you the truth, I'd forgotten how much fun it is to dig up good dirt. Anyway, yeah. Dr. Paula Talbott-Sinclair has only been divorced a couple years. We already knew she'd been in practice in Oregon—Portland. I called one of the assistant producers at our network affiliate out there, and she knew all about our Paula."

Their food arrived, and Camryn picked up her sandwich, nibbled, and sighed happily. "I'll have to do an extra hour on the elliptical to pay for this, but it's worth every calorie."

Grace was surprised by how hungry she was, so they ate in silence for a while. Finally, Camryn finished her sandwich. She picked up the paper plate with the remaining curly fries and dumped them in a nearby trash bin. "I don't need the temptation," she explained.

"You said that producer knew something about Paula?" Grace prompted.

"Mm-hmm. Paula and her husband, Thorsen Sinclair, were in practice together. He was a psychiatrist; she was a therapist. Connie, the woman I talked to at KTXX, says they were pretty prominent, gave workshops all over the Pacific Northwest on 'mindful marriage,' whatever that is. They self-published a book with the same title. And everything was golden with the Sinclairs. Until he fell in love with one of their patients."

"Oh, wow." Grace breathed.

"Uh-huh. Both couples split up, and it made a nice little scandal, because the husband called the state board and filed a formal complaint against Thorsen and then leaked it to the media out there. Connie sent me a link to the story in the Portland paper. 'Mindful Marriage Melt-Down.' Long and short? Thorsen dumped Paula. After their divorce was final, he married the other woman. And Paula, apparently, fell to pieces. She 'borrowed' one of her ex's prescription pads and wrote herself a bunch of scrips for tranquilizers. But she got caught."

"Did she go to jail?" Grace asked, wide-eyed.

"It was a first offense, so the judge agreed to drop the criminal charges and allowed her to check herself into a rehab program for impaired health-care givers," Camryn said. "She must have completed it to the court's satisfaction out there, because Connie couldn't find any record of the arrest."

"Poor Paula," Grace said. "I guess she's been through the wringer, just like all of us. But how did she end up all the way out here?"

"Probably got sick of the rain. You ever been to Portland?"

"No."

"I don't actually know what brought her to Florida," Camryn admitted. "What I do know is, she only set up this divorce and life coaching business six months ago. And it seems like it's just barely legal—as long as she doesn't call herself a therapist or a marriage counselor. Which she doesn't."

"I see," Grace said, toying with a piece of lettuce that had slid off her mahimahi. "So—is Paula actually qualified to do what she's doing? I mean, I thought she was a quack that first week, but honestly, I think she really is trying to help us. And she has some real insights into what goes wrong with marriages."

"When she's sober or not having a 'family emergency,'" Camryn said, still clearly not convinced. "Her credentials are for real. I checked. Her undergrad degree is from the University of Washington, and she got a master's in clinical social work from Portland State. She belonged to a bunch of professional organizations in Portland and was even on the board of a center for battered women, until her life went to shit."

Grace drummed her fingernails on the tabletop. "Obviously, she's back on the pills, self-medicating. It's such a shame."

"She's a grown-up," Camryn pointed out. "Nobody's making her take those pills. What I want to know is, how did she and Stackpole get hooked up?"

"Good question." Grace considered the woman sitting opposite her at the table. "Camryn?"

"Hmm?"

"Why are you telling me all this?"

"You're a member of the group. It affects you as much as it does me."

"There are three other people in our group. You don't even like me."

"Did I ever say I don't like you?"

"Well, it's not like we're buddy-buddy. You've never called me and asked me to go to lunch or anything."

"I don't *do* lunch, Grace. You want to know about the glamorous life of a morning anchor in a third-tier market? I get up at five in the morning, get on the elliptical, haul my ass to the station. I'm in makeup at six, on air at seven. After I get off the air, I've got meetings, I read the wires, the online editions of *The New York Times, Wall Street Journal, Washington Post, Miami Herald*. Since I still do my own enterprise stories, I've got phone calls to make and interviews to set up, and lots of times I go out on remotes with a camera crew. I eat a take-out salad at my desk, go to some more meetings, make some more phone calls. Oh yeah, and I talk to my lawyer about this freakin' divorce and brood about being single again at my age. And that's my day."

Grace still wasn't convinced. "Why me?"

Camryn considered her over the top of her sunglasses. "Because other than me, you're the only normal person in this group."

Grace started to protest.

"Stop!" Camryn took off the sunglasses. "Wyatt doesn't count. He's a guy. A white guy, and I know it's a new century and we finally have a black man in the White House. And I should be better than this, but I still consider him the man. Ashleigh? Pffft. I won't even go there. You and I? Yeah, we did some stuff to our men, but they had it coming. Ashleigh is just all kinds of flaky. I wouldn't trust her any farther than I could throw her."

"What about Suzanne? She's shy, sure, but she's also smart and compassionate, and she seems to understand people."

Camryn shook her head. "No. I can't put my finger on it, but there is something definitely off about that woman."

"She's an introvert," Grace protested.

"It's more than that," Camryn said. Suzanne is damaged goods. Like it or not, Grace, it's you and me."

"You and me—doing what?" Grace said impatiently. "We don't definitely know that Paula and Stackpole are involved. She's not breaking the law billing herself as a divorce coach. I don't see us blowing the whistle on her because she's got a problem with pills. If anything, I think we should try to get her help."

"Help her?" Camryn looked disgusted. "Who's helping us? Who's helping us pay three hundred dollars a session for a 'divorce coach' who can't keep her eyes open for an hour at a time? Who's helping all those other poor women Stackpole sends to Paula for help? You ever consider that? I have. I hung around outside her office yesterday. Yeah. I saw what looked like three different 'divorce recovery' groups filing in there. Total of fifteen people. All women. I did the math. That's 4,500 dollars. In one day. Do you make that kind of money in one day? I sure as hell don't."

It didn't take long for that to sink in. "What do you want from me?" Grace asked.

"You said your lawyer went to law school with Stackpole? You trust her?"

"Yessss?" Grace said reluctantly.

"Talk to her. Ask her to sniff around. I'd ask my lawyer, but he's a man. And he's from Miami, went to law school down there. Balls of brass, great for negotiating your next contract at the station, but he's definitely not in the local courthouse pipeline."

Grace hesitated. "I'll ask Mitzi what she can find out, but in the meantime I've got an idea of what we can do to help Paula. But I'll need your help. The others, too."

"You bleeding-heart liberals," Camryn said. "What have you got in mind?"

"I'll e-mail everybody else in the group, let them know the plan. Wednesday night, assuming Paula shows up, we ambush her. Do an old-school Betty Ford intervention."

Camryn nodded thoughtfully. Put on her sunglasses, picked up the check. "I like it." She pulled her straw hat down so that it put her face in deepest shade. "Don't tell anybody else, but I like you, too, Grace Stanton."

"Davenport," Grace corrected. "It's Davenport now."

Grace watched while Camryn sped purposefully down the pier toward the parking lot. Had Camryn Nobles actually just befriended her? Were they in cahoots? Conspiring against Stackpole? Her life had just taken another unexpected turn. For the better, she hoped.

39.

Grace took the outside stairs to the apartment two at a time. She let herself into her bedroom and set Sweetie on her bed. She knelt beside the bed and whispered into the dog's silky ear. "I've got to take a shower and get ready for tonight. But you have to be really, really quiet, or the bad lady downstairs will kick us both out of here."

Sweetie blinked, gave Grace's nose a lick, then settled herself on one of Grace's pillows, with her head on her paws. By the time Grace emerged from the shower, the dog was asleep. She dressed quietly, in a pair of blue and white seersucker shorts and a scoop-necked white T-shirt that she'd found for a total of five dollars at the Junior League thrift shop.

She found Rochelle downstairs, behind the bar, refereeing a hot argument about politics between two of her regulars.

"You look nice," Rochelle said, raising an eyebrow. "Going somewhere?"

"I promised Wyatt I'd take him dinner when I drop Sweetie off for the night," Grace said.

Rochelle frowned. "Is that dog . . ."

"Sleeping in my room. Don't get your panties in a wad. It's just until I round up some food to take over there. He's got Bo tonight. What do little boys like to eat?"

"I never had a little boy, so I wouldn't know. But I can tell you what the big ones like. Meat. Fried things. Cheesey things. Anything with ketchup or barbecue sauce. Or jalapeños."

"Well, it's after five now, and I promised to have dinner there at six," Grace said. "So I don't have time to fix anything healthy from scratch. What are our specials tonight?"

"Wings. Crab burgers. Fried fish bites. Taco casserole."

"God help me, but the taco casserole hits on all the major male food groups," Grace said.

She went through the swinging doors into the kitchen and found the taco casserole on the steam table. Grace scooped up enough of the casserole to fit into a foil nine-by-twelve to-go tray and fitted it with a cardboard top. She was filling another foil tray with salad when Rochelle joined her.

"What about dessert?"

"Maybe just some fruit?"

Rochelle snorted. "If you're ever gonna land another man you've got to get over this healthy fetish of yours." She turned to one of the big walk-in coolers and lifted out a plastic-covered dish. "Never met a man or a kid yet who didn't love my brownie pie," she said, slicing off a huge slab and placing it in a large Styrofoam clamshell. Then she reached back into the cooler and handed her daughter a white can. "Whipped cream. You know what to do with this. Don't you?"

"Get your mind out of the gutter," Grace said primly. She sorted everything into a large brown paper sack. "Thanks, Mom. This will be great."

Rochelle raised one eyebrow. "Don't forget the damned dog."

* * *

Wyatt Keeler emerged from the shower to find the other male inhabitants of his home immersed in the Rays game. Nelson was stationed in his recliner command center, and Bo was sprawled on his belly on the floor, his face inches from the television. The room was a disaster. A mound of clean, unfolded laundry took up most of the sofa. Bo's mud-grimed T-ball uniform, underpants, socks, cleats, and sweat-soaked cap were tossed on the floor. The wood laminate coffee table was littered with three days' worth of newspapers; dirty dishes, including a half-eaten pot-pie; empty Coke cans; and the remains of their fast-food lunch.

"Hey, you guys," Wyatt started, but then he felt his bare foot impaled with a piece of sharp plastic. He stooped over and held up a yellow Lego. "Ow!"

"Dad!" Bo protested. "You messed up my Mega-Bot." He started to scoop up the scattered red, yellow, green, and blue blocks. "I've been working on this all day. Now I gotta start all over."

"Now you gotta clean up this mess," Wyatt told him. Nelson looked up from his chair.

"Both of you," Wyatt said firmly. "We've got company coming in fifteen minutes, so I need all hands on deck here. Bo, pick up all your Legos and stash them in their basket, where they belong. Get your uniform and put it in the laundry room, then clean up all this trash on the coffee table. Dad? Didn't you say you'd fold the laundry and put it away?"

"*You* said I'd fold the laundry," Nelson muttered, bracing his hands on the recliner's arms as he struggled to stand. "And what are you going to be doing while me and Bo slave away in here?"

"I'm going to clean up the kitchen, sweep the floor, and

take out a week's worth of garbage. I already cleaned and disinfected the bathroom, so don't either of you dare go in there."

"What if I gotta pee?" Bo asked.

"Take it outside," his father said.

"Who's coming over, the queen of England?" Nelson griped. He was folding T-shirts and shorts and underpants, matching socks.

"It's Grace, Dad's new girlfriend," Bo told his grandfather.

"Who told you Grace was my girlfriend?" Wyatt said. "I never said that."

"Well, she is, isn't she?" Nelson asked.

"Anna said it's okay for Dad to have a girlfriend, since Mom already has you know who," Bo commented.

"Remind me to have a discussion with Anna about minding her own business," Wyatt said. "In the meantime, just get busy, you two. She'll be here in, like, ten minutes. And she's bringing dinner, so be nice. And whatever she brings, pretend like you like it."

"What if she brings fried liver?" Bo asked. "Or lima beans?"

"Or tofu?" Nelson said darkly. "I'm warning you right now. I don't do tofu."

"If she tries to make me eat liver and lima beans, I'll blow chow," Bo said.

"She's not bringing liver or tofu," Wyatt said. "Just remember what I told you. Nice."

"I'm always nice," Nelson said under his breath. He looked over at Bo, who was busily wadding up the newspapers and paper bags and stuffing them under the sofa. "Aren't I always nice?"

Bo gave it some thought. "Mostly. Except when my mom calls."

* * *

Wyatt sprayed the chipped Formica countertops with Windex and surveyed the kitchen. He had no idea what Grace's reaction would be to his place. He knew she'd lived in some mansion, because he'd surreptitiously looked at pictures of the place on her old blog. It was huge, with something like five bedrooms and four bathrooms, a screening room, home gym, swimming pool, pool house. Hell, from the looks of it, her pool house was bigger than his crappy little double-wide.

Still, she seemed happy enough, working over at the house on Mandevilla, even admitting she'd fantasized about living there. Maybe she wouldn't turn around and run screaming into the night after she got a look at this dump.

At least it was a fairly tidy dump now. He'd picked some zinnias from the flower bed by the back door and stuck them in an empty jelly jar. The table looked okay, set with his mother's good dishes, the ones with little sprigs of blue cornflowers and gold edges. The silverware all matched, and there were paper napkins at every place, which was a huge step up from the usual roll of paper towels he kept on the table.

But there were only three chairs. How had he missed that? At one time, the dinette set had four chairs, but just a few months ago Bo had been leaning back in his chair when one of the back legs buckled and cracked. He'd meant to try to fix that. But it was too late now. He hurried through the house, looking for an extra chair. Nothing. In desperation, he went out to the carport, found an old plastic beach chair, and dragged it inside. He frowned. It was too short. He went out to the living room, where Nelson and Bo were again wrapped up in the baseball game. He snatched a throw pillow from the sofa and tossed it onto the seat of the chair, just as he heard a knock at the door.

Wyatt wiped his sweaty palms on the seat of his shorts and went to answer the door.

As Rochelle'd predicted, the taco casserole was a hit with the Keeler men.

"Pretty good," Nelson said, scraping a last bit of hamburger, tomato sauce, and cheese from his plate. He pointed at the nearly empty Pyrex dish Grace had used to warm up the casserole. "Is that a Frito?"

"Afraid so," Grace said. "Not very healthy, I know, but . . ."

Before she could apologize further, Nelson reached across the table and scooped up the last remaining spoonful.

"Dad loves Fritos," Wyatt said. "Almost as much as chicken potpie."

"Just the Marie Callender's ones," Nelson said. "Not Swanson. The Marie Callender's are more expensive, but I can usually find a coupon in the Sunday paper."

"Dad does most of the grocery shopping," Wyatt said. "He's a fiend for those coupons. Knows where all the best deals are."

Nelson beamed at the compliment. "Do you like baked beans? Because I've got an extra BOGO for Bush's baked beans at Winn-Dixie this week."

"What's a BOGO?" Wyatt asked.

"Buy one, get one," Grace said. "And yes, I'd love a coupon, if you've got an extra."

Dinner, she thought, had been a breeze. It was so cute, the way Wyatt had obviously gone to such pains to make a good impression. She looked down at her plate. "I know this china pattern. It's Bachelor's Button, right?"

"Uh, maybe," Wyatt said.

"That's right," Nelson volunteered. "It was our wedding china. Peggy picked it out. Blue flowers were always her favorite."

"Mine too," Grace confided. "Bachelor's buttons, or cornflowers, any shade of hydrangea, iris, those deep-blue pansies with the little clown faces . . ."

"Plumbago?" Wyatt said. "You like plumbago?"

"I love it, especially the ferny leaves," Grace said.

"I grow it in our nursery here," Wyatt said. "We could dig up some clumps and plant it at Mandevilla if you want, maybe a swath of it in front of the gardenias by the porch. The lighter green foliage would be a good contrast against the dark-green gardenia leaves."

"Great idea," Grace said. She looked around the table, beaming at the sight of all the empty plates. "I brought dessert, if anyone's interested."

"I'm interested," Bo said.

"You're interested in any kind of food," Nelson observed.

"Except liver and lima beans," the child said. "Gross."

Grace laughed. "I have to agree with you there. Totally, gag-me-with-a-spoon gross."

She'd sliced the brownie pie into generous squares and arranged them on one of the chipped white plates she'd found in the cupboard. Now, she set it in the center of the table. "My mom's brownie pie. It's her secret recipe, so I don't know what's in it, but we always sell out at the Sandbox."

Each of the males at the table immediately reached for a square. They were all munching happily.

"Bo, I meant to ask, how did your big T-ball game go today?" Grace asked.

"We lost," Bo said, spraying crumbs of chocolate over his plate.

"Not with your mouth full," Wyatt warned.

Bo chewed for a moment, then, his eyes on his father, carefully wiped his mouth with his napkin. "We lost to the stinkin' Pythons. Our archenemy."

"I'm sorry," Grace said.

"But we played great," Wyatt said. "Bo hit a triple and a double. And he hit a smokin' line drive that probably would have homered, except their third baseman, who I totally think is on growth hormones, because the kid is six and he's like six feet tall, made a diving catch."

"But then I struck out. Twice," Bo said sadly.

"Boy, you're batting four hundred," Nelson reminded him. "That ain't too shabby."

Bo eyed the last slice of pie on the plate, his hand hovering just above it, until his father nodded approval.

"Granddad, I'm four hundred for the week, three-fifty for the season. This kid on the Wolverines, he's batting six hundred. Scout's striking out, like, two kids an inning."

"Wow," Grace said admiringly. "You really do know your statistics. Your dad told me you're quite a math wizard."

"He's a freak," Wyatt said, gazing fondly at his son. "But he's our freak."

Bo looked longingly toward the other room. "The game's still on, Dad. Can I be excused?"

"After you two clear the dishes. And thank Grace for the dinner she cooked."

"Don't thank me," Grace admitted. "My mom fixed everything. I just carried it over here."

"Dinner was awesome," Bo said, gathering the dishes.

Nelson stood slowly. "Anytime you want to bring over some more of that taco casserole, please feel free."

Wyatt looked at Grace, who was starting to gather up the silverware. "That's Dad's job," he said. "It's not too hot right now. I thought maybe I'd take you on a tour of the park. If you're interested."

"I was hoping you'd ask," Grace said.

40.

The golf cart bumped noiselessly along the crushed-shell pathways, an occasional limb or branch slapping harmlessly at Grace's arm. The air was thick with humidity and the scent of damp earth and tropical flowers. It was twilight, and birds and squirrels twittered from the thick tree canopy. And from somewhere off in the park came an unearthly shriek that made Grace startle, so much that she nearly fell off the cart. "What was that?" she asked, clutching Wyatt's arm for balance.

"Peacocks," Wyatt said. "The bane of my existence. If only that damned coyote had jumped a peacock . . ."

"But they're so beautiful," Grace said. "So elegant."

"So noisy and cranky and a major pain in my ass," Wyatt said firmly. "People in the neighborhood around here are always calling the cops to complain that we're torturing animals over here. We can't make 'em understand that it's just normal peacock behavior."

"Why do you have them if you don't like them?"

"Jungle Jerry's has always had peacocks," Wyatt said. "The first pair, Ike and Mamie, were my grandmother's pets. After they died, we thought we were through with peacocks, but no, somebody was always 'gifting' us with new peacocks. People get them because they think they're such a classy addition to a garden or an estate. Then they hear that ungodly banshee screeching and they can't get rid of them fast enough. They don't even ask us. They just drop the damned things off in the parking lot in the middle of the night, like stray kittens."

He pointed to a huge banyan tree a few hundred yards ahead. "They like to roost there." The path wound around the tree and a clearing came into sight. It was ringed with flowering bushes, and a tall rose-covered arch was centered in a swath of grass.

"That's the butterfly garden," Wyatt said, pointing. "And the wedding chapel, in the middle there."

"How pretty," Grace said. "Do you get many weddings here?"

"Not so many lately," Wyatt said. "Couples seem to want to get married at the beach. Anyway, we don't have the kind of upscale facilities a lot of brides want. The only bathrooms are back at the gift shop, and they're not too glamorous. And let's face it, Jungle Jerry's ain't exactly a classy destination."

"That's a shame," Grace said. "It really is a lovely setting, with all the trees and flowers around, and that sort of meadow in the middle. You could bring in a tent and those fancy port-a-potties that are on trailers, with running water and everything. A good wedding planner could pull off an amazing event here."

"Know any?" Wyatt said gloomily. "Me neither."

The path made a sharp left and suddenly they were surrounded on both sides by a dense wall of bamboo. A light rain had begun falling, so she moved away from the open sides of the cart. Grace caught a glimpse of some kind of structure through the curtain of green.

"What's that back there?"

"That's what's left of Jungle Jerry's big-cat house," Wyatt said. He explained about his grandfather's short-lived career as a lion tamer, and how all the big cats had long ago left the premises.

"From what I've heard, they used to really pack 'em in for the shows," Wyatt said. "At one time we had a 'Safari Train' that ferried people from the parking lot back in here. It was really nothing more than a glorified tractor with a bunch of open cars tacked on the back. Dad sold the train for scrap after we farmed out all the animals more than twenty years ago. But the cages and the remains of the grandstand are still back there. Mostly rust and dust. He planted bamboo to try to provide a natural barrier, but he didn't really understand back then how invasive the stuff is. It's a constant, losing battle, trying to keep it from totally taking over every inch of the park."

"I had no idea what all was involved in running a place like this," Grace said, studying Wyatt's strong, stubborn profile. "I'm amazed you've been able to keep it running after all these years."

He turned and flashed her a rueful grin. "No more amazed than me. But it's not like I really had a choice."

Her hand crept across the bench seat and gave his forearm a squeeze. They rode along for several more minutes with nothing louder than the sound of the rain lightly falling and a breeze ruffling the bamboo until the path took a sharp left.

The bamboo hedge ended abruptly in a large field. Rows of flowers and young trees were laid out in straight lines. A tin-roofed shed was off to one side, under the shade of a large tree.

"This is my favorite place in the park," Wyatt said. "My nursery."

He pulled the golf cart up to the shed and jumped out. "We can hang out here 'til the rain stops." A moment later he was back with a pair of rubber boots. "It's pretty muddy," he warned, handing them to her. "You might want to wear these."

Grace slipped out of her sandals and plunged her feet into the boots, which were four sizes too big and reached nearly to her knees. She giggled as she climbed clumsily out of the cart, lumbering forward in the over-sized boots.

Wyatt offered her his arm to steady her. There was a picnic bench under the tin-roofed shed, and now he turned, reached under the seat of the cart, and produced a paper bag, which he handed to her.

Grace looked inside and found a bottle of wine and two plastic cups. "It's screw-top," he said apologetically. "But the guy at the liquor store swears it's good screw-top. You like red?"

"Sure," Grace said.

"One other thing." He picked up a can of insect repellent and sprayed his own neck, arms, and legs, and did the same for her.

Grace sat down on one side of the bench, and after a moment Wyatt sat beside her. He opened the bottle and poured a bit into the cup, handing it to her to sample.

"The guy at the liquor store was right. This is yummy." She held out her cup and he filled it, then filled his own. They sat with their backs to the table, looking out over the fields, slowly sipping the ruby-colored wine.

"What all do you grow here?" Grace asked.

"Annuals for the flower beds out front and throughout the park, some perennials and shrubs. I've got some saplings going that I started from seeds or grafts from our existing trees," Wyatt said. He nodded toward a row of palm trees at the far edge of the field. "I've had pretty good luck with the palm trees. Those are four years old."

"Isn't it a lot of trouble to grow all your own plants?"

Grace asked. "Especially with everything else you have to do around the park?"

"It's way cheaper than buying from wholesale nurseries, and anyway, I get a kick out of growing our own stock. It scratches my horticulture itch."

"Very impressive," Grace said, tapping her cup against his.

He fumbled in his pocket for a moment, then brought out a carefully folded sheet of paper. "I, uh, well, when I was thinking about you last night, after I got back home and couldn't sleep, I, uh, drew something for you."

She took the paper and unfolded it. "A landscape plan?" It was an elaborate pencil drawing of a garden, with hand-lettered botanical names. Looking closer, she saw "Mandevilla Manor" in neat block letters in the lower right corner of the paper.

"Some nights my mind won't shut up," he said apologetically. "I have to get up and draw. This isn't anything fancy. Just some ideas."

"I get like that, too," Grace admitted. "I'll wake up in the middle of the night with an idea for a recipe I'd like to develop or some crazy scheme for a house. Since I've been working over at Mandevilla, some nights I only sleep a few hours, I'm so stoked. I think that's how creative people operate."

"Callie always said it was how crazy people operate," Wyatt said.

Grace was examining the sketch. "So . . . no more lawn?" She pointed to the tightly packed rows of shrubs he'd sketched for the front yard.

"Very little grass," Wyatt said. "You could change that, if you wanted, but in Florida it takes so much in the way of water and chemicals to keep large chunks of grass healthy. I think it would look better to do these planting beds with native ornamentals, and maybe some seasonal annuals for color. Here," he jabbed a finger, "I'd do a crushed-shell parking pad, and then extend it to a path that winds through the flowers right up to your front door.

"I didn't have time to label everything, but since I know now that you like blue flowers, I'd give you lots of blues and purples, with whites and green and silver," he said.

"If it were my house, it would be perfect," Grace said, leaning over and giving him a peck on the cheek. "I'll keep it. Maybe eventually I'll have a house again, where I could plant something like this. Well, exactly like this."

"Why couldn't you just do it at Mandevilla Manor?" Wyatt asked.

"Arthur would never go for it," Grace said. "I'm still trying to talk him into springing for central air so I can get rid of those hideous rusting window units."

"It wouldn't be all that expensive to install this plan," Wyatt said. "Most of the plants I've drawn I grow right here in my nursery. The big cost would be in the gravel for the parking pad, the pavers, and the walkway. I get that all at wholesale cost."

"And what about the installation?"

Wyatt grinned. "I know a guy. He works cheap. Or in your case, free." He put his arm around her shoulders and drew Grace closer.

She returned her attention to the plan. "Whoa!" She placed her finger on an irregular shape on the plan. "Is this a pool? In the backyard? Are you kidding?"

"It's just a little dip pool," he said. "Nothing like you had at your last address. Nothing big enough to drown a convertible," he added impishly.

Grace gave him the side eye, and then giggled despite herself. She took another sip of wine.

"The backyard is so big at Mandevilla, it would be a shame not to take advantage of it, eventually," he said. "Everything on here could be done in phases. So, phase one is the front yard and trimming and defining the shrubbery on the sides of the house. Phase two would be getting the citrus grove in the backyard looking good. Paint that barn-slash-garage thing, plant some vines to grow on a trellis to try to minimize the scale of it. Phase three would be the dip pool. And the garage-barn is so big, you could section off part of it for a guesthouse. The side that faces the proposed dip pool, you'd put in French doors or maybe a cool, industrial-looking roll-up bay door to a space that becomes your pool house. At the same time, you'd probably want to put a pair of French doors in that bedroom that becomes the master, so you have access to your little private patio out to the pool courtyard."

"You are really, really good at this," Grace marveled, looking from the plan to him. "Everything you've drawn here, it just perfectly fits the scale and sensibility of that little Florida cottage. Nothing too grandiose, just right, so appropriate. I can actually picture all of it."

Wyatt's face shone with pleasure. "It's cool, you know? Creating something out of nothing? I miss the design aspect of landscaping. The rest of the park"—he gestured around—"it's pretty much a done deal. All I can do is try to keep the wheels on the bus."

Grace leaned her head back against Wyatt's arm and stared up at the deepening night sky. The rain drummed softly on the tin roof. "What if money were no object? What would you do here then?"

"If wishes were horses?" He snorted derisively. She nudged him with her elbow.

"Okay, well, I'd do more to emphasize the specimen plants my grandparents brought here from all over the world. I'd eventually phase out the bird show, but not Cookie, of course. She's part of the family. I'd maybe have a big demonstration garden, showing all the fruits and vegetables that we grow well in this climate. I'd love to work with local chefs, have an outdoor kitchen here and do cooking demonstrations using locally harvested produce and seafood and meat. I'd make the park less about tourism and more of a community resource. And, maybe, I'd even enlarge the nursery, make some of the plants we've grown here available to the public."

Grace sat up. "Those are wonderful ideas! Truly."

Wyatt shrugged. "It'll never happen. Not in my lifetime. But yeah, I've got my plans."

She gave him a level look. "Do I fit into any of those plans? Or am I just another complication?"

"You? You're not a complication. You're . . . ah, hell, Grace."

He turned and gathered her into his arms and kissed her softly.

"Mmm," she said after a while. "I do like your plans." Wyatt's arms tightened around her. His tongue tickled hers, and she wrapped her arms around his neck and flattened herself to his chest. A moment later, his warm hands slipped under her T-shirt, and then under the white camisole she wore instead of a bra. He grazed her nipples with his thumbs and she inhaled sharply and twined her hands through his hair.

"Is this okay?" he whispered in her ear. "Should I stop?"

"Never," she breathed.

His kisses grew more urgent as he pushed the fabric of her T-shirt upward. Grace let her hands slide slowly down his chest, to his waist; then, working them under his polo shirt, she flattened her palms on his bare chest, feeling the warmth, sliding her hands upward, brushing her fingertips across his nipples.

A moment later, by mutual, silent agreement, they were both shirtless. Wyatt pulled her onto his lap, kissing the nape of her neck, the hollow of her throat, cupping her breasts with both hands, teasing his tongue across her tightened nipples while she kneaded his shoulders, raking her nails across his bare back. Her breathing grew ragged as he kissed and caressed and, slowly, pushed her backward onto the picnic bench.

"Mmm," she protested, between kisses. "This isn't going to work, this bench is too skinny. We'll both end up in the mud."

He stopped what he was doing, then pulled her to her feet and, without warning, picked her up and plunked her atop the picnic table. She laughed but scooted back on her behind, and soon he was right there beside her, stretched out on top of the picnic table. He worked one thigh between hers, fumbling for the zipper of her shorts. She found his zipper easily, slid it down, and traced his erection with her thumb, while she pushed his shorts down. He was still groping with the button on the waistband of her shorts when she heard a soft buzzing and then a ringtone that sounded like "Take Me Out to the Ball Game" coming from the pocket of his shorts.

"Dammit!" he muttered.

She laughed. "Can't it wait?"

He sat up abruptly, pulling at his shorts. "That's Bo's ringtone," he said, grabbing the phone. "I gotta answer."

41

Hey, buddy, what's up?" Wyatt said softly, turning so that his back was to Grace. She rested her head on his bare shoulder.

The child whispered something incoherent.

"What's that? I can't hear you, Bo."

"I said, Mom called and she sounded really mad," Bo said, his whisper hoarse.

"Why are you whispering?" Wyatt asked.

"I don't want Granddad to hear," Bo said. "He told me not to call you, but I can tell he's all upset."

Wyatt held the phone away from his face and swore softly.

"What did your mom want?"

"She was yelling at me because she said you didn't tell her we had a big game today and she missed it."

Wyatt rolled his eyes. "We gave your mom a schedule of all the games at the beginning of the season, son. I'm sorry she yelled at you, but I'll call her later and we'll get it straightened out."

"Dad, Mom made me put Granddad on the phone when she got done talking to me. And he got super, super angry. He was yelling and saying bad words. Some of it didn't even make any sense. Now he's breathing kind of funny. Dad, can you come back? I'm kind of scared."

"I'll be right there," Wyatt said firmly. "Don't be scared. You did just the right thing to call me. We're just over at the plant nursery. We'll be back at the house in five minutes."

Wyatt stood and pulled his shirt over his head. Grace dressed hurriedly, straightening her hair, and packed the wine bottle and glasses in the brown paper sack.

"Do you want me to stay on the phone with you while we ride back?" Wyatt asked. Grace climbed onto the seat of the golf cart, and a moment later they were rocketing down the path.

"No, that's okay," Bo said.

"Where is Granddad right now?" Wyatt asked. "Is he awake? What's he doing?"

"He's just staring at the television, talking to himself," Bo said. "It's okay now. He's not dead or nothing."

Wyatt laughed, despite himself. "That's good news. I'm on the way."

"Bye."

Grace gripped Wyatt's arm. "I heard part of that. What's the problem? Is your father okay?"

"To quote my son, 'he's not dead or nothing,'" Wyatt said, his facial features taut. "Callie called to ream Bo out because she missed his game today. Then, after she'd finished making him feel like crap, she got on the phone and picked a fight with Dad. She knows just how to push his buttons. Apparently, he was yelling and ranting and raving at her, and of course Bo overheard all of it, and, naturally, it got him pretty worried. He says Dad is breathing funny, just staring at the television, talking to himself. Bo's a smart kid. I think he senses that Dad is starting to slip a little, and he's protective of his grandfather."

"Thank God for that," Grace said. "And thank God we weren't far away."

"I'll just pack up my stuff and get out of your way," Grace said, as the cart approached the double-wide.

"No! This is not how I wanted the evening to end," Wyatt said. "It's probably nothing. I'll get Dad calmed down and pack Bo off to bed. It'll be fine."

"You need to spend time with them, not worry about me," Grace said. "We can have other nights."

"Really? When? We both work all the time, and the rest of the time, my life is like this," he said, pulling the cart beneath the carport. "Just stay a few minutes, please? Just 'til I get these guys sorted out."

"I don't want to be in the way," Grace protested.

"You're not in the way. I promise," he said, squeezing her hand. "Your being there will probably make Bo feel a little better. He likes you."

"He just likes my dog," Grace said, laughing.

"Whatever works."

Bo met them at the door. He was dressed in his pajamas, and his freckled face looked worried. "Don't tell Granddad I called, okay?"

Wyatt leaned down and hugged his son. "It's a deal."

He walked into the living room, where Nelson sat rigidly in his recliner, muttering incoherently. His face was pale except for two scarlet patches on his cheeks. The television volume was turned all the way up.

Wyatt touched his father's shoulder. He found the remote control and turned the television down. "Dad? What's going on?"

Nelson didn't look up. "That woman got no right to talk to me like that. No respect. No morals. I told her that, too. Told her it looks bad for her son, her living in sin with that man. Did I cuss her out? Hell yeah, I cussed her out. Do it again, too, next time."

Wyatt sat on the sofa. "I'm sorry Callie got you so upset. I'll talk to her about that. But maybe it would be better if you just didn't speak to her at all."

"She called me!" Nelson shouted. "Didn't even know she was the one on the phone until Bo said his mom wanted to talk to me. I told Bo to tell her I was asleep, but she could hear me, and she insisted Bo give the phone to me."

"What did she want?" Wyatt asked.

"What she always wants. She wanted to raise hell with me. Wanted to know where you really were. If you were out with your new girlfriend. She claimed you didn't tell her about Bo's game because you wanted your girlfriend to go to the game instead of her. I told her if you did have a girlfriend it was none of her goddamn business. Then she wanted to know why Bo wasn't in bed, since it was after nine, which is his bedtime at her house. I told her it was Saturday night and there's no school tomorrow and I didn't give a tinker's damn what time he went to bed at her house."

Nelson's voice was rising, his breathing getting shallow. He waved his arms as he shouted, and from the corner of his eye, Wyatt saw Bo, standing, wide-eyed in the doorway. A moment later, Grace was behind him, gently shepherding him into the kitchen.

He leaned forward and grasped his father's arms, forcing the old man to look at him. "Okay, Dad, calm down. I am going to have a discussion with Callie and her lawyer, and tell them that she is not to talk to you anymore. All right? This isn't your fault. But you need to settle down. Did you take your blood pressure meds this morning?"

"What? Hell, who remembers that long ago?" Nelson grabbed for the remote control, but Wyatt held it out of his reach.

* * *

Bo sat at the kitchen table, clutching Sweetie in his arms. Huge tears welled in his dark eyes, and he was rhythmically kicking the chrome table leg.

Grace found the foil-wrapped remains of the brownie pie. She cut a generous slice and put it on a plate and poured a glass of milk, which she set in front of the little boy.

Without a word, Bo picked up a fork and took a bite. He gulped his milk and wiped his mouth with the back of his hand. Sweetie wriggled in his lap and licked his neck. Bo giggled.

"She just wants some of your pie, but we can't give her any, because chocolate isn't good for dogs," Grace warned. She gave Sweetie a mock-stern look. "What? Sorry, little girl. There are no leftovers when you feed three hungry single men." She looked around the room until she found the jar of dog treats she'd given Wyatt. She handed one to Bo, who offered it to Sweetie, who snapped it up without hesitation.

Bo ate a few more bites of the pie. He had a milk mustache and his ears were bright pink as he looked at Grace with open curiosity. "I think my mom is mad because I told her Dad took you out to ride around on the golf cart."

Grace nodded. "She's probably mad at me, not you. But that's understandable."

"She thinks you're Dad's new girlfriend."

"I wonder how she got that idea?" Grace said. "Your mom doesn't even know me."

Bo hung his head.

She laughed, leaned over, and ruffled his close-cut hair. "It's okay with me, but I don't know how your dad will feel about hearing that I'm his girlfriend."

"You're my new girlfriend?" Wyatt walked into the kitchen and swiped the last bite of pie from his son's plate.

"That's what Bo's mom apparently thinks," Grace said. She bustled around the kitchen, packing up the empty food containers.

"Hmm," Wyatt said, looking from Bo to Grace. He nodded at Bo. "Wonder where she got that idea?"

Bo's voice was very small. "I told her. She made me very, very mad when she yelled at me about the game. So I told her you have a new girlfriend who is really nice, and whose name is Grace, and who brought us taco casserole and chocolate pie. I told her I get to take care of her dog. And then I told her I do not want to move to stinking Birmingham."

"Okay," Wyatt said. He looked at the clock on the oven. "It's past your bedtime. How about you tell Grace good night and then go brush your teeth and hit the hay?"

Bo looked like he might put up a fight, but then thought better of it. "Is Granddad okay?"

"He's kind of tired right now, so he just went to bed," Wyatt said. "I think maybe he forgot to take his medicine this morning. Guess we'll have to do a better job of reminding him, won't we?"

"Yes, sir," Bo said. He set the dog down on the floor and stood. "Good night, Grace. Thank you for dinner." He thought for a minute, then added, "And for letting Sweetie stay here."

"I'd better get going, too," Grace said, watching the dog follow Bo down the hallway.

"I could make some coffee," Wyatt offered. "Don't run off just yet."

He poured them each a mug of coffee and sat opposite her at the kitchen table. "Sorry about all the drama," he said, taking a sip. His face hardened. "It's like Callie enjoys stirring up trouble. She hasn't been to a single one of

Bo's Saturday games this season. She's always too busy with Luke. Now, suddenly, it's my fault she didn't know about today?"

"It does sound like she's deliberately trying to provoke you, and Nelson," Grace observed. "The question is, Why? What does she get out of it?"

"I'm sure she's got an ulterior motive," Wyatt agreed. "But I have no idea what it could be. And I don't feel like investing a lot of energy trying to predict what her next move will be."

"Maybe just be careful with what information Bo gives her," Grace said. She felt her face warm. "So . . . it's official? I'm your new girlfriend?"

"I hope so," Wyatt told her. "Is that weird?"

"Not weird," she decided. "Different. New. I haven't been anybody's girlfriend in a really long time."

"It's new to me, too," he admitted. "Not at all what I expected when Stackpole ordered me to attend divorce camp."

"Speaking of," Grace said. "I had lunch with Camryn Nobles today."

"Camryn? Why? I didn't know you two were buddy-buddy."

"Neither did I. She's been doing some investigating. She found out Paula lost her therapist accreditation out in Oregon, after she got caught forging her ex-husband's name on some prescriptions for tranquilizers."

"No shit?"

"It's kind of a sad story." Grace filled him in on everything Camryn had confided in her at the Rod and Reel pier and about Paula's new career as a divorce coach.

"We know she's taking pills again," Wyatt said. "I wonder if they have something to do with her family emergency the other night?"

"I'm thinking the same thing," Grace agreed. "Camryn wants to report her to the authorities here. But what good does that do? I think we have to help her."

"And how do we do that?"

"I think we, that is, the group, have to confront her," Grace said. "Tell her we know she's self-medicating and that we know she was in rehab for the same thing. Maybe she'll open up and talk to us."

"Or . . . maybe she'll tell us all to fuck off and then rat us out to Stackpole for spying on her," Wyatt said. "And then we're all really, really screwed with the judge who has life-or-death jurisdiction over our divorces. Have you considered that possibility?"

Grace sighed. "Stackpole's the bad guy in all of this. I really think Paula is like us, another one of his victims."

"But we can't prove they're involved or that Stackpole is doing anything illegal, right?" Wyatt asked. "And in the meantime, it's hard for me to feel sorry for a phony therapist who's ripping us off."

"I disagree," Grace said lightly. "I just don't believe Paula is the one getting as rich as Camryn believes she must be. I'm going to call Mitzi tomorrow, just to let her know what we've found out about Paula. And I think we ought to at least let Ashleigh and Suzanne know what Camryn discovered."

She took her coffee mug and set it in the sink. "But now, I think I'd better head home. Thanks for a lovely evening, Wyatt."

He walked her outside to her car, his arm slung casually over her shoulder. "I just wish things had gone differently tonight. I wish . . ."

She turned and wrapped her arms around his neck. "I wish it, too. It was nice while it lasted, though."

He kissed her. "Nelson wanted me to apologize for him.

For ruining our 'date,' as he called it. He keeps asking me if we've slept together!"

"Oh my God," Grace said with a giggle. "I should not be telling you this, but Rochelle keeps asking me the same thing."

"So why haven't we?"

Grace arched an eyebrow in response.

"I'm a slow starter," Wyatt admitted. "But once I build up steam . . . I won't lie. I've been trying to figure out how we can be alone since last week."

"We can't be together at the Sandbox, that's for sure," Grace said.

"Ditto for here," Wyatt said, resting his hands lightly on her waist. "Bo and I share a room, and even on nights he's with Callie, Dad's room is right next door, and the walls in this trailer are like toilet paper."

"Poor us," Grace said mockingly.

"I'll think of something," Wyatt said. He lifted her chin and kissed her hungrily. "Soon. Very soon."

42.

The coffee shop was only two blocks from the Manatee County Courthouse in downtown Bradenton. The lunch-hour rush was over, and Grace and Mitzi Stillwell were alone at a booth near the front window, sipping watered-down iced teas while the hostess counted down the money in her cash register.

"I've got a little good news for you," Mitzi said. "After much arm-twisting and hand-wringing, I heard from Ben's lawyer today. You'll have your first check tomorrow."

"It's about damn time," Grace said. "How'd you manage it?"

"A combination of threats, nonstop phone calls and e-mails, and borderline harassment," Mitzi said. "It's not nearly enough, but it's a start."

"I cannot wait to buy myself a decent pair of shoes. And some new underwear," Grace added.

Mitzi gave Grace a critical glance. "You're looking good, Grace. I think the single life must suit you."

"Thanks. I'm busy, working on a house, and that makes

me happy. As for single life? Things are getting, um, interesting."

"Hmm. Interesting as in good?"

"Very good," Grace assured her.

"And how's Rochelle? Do you think she'll ever get back in the game?"

"Mom?" Grace looked puzzled. "Date? We've never discussed it. To tell you the truth, the idea of her going out never entered my mind. Why do you ask?"

"No reason," Mitzi said quickly. "She's not that old, not even sixty, right? My mom married her second husband at seventy, and when he dropped dead five years later, she picked right back up again. She's always got a guy in the wings. Rochelle's a very attractive lady, very young-thinking. I just think it would be a shame if she turned into one of those dried-up mean widow women you always see in every retirement community in Florida."

"Mom. Dating?" Grace couldn't quite seem to put the words together, in her mouth or in her mind.

"Never mind," Mitzi said. "Tell me how it's going in divorce-recovery group. Does your therapist seem to have recovered from her episode?"

"That's why I called you," Grace said eagerly. "Camryn—she's that reporter from channel four. Stackpole sentenced her to group after she put a video of her husband parading around in a pair of red satin women's thong panties up on YouTube . . ."

Mitzi coughed violently, and dabbed at her face with a paper napkin. "Oh my God! That's her husband? Camryn Nobles, News Four You? What's that song he's dancing to in the video? Have you seen it? It's hysterical!"

"No, I haven't seen it. Stackpole made her take it down," Grace said. "But listen to what Camryn found out about Paula."

* * *

"Really? I'm impressed. Camryn Nobles figured this out? I always thought she was just a pretty face. Who knew she could actually do real journalism?"

"Paula's not even a licensed therapist in this state. She gets around that by calling herself a divorce coach. Mitzi, she doesn't even have a Web site. So how did she get that successful that fast?"

"Her book?"

"It's only available as an e-book, and *Mindful Marriage*'s Amazon ranking is 367,459," Grace said.

Mitzi chewed on some ice. "Those people in the other divorce-therapy sessions, were they all women?"

"Yes."

"Well . . . if we knew that all of them were referred to Paula by Stackpole, that might be a very useful piece of information," Mitzi allowed.

"How could we find that out?"

"I guess you could ask them," Mitzi said.

"I think our group should have an intervention with Paula," Grace said. "We could confront her about the pills and her odd behavior. But Wyatt thinks if it goes wrong, it could make things even worse for all of us. With Stackpole."

"Wyatt?" Mitzi pursed her lips. "He's the guy we saw in court that day? The one who put his fist through his wife's car window? Are you two seeing each other?"

Grace blushed.

"Is it serious?"

"I hope so," Grace said quietly. "He's a good person, Mitzi. He doesn't deserve the crap his wife is handing him."

"I remember the wife from court. She was a terror."

"You don't know the half of it," Grace told her. "Wyatt is sick with worry that Stackpole will allow Callie to move to Birmingham with his son, Bo."

"About Stackpole," Mitzi said. "I've been asking around, very quietly. He and his wife used to be quite the social butterflies around town. She chaired the big Heart Fund ball last year, and they're members at the Longboat Key Club, where he plays a lot of tennis, but nobody's seen them out and about together much these past few months."

"Maybe the wife found out about Paula."

"Could be," Mitzi allowed. "Or maybe it's just that it's July. The Stackpoles have a house in the mountains in North Carolina. One of those woodsy, social places like Highlands or Flat Rock. I think she spends most of the summer up there."

"And while the cat's away, the rat will play," Grace said. "Mitzi, I just know Stackpole and Paula are having an affair. I can't prove it, but if you'd seen them that night when he showed up at group, it was just so obvious."

Mitzi stirred the dregs of her ice with her straw. "So what? You've only got two more weeks of divorce camp left, and then Stackpole will sign off on your divorce."

"I know," Grace said resignedly.

"Isn't that what we want? You—divorced? Free to get on with your life? Free to have a relationship with Wyatt or anybody else of your choosing?"

"The whole thing with Stackpole and Paula—it's wrong, Mitzi! And there's nothing I can do about it."

"You *are* doing something, Grace. You're building a new life for yourself. The financial aspect aside—I still haven't given up on that—I still think we can argue that you're entitled to your equity in the house since so much of the labor and materials were given to you as compensation for exposure on your blog . . . All that aside, you are doing what I preach to all my women clients. You are not letting this divorce define you. You're not letting bitterness defeat you. Grace, you're a rock star!"

Grace snorted. "I don't even have a place to shack up

with the new man in my life! So what kind of rock star does that make me?"

Mitzi's eyes lit up. "Ohhhh. So it really is getting serious with Wyatt. Why didn't you say something earlier?" She dug a key ring from her purse and extracted a key, which she pressed into Grace's hand.

"Here. This is to my condo at Anna Maria. My long-term tenant just moved out, and I'm converting it to a vacation rental. I've bought some furniture and had it painted and recarpeted, but that's as far as I've gotten with the place. Decorating is just not my thing. I've been planning on hiring a decorator to finish it, but maybe that's something you could do?"

Grace flushed and tried to return the key. "Oh, Mitzi, no. I couldn't. I really wasn't asking for your charity. I just needed to vent for a minute."

"I'm not trying to give you charity," Mitzi exclaimed. "I'll pay you, for God's sake! You'd be doing me a huge favor. The management company that's going to handle the rentals has been after me to get the place ready to be photographed for their Web site, but I hate shopping, and I suck at decorating. You'd be doing me a huge favor if you'd agree to fluff the place. Please?" She grinned. "It's not fancy, but there's a sofa and a bed and sheets and towels and a flat-screen television. What more do you need for a romantic evening? Say you'll take the job, and I'll stock the fridge with champagne and chocolate."

"I don't know," Grace demurred, but Mitzi grabbed her hand and closed her palm over the key. "You've got a credit card again, right?"

"Yes, with a five-thousand-dollar limit," Grace said.

"Great. So that'll be your budget for the condo. Five thousand will be enough to get some curtains and some rugs and doodads, won't it?"

"Sure, as long as I don't have to buy the big-ticket items

like mattresses or sofas or furniture, I should be able to fluff it for that much. When do you need it ready?"

"Like, yesterday, according to the property-management people. They wanted it done before Memorial Day, but that ship has sailed."

Grace gave it some thought. "Give me two weeks. Is that okay?"

"Works for me," Mitzi said. She reached into her purse and pulled out her checkbook. "Designers work on retainer, right? So, how much?"

"No retainer," Grace said firmly.

Mitzi's eyes narrowed. "Then give me back my key. Because I won't let you work for me for free. Listen to me, Grace. I have to remind my women clients about this all the time. Just because your spouse didn't recognize your worth doesn't mean you have no value. You're a professional interior designer, not some little dabbler who does this as a hobby. Don't devalue yourself by refusing to be fairly compensated. Now. What do you bill out at?"

Grace opened her mouth to argue, then closed it. Finally, she said, "Going rate here is about 125 dollars an hour, but since I won't actually be doing any sketches, and since it'll mostly be a matter of shopping and installing, I charge a hundred dollars an hour."

"Fine." Mitzi wrote the check and handed it to her client. "That's fifteen hundred. If you think it's going to take you more time than that after looking at the place, let me know."

Grace took the check and looked at it. It was written to Grace Davenport, her first paycheck under her born-again maiden name.

"Thanks," she said, her eyes shining with barely suppressed tears. And then she remembered the reason she'd asked for this meeting with her lawyer.

"Okay. What about Stackpole?"

"Oh, all right," Mitzi grumbled. "I'll take a look at his recent dockets to see what other attorneys I know have had cases before him. I'll ask around, to see if any of their clients have been sentenced to divorce camp with Paula Talbott-Sinclair. Satisfied?"

"Yes," Grace said. "Totally satisfied."

"In the meantime," Mitzi wagged a finger at Grace, "stay away from Wyatt Keeler's wife. That woman is trouble."

Grace shuddered. "Don't worry. I have no plans to get anywhere near Callie Keeler."

Wyatt Keeler spent the morning in his tiny office at Jungle Jerry's, staring at a mounting pile of bills. When his cell phone rang and he saw who was calling, he snatched it from his desktop.

"Betsy? Hey! How are you?"

"I'm fine. How's the rash?"

"Mostly gone, thanks to you. Guess I should listen to my elders more often."

"I'll have to remind you of that in the future," Betsy said drily. "Look, I won't beat around the bush. I just got a call from Callie's lawyer. They're asking Stackpole for an emergency hearing."

Wyatt's throat went dry. "What's the emergency?"

"Oh, Christ," Betsy said. "Promise me you will not go crazy when you hear."

"I won't go crazy," Wyatt said automatically. "Now tell me what's going on. Please."

He heard the sound of pages being turned. "Callie is now claiming that Nelson is suffering from acute dementia. Her filing says that when he is not confused and nonresponsive, he is verbally abusive and threatening, and he uses profane language in front of Bo, and he's capable of violence. In short, she's saying that as long as Nelson is living with you, your home is an unfit atmosphere for a child."

"What!" Wyatt put the phone down on the desk. He stood back and kicked his old army-surplus battleship-gray desk so viciously his work boot left a hollow impression in the bottom file drawer.

He sat back down and took several deep breaths.

"Wyatt?"

"I'm here," he said quietly.

"Do you have any idea what prompted this piece of garbage?"

"I do," he said grimly. He quickly recounted Saturday evening's events for his aunt.

"Well." Betsy sighed. "You and I know Callie deliberately provoked Nelson into a tirade. Is any of what she's claiming true? Is your Dad suffering from dementia?"

"No. Betsy, you know what Dad's like. He's slowing down, no question about it. Sometimes, usually in the evenings, he gets a little . . . foggy. And sometimes, again, usually when he's overtired, he can get a little verbally combative. But most days, he's still sharp as a tack. And he's a sweetheart, you know that. He adores Bo. Being around Bo, helping take care of him, it's given him a real sense of purpose. Of responsibility. And it's good for Bo, too. There is no way Dad is capable of violence. Ever! He might rant and rave at Callie, because as far as he's concerned, she abandoned us. But he would never act on his threats."

"That's what I think, too," Betsy said. "But this latest ploy has me worried. Stackpole really chewed her out last time around. I'm thinking she wouldn't risk annoying him again unless she thinks she really has something that will stick."

Wyatt buried his head in his hands. "Oh my God," he said softly. "This is like a nightmare that never ends. She really will stop at nothing."

"I know," Betsy agreed. "Stackpole wants to see us at eleven A.M. tomorrow. In the meantime, I went ahead and made an appointment with Margaret-Ellen Shank. She's a really well-respected geriatrician on staff at Sarasota Memorial. Fortunately for us, she had a really messy divorce a couple years ago, and I was able to help her out. Can you have your dad over there by four this afternoon? She's agreed to juggle her schedule to see him."

"I'll have him there," Wyatt said wearily. "But what do I tell him? He's gotta see a doctor to prove he's not senile so I don't lose custody of my son?"

"Tell him the truth," Betsy said. "I'll see you there."

43.

Arthur Cater stood on the porch staring into the doorway at the little cottage on Mandevilla. He wore an ancient T-shirt with chopped-off sleeves; shapeless, colorless green pants; and a dubious expression. He poked his nose inside the living room. He sniffed. His craggy face scrunched into some indefinable expression that threatened to give Grace an anxiety attack.

"What?" she asked. "What's wrong?" She'd spent all day Sunday using a rented floor sander to take the dirty, scuffed finish off the oak floors. She'd worked all night, mopping every last particle of sawdust before staining the floors a rich, dark walnut color. Her arms and lower back were still throbbing from her efforts.

When Arthur Cater called to casually announce his intention to drop by and check on her progress, Grace had only managed to stall him until after her meeting with Mitzi. Her stomach had been in knots all morning, wondering what Arthur's reaction would be to her progress.

Now she had it, and judging by the look on his face, the news was not good.

Suddenly, she got angry. And defensive.

"Arthur," she exclaimed, "it's just paint. If you hate it, I can repaint. But I wanted a higher contrast between the floors and the walls, which is why I chose the dark stain for the floors."

"Hush!" Arthur turned on his heel and walked rapidly out to the porch and into the yard.

Grace stared, speechless. Was he leaving?

No. A moment later he was back, carrying a bulky leather-covered camera. It was an old 35-millimeter.

He stood in the doorway and clicked the shutter. He walked into the dining room and snapped another picture. When he got to the kitchen, he stopped in his tracks.

"Well, I'll be damned." When he turned to Grace, his face was actually wreathed in smiles.

"You did all this?"

"I did," Grace assured him.

"By yourself?"

"With a little help."

He gestured at the secondhand Craigslist range, fridge, and dishwasher. "How the hell did you get those in there?"

"Some guys I used to work with back in my model-home days. Jimmy and Eduardo. I hired them to pick up the appliances in their truck and to install them. I don't do wiring, Arthur."

He gestured at the floor, with its gleaming red-checkerboard pattern. "What's that made out of?"

She gulped. "It's marine-grade plywood. The old linoleum tiles just were not coming up. So I nailed the plywood down, primed it, then taped off the squares and painted it with deck paint. Do you hate it?" She prayed he didn't. Her knees still had bruises from all the hours she'd spent taping and painting.

"It's good," Arthur said, nodding and flashing that rare-as-diamonds smile again. "Better than good. It's great. This floor—it looks just like the tiles my grandmother used to have in here. I'd forgotten that until just this minute."

"How about the open shelves?" Grace asked, still anxious for his approval. "The old cabinet doors were warped and gummy with all those old layers of paint, and the only way to clean them up would have been to strip them all down to the bare wood, and I just didn't have the time or the patience for that."

"Hush," Arthur commanded. He snapped two more pictures of the kitchen in rapid succession. "Wait until my wife sees this." He chortled. "She's said all along that we should just get rid of the darned cupboard doors. She even showed me a picture in one of her magazines, but I told her she was crazy. Just shows you how much I know."

He walked back through the abbreviated hallway and poked his head into both bedrooms, nodding and snapping more exposures.

"I can't believe it," he said, shaking his head. He looked over at Grace, still dressed in a simple cotton sundress for her coffee date with her lawyer.

"A little bitty gal like you got all this done, just like that," he said, snapping his fingers.

If only he knew, Grace mused, the untold hours she'd spent working on the house, for which she'd never be compensated—not in money, anyway.

"So, do you like it?" she asked.

"I do," he said, patting her shoulder awkwardly.

"There's still so much more to accomplish," she cautioned. "The bathroom vanity—I know I told you all the fixtures were okay, but the sink has a leak, and that vanity is all rotted out underneath. I'd like to replace it with a pedestal sink with more of a period look. And the tub—I've scrubbed it and scrubbed it, but it's pitted and chipped, and it's going to look even nastier once I get the bathroom painted. I'd love to have it reglazed."

"Do it," Arthur said expansively. He was in a rare mood, Grace thought. Maybe now was the time to spring the rest of her wish list on him.

She followed him onto the front porch, where he gazed out at the yard. "What the hell have you done out here?" he asked wonderingly.

Grace blushed. "I have a friend, he's a landscape architect, and he gave me some suggestions about cutting things back, reshaping the beds. There's a lot more I'd like to do in the yard, eventually. This house has such incredible curb appeal now, but it could be even better."

"It looks grand," Arthur said, and he was actually beaming. "It looks better than it has in twenty years. Not just the yard, everything."

"I'm so glad you like it," Grace told him. "Once I get some poly on those floors, they'll really look sharp. And then I was thinking, I could probably start furnishing it in the next week or so."

"Fine," Arthur said. "That sounds fine."

"About the air-conditioning, Arthur," Grace began.

He scowled.

Grace picked up a wooden paint-stir stick from her stack of supplies in the corner of the front porch. She poked the outside of the air-conditioning unit protruding from the living room window. A flurry of rust chips fell to the porch floor.

"The salt air has completely rusted this unit out," Grace said. "It's on its last legs. And the other units aren't much better."

"No ma'am," he said firmly. "Why, those units aren't that old. I put them in here myself."

"In 1982. I found the owner's manual in the hall linen closet. Arthur, these units are almost as old as me. They've outlived their useful life."

"Then I'll buy some new ones," he said, his face set in a mulish expression.

"You'll need five window units, at the very least," Grace said, consulting the notes she'd scribbled on her last shopping trip. "I checked at Sears and Home Depot, for the BTUs we need in the main rooms, meaning, the living room, dining room, kitchen, and both bedrooms, that's a little over two thousand dollars."

"Nonsense," Arthur said. "I can buy those units for under a hundred bucks apiece."

She handed him the most recent sales flyer she'd picked up at Sears. "Maybe thirty years ago you could buy them for that, but not these days."

He scowled down at the flyer. "I suppose you're going to keep after me about putting in central air-conditioning?"

"Yes, I am," Grace said emphatically. She handed him another brochure. "That's an estimate I had worked up by a very reliable HVAC guy who my mom uses at the Sandbox. It'll cost less than five thousand dollars! You'll get an up-to-the-minute energy-efficient unit, and there may be tax breaks involved as well. And, since you pay the utilities, there will be a substantial savings on your electric bills."

He ran a bony finger down the printed estimate, frowning. "I never figured to put all this much money in this little house." He looked up at her. "There's hardly any sense fixing it up this grand, just so the next bunch of tenants can come in here and ruin all our hard work."

Now, Grace told herself. Ask him now.

"About the next tenants," she said, fixing him with her most winning smile. "What would you say to renting this place to me?"

"Ah-hah!" he cried. "At last the other shoe drops. I should have known you had an ulterior motive for wanting me to spend all this money."

"I want you to spend what is really a very reasonable amount of money to maintain and improve this lovely property," Grace said, willing herself to keep calm and use all the arguments she'd gone over and over in her head. "I really didn't intend to ask about renting it, but then, once I got it cleaned up and saw just what a nice place it could be, it occurred to me to inquire about renting it."

His smile grew crafty. "All this money of mine you've been spending, you realize the rent's going up, right?"

"Of course. If you'll recall, that was one of the arguments I gave you for fixing it up. You've rented it so cheaply in the past, it's no wonder you've gotten deadbeats and low-lifes as tenants. But if you rent it to me, at a fair market price, I'll be a model tenant. I'll pay on time, every month, no excuses. I'll keep the property in pristine condition. And I'll continue to make improvements, provided you pay for them."

"Like what?"

He hadn't, Grace realized, said no yet.

"The kitchen still needs more work," she pointed out. "Better lighting, especially under the cabinets. There's that big dead space by the back door; I think it could be made into a nice laundry room, with a stacked washer/dryer and a shelf for folding clothes. All the windows need caulking, which should also help make the house more energy-efficient. The garage needs paint; it's a major eyesore. And then there are tons of little things. Like replacing all the nasty old electrical outlets, maybe installing ceiling fans in the bedrooms . . ."

"You love spending other people's money, don't you?" Arthur complained.

She ignored him and went on with her list of improvements. "My friend drew up a wonderful landscape plan for the yard. Did you know there are half a dozen fruit trees in the backyard? Lemon, lime, grapefruit, tangerines. He'll show me how to trim them and fertilize them so they produce again. I'd plant more flowers in the front beds, maybe do away with some of that grass . . ."

"Get rid of grass?" he squawked. "What do you want to do, pave the yard?"

"Not at all," she said calmly. "Maintaining all that grass takes so much time and energy, water and chemicals, my friend thinks flower beds might be a better solution. Oh, and did you know there's a sprinkler system out there?"

"Of course," Arthur said. "Not much good, since it hasn't worked in years and years."

"My friend thinks he can probably get it working again without spending much money," Grace said. "This could be the beauty spot in the neighborhood."

"Not to mention my water bill would go sky-high," he muttered.

"Come on, Arthur," Grace coaxed. "Quit making excuses for why it won't work. Won't you at least consider it?"

He folded the brochures and stuffed them in his back pocket. "I'll give it some thought," he said finally. "Have to discuss it with my wife. She's the real boss, you know."

"That's all I ask," Grace said. "Show her the pictures you took today, tell her my ideas, see what she says."

"Can't promise anything," he warned. "We're busy, getting ready to head up to the mountains."

"That's fine," Grace repeated. "Just let me know. And Arthur?"

"What now?"

"Thanks for the vote of confidence. I'm really thrilled you like what I've done."

Truegrace

One of my favorite old movies is Mr. Blandings Builds His Dream House. *Poor Mr. Blandings (played by*

Cary Grant) is a harried advertising copywriter living with his happy nuclear family in a cramped city apartment who just wants to build a simple little cottage in the country, but when the dream starts to take on grandiose proportions, Mr. Blandings's sunny version of utopia suddenly turns cloudy. I've thought of that movie a lot lately, as my own home life was dramatically disrupted, and then destroyed. Up until three months ago, I was living in a 6,500-square-foot mansion, that I thought was my own dream house. Now, with the clarity that only hindsight can bring, I realize that dream was mostly spun of high-fructose fantasy.

These days, I'm finding intense satisfaction in the transformation of a weather-beaten little 1,200-square-foot Florida "cracker cottage" into what I think will be a cozy jewel of a home—maybe even, eventually, my home. I feel a little like Goldilocks, who found one chair too big, another chair too small, but, finally, an exactly-perfect-fit chair that feels "just right." My work on Mandevilla Manor is far from done, but already it's feeling "just right."

44.

Nelson Keeler was having one of his good days. "God-damn it," he roared, when Wyatt told him of his impending doctor's appointment. "I do not have Alzheimer's! I'm fine! That scheming woman . . . you call up that judge, tell him I'll go to the courthouse right now. I'll recite the Declaration of Independence by heart, balance my checkbook, balance his checkbook, and then I'll drop and give him fifty, by God!"

"No, Dad, that's all right," Wyatt protested, but it was too late.

Nelson proceeded to do just that, right there in the living room of the trailer, flattening himself on the floor, doing fifty straight-arm push-ups, counting aloud in a wheezy voice, then sitting up, cross-legged, wiping his perspiring brow with the sleeve of his shirt.

"How many other seventy-four-year-olds you think can do that?"

"None." Wyatt gave his father a hand up. "I know you've got all your marbles. But we've got to prove it to the judge, and to do that, you've got to go see this doctor and get a bunch of tests done. Just remember, you're doing this for Bo, not for Callie."

"Callie!" Nelson spat the name. "Somebody should have knocked some sense into that woman years ago. When this is all over, I'm gonna . . ."

Wyatt steered his father toward the door. "When this is all over, we're gonna laugh about it, but until then, neither of us can afford to do or say anything that might make anyone believe we're a couple of dangerously violent misfits. Right, Dad?"

"If you say so," Nelson muttered.

"One more thing," Wyatt said. "If you're going to convince this doctor, and then the judge, that you're harmless, you've got to keep your temper under check. This means no debating Alex Trebek or the designated-hitter rule. And it especially means no discussion of your bowel movements. Right?"

"Unless the doctor asks," Nelson countered.

"But only if she asks."

It was after six o'clock. Nelson Keeler was sitting upright in a chair in the doctor's office, snoring.

"He's had a really long day," Wyatt told Margaret-Ellen Shank. "He gets up at six, always has, and some nights he doesn't sleep all that well. He usually has a midday nap, but he didn't get that today."

"No need to apologize," Dr. Shank said, her voice soft. "Your dad is quite a guy. I really enjoyed meeting and talking to him today. One thing. What's his diet like?"

Wyatt shrugged. "Dad has a sweet tooth. He likes Pop-Tarts or Twinkies for breakfast. He might eat some canned soup for lunch, and a lot of nights he'll have a frozen chicken potpie for dinner. Or, and I'm not proud of this, a quart of ice cream or some more Twinkies."

Dr. Stark was still making notes. "What did he have for lunch today, do you know?"

"I don't," Wyatt admitted. "I was out in the park working until right before time for his appointment with you."

She frowned and consulted her notes. "Your dad has good balance and coordination, is able to communicate clearly, and his short- and long-term memory seemed to be in an acceptable range for his age. But as the day wore on, his personality changed drastically. I'm not an endocrinologist, but I think there really is a good possibility that your dad might be suffering from diabetes."

Wyatt stared at her. "So . . . you don't think he has Alzheimer's?"

"We'll need to take a look at all the test results, but my initial impression is that he does not. Your Aunt Betsy called him cantankerous, but I'd prefer the word 'spirited.' He clearly adores you and your son and is not an admirer of the boy's mother."

"That's putting it mildly," Wyatt said. "As far as Dad is concerned, Callie is the enemy, because she wants to move to Birmingham and take Bo with her. And, of course, she's now trying to prove that he's senile."

"He's pretty adamant on that subject," Dr. Shank said, smiling. "And I can't blame him. By the way," she added, her eyes twinkling, "I don't agree with him on the subject of Alex Trebek. At all. I think he's every bit as intelligent and talented as Art Fleming."

Wyatt let out a sigh of relief. "We've got to meet with the judge at eleven tomorrow morning. Is there any way you can give us some kind of report?"

She glanced at her watch. "I'll fax over something by ten tomorrow. Will that work?"

"That would be great," Wyatt said, jumping to his feet and pumping her hand. "I can't thank you enough,

Dr. Shank. For seeing Dad so quickly and, just, everything. You've been a huge help."

Margaret-Ellen Shank leaned over and tapped Nelson
gently on the shoulder. "Mr. Keeler?"

Nelson yawned widely. "What's that?" he asked grog-
gily.

"It's nearly seven o'clock," she told him. She offered her
hand; he took it and stood slowly.

"I told Wyatt you need to eat more sensibly," she said,
giving him a look of mock disapproval. "No more Pop-
Tarts for dinner. Right?"

"Right," he agreed.

45.

Grace heard the muffled pinging of an incoming text coming from somewhere beneath the towering pile of merchandise in her shopping cart. She shoved aside the quilt with its vivid orange and green chinoiserie print, the four turquoise and green quilted throw pillows, the green and blue striped dhurrie, and the stack of turquoise and white polka-dotted bath towels.

The pair of green chevron-striped shower curtains she'd bought for the condo's dining room windows slid off the top of the stack and onto the floor. Finally, burrowing deep down into her pocketbook, she brought up the phone.

The text was from Camryn Nobles.

Where r u?

HomeGoods. What's up?

While she waited for a reply, Grace studied the store's furniture selection. Mitzi Stillwell's kitchen had an island crying out for barstools. Here were a pair of barstools with a perfectly acceptable look, clean lines, and a great price, $59.99 a pair. The problem was that they were white. And that was the problem with Mitzi's condo. Every single thing in it was white.

The walls were dead white. The tile floors were white. The sectional sofa in the living room was white, the pair of armchairs facing it was white, the sheer draperies hung from the floor-to-ceiling windows looking out at the sparkling blue Gulf of Mexico were white. In the kitchen, the countertops were white Corian, with a white subway-tile backsplash. The master bedroom had a king-sized bed with an upholstered, tufted white headboard and footboard. The carpet was an off-white flat weave. The guest bedroom featured a pair of twin beds with no headboards at all, just an expanse of white quilted-cotton bedspreads.

Just thinking of all that arctic white made Grace shiver. Maybe, she thought, running a finger over the back of one of the barstools, she could paint the stools a high-gloss tangerine.

Her phone dinged again with a reply from Camryn.

Been digging into Stackpole's financials and hit paydirt. Lunch?

Grace shook her head, annoyed. She had just begun shopping for Mitzi's place. She still needed lamps, bed-spreads for the guest bedroom, and a new chandelier to replace the hideous builder-brass one in the dining room—and art. And those was just the accessories. She still needed dining room furniture, dressers for both bedrooms, coffee tables and end tables . . .

Can't it wait til tonight? she typed. With her pocket calculator, she began adding up the tab for the merchandise in her cart. She frowned. She was already at $431.99, not counting the two barstools.

Another ding interrupted her mental mathematics.

Got good stuff. How 'bout meet @Sandbox @2?

Grace shrugged and typed.

See u there.

* * *

Cedric Stackpole drummed his fingers on his desktop. He looked down at the faxed report from Dr. Shank, then up at Nelson Keeler. "Mr. Keeler? I understand you are a Vietnam veteran, is that right? In what branch of the service did you serve, sir?"

Was this some kind of trick question? Nelson looked to his son for some kind of signal, but Wyatt remained expressionless.

"That's correct, Judge," Nelson said finally. "I was in the army. Fifth Infantry. Did two tours, managed to get home in one piece. How about you?"

"Er, no," Stackpole said. "I like to think that my time in the judiciary is of some small benefit to my community. But I thank you for your service to this great country."

"You're welcome," Nelson said. "I got drafted, so it wasn't like I had a choice or anything."

Stackpole looked at Nelson over the rim of his glasses. "I understand you had some kind of verbal altercation recently with your daughter-in-law?"

"Altercation's a big word for what we had," Nelson replied calmly.

"Your daughter-in-law is saying that you did use strong language in your conversation with her. In fact, she says you actually threatened her. Did your grandson hear you making threats against his mother, hear you using strong language?"

"I reckon he did," Nelson said, his chin dropping. "I'm ashamed of that, Judge. Ashamed I let her get me riled up like that. And I'm here to promise, I won't let her get my goat again. No sir."

Betsy Entwhistle cleared her voice. "Judge? If I may?"

Stackpole gave her a curt nod.

"I'd just like to point out that Mrs. Keeler is not charging that Nelson Keeler has ever neglected or in any way harmed his grandson. Because he hasn't, and he wouldn't.

And if you've read Dr. Shank's report, you can see that Mrs. Keeler's assertion that Nelson is suffering from dementia or the onset of Alzheimer's disease is totally untrue."

Betsy took a deep breath. "Dr. Shank is waiting on the rest of the test results, but she believes Mr. Keeler's occasional, er, bellicosity, could be simply the result of low blood sugar. In fact, she's suggested that Nelson Keeler might be suffering from diabetes, which could be responsible for all these symptoms Mrs. Keeler seems to want to believe are Alzheimer's."

The judge glanced over at Nelson Keeler and considered the old man sitting in the armchair across from him.

Nelson's thinning gray hair was neatly trimmed and combed. He wore a pair of navy dress pants, a white dress shirt that he hadn't donned since his late wife's funeral, and a pair of well-polished black lace-up dress shoes.

"I'm not senile," Nelson volunteered. "There is nothing in the world wrong with me, except maybe a little sugar diabetes, and I told the doctor I'd get that checked out and lay off the Pop-Tarts."

"You do that," Stackpole said finally. He closed the file folder. "I'm going to tell Mrs. Keeler and her lawyer that for now, I agree with your Dr. Shank. It appears to me that you have all your mental faculties and that you pose no threat at all to your grandson."

"Good!" Nelson exclaimed. He pulled himself to a standing position and extended a hand to the judge, who took it, somewhat reluctantly.

"Judge," Betsy said hurriedly. "This is the second time in as many weeks that Mrs. Keeler and her attorney have launched one of these baseless attacks on my client and his father. I hope this will reinforce our argument that it is not in Bo's best interest for you to allow his mother to move her son out of state and away from his father's care."

"You've made your point, Ms. Entwhistle," Stackpole said. "I'll take it under advisement."

Camryn Nobles was sitting at their regular corner table at the Sandbox, with Rochelle seated right across from her, their heads nearly touching, deep in conversation.

Grace dropped down into a chair beside her mother. "I'm starved," she announced. "What's the lunch special?"

"Shrimp burger, tuna melt, gazpacho," Rochelle said.

"Gazpacho?" Grace raised one eyebrow askance.

"My produce supplier gave me a whole bushel of tomatoes with bad spots, for next to nothing," Rochelle said. "Do you have something against gazpacho?"

"I love gazpacho," Camryn said. "Unless it's got green peppers, which don't agree with me."

"This recipe is straight off Grace's Web site," Rochelle said. "No green peppers. Cucumbers, garlic, cilantro . . ."

"You read my blog?"

"When it's interesting, which I occasionally find it is," Rochelle said.

"You bought cilantro?" Grace's second interruption was a clear annoyance to her mother.

"Yes," Rochelle said. "And I peeled the cucumbers, just as your recipe specified, for your information. With, I might add, a garnish of diced avocado and shrimp. Now, is there anything else?"

"No," Grace said, somewhat meekly.

"Would you like a bowl of gazpacho?"

"Yes, please," Grace and Camryn said in unison.

When they'd spooned up the last traces of cold soup and drained their iced tea glasses, Grace and Camryn sat back in their chairs.

"That was pretty damned good," Camryn said with a sigh.

"Better than my original recipe," Grace admitted. "But she'll never tell me how she changed it."

"Mothers," Camryn said, in unspoken agreement.

"Yeah," Grace said. "Now. What kind of dirt did you dig up on Stackpole?"

Camryn reached for her Yves St. Laurent tote bag and extracted a sheaf of computer printouts.

"Judge Cedric N. Stackpole Jr.," she said, with a flourish, "is in debt up to his pointy little ears."

Grace rubbed her hands together gleefully. "Oooh. Goody. Do tell."

"This is a list of bank-foreclosed properties I pulled from the county's Web site," Camryn said, tapping a fingernail on the first sheet of paper on the stack. She ran her finger down the columns of tiny print and then jabbed one line, highlighted with a yellow marker.

"See here? 1454 Altadora Way, unit C. Siesta Key." Her finger trailed down the page until it stopped at another yellow-highlighted line of print. "1454 Altadora Way, unit B." Grace's eyes skipped down to the next line, which she read aloud.

"1463 Altadora Circle, unit A. But the mortgage holder is listed as Solomon Holdings," Grace said, squinting at the fine print.

"Solomon, as in, wise King Solomon, biblical judge," Camryn said, deadpan. "I looked it up. C. N. Stackpole is the sole corporate officer of Solomon Holdings. And then I took a ride over to Altadora Commons. It's a development of new town houses not far from his address on Longboat Key. I'll tell you a funny coincidence. I didn't realize it until I pulled up in front of the complex, but I actually looked at one of those town houses with my real estate agent, right after I kicked Dexter out of the house. Prices aren't bad, for Siesta, the unit I looked at was a resale, and they only wanted 575,000 dollars, but it was still way too pricey for my budget, and besides, I didn't like the floor plan."

Camryn leafed through the pages of documents until she found one she wanted, a computer printout of a real estate listing for Altadora Commons. The picture showed a series of tasteful cream stucco two-story town houses with orange stucco barrel-tile roofs, and a not-so-tasteful billboard seemingly mushrooming from a postage-stamp-sized lawn that proclaimed, "Bank Owned. Prestige Homes at Distressed Prices!"

"Wow. And Stackpole owns three of these?"

"Judge Stackpole? Your divorce judge?" Rochelle had come up behind them while they were studying the printouts. She leaned over Camryn's shoulder, staring at the photo of Altadora Commons.

"That's right," Camryn told her. "According to my real estate agent, the original sales price, back in 2007, was between 875,000 and 1.6 million dollars for the biggest units, which were actually two town houses joined together. Then, well, you know what happened to real estate around here. You couldn't give a town house away. Stackpole bought three units from the developer, at what looked like fire-sale prices, in 2010. He paid 420,000 dollars apiece. Which would have been a great deal . . ."

"Except?" Grace asked.

"Except that the county's tax digest was reworked in 2011, and now those units are only appraised at 120,000 apiece," Camryn said, sounding absolutely elated. "He's underwater, in a major way."

"But he can't be broke," Grace objected. "He lives at Longboat Key, and you told us his wife's family has gobs of money."

"The wife's family has money. Stackpole doesn't have

squat," Camryn said. "I checked. The house is in her name. And incidentally? It's apparently a lot bigger than it looks from the street. It's on the market for 3.2 million."

Rochelle had eased herself onto a chair. "Bring me up to speed here, Camryn. What does any of this mean to you and Grace?"

"It's just a wild theory we've been tossing back and forth," Grace cautioned.

"It's not a wild theory," Camryn said, tapping the documents on the table. "These printouts prove it. Stackpole's in debt. His wife has money, but he probably can't touch it. He's having an affair with Paula Talbott-Sinclair, and one of them comes up with the idea to mandate women going through his divorce court to seek counseling from Paula, his girlfriend. She gets to soak each of us three hundred dollars per session, for a total of six sessions. There are five people in our group alone, and on the one day I watched her office, I saw three other groups arriving for divorce counseling. Do the math, Grace. They're getting rich off our misery."

"You should do a story about this on the news," Rochelle said excitedly. "Blow the lid off the whole big scam."

"I intend to," Camryn said.

"Isn't it a conflict of interest for you to report on a story you're involved in?" Grace asked.

"It'd be a first-person piece," Camryn said. "And if the story's big enough, I don't see how my station manager can turn it down."

"Look, I'd love it if we could prove those two were in cahoots," Grace said. "But I talked to Mitzi about this yesterday. Even if you did see all those people going into Paula's office, how do you know they didn't go there of their own free will?"

"Can't you just ask her other patients whether or not

Stackpole ordered them to attend therapy with her?" Rochelle asked.

"I wish," Camryn said. "I told you I hung around outside Paula's office last Friday. What I didn't tell you was that she apparently saw me standing there in the parking lot. She came outside and asked me what I was doing! I made up some lame story about looking for a diamond earring I'd dropped Wednesday night but I think she realized there was something fishy going on."

"Mitzi did say she'd take a look at Stackpole's dockets and talk to any attorneys she knows that have had divorce cases before him," Grace said.

"But who knows how long that will take?" Rochelle demanded. "We need action!"

Grace gave her mother the look. "What kind of action would you suggest?"

Rochelle thought. She smiled. She walked away from the table, and when she returned, she brought a handful of flyers, which she offered to Grace.

*Come play in the Sandbox. Good for one free
appetizer or drink*

"I remember these. Dad hired kids to put them on car windshields at the new Publix, right after it opened."

"Until I made him stop, because we were nearly run out of business, giving away all those free drinks and stuffed potato skins," Rochelle said.

"So?" Grace asked. "Am I missing something?"

"I'm not. Rochelle, if you ever get tired of running this bar, you might have a future as an investigative reporter. This," Camryn said admiringly, "is brilliant."

"I still don't get it," Grace said, looking from one woman to the other.

"It's simple," Rochelle said. "Tomorrow morning, I go over to Paula's office. I watch cars pulling up and pay attention to who goes inside. Then, I plaster these coupons all over their windshields. When they bring in the coupons for their freebies, you two swoop in and ask them what you need to know."

"And how do you know they'll use the coupons? Or when they'll use them?" Grace asked.

"I'll just write on the bottom of each coupon that the deal's good for one day only," Rochelle said. "Trust me. Nobody turns down a free drink in this town."

46.

Paula Talbott-Sinclair clasped her hands together prayerfully as she stood in the front of the room. She took a deep breath and let it out so s-l-o-w-l-y that the members of the group all subconsciously held their own breaths, wondering what would happen next.

"Hi, friends." Her voice was clear and unusually calm. "I want to start our session tonight by talking about personal responsibility." She looked around the room. "All of you are here, in a way, because you were forced to take personal responsibility for some action you took against your partner.

"Ashleigh, you were stalking your husband's new lover. You vandalized her home in what was a very terrifying and thoughtless act of vengeance.

"Wyatt, you punched out the window of your wife's boyfriend's car so violently that you smashed his window and injured your own hand.

"Grace, you deliberately drove your husband's car into a swimming pool and destroyed it.

"Camryn, you discovered a provocative and salacious

video of your husband and put it on YouTube, thus exposing him to public ridicule and humiliation."

Paula nodded at Suzanne. "Suzanne, we've all been very patient, waiting for you to admit to us the actions you took that caused you to join this group. Because I'm such a strong believer in personal responsibility, I've been reluctant to force your hand. Up until now."

Suzanne lifted her chin. "I'm ready, Paula. I want to tell the group . . ."

"Are you sure?"

"No," Suzanne said, with a nervous laugh. "I'll never be ready. But I'm willing, and that's the best I can do."

"Did I tell you all that Eric, my husband, is also a professor at Ringling?" Suzanne didn't wait for a reply. "He's in the English department, too. Anyway, I discovered, by accident, that he was sleeping with a co-worker, a woman who'd been my grad assistant last year."

"How'd you figure it out?" Ashleigh asked.

Suzanne's smile was wry. "Modern technology. Eric had gone out for a run. I was doing the laundry and found his phone in the pocket of his pants. As I was putting it on the counter, it pinged, and I saw he'd gotten a text. Darby was at soccer practice, and she was supposed to text one of us to let us know she was on her way home. I just assumed the text would be from her, so I read it. It wasn't from Darby. It was from her."

"The other woman?" Camryn asked.

"Yup. I'll spare you the nitty-gritty. Let's just say she was suggesting a time and place for their next assignation. 'Come horny,' the text said, so that let me know I wasn't overreacting. Just to be sure, I scrolled down the other texts from her. They were all just as graphic, if not more so. And it had been going on for months."

"Did you confront him?" Grace asked.

"No." Suzanne's hands shook as she uncapped the bottle of water she'd been clutching all evening. "I . . . I guess a part of me still didn't want to believe it was true. But another part of me, the cold, analytical researcher, needed data. While I was going through his phone, reading the texts, I found texts from other people, women, but I had no idea who they were."

"He had more than one girlfriend?" Camryn asked. "Just like my cheating husband."

"It gets better, or worse," Suzanne said sadly. "I went online and found something called keystroke software. It's a program you can surreptitiously load onto somebody's computer, and once it's activated, everything that person does on their computer, every e-mail they write or receive, every Web site they visit, you have access to."

"You became your own private detective," Camryn said. "That's so smart!"

"Not really," Suzanne said. "Remember, Camryn, when you said you wished you could take Scopolamine, to for get about your daughter catching Dexter in bed with her roommate? Well, I learned so much about Eric's secret life, I wish the data bank in my head could be wiped clean. But I'm afraid now it's hardwired into my brain."

She took a sip of water. "Those other women? He was meeting them on Craigslist! For hookups."

"Dear God," Grace muttered.

"Exactly," Suzanne said. "He was meeting strange women in sleazy motel rooms for casual sex. And when he wasn't meeting them in person, they were sexting back and forth. It had been going on for years."

"That's just nasty," Ashleigh said. "At least Boyce . . ."

Camryn reached over and grabbed Ashleigh's arm. "Let Suzanne get through this without editorializing. Okay? Otherwise, I will have to pinch your head off of your scrawny little neck." Ashleigh jerked her arm away.

"Camryn?" Paula's voice had a warning note.

Camryn glared at Paula. "I am dead-dog serious. I will hurt her if you do not make her be quiet."

"And I'll help," Grace offered, glaring, in turn, at Ashleigh.

"Everybody?" Suzanne looked amused. "I'm fine. Really. I've been living with this for months and months now. Now? I don't want this slime taking up any more room in my brain. You know?"

They all nodded in unison. They all did know.

"You wouldn't think this could get worse," Suzanne said with a self-conscious laugh. "But it does! Not long after I found out about Eric, I had a regular checkup with my gynecologist, and I had an abnormal pap test."

She looked at Wyatt and blushed. "I'm sorry you have to hear such personal stuff. About my lady parts. But there's just no way to get around this."

"I'll survive," he said, his voice gruff.

Suzanne took a gulp of water. And then the words came tumbling out in an unstoppable torrent. "I had HPV. I didn't even know what it was. My doctor—the same doctor who delivered Darby, who's known me since I was a teenager, had to explain it to me. It was an STD. A sexually transmitted disease."

Grace had to clamp her hand over her mouth to keep from gasping aloud.

"Eric . . . having unprotected sex with those women. He'd given me an STD. I thought I would die of humiliation, the day my doctor told me. Of course, he was as embarrassed as I was. Long story short, I had cervical cancer.

"I had a total hysterectomy, because my husband gave me a sexually transmitted virus. Which, incidentally, could still come back, as something like anal cancer. My doctor had been quietly urging me to tell Eric what was going on, so he could at least notify the women he'd had sex with. You know, so they could see a doctor. I was so calm on the outside, it was frightening. I scared myself. One day, a week before I was scheduled for surgery, I went on Craigslist. I posted a picture of Eric and advised that any woman who'd ever had a hookup with him should get themselves checked. Because he had an STD. And they were at risk, too."

Suzanne gulped more water. "Then I texted my colleague at the college. I told her I knew about her and Eric. But here was a piece of news she wasn't privy to. And I told her. The day I was scheduled to have my surgery, I told Eric what I'd done. And I told him I wanted him out of our house by the time I got home from the hospital."

"Does Darby know?" Camryn asked. "Why you split up?"

"No," Suzanne said. "I couldn't do that to her. It's bad enough I have this stuff in my head. She's only eighteen. I don't want her hating men for the rest of her life. I don't even want her hating her father."

"But   " Ashleigh sputtered. "You let Eric off the hook. He doesn't even have to take responsibility for what he did!"

"He's not off the hook," Suzanne said. "His girlfriend filed a grievance against him with the college, and he was fired. One of the women he met on Craigslist claims he gave her HPV, too, although I don't know how someone who's in the habit of having unprotected sex with strangers can ever figure out how she got an STD. She's hired a lawyer. And so it goes. I think it's safe to say his life is ruined."

"And yours isn't?" Wyatt's face was pink with indignation. "I'm sorry, Suzanne. As a man, I'm sorry. As a husband, I'm sorry." He looked at the others. "We're not all like that. I swear."

"I know you're nothing like that, Wyatt," Suzanne said. "And I don't think every man is like Eric. But you're wrong about one thing. My life isn't ruined. I'm not about to give him that power."

"Right on, sister," Camryn said fiercely.

"Thank you, Suzanne," Paula said quietly. "I can see now why you needed time to find the words to tell your story. We're all full of admiration for your honesty. Right, friends?" She started clapping her hands, slowly, until the others in the semicircle joined in. Paula motioned for Suzanne to stand, and she hugged her. One by one, the others stood and joined the group hug, awkwardly at first, and then, as the moment grew, they stood together, their first real campfire moment.

The members of the group drifted back to their chairs. Paula went on.

"We're in week five of our sessions, and we've got lots of work yet to do before we conclude next week. Tonight, I'm going to ask all of you to think about writing an action plan.

"It's a sort of manifesto for yourselves," Paula explained. "You're all starting a new chapter of your lives. I'd like you to put some thought into how you'll move forward, personally and professionally, physically and emotionally, in a really mindful way."

She glanced at her watch. "This has been pretty intense tonight. Let's take a ten-minute break, and when we come back, we'll talk. Okay?"

Camryn blew her nose. "What's Suzanne's action plan gonna be, Paula? What's she gonna do, grow a new cervix?"

47.

Wyatt was the first one to arrive at their table at the Sandbox. He pulled Grace's chair out for her, letting his hand rest, just for a second, on her arm. "Thanks," she said, shooting him a quick, private smile.

Rochelle was at the table in a shot, bringing a pitcher of beer and menus. "Where are the others?"

"They're on their way," Wyatt told her. "I've got a feeling we're going to need a lot of alcohol tonight, Rochelle. In fact, why don't you go ahead and bring Suzanne whatever it is she usually orders?"

"God, yes," Grace said emphatically. "I think she drinks wine spritzers. And I'm gonna need a big old glass of wine myself."

"Why?" Rochelle asked eagerly. "Did something happen tonight? To Suzanne?"

Wyatt's voice was solemn. "Suzanne finally shared tonight. Her husband was having unprotected sex with total strangers he met through Craigslist. He gave her an STD."

"You mean, like venereal disease?"

"Something like that," Grace said. "Only this disease

can't be cleared up with penicillin. Suzanne had to have a hysterectomy because of it, and it could still come back."

"Sweet Jesus, Mary, and Joseph!" Rochelle exclaimed. "This really happened to our darling Suzanne?"

"Yes. And she just pulled into the parking lot, so please don't mention it. I mean it, Mom. Not one word."

"I would never," Rochelle said indignantly. She sketched a quick cross on her chest. "So help me."

Suzanne looked from the wine spritzer sitting on the table to Grace. "Thanks." She took a sip. "I needed this."

"You were amazing in group tonight," Ashleigh said, leaning across the table.

"You're our she-roe," Camryn chimed in. "You're like a divorce superhero."

Suzanne sipped her drink. "Not at all. The rest of you spilled your guts that first awful night of group session, when we were all total strangers. It's taken me five weeks to get up the nerve. I'm the biggest wimp in the world."

"No, you're not," Wyatt said. "You're . . . an inspiration."

"Okay, enough," Suzanne said. "You're going to make me start blubbering again. Can we please talk about something else? Anything else?"

Camryn and Grace locked eyes, then looked away. But their expression didn't escape Ashleigh.

"What?" she cried. "You guys know something. Come on, spill. Is it about Paula?"

Grace shrugged. "Camryn found out some stuff about Paula's past."

Suzanne regarded Camryn carefully. "This has something to do with why Paula isn't licensed to practice therapy in Florida, doesn't it?"

"Yeah," Camryn said, surprised. "How'd you know?"

Suzanne hesitated. "Okay, one more thing I've been

keeping from you guys. I swear, it's the very last secret. Or, the last one that concerns you. Here it is. Stackpole didn't send me to Paula. I came on my own."

"You mean, you came voluntarily? Why would you do that?" Ashleigh asked.

"After I found out what Eric had done, I was so angry, in such a rage, I scared even myself," Suzanne said. "I had all these awful ideas about how to get my revenge. Fantasies about physically harming him. That's when I knew I had to get help. I went online and googled divorce and therapy and Sarasota, and Paula's name popped up.

"After that first night, I knew there was something off about Paula. Her credentials are actually pretty impressive, but she's very careful not to advertise herself as a therapist or a marriage counselor. She just calls herself a divorce coach. Which got me to wondering."

"Why'd you even keep coming to group after that first night? Or even after the second night, when Paula passed out cold?" Grace asked.

Suzanne looked at the faces sitting around the table. "By then, I knew it wasn't really about her helping me. You all had shared your stories. I knew you were hurting as badly as I was, and I thought maybe you'd help me find a way to deal with this horrible sadness and bitterness that was engulfing me. Turns out, I was right."

"Awwww," Ashleigh said, beaming. "That's so sweet."

"But Paula's helped me, too," Suzanne said. "In her own way. Of course, that doesn't mean I'm not curious about what you discovered, Camryn."

"Okay," Camyrn said. "Here goes."

Rochelle brought another round of drinks, but Suzanne pushed hers away, untouched. "I did wonder if it was something like that. Paula's not a bad person, you know. Just . . . damaged. Like all of us."

Ashleigh was not convinced. "You mean, I'm paying three hundred dollars an hour to get counseling from a convicted drug addict?"

"Recovering drug addict," Grace said. "And remember, Paula doesn't call herself a counselor or a therapist. Just a divorce coach. And who better to coach people through this kind of crap than somebody who's been through it herself?"

"I still think it's a rip-off," Ashleigh insisted. But a moment later, she lowered her voice. "But I don't even care about Paula anymore. I don't even care about that stinker Judge Stackpole. I've got news, y'all. Boyce called! He wants to meet me for lunch next week. And here's the best part. We're meeting at the Ritz!"

"I've never eaten at the Ritz-Carlton," Rochelle said, alighting on an empty chair next to Ashleigh. "Is the food as good as they say?"

"Oh, Rochelle, you're so cute," Ashleigh said, with her tinkling laugh. "Do you know, I've never actually eaten there? As far as I'm concerned, lunch at the Ritz is totally not about the food."

"It's not?" Rochelle looked puzzled.

"Now you're going to make me tell all my naughty secrets," Ashleigh said. She cupped her hands and whispered in Rochelle's ear.

"Ohhh," Rochelle said knowingly. "Now I get it. The Ritz-Carlton is like a high-priced no-tell motel."

"Exactly." Ashleigh giggled.

"Did he say why he wants to have lunch?" Grace asked.

"He didn't have to," Ashleigh said. "It's perfectly clear. He wants me back! I wasn't going to tell y'all this, but since it's kind of a moot point, I will. I saw Suchita, that's his girlfriend, leaving Boyce's office the other day. She's getting fat! And Boyce does not DO fat. He's a plastic surgeon, and appearances have always been important to him." She looked around the table, pausing when she saw Camryn's face.

"And before you say one word, let me just say that I don't intend to let him wriggle off the hook that easily. I mean, please! I do have my pride. I mean to make him pay for what he put me through. Boyce doesn't know it yet, but he's going to be buying a major piece of jewelry to make it up to me."

"Ashleigh," Grace said, "have you really thought this through? You know Boyce was keeping a mistress. You know he cheated on his first wife when he started dating you. What makes you think he won't do it again?"

"Yeah, baby," Camryn said. "I'm sorry, but I do not see this tiger changing his stripes."

"It's different with us," Ashleigh said. "Boyce never loved his first wife. Ever. Their marriage was a joke. I didn't have to break it up. It was already a done deal. So yes, Boyce cheated on me. I've accepted that. Hasn't Paula been yammering for weeks now about acceptance and finding peace?"

Suzanne patted Ashleigh's hand. "We just don't want to see you get hurt again."

"I'm *not* going to get hurt," Ashleigh said. "This is a love story. Plain and simple. Happy ever after. Is that so hard for y'all to believe?"

"It's not that I don't believe it," Camryn said. "It's just that, so far, I've never experienced it."

Ashleigh tossed her hair over one shoulder. "Rochelle, you're my side, right? And you were married a really long time to Grace's daddy, right? Will you please tell these people that there is such a thing as a happy marriage?"

Rochelle pressed her lips together. "Sorry, honey, that's one thing I wouldn't know about." She looked over Ashleigh's head, her eyes focused on the bar. "Dammit, there's Miller and Bud again, taking up space and hogging the popcorn." She stood. "Next thing you know they'll be having their welfare checks forwarded here. I've gotta go chase them off."

Grace watched her mother hurry away. What was that crack about not knowing anything about happy marriages? She thought back to all the barbed remarks Rochelle had made recently about Butch. At some point, Grace thought, she and Rochelle needed to sit down and really talk about this stuff. Butch had been dead three years now. Was there something about her parents' marriage Rochelle had been keeping from her?

"Grace?" Suzanne waved a hand in front of her face. "Earth to Grace. Come in Grace."

"What?" The others were looking at her expectantly. "Sorry, guess I zoned out for a minute there."

"I was just asking what you thought about Paula's assignment. You know—the action plan?"

"I think it's a good idea," Grace said. "I know for myself, after I walked out on Ben, I was really sort of . . . rudderless, I guess would be the word."

"Paralyzed," Camryn agreed. "After I kicked Dexter to the curb, I couldn't make the simplest decision. And y'all know that is not like me. I pulled through Starbucks one morning, and when the barista asked if I wanted extra sugars, I just burst into tears."

"I already know step one of my action plan," Ashleigh confided. "As soon as I get rid of that Suchita hag, I'm taking my old job back as Boyce's office manager. And let me tell you, I'll be the one doing the meetings with those cute little drug reps from now on."

"I'm sort of undecided," Suzanne said. "Darby's been offered a chance for early enrollment at Elon, a small liberal arts college in North Carolina. Their soccer team was

NCAA runner-ups last year, and the head coach personally flew all the way here in the spring to watch Darby play. She turned it down, saying she couldn't imagine missing her senior year of high school, but I think the real reason was that she didn't want to go away and leave me alone so soon after Eric and I split."

"Your daughter sounds like a great kid," Wyatt said.

"I don't know how I got so lucky with her," Suzanne said. "The Elon coach is still calling the house, begging Darby to reconsider. They'd like her to come out right now, to start practicing with the team. Selfishly, I wish she would stay home, finish her senior year, and then go off to college. I want one more year of fixing her breakfast and washing her stinky practice clothes every night! But realistically, there's no reason why she shouldn't do early decision. Darby's a bright kid. She's taken enough Advanced Placement classes at her high school that college work won't be that much of a challenge. This is a terrific opportunity for her."

"Then let her go."

Their heads swung around in unison. Rochelle stood with her hands on the back of Suzanne's chair. "I know, it's none of my business. But it sounds to me like you already know what you should do."

Suzanne swiveled around in her chair. "Thanks, Rochelle. I guess that gives me step one of my plan. Now I just have to persuade Darby that her mother isn't as needy as she thinks."

"I hate to admit that Paula may finally have a good idea," Camryn said. "But what she said tonight does make sense. I've been thinking a lot lately about my career at the station, and where I want it to go."

"You're not thinking of moving, are you?" Grace asked.

"You obviously don't know much about the television news business. Women don't move to other markets at my age. At least, not voluntarily. No, this little bit of investigative journalism I've been doing has been a real kick. I've actually been thinking this might be a good time to go off-camera. Maybe consider producing." She grinned widely. "I've always been great at telling other people what to do."

"What about you, Grace?" Ashleigh asked pointedly. "What would be your step one?"

"I've already taken it," Grace said. "I've asked Arthur, the man who owns the house I've been restoring, if he'd let me rent it. If he says yes, I could move in within a week or so."

"You're moving?" Rochelle looked stricken.

"Don't turn my bedroom into an office just yet," Grace warned. "Arthur didn't seem all that wild about the idea, but he didn't say no. He said he'd have to talk it over with his wife. But I'm hopeful."

48.

Grace mopped the floor while Rochelle counted down the cash register and bundled up the money for the morning's bank deposit. She double-checked the front door to make sure it was locked and flipped the switch for the neon sign. Then, she went behind the bar, poured herself a glass of wine, and took a seat on the barstool next to Rochelle.

"It's after one," her mother said, looking up from her counting. "I don't mind the company, but you've been getting up and leaving pretty early most mornings lately."

"I'll go to bed in a little while," Grace said. "Can I ask you something?"

"Hmm?" Rochelle was jotting figures in the ledger where she always recorded each day's tally. "This divorce group of yours is good for business. Last year, this same date, we did eighteen hundred dollars. Today, we did twenty-one hundred. And the softball guys didn't even have a game tonight."

Grace closed the book. "Mom, what did you mean earlier, when you said you didn't know anything about happy marriages?"

"Nothing," Rochelle said casually. "You know me, sometimes I run my mouth without thinking."

"Sometimes you do, but I don't think that was the case tonight. Lately, you've been dropping these little . . . I don't know, hints? Is there something about you and Dad's marriage that I don't know?"

"Your dad's dead and buried, Grace. That's all old history."

"I don't think so," Grace said slowly. "Come on, Mom. Be honest with me."

Rochelle took off her reading glasses and buffed them on the hem of her blouse. "Your dad was a good man, Grace. He loved you beyond all reason and was so proud of you and the life you were building. That's what's important for you to know."

"Nuh-uh," Grace said, shaking her head. "There's more to it than that. Ever since I started this divorce-recovery group, you've been hanging around, super interested in everything everybody has to say . . ."

"I'm a nosy old lady," Rochelle said.

"What was going on with you and Dad? Whatever it is, I need to know."

Rochelle let out a long sigh. "Since you insist, I'll tell you. Four years ago, I was ready to divorce your dad. I'd hired a lawyer. I'd even found an apartment to move into. And then we found out he was sick. I couldn't walk out on him like that. He was dying. So I stayed. End of story."

She saw the stunned expression on Grace's face. "I'm sorry, honey. I really never meant for you to hear this, but you asked, and I just couldn't keep dancing around the truth any longer."

Grace felt like she'd had the wind knocked out of her. "Why? What did Dad do? Please don't tell me he had another woman."

Rochelle opened the ledger again. "Some things are best left unsaid, you know? And this is one of them."

"Just tell me, please? So, he had an affair? Was it somebody I knew?"

"It was nobody. A snowbird from Buffalo whose husband used to keep a boat here in the marina during the winter. Her husband died the summer before, and she was down here by herself, and I guess . . . she got lonely."

"Oh, God." Grace felt physically sick. Her father? Butch? The same guy who wore loud Hawaiian shirts and loved country music? The man who gave both Rochelle and Grace the same Whitman Sampler of chocolates every Valentine's Day? Butch had a girlfriend?

"It didn't last very long," Rochelle said quietly. "Your dad was a lousy sneak."

Grace swallowed hard. "How . . . how did you figure it out?"

"He was acting funny. Not like himself. You know how Butch was; he liked his set routine. But that January, he switched barbers. After twenty years of the same haircut, he grows sideburns, for God's sake. He started taking an extra shower, in the middle of the day. You know how I always went to the wholesale house for supplies, right? Well, suddenly, he insisted he should be the one to go pick up our order. He'd be gone two, three hours. One time, he came back without the paper napkins and take-out containers. He had some lame excuse that they were out. Of paper napkins?" She shook her head. "He never did have much of an imagination."

"I don't know what to say," Grace said. "You must have been devastated."

"Mad as hell, more like. Because he'd promised—promised on his mother's grave—he wouldn't put me through that crap again."

"Again? It wasn't the first time?" Grace found herself

staring into her own image in the mirror behind the bar, and then at herself, and then at Rochelle, and at Rochelle's image. Who were these strangers?

"No. Not the first time." Rochelle's lips were set in a grim smile. "You were only three the first time he cheated. I found out then, and I left. I took you to my cousin's house in Jacksonville, and we stayed three weeks. Butch was heartbroken. He couldn't stand the idea of not having his baby girl around. He knew he'd messed up. He begged me to take him back, said he'd be a different man. And he was, for a long time."

"I just . . ." Grace swallowed hard. "I don't know what to think. You never said a word. The two of you never fought. My friends' parents were splitting up while we were in high school, and they used to tell me they envied me, because Butch and Rochelle—you know, Butch and Rochelle were solid."

Rochelle reached out and stroked Grace's hair. "Maybe I should have divorced him back then, after the first time. But where would I have gone with a little kid in tow? I had no real job skills; certainly I didn't have any money. And I was too proud to admit to my parents that I'd made a mistake. So I did the easy thing. I went back to Butch. And I stayed."

"All those years? When I thought you guys had the model marriage? That was all a lie? You only stayed together because of me?"

"It wasn't *all* a lie," Rochelle said. "We had some good times. We made a life here, had friends. Had you. I don't want you to think it was a bad life, Grace, which is why I never told any of this to you."

"You could have told me. Especially once I was an adult. I would have understood," Grace said. "It makes me sad to think that you were that unhappy, and I was just . . . oblivious."

"You weren't oblivious. You were busy, spreading your wings, starting a career. A marriage. But now I think, I wonder, if I didn't set you up for failure by giving you un-realistic expectations of your own marriage. Does it make me pathetic, how much vicarious pleasure I got seeing what an amazing woman you were becoming?"

"You've never been pathetic," Grace said. "But what made you finally decide to leave?"

Rochelle fidgeted with her glasses. "Besides Edwina? That was her name. Edwina! I'd say it was just a slow build. One morning, Butch was fussing at me, because I'd bought Chock full o'Nuts instead of Folgers without consulting him."

Grace rolled her eyes. "God. Dad and his coffee."

"I picked up the whole bag of beans and dumped it in the trash. I walked upstairs, packed a bag. When I got downstairs, he looked at me like I'd lost my mind. 'You're leaving over a bag of coffee?' So I looked at him and I said, 'It's not about coffee. It's about Edwina.'"

"Did you think about going to counseling?" Grace asked.

"I went to counseling. Your dad refused to go. He thought it was a waste of his hard-earned money."

"That sounds like Dad," Grace said with a sigh. "I still can't believe you got as far as hiring a divorce lawyer with-out telling me. Wait a minute. Mitzi? Mitzi was the law-yer you hired?"

Rochelle nodded. "You and Ben hadn't been married that long at the time. You were deliriously happy. I didn't want to upset you. And then, of course, we found out how sick Butch was. I wasn't even gone a week."

"Did he beg you to come back?" Grace asked, teary-eyed now, thinking about her father's last months of life, growing thinner, using a walker, and then, finally, a wheelchair.

"Butch? Never. He didn't have to ask. I knew he needed me, so I came. We never even discussed that week. It was like it never happened." Rochelle got a glint in her eye. She laughed.

"What's so funny?" Grace asked.

"Nothing. I was just thinking about the coffee. When I moved back here, that first morning, I went out to the kitchen to make coffee. There sat a brand-new bag of Chock full o'Nuts. That was Butch's idea of an apology."

Grace laughed until the tears were rolling down her cheeks. "Mom? You know what I remember that last year? When Dad was so sick? You were so strong. You kept the bar running, took him to all his doctors' appointments, to chemo. You bathed him and spoon-fed him when he was too sick to eat, fixed his bed in the living room so he could look out at the water those last few weeks."

Rochelle blinked back her own tears. "He made me promise I wouldn't let him die in the hospital. It was a small enough thing to do."

"So you forgave him?" Grace searched her mother's face for an answer.

"You know? I guess I did," Rochelle said, wonderingly. "At the time, I told myself I was doing it for you—because he was your daddy. But now, I think maybe I did it for me. I hated what Butch did—cheating on me—but I guess at the end, even after everything, I did still love him."

"I'm glad you told me," Grace said. "Thanks for that, Mom."

49

Good morning Grace. Don't know if you'll remember me, but you and I had some dealings a few years ago when I was an assistant to Lily Soo at House Beautiful. I'm now features editor at Veranda, and I've been following your new blog and your new project with such delight. We think our readers would love it, too. Wondering if we might discuss having you write and photograph a monthly feature about your progress at Mandevilla Manor? Can't wait to discuss! All best, Doreen Zelen. P.S. Adore that checkerboard kitchen floor!

Grace read the e-mail three times, just to make sure it wasn't a figment of her imagination. Then she tucked her laptop under her arm and went running downstairs to the bar.

Rochelle was directing the beer-delivery guy into the storeroom. "Mom!" Grace cried.

Her mother whirled around, knocking her cup of coffee to the floor. "What is it?"

"*Veranda!* They want to hire me to write a series about

Mandevilla. Can you believe it? I've subscribed to *Veranda* since forever. And they want me!"

Rochelle grabbed a bar towel and dropped it to the floor, mopping the spilled coffee with her sneaker-clad foot. "Honey, that's fantastic!"

"I know," Grace said. She was hopping up and down with excitement. "*Veranda!* This is a dream assignment."

"How about some breakfast?" Rochelle asked. "You can tell me all the details and I'll cook you some eggs and bacon."

"Can't," Grace said. "I've got to get over to the cottage and get to work. I want to be able to move some furniture in by the end of the week so I'll have some new photographs to show Doreen; she's the *Veranda* editor who e-mailed me. I did a freelance piece for her years ago, when she was at another magazine. I was supposed to stop and pick up Sweetie, but I'm going to text Wyatt and see if he'll drop her off. Talk to you later!"

Arthur Cater was sitting on the front steps of the cottage on Mandevilla when she pulled into the driveway.

"Arthur!" Grace called, as she crossed the lawn. "I'm so glad you're here. Wait 'til I tell you my news."

As soon as she got closer, she saw by the expression on Arthur's face that something was terribly wrong. His face was streaked with what looked like soot, and he suddenly looked like a very, very old man.

"What's wrong?" she asked. "Is it your wife? Is she sick?"

"My wife is fine," Arthur said. "It's the house, Grace. Somebody tried to burn down the house last night."

Grace stood in the living room, staring down at the charred floorboards in the corner closest to the dining room. Soot marks streaked the white walls, and shards of broken glass

sparkled from the shattered front windows. She clutched
her laptop tightly against her chest and willed herself not
to cry.

"The neighbor next door smelled something burning
when he got up to let his dog out at six this morning," Arthur said sadly. "He called me, then he called the fire department, then he came over here himself. As soon as he
got onto the porch, he saw the flames, right over there. It
was just a small blaze, looked like a bundle of rags or
something, he said. He broke the window and climbed in.
He found the mop bucket you'd been using and doused the
fire with water. If he hadn't done that, I don't guess this
place would be standing. This house is mostly wood. Heart
pine that burns like kindling."

"I don't know what to say," Grace said, her words catching in her throat.

"There's more," Arthur said grimly, jerking his head in
the direction of the kitchen. Grace's footsteps echoed in
the high-ceilinged empty room. She stood in the doorway
of the kitchen, and now she did cry.

Black paint had been spattered all over the kitchen. It
oozed down the faces of the new refrigerator and range and
trickled down the cabinet faces. Paint pooled on her freshly
painted checkerboard floor. "Fuck the Man" had been
painted in wobbly black letters across the kitchen window.

"Kids." Arthur spat the word. He pointed at the sink,
where an empty plastic half gallon of cheap vodka had
been tossed, along with empty cans of Red Bull and assorted brands of beer cans.

"Oh my God." Grace breathed the words. She backed
away from the doorway and into the hallway, where half
an inch of water sloshed over the floorboards. Wadded up
towels littered the floor.

The bathroom door was closed. She was about to open
the door when Arthur closed his own gnarled hand over

hers. "Don't," he warned. "It's awful bad." He swallowed.
"They . . . Grace. They took a dump in the tub and smeared
it all over the walls. Then they shoved a towel down the
toilet, to back up the plumbing, and did the same thing
with the sink. I've shut the water off now, but hadn't had
time to clean everything up before you got here."

The bedroom doors were closed, too. Before he could
stop her, Grace opened the door to the front bedroom.
Day-Glo orange paint festooned the walls. The empty paint
bucket lay on its side, a river of orange paint spilling onto
the newly refinished hardwood floor. More empty beer
cans were scattered over the floor, and the room reeked of
urine and marijuana smoke.

"Who would do this?" she whispered.

She heard the front door opening then and the sound
of boots on the floorboards, and then the skittering of a
dog's nails clicking across the floors. "Grace?" Wyatt's
voice sounded panicky.

Sweetie came speeding around the corner, and Grace
grabbed her up in her arms before the dog could go track-
ing across the orange paint.

"I'm back here," she called, her voice breaking. A moment later, he was there, by her side. Without another word,
he wrapped his arms around both her and the dog, and held
them close.

"I'm so sorry," he murmured into her hair. "Are you all
right?"

Finally, she sniffed and wiped at her eyes. "I'm okay,"
she insisted, pulling free.

Arthur stood awkwardly in the middle of the room,
brandishing a push broom.

"Wyatt, this is Arthur Cater. He owns the house. Arthur, this is my friend Wyatt, the one I told you about who
had the ideas for the garden."

The two men nodded at one another. "What happened

here?" Wyatt asked. "I saw the burned places in the living room."

"Somebody broke in and tried to burn it down." Arthur gestured around the bedroom. "But before they got around to that, they did all this. More in the kitchen. The bathroom's worse."

"Who?" Wyatt asked. "Do you have any idea?"

"Kids is my guess," Arthur said. "The neighbor said he noticed a car parked in the driveway last night, around ten. I'd told him about Grace working over here, and he just figured it was her, so he didn't think any more of it. He's the one that called me this morning."

"They had themselves a big ol' party," Grace said bitterly. "You can smell the weed in here. And there are beer cans and a vodka bottle in the kitchen."

"Damned kids," Arthur growled.

"I guess it's too much to hope the neighbor got a description of the car or a license number," Wyatt asked.

"Coulda been blue, coulda been green. It was dark, and he only just glimpsed the car from his own front porch," Arthur said. "Probably doesn't matter. They're long gone by now."

"And nobody heard anything over here?" Grace asked.

"It's been a rental house so long, and we've had so many tenants in and out, the neighbors just started tuning out what goes on over here," Arthur said. "The lady across the street came over this morning when she saw the fire truck to tell me she'd called the police twice on my former tenants, but the cops just issued them a warning. Wish she'd have told me."

"All your hard work," Wyatt said, squeezing Grace's hand. "You had the place looking so good."

"It looked real nice," Arthur agreed. "I'm glad I took those pictures to show my wife, before all of this happened."

Grace dabbed at her eyes with the hem of her oversized T-shirt. "I'll just have to start over, that's all." She picked up the paint can and looked at the label. "At least it's latex. I'll have to repaint the walls, but if I get some rags and get to work on these floors before the paint really hardens, it may be that I won't have to strip the floors again. Thank God this happened after I'd gotten the poly down."

"There's nothing much happening at the park today," Wyatt said. "I'll call my Dad and tell him I'm going to hang around here today and give you a hand. Bo's at his mom's, so I've got the day and the evening free, if you need me."

"Oh no," Grace started to say. Then she shrugged. "Who am I kidding? If you really can spare the time, it would be a lifesaver."

"Sorry, but I won't be much help to you," Arthur said. "I've got a doctor's appointment in an hour, and after that, I've got to take my wife to her doctor. It takes forever to get on his schedule, so I can't change it. Anyway, my bursitis has flared up again. It's hell getting old."

"We'll manage," Grace assured him.

"I'll check back with you later in the day," Arthur said. He looked around at the bedroom walls and shook his head again. "What gets into kids' heads these days? What's the fun of destroying property? Where are their parents? That's what I'd like to know."

He pulled a handkerchief from his pocket and wiped his paint-smeared hands on it. "I took more pictures before you got here," he told Grace. "And the police were here, right after the firemen left. I'll file a claim with the insurance company in between the doctors' visits."

"Thanks, Arthur," Grace said, following him onto the front porch.

He turned just before reaching the door. "You sure you want to bother with doing this all over again? Maybe I should just hire some young fella to come in and clean it up and paint it all and be done with it. Get it rented again and quit worrying."

"No!" Grace said sharply. She smiled sheepishly. "I mean, I wish you wouldn't. I've got so much invested here. I really want to see it through to completion. Besides, I'm still hoping you'll decide to let me rent it when it's done. So I really do have an ulterior motive."

"I'll tackle the kitchen if you want to concentrate on this bedroom," Wyatt offered.

Grace planted a kiss on his chin. "You're a good guy, Wyatt Keeler." Then she went back to work.

It was nearly two o'clock when he poked his head in the bedroom again. She'd managed to mop most of the orange paint off the floors. She'd scraped the dried paint from the windowpanes and had even put a coat of primer on the walls. The orange paint was so vivid, she was sure it would take at least two coats of primer, plus two coats of the Benjamin Moore. At some point, she'd have to make another trip to the hardware store to buy more paint.

"Looking good," Wyatt said. He held out a white paper sack. "I went and got us some lunch. You ready for a break?"

They sat cross-legged on the front porch to eat their turkey sandwiches. Grace rested her aching back against the wall and took a swig of her Diet Coke. "How's it coming in the kitchen?"

"There's good news and bad news. Which do you want first?"

She made a face. "Tell me the good stuff first."

"I managed to get all the paint off the fridge and stove. We didn't get so lucky with the cupboards. They'll all have to be repainted."

Grace sighed and pushed a strand of sweaty orange-streaked hair off her forehead. "What's the floor looking like?"

Sweetie, who'd been sitting politely on her haunches, stared hungrily at the sandwich wrappings and whined softly. Grace tore off a bit of turkey and tossed it to the dog, who caught it in midair.

"Like a really long night of repainting red and white checkerboards," Wyatt said, grimacing.

Grace groaned and rolled up the legs of her jeans to show him her bruised knees. "I'm still not recovered from the first time I painted that floor. Me and my big ideas."

"I know this is probably a silly question, but couldn't we just paint the whole thing one color?"

"We could—except that I got an e-mail from an editor at *Veranda* magazine this morning. They want me to do a series for them—story and photographs, of my redo of the cottage. And the editor very specifically mentioned that she adores that floor."

"Oh." Wyatt munched on a potato chip. "*Veranda* magazine. That's good?"

"Very good. Especially in my world. It's huge."

"I'd slide over there and give you a congratulatory hug, but I'm too tired."

She smiled. "I'll consider myself hugged. Anyway, who knows if I can get this place cleaned up enough now to even do the story?"

He chewed and thought. "Maybe you could make this"—he swept his hand, indicating the charred porch floor and broken windows—"part of the story. You know, intrepid girl rescues house from fire and paint bomb?"

She raised an eyebrow. "That's actually not a bad idea. Now I wish I'd taken some pictures of the bedroom before I started cleaning it up."

"Could you use the pictures Arthur took?"

"Maybe. I guess they'd have to be scanned or something." She finished off her sandwich and threw a last chunk of turkey to Sweetie, who'd been stealthily creeping closer to the source of the food while she talked.

Wyatt stood and helped her to her feet.

"Guess I'd better grit my teeth and check out the damage in the bathroom," Grace said, making a face. "Arthur wouldn't even let me look in there when I got here this morning. He said it was pretty gross."

"It was," Wyatt said. "Nothing I'd want you to have to deal with. I got the tub and all the walls wiped down with bleach, and I managed to unstop the toilet and mop up most of the water. All I can say is, if I ever get hold of the punks who did all this . . ." He made a fist. "Pow!"

"Yeah," Grace said. "About those punks. I'm not so sure this was the random act of vandalism that Arthur assumes it is."

"Really? Then . . . You're not saying your ex did this, are you?"

"Maybe. Although this—especially the way Arthur described the bathroom—that's not really Ben's style. J'Aimee, on the other hand? I'm not so sure it wasn't her. Or maybe she put somebody else up to it."

"I don't know, Grace," Wyatt said. "What happened here is pretty extreme—even for a pissed-off ex-husband. Besides the fact that the two of them are scum, what makes you think they're behind this?"

"For one thing, the paint. That was a brand-new can of orange paint, and a brand-new can of black paint. I didn't have either of those here in the house, so whoever did it took the trouble to go buy paint and bring it along. So not really a crime of opportunity. Same with the fire. That wasn't just a bunch of rags they used to start the fire in the living room. There were loads of old towels and sheets in the linen closet, but they didn't use them to start it. They brought what looks like a new canvas drop cloth.

Because, again, whoever set that fire was quite the little planner. Does that sound like kids to you?"

He stared at her. "Are you sure you haven't been watching too much *CSI*?"

"I've had a lot of time to think while I scrubbed that floor," Grace said. "Shall I tell you what else I think is suspicious?"

"Shoot."

Grace pointed toward the house across the street. The lawn was neatly mowed, and two green recycling bins stood at the curb. "There were three or four different kinds of beer cans in the kitchen sink, plus the Red Bull, plus the vodka. I think whoever did this caper wanted us to think they had a party, so they probably just scooped up some empty bottles and cans along the way. Today was recycling day, so every house on this street had full bins sitting on the curb last night."

"Anything else?" Wyatt asked.

She walked into the living room, and he followed. She kicked at the remains of the charred thing on the floor. "I don't think J'Aimee intended to burn the house down. That's pretty scary, even for her. I think she just wanted to make a little fire. Why else just set fire to something like this? If someone really wanted a fire, they would have poured lighter fluid, or kerosene, or whatever all over the house. But it's just this one little corner of the room that's charred."

"Why would she, or Ben, do any of this?" Wyatt asked. "How do they even know you're working on this house?"

"Trust me, they read TrueGrace every day. J'Aimee steals my pictures and recipes all the time. Both of them have stopped by here. As to why, that's simple. For revenge. The last time J'Aimee lifted one of my blog posts, and the photos and posted them on Gracenotes as her own, I got fed up. It's copyright infringement, pure and simple. I e-mailed all their advertisers to let them know what was going on. I know at least one of their biggest accounts pulled their ads because of that."

"Will you tell the cops?"

"I would if I thought it would do any good," Grace said. "But all I have is a lot of theories. So I'm going to do the one thing that will piss them off the most. I'm going to start all over, and I'm going to make this house fabulous, even if it kills me."

"Okay," he said. "Count me in."

50.

Grace stood in the middle of the living room, her hands on her hips, and scowled. Wyatt came in just in time to catch her angry expression. "What now?"

"On top of everything else, she stole my damn iPod," Grace said. "I left it in here the other night. The thing was, like, four years old, but it had all my music; my running music, my painting music, everything. Now it's all gone. Dammit. I need my music to paint by."

"I've got my iPod out in the truck," Wyatt said cautiously. "But it's getting kind of late, isn't it?"

Grace looked out the shattered front window. The sun was hanging low in a bright orange-tinged sky. "Wow, it's almost sunset. What is it, after eight?"

"Five after eight," Wyatt said. "Are you ready to quit yet?"

"Are you?"

"I'll keep working as long as you want to. But you've been at it all day, Grace. Since nine this morning, with only a half-hour break at lunch. Do you really want to keep going?"

"No," she admitted. "As Rochelle would say, my get up and go got up and went. Maybe I'll head home."

"Good idea," Wyatt said.

"Unless . . ." A smile crept over her face.

"Unless what?"

"I was just thinking, you might like to see my other design project."

"I didn't know you had another project."

"It's Mitzi's condo over on Gulf Drive. She's turning it into a furnished vacation rental, and she's hired me to fluff it. The back of my car is actually full of towels and rugs and bedspreads and curtains for the place. I just started shopping for it yesterday."

"Sounds nice," Wyatt said, wondering where this conversation was headed. "But it's getting kind of late for a sightseeing tour. Maybe you could show it to me this weekend?"

"It sits right on the gulf," Grace told him. "The master bedroom has a balcony with a spectacular sunset view. And it has a king-sized bed. And I have the key."

Wyatt's eyes lit up. "Are you propositioning me?"

"Would you think less of me if I were?"

"Not at all," he assured her. "And I promise. I'll still respect you in the morning."

They left Wyatt's truck at Mandevilla Manor and drove to the Publix on Holmes Beach to pick up supplies. While he circled the parking lot, Grace made a sweep of the supermarket. She hummed as she careened through the aisles, tossing a bag of dog food, a bottle of wine, a six-pack of beer, a pound of boiled shrimp, some good cheese, a loaf of French bread, and some grapes into the cart. On her way to the cash register, she caught sight of herself in a mirrored display in the floral department. Ugh! She was a mess. She backtracked through the store and added a bar of scented soap and some shampoo and conditioner to the cart, and then, in a flash of genius, she added a jug of detergent because the condo had a laundry room.

"Get everything we need?" Wyatt asked, pulling alongside her at the entrance to the store.

"I think so," she said, holding up the wine.

When they got to the condo, Wyatt snapped a leash to Sweetie's collar and carried the grocery sacks, and Grace loaded her arms with the linens she'd bought. She juggled the packages while she dug in her pocket for the key. When they entered the apartment, it was already flooded with the dying light of the sunset.

Grace glanced down at her paint-spattered sneakers and kicked them off before stepping onto Mitzi's pristine white carpet, and Wyatt followed suit.

Wyatt dropped the groceries on the kitchen counter and walked back to the living room, standing in front of the sliding glass doors that led out to the balcony. The sky was streaked with brilliant layers of colors, from navy to violet to scarlet, orange, and pink. "Awesome," he breathed. Grace hurried into the bedroom and dropped her packages. By the time she got back to the living room, Wyatt had opened the wine and poured glasses for both of them, and Sweetie was curled up on the rug in front of the television.

"Come here," he said, holding out her glass. She took a sip of the wine. He put his arm around her, and she rested her head against his shoulder.

"Nice place," he said, looking around the room. "Kinda white, though, isn't it?"

"Mitzi's a great lawyer, but, as she herself admits, she sucks at decorating. She gave me a five-thousand-dollar budget and a deadline of two weeks, but otherwise no restrictions."

"Hmm." He was nuzzling her neck. "Is it okay for me to be here?"

Grace chuckled, thinking of her conversation with her lawyer. "I think she'd be okay with it."

He turned her toward him and slid his hands around her waist. "Pardon me for being forward, but didn't you say something about a king-sized bed?"

"Mm-hmm." She gave him a lingering kiss. "What about the sunset?"

"I thought you said the bedroom looked out onto the gulf."

"So I did." She kissed him again, then pulled away.

"Much as I hate to bring up the subject, I am absolutely filthy, and I smell like a goat. I'm just going to jump in the shower, and then maybe we can continue this discussion somewhere else?"

"Okay," he said, running a finger slowly down her arm. "Need anybody to scrub your back?"

"Mmmm. Hold that thought."

The master bedroom had a huge tiled walk-in shower with an adjustable rain-forest showerhead. Grace hummed as she lathered her entire body, scrubbing at the streaks and specks of orange paint that seemed to coat every inch of her exposed skin. The hot water sluiced down her back and over her chest and her head. She washed and rinsed her hair and wished she'd brought along a razor to shave her legs. The thought struck her that she still had two weeks to work on the condo. She'd make sure and stock the bathroom with a razor—and a toothbrush and toothpaste—after her next shopping trip.

She towel-dried her hair and finger-combed it as best she could, then wrapped herself in another one of the big fluffy towels she'd bought. Then she gathered up the clothes she'd left on the bathroom floor.

Wyatt's voice drifted in from the other room. It sounded like he was on the phone. She hesitated, then pressed her ear to the door.

"Hey, Dad." His voice was low. "How're you feeling?

"That's good. Did you have dinner? Did you eat the vegetables I bought you? No, Dad, Tater Tots don't count. Yeah. Salad's good. Did you take the new medicine the doctor gave you?"

He sighed. "Yeah, I know you're a grown-up, but I just want to make sure you take your pills. Is that a crime? Okay, great. Callie didn't call, did she? No, Dad, remember? You promised the judge you wouldn't call her that anymore.

"Listen, Dad, I'm, uh, probably not coming home tonight, but I'll be back first thing tomorrow to get the animals fed and open up.

"What? None of your business. I'll see you in the morning."

How sweet is it that he calls his dad to check on him? Grace thought. *This is somebody I could love.*

And then something else occurred to her. She grabbed the jeans she'd dropped on the floor and dug her cell phone out of the pocket. It was Thursday night, which was ten-dollar-pitcher night. Hopefully, Rochelle would be too busy to answer her phone. She really did not want to have a variation of the same conversation Wyatt had just had with his father.

The phone rang once and went right to voice mail. "Hi, Mom. Just wanted to let you know I'm not coming home tonight. I've got so much to do, I think I'll just camp over here tonight. See you in the morning." She disconnected hurriedly.

Wyatt was standing by the sliding glass doors in the bedroom when she emerged from the bathroom dressed only in a towel and a smile.

He gave a long, low wolf whistle when he saw her and held his arms open.

Grace padded across the room to him. "Take off your clothes."

He grinned. "If this is your idea of foreplay I can't wait to see what happens next."

"Don't be smutty," Grace said primly. "I bought detergent at Publix, and I'm going to wash our clothes so we have something clean to wear after . . . dinner."

He reached out and grabbed her. "Does this mean we get to have dessert before . . . dinner?"

She kissed him lightly. "We'll see."

He set his wineglass on a table by the window and made a huge production out of stretching and yawning.

"Oh man," he said. "I am soooo tired. I think I'm so tired I'm gonna need you to undress me."

Grace wrapped her arms around his neck. "Is that so?"

"Yes," he said solemnly. "Please."

Grace blushed. "You know I haven't been with another man in a really long time, right?"

He cradled her face between his hands and kissed her again. "It'll come back to you. It's like riding a bike."

She tugged his T-shirt over his head and tossed it to the floor, then ran her hands over the flat planes of his bare chest, resting her fingertips on his nipples. She kissed his ear, then his collarbone, and worked her way to his chest. Wyatt slid his hands around her waist and kissed her hungrily.

Grace slid her hands down lower and felt him inhale sharply. She worked her fingers inside the waistband of his jeans and nimbly unfastened the metal snap before slowly easing the zipper down. She rolled the waistband of his cotton briefs over his slim hips, brushing her hand lightly over his erection.

"Oh God, Grace," he whispered in her ear. She slid her

hands around to his rear, cupping her hands on the smooth, cool flesh of his butt, while he kissed her neck, the warm spot at the base of her throat, and then her lips again, parting them with his tongue, both hands entwined in her damp hair.

Grace tugged the waist of his jeans and briefs lower, past his hips, feeling the bulge of his erection pressed against her groin, lower, until she could wrap one bare leg around his and ease the jeans down to his ankles with her toes.

"Nice trick," he murmured in her ear. He released her long enough to kick free of his jeans, then, naked, pulled her to him again.

He flicked the edge of her towel and it dropped to the floor. He took a step backward and gazed at her pale body, silhouetted against the deep-purple sky outside. "You're beautiful," he said. "So beautiful." His hands roamed slowly, lingering on her butt, traveling up her spine and then around her ribs, until he cupped a breast in each hand. His head dipped, nuzzling and suckling each nipple until Grace could hear her own ragged breaths in the still of the darkening room.

She ducked her head and felt the blush starting at the roots of her hair and spreading downward. He pressed a finger under her chin and she looked at him from beneath her lowered lashes.

"I'll take it from here," he said. He took her hand and led her toward the bed.

51.

Grace lay on her side, gazing out the sliding glass doors at the deep-blue sky. At some point, Wyatt had opened the doors, and they could hear the waves washing ashore. He was spooned up against her back, his arm draped over her side, with his hand cupped against her breast, his thumb rhythmically brushing against her nipple. He was already aroused again. For that matter, so was she.

She rolled over to face him. "You've got to stop that, or we'll never get any dinner."

Instead, he bent his head and kissed her other nipple. "Would that be such a bad thing?"

"I'm starved," she announced. He caught at her hand, but she neatly slid out of the bed. Still self-conscious, she groped around on the floor for her forgotten bath towel, finally crawling over to where Wyatt had dropped it, several feet from the bed.

As she fastened it, she glanced over her shoulder and saw him, propped up in bed, watching her with amusement.

She gathered up their clothes and went out to the laundry room to load them into the washer. When she'd started the wash, she went to the kitchen and poured herself a glass of the chilled white wine. Through the open bedroom door she heard the sound of the shower starting.

Grace found a large bowl—white pottery, of course, in one of the kitchen cabinets. She dumped in the bag of boiled shrimp, cut up a lemon, and arranged the slices around the edge of the bowl, humming as she worked. She rinsed the green grapes and placed them on a cutting board, next to the loaf of French bread. There was no bread knife in the scarcely appointed drawer of kitchen implements, so she simply tore the bread in hunks and heaped them beside the grapes along with the cheeses she'd picked up in the deli department.

She heard the clicking of nails on the tile floor and looked down. Sweetie jumped up, her front paws scratching at Grace's bare knees.

"Ow," Grace said, leaning down to scratch the little dog's silky ears. "We've got to get you to the groomers to get your nails trimmed. In the meantime, thanks for reminding me. I actually did bring some dinner for you, too."

She poured dog food into one bowl and water into another and set them on the floor, then went back to her preparations, loading all the food, along with the wine bottle and two glasses, onto a large wicker tray.

Wyatt was just emerging from the bathroom as she walked into the bedroom. He had a towel wrapped loosely around his hips, and, with a hand towel, he was rubbing his closely shaven head. His chest was muscled and his abs were not quite male-porn-star tight, but close enough. His skin gleamed darkly tan in contrast to the white towel. She stopped dead in her tracks, forgetting what she'd been about to say.

"You're staring at me," Wyatt pointed out.

"That's not staring. That's lusting." Grace set the tray

with the food on the nightstand. She wrapped her arms around his waist and backed him toward the bed.

He laughed, but offered no resistance.

When she had him right where she wanted him, she placed one hand on his chest and toppled him backward.

"You're freaking gorgeous," she said, looking down at him, spread-eagled across the bed. "I thought I liked you best dressed in your little Ranger Rick safari outfit, but that was because I'd never seen you naked. Or in a towel. I definitely like the towel best."

She leaned forward and brushed her fingertips lightly across his chest. Wyatt caught her hand and pulled her down beside him. He pinned her arms to the bed and rolled until he was on top of her.

He frowned down at her. "That is not a Ranger Rick outfit. I'll have you know it's an official Jungle Jerry uniform. My grandmother had them made for everybody who used to work at the park. The one you've seen me wearing is the last one left. The rest are all in tatters, and that one is one rip away from the trash."

She easily worked her hands free from his and ran her palms down his flanks. "You can never throw that uniform away," Grace said sternly. "It's what you were wearing the night we met."

"Minus the parrot poop," he reminded her. "But that wasn't the first time we met. The first time was that day we both went before Stackpole. Remember? I have to confess, I have no idea what you were wearing either time. You looked so angry and intimidating, I was about to flee the premises." He pointed at the tray. "Room service? I like your style."

"There's no dining room furniture yet," she said. "And I still have to buy barstools for the island in the kitchen. And I don't want to eat on that white sofa, not until I have a chance to spray it with a stain repellant. So . . . dinner in bed."

She crawled onto the bed and propped herself up against the padded headboard. Wyatt handed her a glass of wine and took his own. He lightly clinked his glass against hers. "Here's to divorce camp."

An hour later, they'd devoured every morsel of food on the tray and drained the bottle of wine. The towels were scattered about the floor, and after another longer, more leisurely session of lovemaking, they were spooned together on the big bed, Sweetie asleep on the floor beside them, moonlight pouring in through the open doors.

At some point, Grace was vaguely aware of her cell phone, which she'd left on the dresser, dinging softly to indicate an incoming voice mail, and then another, and then another. But she was still too drowsy, too warm and happy and overwhelmingly, bone-deep contented, to rouse herself and see what was going on in the rest of the world.

52.

Driving back to the Sandbox the next morning, Sweetie sleeping on the front seat beside her, Grace finally took the time to check the voice mails from the night before.

The first, at 9:45 P.M., was from Rochelle.

"Grace! Those women from the other divorce camp sessions are here. They're on their second round of free drinks. You need to get back here and talk to them."

Shit! She'd totally forgotten her mother's plan to leave free-drink coupons on the windshields of Paula's other divorce campers. She couldn't believe her mother's crazy scheme had actually borne fruit.

The second call, ten minutes later, was also from her mother. "There must be seven or eight of those divorce women in here," Rochelle said, her voice cracking, either from excitement or desperation, Grace didn't know. "What the hell are you doing? Why aren't you here? These women all have hollow legs. They're drinking me broke!"

The third call was from Mitzi Stillwell, and she didn't sound happy. "Grace? It's ten fifteen in the evening. And I have a deposition at 8:00 A.M. I just got a call from your mom, insisting I get over to the Sandbox, to talk to some women she claims have some important information about Stackpole and your therapist. I have a vague idea where you might be right now, but I'm going to claim attorney-client privilege and not divulge that to Rochelle. Instead, I'm going to get out of bed, get dressed, and drive over to that bar to check this out. All I can say is, this had better be good. And he better be good, too."

Rochelle was practically beside herself by the time Grace walked into the bar, shortly before nine.

"Didn't you get any of my messages last night?" her mother demanded. "I kept calling and calling!"

"I'm sorry," Grace said. "Vandals broke into the cottage on Mandevilla sometime Wednesday night. It was a huge mess. They splattered paint all over the place and tried to burn it down. I kind of had my hands full. I had to try to get the paint off the floors and the appliances before it dried, and wash everything down. It was late by the time I got done, and I kind of just collapsed. I didn't get your messages until this morning."

"Vandals?" Rochelle asked. "Did you report it to the police?"

"Arthur did," she replied. "He's dealing with them." She walked around to the back of the bar and poured herself a mug of coffee. She took a sip and seated herself on a barstool. "Did you find out anything from the women who showed up here last night?"

Rochelle took a sip of her own coffee. "I found out a lot of stuff I didn't want to know, that's for sure. Husbands who are cross-dressers. Husbands who like to hang out in public bathrooms and expose themselves to little boys. Husbands who like to watch their wives have sex with strangers . . ."

"Eewww," Grace said. "Stop. I get the picture. I mean,

did you find out anything about people who've been referred to Paula by Judge Stackpole?"

"Yup," Rochelle said, looking immensely pleased with
herself. She turned to the bar back and pulled a spiral-
bound stenographer's notebook from the drawer. "I took
notes," she added.

"I must have put twenty or thirty of those coupons on
the cars in that therapist's parking lot," she continued. "I
didn't get over there 'til nearly eleven yesterday, and by that
time, there were five women coming out of her office. I just
handed them the coupons, and, since they were watching,
I had to put them on the other cars. I got back over there
after the lunch hour and hung around an hour, and another
group of women, and one man, drove up and went into her
office, so I put coupons on their cars. Then this big, burly,
scary-looking guy came out of that tattoo place, and he
wanted a coupon, so what could I do? I had to give him
one. And then . . ."

"Mom," Grace said gently. "You did a great job handing out the coupons. But could you just cut to the chase?
How many people actually showed up here last night who
said they were in Paula's divorce camp?"

Rochelle didn't like having her story interrupted. "I was
getting to that. I guess there were nine women who came
in last night over the course of the evening with those free-
drink coupons. I was trying not to act too nosy, just, you
know, talking them up, asking how their day was going.
A couple of them got kind of snotty with me. Just drank
their free drink and left, without even leaving me a tip!
What kind of woman stiffs a bartender who's giving her
free drinks?"

"Probably one whose husband got to keep all the money
in the divorce," Grace said.

"Eventually, though, four women sat right here at the
bar. I think they were all in the same divorce group,

because they were calling each other by their first names and kind of joking about their action plans. One of them said her action plan was to find herself a new sugar daddy. So I kept pouring the free drinks and playing dumb. Finally, I asked the chattiest one, this gal named Ginger, how they all knew each other, and she said they were in the same divorce-recovery group. I told Ginger I was going through a divorce myself, and how did she find out about something like that. And she said it wasn't her idea. The judge in her divorce case told her she *had* to go to a therapist. And not just any therapist. It had to be a therapist named Paula Talbott-Sinclair. That's when I started calling you."

She glared accusingly at her daughter. "And when you didn't call me back, I called Mitzi Stillwell. And she came right away."

"And that's when things started getting really interesting." A woman's dry voice came from behind them. Grace swiveled around on her barstool. "Mitzi! I thought you had an early deposition."

"I did, but when I got to the other attorney's office, he asked if we could reschedule. So here I am."

Rochelle took a mug and filled it with coffee before handing it over to the lawyer.

Mitzi sat down beside Grace. "I'm seriously thinking of hiring your mother as a private investigator. She's *that* good at asking dumb questions and drawing people out without raising their suspicions."

"That's what happens after you've tended bar for thirty years," Rochelle said modestly.

"What did you find out?" Grace begged. "Give me the nitty-gritty, please. I'm dying here."

Mitzi nodded deferentially to Rochelle. "Go ahead."

"All four of those gals, Ginger, Angie, Becky and Harriett, had your judge in their divorces," Rochelle said.

"The Honorable Cedric N. Stackpole Jr." Mitzi put in.

"Right. Harriett Porter, she was the oldest one, probably around my age, her husband owns a Cadillac dealership up north in Indiana, but they live down here full-time now," Rochelle reported. "She discovered her husband was having himself a fling with a male stripper in Tampa. She waited for him outside that club, and when he came outside at two in the morning, she sort of lost her temper and accidentally ran over his Gucci loafers with her SRX Crossover." Rochelle took a sip of coffee. "I'd never heard of such a car, but Harriett says it's sort of a cross between a real Cadillac and an Escalade. Escalades are what all the rappers drive, Harriett says . . ."

"Mom!"

"Right," Rochelle said, without missing a beat. "Stackpole threatened to throw Harriett in jail for aggravated assault, which her lawyer later told her was bullshit, because her husband did not want to have it get in the papers that he'd been run over in the parking lot at Jeepers Peepers. Instead, Stackpole told her she had to attend divorce-recovery group. With Paula."

"And the rest of the women in the group?" Grace asked.

"Different stories, same endings," Rochelle said smugly.

"By the time I got here last night, dear Harriett was fairly intoxicated," Mitzi said. "Lovely lady, but I think she probably needs AA more than she needs divorce recovery. I sat with all the girls for a while; then, I volunteered to make sure Harriett got home safely." She raised an eyebrow. "While she waits for her divorce to get settled, she's living in an enormous rented mansion on Siesta Key. Before I walked her to her door, I casually asked how much she's paying for her divorce-group sessions. Grace, she's paying nine hundred dollars!"

"That's three times as much as the rest of us," Grace said.

"I know," Mitzi said. "I was as stunned as you are. It

didn't seem to bother Harriett. I think she's actually enjoying the sessions with Paula. She apparently hasn't made
a lot of friends since moving here. Before I told her good
night, I asked for her lawyer's name." Mitzi sighed happily. "It's Carlton Towne. He's senior partner in my old law
firm, and a prince of a guy. I put in a call to him first thing
this morning."

Rochelle pushed her steno notebook across the bar to
Grace. "Here're the names of the other gals in Harriett's
group. They even have a name for themselves. The Diva
Divorcées. Cute, huh?"

Grace read the names scrawled on the notepad. "Are
these their lawyers' names, too?"

"You bet," Rochelle said.

"I only know one of these lawyers personally," Mitzi
said, running her finger down the list of names. "And because we have to do this very quietly, with an abundance
of caution, I'm not going to call them until absolutely necessary."

Grace nodded. "Just what is it you're planning to do?"

"First, I'm going to call Betsy Entwhistle and chat with
her about Wyatt's experience with Stackpole. Then, I'm
hoping Carlton Towne will be as frank with me as his client was last night. Then, I think it's time we talked to the
other members of your group, Grace, to see what their lawyers have to say. If that goes well, I think we'll probably
have enough to file a complaint against Stackpole with the
state Judicial Qualifications Committee."

"How long will all that take?" Grace asked. "After next
week, we've only got one week of divorce camp left. Then,
Stackpole's supposed to rule on my divorce. What if he
finds out what we're up to?"

"Leave that to me," Mitzi said. "We're going to gather
every bit of documentation possible, and I can be very,
very discreet and low-key."

53.

Grace, can I speak with you privately for a minute?" Mitzi asked. Rochelle gave them a questioning look but retreated to the kitchen.

Mitzi lowered her voice. "How's the condo coming along?"

Grace blinked. "Good. I went shopping Thursday and picked up a lot of things to bring in some color, since you've got so much white. I don't want it to look too sterile. You're going to have turquoise and lime green, and pops of tangerine . . ."

"How about the bed? I paid nearly two thousand dollars for that mattress, you know."

Grace felt herself blushing and glanced toward the kitchen to make sure her mother was not within earshot. "The mattress is amazing. Totally."

Mitzi smirked. "I just like knowing I've gotten my money's worth."

"Trust me," Grace said. "You did."

Wyatt pulled up in front of Luke Grigsby's house shortly after ten. He'd averted his eyes as he passed his old house, just down the street. It pained him to see the smudged windows, the stack of yellowing plastic-wrapped newspapers at the edge of the driveway, and the forlorn tire swing hanging from a rotted rope tied to a spindly tree in the side yard. Mostly, it pained him to see the "Bank Owned: For Sale" sign in the weed-strewn front yard.

Losing the house to the bank, he realized, was probably more painful than losing Callie.

He glanced at the clock on the truck's dashboard, then at Luke's front door and, as always, felt the same familiar, simmering resentment replace his previously cheerful, even joyous, demeanor.

According to the written agreement they'd hashed out during their separation, Callie was supposed to deliver Bo to Jungle Jerry's on the days Wyatt had custody. In reality, Wyatt usually ended up going to get his son on what he thought of as "hand-off days," because Callie was rarely even remotely on time, which always made Bo anxious and agitated, afraid his mother would change her mind and refuse to allow him to see his father.

Wyatt tapped his fingers impatiently, the back of his wedding ring sounding a *ching-ching-ching* against the hard plastic of the steering wheel. He'd been sitting there for ten, then fifteen minutes. He was reluctant to tap his horn or even go to the front door, because the last person he wanted to see that day was his soon-to-be ex-wife.

He found his mind wandering back to the previous evening, and then this morning. He'd awakened early, as always, shortly after six. It was still dark outside, and Grace was sleeping on her side, faced away from him, moonlight silvering her slumbering form. The quilt had slipped from her bare shoulder. Carefully, he pulled it lower until her back was exposed. He marveled at the elegant curve of her spine, the way her soft brown hair spilled onto the pillow, the way her full hips flowed from her narrow waist. She had a tiny mole on her left shoulder; he could just barely see it. He'd pressed his lips to her shoulder, not really meaning to awaken her, but she'd turned, and seeing his face inches from hers, smiled lazily. He'd thought her beautiful the night before, but finding her like this, tousled and sleep-drunk, he decided she was the most exquisite woman he'd ever known.

The passenger-side door opened abruptly and Bo hopped onto the seat and slammed the door hard. He folded his arms across his chest and grunted. "Let's go."

His son's face was set in anger, his eyes red-rimmed.

"Hey, dude," Wyatt said cheerily. "Something wrong?"

"Mom's really upset," Bo said. "Some guy came over this morning and took her new car, and she's been on the phone hollering and yelling at you know who. Can we just go now?"

What now? Wyatt wondered. Callie's car was a flashy red Mustang convertible. Bo told him Luke had given it to her for her birthday a few months earlier, complete with a vanity tag that read HOTMAMA.

"Is your mom's car not working?"

"No. I mean, yeah, it works good. We were asleep, and then I heard something outside and it was still dark, so I snuck out to the living room window to see if was like a burglar or something, and I saw this guy breaking into Mom's car! I went in and woke her up and told her, and she went and got this like gun out of the dresser. Then she went running outside, but the guy was already inside her car. She was screaming at him to stop, but he just rolled the window down and threw a piece of paper at her, and then he peeled off down the street, going really fast."

Uh-oh. Sounds like the repo man had paid a visit this morning. Mr. Bigshot must have missed a car payment. Or two.

Wyatt would have found it comical, except that witnessing the unpleasant scene had clearly upset the child.

"Well, I'm sure your mom will get it figured out," Wyatt said for lack of anything better to say.

"She's really, really mad at him," Bo said. He gave his father a hopeful look. "Maybe she'll change her mind and they won't get married, and we won't have to move to stinkin' Alabama."

Wyatt was about to pull away from the curb when out of the corner of his eye he saw Luke's front door open. Callie stood in the doorway, dressed only in an oversized T-shirt that barely touched her thighs. Her hair was mussed and rivers of black mascara streamed down her cheeks.

"Wyatt!" she screamed. And then she came running toward the truck in her bare feet.

Bo's eyes were the size of saucers. "Stay here," Wyatt said. He jumped out of the truck and met Callie at the sidewalk. "They repossessed my Mustang," she cried. "It's gone! Luke swears he doesn't know what happened, but I know he's lying. He lied about everything."

Callie threw herself into his arms. He closed them uneasily about her shoulder, turning to see that Bo was still in the truck, his eyes riveted to the unfolding scene.

"Shh," Wyatt said, patting her shoulder. "It's probably just a misunderstanding. Maybe the car payments got posted wrong or something."

"No," she sobbed. "Luke's broke. He's been lying all along. Oh my God, Wyatt. It was all just a big lie. What am I going to do?"

"Hey," he said softly. "We'll figure it out. Look, this is upsetting Bo. Why don't you go inside and get dressed? Let me take him over to the park and get him settled with Dad; then I'll give you a call and we can talk about it. Okay?"

"A call?" Her voice was wobbly. Snot trails dribbled

down her face. "Can't you come back here and talk? I could make us some coffee . . ."

"Not here," Wyatt said, his spine stiffening. There was no way he was setting foot inside Luke Grigsby's house again. Not ever.

"Oh," she said. "I get it. Okay. I could come over to the park . . ."

"God no," he replied. "You're not exactly Dad's favorite person these days, Callie."

"That was all Luke's idea," she said quickly. "I never meant anything by it . . ."

Wyatt sighed. "I'll meet you at Starbucks in an hour. Okay? But I can't stay long."

"All right," she said. "Oh my God. This is all such a nightmare."

For once, Wyatt thought bleakly, he'd have to agree with her.

54.

Callie had managed a remarkable transformation in the hour since he'd last seen her. Her hair was now clean and shiny and pulled back in a ponytail, she had fresh makeup, and she was dressed in a low-cut pink top and tight white jeans. And, Wyatt noticed, as she clutched the mug of coffee he'd just brought to the table, she wasn't wearing Luke's flashy diamond engagement ring.

"Thanks for coming," she said, her voice low. "I'm sorry I got all hysterical in front of Bo. That was bad. But everything happened so fast . . . I completely lost it."

"He's a sensitive kid," Wyatt said. "I know it's hard to do, but, for his sake, we really have to try to keep things on an even keel."

"I know." Callie nodded and took a sip of coffee. She gazed out the window at the parking lot. When she turned to look at him, her eyes were brimming with fresh tears.

"It's over between me and Luke," she said, her lower lip trembling. "And not just because of the car. Everything he told me? Everything he promised me? It was all just a big fat lie. He lost his job. There is no transfer to Birmingham. He just told me that because he assumed he'd get a new one with another company there. He's known for three weeks now, and he never said a word. Just kept bullshitting me. About everything." She held up her naked left hand. "My ring? Not real. Not even a good fake. And you know how I found out? I took it to the jewelry store in the mall yesterday, because I wanted to have it sized, and the girl behind the counter actually laughed at me when she saw it. It's a friggin' cubic zirconia."

Wyatt winced. "Did you ask Luke about that?"

"Yes. Of course, he had all these bullshit excuses. He tried to tell me he gave me a fake ring because he was having the real one custom-made, and it wasn't ready yet. He's got lies and excuses for everything."

"Geez. I'm sorry, Callie."

"Not as sorry as me," she said bitterly. "What do I do now? I can't stay with him. I won't. I told him that this morning. I can't marry a liar."

"What'll you do?" he asked.

She shrugged. "I have no idea. I just know I won't stay under the same roof with him. Not another night. I can't have Bo exposed to somebody like that."

"Well, of course, Bo can stay with Dad and me for as long as you need him to. But where will you go?"

"Good question. I don't exactly have a lot of options. Most of my girlfriends? As far as they're concerned, I'm the slut who cheated on her husband. They all made it pretty clear they couldn't stand Luke."

"What about your family?"

"Ha! My parents are barely speaking to me since our breakup. They always thought you walked on water, Wyatt. Anyway, I'm not about to move back to South Carolina. What would I do there? Get a job selling made-in-China sombreros at South of the Border? Anyway, Bo would hate it there. And the schools suck."

You didn't care what Bo thought about Birmingham

when you thought you and Luke were moving there, Luke thought.

"What about Kendra?" he asked.

Her lips twisted. "My baby sister is just itching to get a chance to say, 'I told you so.' She never liked Luke, either. Guess maybe I should have polled all my friends and family before falling in love with him and ruining my life, huh?"

Funny how it didn't occur to Callie that she wasn't the only one affected by her affair with Luke Grigsby. She probably just considered her husband and son as collateral damage.

"You've always gotten along with Kendra. Surely she wouldn't turn you away, right? Until you get things figured out?"

"Maybe." Callie didn't sound convinced. She grabbed a paper napkin from the stack Wyatt had brought to the table and used it to blot her eyes.

"Oh God, Wy," she whispered. "How could this have happened? You were the best thing that ever happened to me. And I let you walk away. Can you ever forgive me?"

Wyatt twisted his own paper napkin into a tightly wound ribbon. "What's done is done." *What does she want from me?* he wondered. "You just need to figure out how to get your life back on track, with the least amount of disruption to Bo. He's had more than enough of that in the last year."

"I know, I know," Callie agreed. "I'll call Kendra right now. I can probably stay with her for tonight, at least."

"What about a car?" Wyatt asked.

"That bastard Luke traded my Civic in when he got the Mustang," Callie said. "I drove his old Jeep over here. And he's crazy if he thinks I'll give it back. He owes me. Big-time."

"At least that's something," he said. "Look, Callie. I'm

sorry, but I really need to get back to the park. We've got a group of thirty kids coming in with a day camp in an hour, and they're expecting a guided tour and a performance from Cookie."

"I know you're busy," Callie said. "You don't have time for my soap opera. Go on. I'm just going to sit here for a while and try to get my wits about me before I go back to Luke's and start packing up my stuff."

He hesitated. "So . . . we'll plan on keeping Bo at the park, at least through the weekend. Is that okay with you?"

"Sure," she said, shrugging. "What are you going to tell him? About Luke and me?"

"Nothing," Wyatt said. "I'll leave that to you to figure out. You should probably call him later today, when you're calmer. You don't have to tell him the gory details yet. Just let him know you're okay."

Callie reached across the table and squeezed his hand, clinging to him. "I will. And I won't cry anymore. Not in front of him, anyway. Thanks, Wy."

"You're welcome," he said, slowly sliding his hand away from hers. "Good luck with Kendra."

On Monday, Grace was just unloading the last of her second batch of painting supplies from her car when Arthur's car pulled up to the driveway.

It took him a few minutes to emerge from the car, and when he did, Grace thought he looked tired. Tired and defeated. He walked, stiff-legged, toward where she stood, right outside the front porch.

"Hi, Arthur," she called.

"Hi there, Grace." He looked down at the buckets of paint she'd stacked on the porch steps and sighed and looked away. His shoulders slumped.

"I know, it's a hit to our budget," she said. "But hopefully the insurance will pay for it, right? Anyway, Wyatt and I managed to get all the paint off the floors and the appliances, so I'm just repainting the walls in the bedroom and the kitchen cabinets. And the kitchen floor. Again. That's a pain in the butt, for sure. We'll have to get a floor guy to take a look at the scorched floor in the living room, but maybe that can just be patched."

"Come on inside, Grace. I need to talk to you."

Theirs footsteps echoed in the high-ceilinged rooms. Arthur looked in at the kitchen, and the bedroom and bathroom.

"You've done real good work here, Grace," he said finally. "And I'm gonna pay you for everything you've done. I want to do right by you."

"But?" She dreaded what he was going to say next. It would not be good news, she knew.

"The wife and I had a long talk yesterday. My blood pressure was up pretty high by the time I got to see my doctor, and that got her all upset and worried. And the thing is, at my age, I just don't need the hassle."

"Arthur, once somebody's living here, I seriously doubt you'll have anything like this happen again," Grace said. "Even if you don't rent it to me . . ."

"If we rented it to anybody, it'd be you, Grace. But we're not going to rent it. We talked it over, and what with the money it'll take to put in that central air-conditioning you keep talking about, well, I just don't see putting that much money into the place right now. So we're going to sell it."

"Oh." Grace felt herself sag against the kitchen doorway. "I see."

He swallowed and she saw his Adam's apple bob up and down as he worked through what he was going to say.

"I hate like the dickens to let the place go," he said, running a gnarled hand over the door frame. "The way you had it looking, just these past couple of weeks, my folks would have been proud of that. This was their home place, and they always took pride in it. But my wife, she helped me see, the time has come to let it go to somebody else."

Grace couldn't trust herself to speak. She just nodded.

"I've got a real estate agent coming over on Saturday, to look the place over and tell me what she thinks I could sell it for," Arthur said. He looked up at her. "My wife was wondering if maybe you'd be interested in buying it. If you were, we'd try to make you a fair price, taking into consideration how much time you've already put into the house. But we'd need you to make a decision pretty quick, before we go ahead and list it with an agent."

She bit her lip. "If my divorce were final today, and I had the money, I'd love to buy this house," Grace said. "But to be honest with you, I can't say exactly when that's going to happen, or how much of a financial settlement I'm going to get from my ex. The judge in my case . . . well, let's just say he doesn't exactly see things the way my lawyer and I do."

"That's a damn shame," Arthur said. "And that fella, that friend of yours? I don't guess he's in any position . . ."

"He's in almost the same position I am, except he's also got child-support payments," Grace told him. "Anyway, Wyatt and I . . . well, he's a very nice person. But we just started seeing each other. It's way too early to know how that's going to turn out."

"I see. Well, I guess that's that then," he said. "I'm real sorry it had to end like this, Grace. I liked the idea of you fixing up this place, moving in and living here, starting all over again. Don't guess there's any need for you to do any more painting now. I feel bad enough that you put all this time into the place, for nothing."

"Not for nothing," Grace said. "I enjoyed the process. I just hope whoever buys the place will finish the job and do justice to it."

She followed the older man out to the front porch. "I

meant to ask you," she said, as he fumbled in his pocket for his car keys. "Did you report the vandalism to the police?"

"Yes. I filed a report. I showed them the pictures I took with my camera. They didn't seem too interested. I guess they see a lot of that type of thing."

"I've got an idea about who might have done it," Grace said slowly. "Would it be okay if I talked to a cop I know?"

He gave her an odd look. "Grace, it's over. I appreciate your wanting to catch whoever did this, but don't you have something better to do with your time?"

"Humor me, will you, Arthur? You're probably right. It'll probably come to nothing. But this is personal now. I'd like to see it all the way through, whatever happens."

Arthur patted her shoulder. "You're a stubborn little gal. Guess I should have figured you'd want to get to the bottom of things. All right. Go ahead. And if this cop friend of yours has any questions, have him give me a call."

55.

In a pair of frayed jeans with holes at the knees, a Tampa Bay Rays T-shirt, and Wayfarer sunglasses, Pete Strivecky looked nothing like a cop and everything like a too-cool-for-school teenager as he stood on the doorstep of the cottage on Mandevilla, holding his motorcycle helmet under one arm.

"Awesome house," he said when Grace greeted him Tuesday morning. "I'm glad you gave me a call. I've been reading about it on your blog. I even rode my girlfriend over here last weekend so she could take a look at it in person."

"It is an awesome house, or it will be, when whoever buys it gets done," Grace said sadly.

Officer Strivecky stepped inside and immediately walked over to the scorched corner of the living room. "So, you said the fire started here? Looks like it didn't do much damage."

"They poured some kind of lighter fluid or something on a new canvas drop cloth," Grace said. "Fortunately, the neighbor saw the flames through the porch windows, and he was able to put it out before the fire spread."

"Did you happen to save the drop cloth?"

"What was left. I put it out in the garage," Grace said. "Along with the empty paint cans they used in the kitchen and living room."

"Good idea." Strivecky nodded his approval. "Like I told you on the phone, I'm not a detective, and I'm sure not an arson investigator. But I don't think it would hurt to take a look around."

Strivecky walked through all the rooms in the house while Grace gave her running narrative on all that she'd accomplished in rehabbing the house—and what the vandal did to ruin her handiwork.

When they were done, they sat on the front porch steps, and Grace handed him a bottle of water.

"You really think it's your ex-husband's girlfriend? Why would she do something like that?" he asked.

"Revenge," Grace said succinctly. "She and Ben were blatantly ripping off material from my new blog for Grace-notes. So I e-mailed most of my old advertisers to let them know what was happening. I thought they should know they were spending money with people who have no ethics. At least a couple of them dropped their ads. J'Aimee came over here last week, and she threatened that she'd make me sorry. So yes, I think she's behind this."

"She sounds like a head case," Strivecky said. He took a swig of water. "I can talk to one of our detectives about your suspicions, but I can tell you right now he'll probably say that unless somebody catches her in the act, there's nothing he can do."

"What about if she left fingerprints? On the paint cans, or even in the bathroom, where she did the cute finger-painting?"

"The bathroom was wiped clean," Strivecky reminded her. "And what if she did leave fingerprints? You said she came over here last week. She could claim she left fingerprints then. But it's not going to get that far, Grace. We already know there's bad blood between you and your ex and this woman. Our detective is going to say this is just another domestic dispute. Nasty, yes. Criminal? Probably not."

Grace kicked at the porch railing with the toe of her sneaker. "This day just keeps getting better and better. Because of *her,* the owner of the house has decided to just sell it, instead of renting it to me. And I can't afford to buy the place myself, because I don't have any money. And now you tell me, even if I could prove it was *her,* there's nothing the police will do."

She glared defiantly at Strivecky. "Now I know why people take the law into their own hands. I feel so powerless—it's infuriating!"

"But you won't do anything to get back at her—right?" Strivecky said. "We didn't have this conversation. Right?"

"Right," she said glumly. "No violence. I'll just have to figure out how to get back at Ben—and her—legally."

Dear Lily: Thanks for your recent e-mail and your kind words about TrueGrace and the cottage on Mandevilla. It was a dream project—while it lasted. Unfortunately, the owner notified me today that he intends to sell the cottage, as is, meaning that my work there will go unfinished. I'd be happy to send you photos of my other current project, although it is not on the same scope as Mandevilla. And I'd love the chance to land an assignment for Veranda. Regretfully, Grace Davenport, TrueGrace.com

When she'd sent the e-mail, Grace flopped facedown on her bed and screamed into her pillow. Then she stood up, combed her hair, and called her lawyer.

Nelson Keeler was kitted out in his Jungle Jerry's uniform, khaki safari shirt, khaki slacks (his old khaki shorts no longer fit around his thickened waist), and his battered old safari hat—the leather-lined one that had been handed down to him by his father. He was happily chatting with a half-dozen members of the Hibiscus Garden Club who'd gathered around him in the gift shop after buying their senior-citizen-discounted tickets.

"Now, ladies, we're going to start your tour with a little history of the park," he was saying.

Joyce Barrett, their only other full-time employee, was staring out the glass door leading into the gift shop and ticket area when she saw Callie Keeler briskly approaching.

She was in her eighties and had silver hair she wore in a long braid down her back, and her own Jungle Jerry's costume was immaculately pressed, as always.

"Uh-oh," she whispered under her breath. She glanced back at Nelson, who'd already briefed her on Callie's latest attempt to torpedo Wyatt's happiness. She reached for the walkie-talkie they kept under the ticket counter.

"Wyatt? Office to Wyatt. Storm on the horizon. Repeat. Storm on the horizon."

There was a burst of crackling static. "Shit. Copy that, Joyce. On my way. Be there in five."

Joyce tugged at Nelson's arm. "Er, Nelson?" He looked up, and she jerked her head in the direction of the door just as Callie pushed through it.

Nelson stopped speaking, midsentence. His expression darkened. "What's she doing here?"

"Don't know," Joyce murmured. "But Wyatt's heading back here right now."

"Ladies," Nelson said loudly, turning so that his back was to the door. "Let's head out to the garden now, and I'll fill you in on what's in bloom as we walk." He strode out the double doors to the park without a backward glance.

"Joyce," Callie cooed, when the older woman returned

to the ticket counter. "How nice to see you. How are the grandkids?"

"Fine," Joyce said, stone-faced.

"Quite a few cars in the parking lot," Callie said, leaning against the counter. "Business must be picking up, huh?"

"It's all right," Joyce said, her voice a monotone. "We get by."

"Is Wyatt around?" Callie asked, craning her neck to try to see around the bookkeeper.

"He's been out with a group from summer day camp, but he's on his way back now," Joyce said. "Excuse me, Callie. I need to get the snacks ready for those kids. They're always hungry and thirsty when they come back in out of that heat."

She turned to go, but Callie placed a hand on her arm. "Oh, let me help, Joyce. I know where everything is." Callie stepped neatly under the old-fashioned wooden turnstile and bustled into the office.

Two minutes later, when Wyatt hurried into the lobby, followed by thirty clamoring children, Callie was setting juice boxes and plates full of graham crackers and apple slices on the long table in the snack bar.

Bo brought up the rear of the group. He was dressed in a faded and somewhat shrunken Jungle Jerry's T-shirt, and Cookie the parrot was perched on his shoulder. He beamed at the sight of his mother. "Mom!"

"Hey, Bo-Boy," she said, looking up from her task. She met her husband's unsmiling eyes. "Hi, Wy."

"Shots and beer!" the parrot demanded. "Gimme whiskey. Gimme beer."

Callie broke off a piece of graham cracker and held it out for Cookie, who snapped her beak around the cracker—taking with it a sizable chunk of Callie's fingertip.

"Owww," Callie screeched. "Son of a bitch!"

Startled, the parrot squawked and flew crazily around the room, while the day campers alternately screamed, giggled, ducked under tables, and covered their heads with their arms.

After circling the room a couple of times, Cookie finally settled on Wyatt's shoulder. He tried to soothe the agitated bird. "Shhh," he said, stroking the bird's head. "Quiet, Cookie. It's all right."

Callie held her bleeding finger out for inspection. "It is not all right. Look at this! I think I might need stitches."

Bo studied his mother's wound. "Awww, Mom, it's hardly a scratch. Cookie wouldn't really bite you. She just thought your finger was part of the graham cracker."

Callie frowned. Her eyes rolled back. "I think . . . I think I might faint." She looked around the room. "Wyatt! I feel faint!"

Before he could respond, Joyce Barrett swung into action. She bustled to Callie's side and looped an arm around her waist. "Come into the office and let me get you some antiseptic and a Band-Aid." She lowered her voice to a near whisper. "We don't want to upset the children or make them afraid of Cookie, do we?"

Callie scowled but reluctantly allowed herself to be led away. "That bird never did like me."

Later, after he'd loaded the children back on their day-camp bus, returned Cookie to her aviary, and settled Bo in the trailer for a late lunch, Wyatt walked into his office to find Callie seated in the chair in front of his desk.

"There you are," Callie said, holding up her bandaged finger. "See what that stupid bird of yours did to me?"

"Sorry," he said with a shrug. "I think maybe she got a little overexcited with all the kids around. She's never bit Bo or me or Dad before. Did you get yourself set up over at your sister's?"

"Sort of. Kendra's out of town, but she called her next-door neighbor to meet me over there with the key, so I dropped off a load of my stuff there before I stopped off here. At least I don't have to deal with her holier-than-thou crap right now."

"What's Luke have to say about you bailing out on him?"

"Don't know," she said. "He's been calling and texting me all day, but I've been ignoring him. To tell you the truth, I really don't care what that piece of garbage has to say."

Wyatt spread his hands out across his desktop. "What is it you want from me, Callie?"

"Who says I want anything? Can't I just drop by to visit with my son?"

"You've had Bo for the first half of the week. He was with you until a few hours ago. So you'll forgive me if I'm a little suspicious about your motives."

Callie gazed around the office. "God, this place is depressing. When was the last time you painted this room? Or had the floors mopped?"

"I don't have a lot of extra time or money for things like paint jobs these days," he said, struggling to remain civil. "What with legal fees, child support, and the three hundred dollars a week I have to pay for divorce camp."

"Three hundred dollars! Are you serious? That's crazy. That's money your family needs."

"Seriously crazy," Wyatt agreed, his face darkening. "But that's what Judge Stackpole mandated. After your lawyer showed him that video of me smashing Luke's car window. Which the two of you deliberately provoked me into doing."

Callie picked up an old plastic Jungle Jerry's snow globe from the corner of his desk and studied it, deliberately averting her eyes from his.

"That was all Luke's doing," she said, her voice low. "I never thought you'd go crazy and break your hand. I never intended things to go as far as they did."

"You filmed me with your cell phone," Wyatt said. "And then you called the cops. It's a little too convenient to blame everything on Luke, don't you think? You're thirty-six, Callie. Don't you think you bear some responsibility for what happened in our marriage?"

"Some of it," she said, shaking the snow globe, watching the glittering synthetic flakes settle over a tiny plastic replica of the Jungle Jerry's neon sign.

She looked up. "What if I told you I wished none of this had ever happened?"

"But it did happen," he reminded her. "You decided you were in love with somebody else and that you wanted to be with him more than you wanted to be married to me. You chose Luke over me. And our family. That's something I can't just forget."

She turned the snow globe over and picked at the yellowing price sticker with her fingernail. "Sixty-nine cents! How old is this thing?"

"It's ancient," he said. "As old as I feel right now."

Callie looked up. "Bo tells me you have a 'friend.' Is it serious?"

"Maybe. She's a nice woman. Look, Callie. I don't feel comfortable discussing her with you. I'm trying very hard to have a normal life now, to see to it that our son feels loved and safe."

"Is this your way of telling me you're moving on? That you're completely over me?"

Wyatt ran his hands over his head. "Over you? No. I'm trying, but I can't say I'm there yet."

She looked up at him through lowered lashes. "I hope you never get over me. I'm not over you. At all."

56.

Grace was the first to arrive at Paula's office. She found the therapist sitting at the desk in the reception area, staring down at something on the computer screen and frowning. There were dark circles under her eyes that even a careful application of concealer couldn't hide.

Paula looked up and immediately clicked to close out the screen. "Hi, Grace," she said. "How's your week going?"

"My week sucks," Grace said flatly. "Thanks for asking."

Paula sighed. "Is there something you'd like to discuss with the group? Is this about your divorce?"

"It's about my life, and right now everything in my life has been screwed up by my divorce, so yeah, I think you could safely say that." Grace felt the tote bag slung over her shoulder move ever so slightly. She started to walk into the inner office.

"Grace?"

She turned to face the therapist.

"Things will get better. I know you think they won't. I know it's hard. But you have to trust me. I've been there,"

Paula said. "The pain, the rage, the bitterness—if you can find a way to let go of all that, a huge weight will be lifted from your soul."

Grace bit her lip. She wanted to confront Paula with everything she knew or thought she knew about her arrangement with Stackpole. But she'd promised Mitzi to stay quiet until they could absolutely prove their suspicions.

"You've been there?" She couldn't resist. "Through a divorce? Where you lost everything?"

"That's right." Paula's eyes met hers. "I moved here to Florida . . . afterwards. I started over with nothing. Well, next to nothing. It hasn't been easy."

The outer door opened, and Camryn and Suzanne came in. Their conversation came to an abrupt end.

"We'll talk later," Paula said.

"Friends?" Paula gestured around the circle. "We've got so much ground to cover before your completion ceremony next week. But first, I'd like to hear about how your life is going—recovery-wise."

She was met with five blank expressions. "Anybody?" Nothing.

"All right. I suppose we'll just do this the old-fashioned way. I'll call on you, and you'll share. Camryn?"

"Recovery-wise? Dexter's lawyer called my lawyer this week. He wants his mother's dining room table. Claims it has happy family memories, and it's the only piece of furniture he wants."

"Did you give it to him?" Ashleigh asked.

"Umm-humm," Camryn said, looking pleased with herself. "I hope he can find a good furniture refinisher, though."

Paula looked at her over the top of her wire-framed glasses. "Did you damage the table?"

"Not me," Camryn said, feigning innocence. "But the movers I hired, they were sooooo clumsy. They must have just thrown it into their truck, because when Dexter got it, the top was all scratched up and gouged. I guess it looked pretty bad."

"How bad?" Grace couldn't resist.

Camryn held up her iPhone and scrolled through her photo roll and tapped the screen. She held up the phone for the others to see.

"What's that say?" Suzanne asked. "It looks like writing, on the tabletop, but it's kind of dark."

She handed the phone to Wyatt, who looked, squinted, and laughed. "It's writing. Looks like it says . . . 'Eat shit and die'? Is that right?" He looked to Camryn for confirmation.

"I was shocked," Camryn said, barely able to contain merriment.

"Never mind," Paula said, annoyed. "You know, Camryn, if you keep regressing, acting out in these childish and vindictive ways, I'm not going to be able to sign off on your successful completion of these sessions. Truly, you're only hurting yourself."

Camryn muttered something under her breath.

"Ashleigh?" Paula turned to the next person.

"Recovery-wise, I am fantastic," Ashleigh said. "Really. Forgive and forget. I even went out to lunch today with one of the girls in Boyce's office, and I never asked one question about Suchita. I've quit driving by her house, too."

Paula frowned. "I'm glad to hear that, but I wasn't aware you were engaging in such unhealthy, obsessive activities. Remember, Ashleigh, the other woman wasn't the problem in your marriage. She was only a symptom."

"Whatever," Ashleigh said. "I am in a very good place right now. An awesome place."

"Happy to hear it," Paula said. "I wish everybody could

move in that direction. Suzanne? Are things going better for you?"

"Maybe a little better," Suzanne admitted. "It's still too painful to talk to Eric, but I finally e-mailed him and told him that Darby has been accepted for early admission to Elon."

Paula beamed at her star patient. "Suzanne! That's a real breakthrough." She looked around the circle. "Friends? Let's give Suzanne our approval."

The others clapped politely.

"Darby's his daughter, too," Suzanne said. "I know she's conflicted—she feels loyalty to me, but she misses seeing him."

"Hmm. Maybe Darby would like to attend one of the 'Daughters of Divorce' seminars I'm going to be giving," Paula suggested. "And I've been thinking that might be helpful for your daughter, too, Camryn."

"No offense, Paula, but right now I can't afford to pay for any more of your sessions," Suzanne said. "Maybe I'll get her some books from the library."

Camryn coughed loudly and looked away.

"Grace? When you came in tonight, you seemed very down about things," Paula said. "Anything specific going on?"

"Very specific," Grace said, biting the words out. She recounted the events of the past few days in vivid detail. "Arthur's going to sell the house. And I'm back where I started."

"That's such a shame," Suzanne said. "I've been following your blog. It was such an adorable house. Do you have any idea who would do such a thing?"

"A very good idea. J'Aimee. My former assistant and my ex's new girlfriend," Grace said. "This is totally her handiwork. And, of course, now the house is out of my reach, because I can't afford to buy a house, because, so far, Judge Stackpole's idea of a property settlement is to give Ben the gold mine and me the shaft. Ben is entitled to everything, and I get nothing. Because he hates women."

"Fucker." Camryn said it quite distinctly.

Paula's face turned pink. "I'm sure that's not the case . . ."

"Not the case?" Ashleigh hooted. "Paula, get a grip! Those pills you've been taking have seriously pickled your punkin'."

The therapist's face paled. "That's very unfair."

"But it's true," Ashleigh insisted. "Nobody else wants to speak out, because they're all soooo afraid Stackpole will screw them even worse than he already has. Not me. I don't care what you or Stackpole say or do. Because after Monday, this is all a moot point anyway. I am so out of here."

She hopped out of her chair. "I'll see y'all later. At the Sandbox. Right?"

"Man, Ashleigh, you knocked Paula for a loop tonight," Camryn said later, with something akin to admiration. "After you left, she was back to her old self. Just going through the motions until eight o'clock rolled around. She didn't even have us read from our journals."

Ashleigh dipped a finger in her margarita and licked it. "I'm not going back for any completion ceremony, y'all." She looked around the table. "This has been kind of fun, in a weird way, but it's not an experience I want to repeat. But hey, if any of y'all ever want a little nip or a tuck, give me a call. I'll make sure Boyce gives you our professional discount."

"What about me?" Wyatt asked.

"What? You think men don't have plastic surgery?" Ashleigh chortled. "Eyelid lifts, chin implants, tummy tucks, breast reductions—honey, you'd be amazed how many men walk into our office. Not to mention all the prescriptions for Rogaine we write." She gazed meaningfully at Wyatt's gleaming dome.

He ran his hand over his head, immediately feeling defensive. "I'm not bald. I've got plenty of hair. I shave my head because I work outdoors all day. It's cooler. And there's less chance of ticks hiding in my hair."

"Ticks. Eeew." Ashleigh shuddered.

At the other end of the table, Grace waited until the others were engaged in a lively conversation about the cause for Paula's demeanor. She leaned over and spoke in a low voice.

"Camryn? Remember the morning you and your cameraman came to my house? The day after I left Ben?"

"How could I forget?" Camryn said. "Best story of the year."

"I've been wondering. How'd you get past the guard gates?" Grace asked. "None of those other news crews were able to get through security. How'd you do it?"

"Mmm. Trade secret," Camryn said, sipping her drink. "Why do you care?"

"Because I want to go back to the house. And get the rest of my things. But Ben got the security guards to deactivate my key card."

"Gotcha," Camryn said. "Let me call my friend in the morning. See if she can help us out."

"We?"

"You're gonna need a wingman, right?"

Wyatt watched Grace, her head bent close to Camryn's, as they whispered and plotted. He felt an irrational stab of jealousy. All night, he'd tried to catch Grace alone, if only for a moment. He needed to reassure himself that what was between them was real and that they had a future together. But there was always somebody around. He took a sip of his beer, then pushed it aside. He yawned widely, hoping the exaggerated movement would catch her eye.

Finally, she glanced his way, smiling ruefully. He got up and made his way toward the men's bathroom. Grace followed, pausing at the door to the ladies' room. She opened the door, and in the next instant, he'd pushed his way inside, slamming the door and locking it in one fluid movement.

"What are you . . ."

He silenced her with a kiss. "This," he said, his voice muffled.

"And this." His hands slid under the back of her sleeve-less cotton top, nimbly unsnapping her bra.

"Also this." He worked his knee between her thighs, her skirt riding up and baring her thighs, pinning her up against the sink vanity. Grace's body arched into his, and he lifted her effortlessly atop the vanity. She leaned back and ran her hand over his cheek. He caught her hand in his and kissed it, then yanked her top over her head in one fluid movement.

She laughed uneasily and crossed her arms over her bare chest. "We can't do this! Everybody's out there. My mother is out there. Somebody's going to notice . . ."

"I've been thinking about you all day, and I have wanted to do this all night," he whispered, cupping one of her breasts and kissing it. She let out a soft, low-pitched moan, then grabbed the waistband of his jeans and traced the zipper's path slowly with her thumb until she heard the sharp intake of his breath against her nipple.

"God, Grace," he breathed. She worked the zipper downward, stroking his erection. His hands fumbled with her skirt. "How does this damned thing come off?"

There was a sharp rap at the door. Grace froze.

"It's occupied," she croaked, hopping down from the vanity and hastily pulling on her top.

Wyatt grabbed for her, but she was too fast for him. He chuckled, despite himself, but she frantically shushed him.

Grace flushed the toilet twice, then groaned loudly and followed that with a remarkably authentic sound effect mimicking violent nausea.

"Come on, already," a girl's annoyed voice came. "I'm about to pee my pants."

"Employee bathroom near kitchen door," Grace called. "Sorry." She gagged violently, for good measure.

"Goddamned amateur," came the girl's parting shot.

When she was sure the girl was gone, Grace collapsed against Wyatt in a fit of giggles. "I'm sorry," she said, turning to the mirror to fix her disheveled clothing and hair. "But we've got to get out of here before we get busted."

She turned and gave him an appraising look, tugging at the hem of his shirt. "I had no idea that the scent of hand sanitizer could be such a turn-on." She opened the door and peeked out. "Okay, coast is clear." She shoved him out. "Go on. Go! I'll wait a minute and then come back to the table."

"Later?" Wyatt asked, kissing her neck. "We need to talk." But somehow, later never arrived that night.

57.

"Dad?" Bo walked into the kitchen, where Wyatt was shaping hamburger patties. Sweetie followed close on the child's heels, sniffing the air expectantly.

"I know it's late and you're hungry, but dinner's almost ready," Wyatt assured, seasoning the burgers with salt and pepper, stopping to toss a bit of meat to the dog.

"I'm okay." Bo plopped down at his place at the kitchen table. "Can I ask you something?"

"Sure thing." Wyatt put the griddle pan on the burner and turned on the heat. "You want cheese or no on your burger?"

"Cheese," Bo said. "The yellow kind, not the white."

"Got it. What did you want to ask me?"

Bo kicked the table leg. "Do you still hate Mom?"

"Hate her?" Wyatt asked cautiously. "I don't hate your mom, Bo. Is that what you think?"

"Sometimes," the boy said. He helped himself to a handful of potato chips from the bowl on the table and tossed one to Sweetie, who caught it midair. "Mom thinks you hate her. She's pretty sad. Because now she's not gonna marry you know who. And Aunt Kendra is a big bee-yotch." He shoved all the chips in his mouth and chewed furiously.

"You probably shouldn't call your aunt that word, pal," Wyatt said. "It's kind of a bad, grown-up word. So . . . you talked to your mom today?"

"Do we have any onion dip?" Bo asked hopefully.

"Sorry, no. But we've got salad. Did your mom call you today?"

"Yeah," Bo said. "She says we're not gonna live with you know who anymore. Do you think we can get our old house back instead? I kind of miss my room there."

Wyatt sighed. "That's complicated, pal. I wish we could get the old house back, but right now we can't. So I guess you're stuck sharing a room with me. Is that so bad? I mean, I don't snore too loud, do I?"

"Not as loud as Granddad," Bo said, giggling. A moment later, he was serious again. "What about Mom? Where's she going to live?"

Wyatt got up and turned the burner on again. He waited until the eye glowed red, then added the hamburger patties to the grill pan.

Obviously, Callie had unburdened herself to their son at some point during the day. What the hell was she thinking, worrying a six-year-old with this stuff? Did she seriously think she could use Bo to guilt-trip him into taking her back?

"For now, your mom's going to stay with Aunt Kendra," Wyatt said finally. "And then she's going to find a new place to live. And you'll have a new room. Okay? Is that cool with you?"

"I guess," Bo said. He kicked the table leg rhythmically. "But it would be cooler if Mom and me could just live with you. Like we did before." He took another handful of potato chips and shoved them into his mouth and chewed furiously.

Shit. Shit. Shit. Wyatt thought. Callie was really pulling out all the stops. He should have seen this coming.

Wyatt heard the meat sizzling on the cast-iron grill pan. Smoke rose from the stove. He jumped up and flipped the burgers, his mind working furiously to find a way to be honest with the child. Finally, he sat down and reached across the table and took his son's hand in his.

"Look at me, Bo," he said calmly. "Mom and I both love you. More than anything. And that will never change. But she and I, we're probably not ever going to live together again. Not because I hate her, but because we don't love each other the way married people should love each other. I'm sad about that, and I know you're sad about it, too. But that's just the way it has to be. Okay?"

"Okay," Bo said. "Can Sweetie have a hamburger, too?"

"Afraid not," Wyatt said. "Now, go wash your hands and tell Granddad dinner is ready."

Their Friday-night routine seldom varied. Nelson took himself off to bed around nine, and then Wyatt and Bo either watched a movie or played video games, until one or both of them fell asleep. Right now, Bo was sprawled on the floor, scraping the last bit of ice cream from the carton as he watched *The Bad News Bears*—the old Walter Matthau version—for maybe the tenth time since the start of summer. Sweetie was curled up on the floor beside him, her snout resting in his lap.

It had started drizzling shortly after dinner. Now the rain fell steadily, beating a noisy tattoo on the trailer's metal roof and siding.

Wyatt had texted Grace earlier in the afternoon, proposing that they meet somewhere, but discarded that idea after realizing how anxious Bo was about his parents' marital status.

After dinner, he'd managed a furtive phone call while

Bo and Nelson did the dishes. "Hey," he'd said, his voice low. "I don't think I can get away tonight after all. Bo is having some issues, and I think I'd better stick close to home."

"Everything okay?" Grace asked. "Your dad's not sick again, is he?"

"Nothing like that," Wyatt said. He knew he should tell Grace what was going on with Callie, but something held him back. All he knew was that he was tired of the tug-of-war. Callie was the past. And Grace was his future. He and Bo deserved a happy future, didn't they?

"I'll call you tomorrow," Wyatt promised. He glanced back toward the kitchen to make sure he couldn't be overheard. "I've got some stuff to tell you. Maybe we could have another sunset viewing at that condo?"

Grace laughed throatily. "I think that could probably be arranged."

He must have dozed off sometime between the end of *The Bad News Bears* and the beginning of *Field of Dreams*. Somebody was banging on the trailer's aluminum storm door. Wyatt jumped up, startled by the noise, but Bo, always a heavy sleeper, didn't move. Sweetie, on the other hand, went on instant alert, running toward the door and barking.

"Wyatt? It's me."

He cursed softly. His midnight caller was Callie. "Shush, Sweetie," Wyatt grumbled. He flipped on the porch light and opened the door.

She was barefoot and rain-soaked, dressed in a low-cut tank top and shorts so tight he could clearly see the outline of her panties. She'd been crying again. And this time, she'd brought baggage. Literally. A large wheeled suitcase rested on the porch, and next to it sat a plastic laundry basket heaped with her belongings.

"Can I come in?" She didn't wait for an answer, picking up the basket of clothes and stepping inside, out of the rain. He hesitated, then grabbed the suitcase, too.

"What's all this?" he asked, gesturing at the luggage.

"My stuff. Can you at least get me a towel so I can dry off before you start yelling at me?"

As she walked past him toward the bathroom, Wyatt detected the smell of alcohol and cigarette smoke. She took her time in the bathroom. He heard water running, and then the sound of a hair-dryer. He waited outside the bathroom door, arms folded across his chest, gathering resolve.

Finally, she emerged, her face pink from heat, hair fluffed, dressed only in his worn terrycloth bathrobe. "You don't mind, right?" Callie asked. "Just until my stuff dries out, okay?"

"You can have the bathrobe," he said, keeping his voice low, "but then you have to leave."

"And go where?" she asked, running her fingers through her hair. "My baby sister kicked me out. You believe that? It's midnight and we're in the middle of a monsoon, and she kicks me out. So for tonight, anyway, you're stuck with me. And I hate to ask, but do you have anything to eat? I didn't get dinner."

He took her by the arm and steered her toward the kitchen. "I'll fix you a sandwich. Keep your voice down," he warned. "Bo's asleep on the living room floor. I don't want him waking up and asking why you're here."

She yanked her arm from his grip and followed him into the kitchen. "We're still married, technically. So why shouldn't I be here?" She looked around the room and frowned. "Unless your new girlfriend is having a sleepover?"

Wyatt took a package of lunch meat from the fridge, along with a jar of mustard. He slapped the meat between two slices of bread, which he slathered with the yellow mustard, then slid the sandwich in front of her.

He decided not to allow Callie to bait him. "What are you doing here, Callie? What did you do to make Kendra kick you out?"

"Nothing!" she said, biting into the sandwich. "Kendra's just a bitch, okay? She resents me. Always has. She was always on your side after we split. And she hated Luke, of course."

She'd knotted the bathrobe loosely around her waist, and it gapped widely at the neck, giving him a too-generous view of her cleavage and a provocative expanse of her bare legs.

The truth was beginning to dawn on him. "Luke came over there tonight, didn't he? That's why Kendra kicked you out. Right?"

"I didn't *invite* him," she said indignantly. "He just showed up. He promised to get my car back for me. So I let him in, but then he started with the same old bullshit, and I called him on it. We were not fighting. It was a *discussion*. But all of a sudden, Kendra goes bat-shit crazy and starts threatening to call the cops on both of us."

"The two of you'd been drinking, right? And don't try to deny it, because you smell like a brewery," Wyatt said.

"What are you, my parole officer? Yes, we had a few beers," Callie said. "But I am not drunk. And anyway, what kind of sister throws somebody out in the middle of a tornado? Kendra wouldn't even listen to me. She literally grabbed my suitcase and pitched it out her window. And she lives on the second floor. I was barely able to grab the basket with the rest of my stuff before she locked me out in the rain."

Callie took another bite of her sandwich, and then another, chewing calmly. "God, I'm hungry. I bet I could eat another sandwich." She looked down at Sweetie, who was crouched on the floor, her liquid brown eyes focused on her.

"Is this the girlfriend's dog?" She tore off a bit of bread and tossed it to the little dog, who caught it in midair. "She's kind of cute, isn't she? What's her name?"

"We're not discussing the dog. And I'm not fixing you another sandwich," Wyatt said. "You can't stay here to-night, Callie."

She raised an eyebrow. "You're kicking me out? Where do you expect me to go at this hour? And don't suggest a motel. You might as well know. I'm flat broke."

"Dammit, Callie!" Wyatt whispered hoarsely. "I'm not going to let you manipulate me like this. I just sent your child-support check."

"And Bo needed new sneakers. And he's outgrown all his clothes," Callie said. "What is the big deal? It's just one night, okay? I'll sleep on the sofa. You won't even know I'm here."

"I will know. More importantly, Bo will know. You've already managed to get him freaked out about where he's going to live now that you and Luke are broken up. I don't want him any more confused than he already is."

But it was too late. They heard light footsteps in the hall-way, then the sound of the bathroom door being opened, and then a toilet flushing. A moment later, the sleepy-eyed child rounded the hallway into the kitchen.

"Mom?" he said softly.

She held out her arms and the boy dutifully allowed himself to be folded into an embrace. "Hey, Bo-man," Callie said, hugging him tight. "Are you surprised to see me?"

"Yeah. I mean, no," Bo said, yawning widely. "I thought you were at Aunt Kendra's house."

Callie made a face. "Your Aunt Kendra is a big doo-doo head," she said, laughing as though it were all a joke.

"So I came over here to see what you and your dad were up to."

"Are you gonna spend the night?" He shot his father a hopeful look. "Please, Dad? Mom can have my bed. I'll sleep on the sofa."

"Absolutely not!" Callie said. "If anybody gets to sleep on the sofa, it's me." She tousled her son's hair and looked defiantly at Wyatt. "Right, Dad?"

Bo's eyes were pleading. "Okay?"

Wyatt knew when he'd been beaten. "Fine," he said brusquely. "Come on, Bo," he said, holding out his hand for his son. "You're going to bed. I'll get your mom a pillow and a blanket. But this is just for tonight. Tomorrow, she's going to find a new place to live." He glared at his wife. "Right, Mom?"

Callie smiled weakly. "Right."

58.

Grace pulled alongside Camryn's car in the Publix shopping center Saturday morning. She hopped into Camryn's car, and moments later the two of them were heading west toward Gulf Vista.

"Nice car," Grace said. She wiped her sweaty palms on her jeans and lightly stroked the Jaguar's sleek leather upholstery.

"It was an anniversary gift from Dexter," Camryn said. "The man does love to buy nice things. Of course, mostly it's to show all his friends how much money he makes and what a big man he is."

"Are you sure your friend is okay with doing this?" Grace asked as they approached the Gulf Vista security gate. "She's not worried Ben might find out?"

"Marissa?" Camryn laughed. "She and LaDarion think your ex is a stuck-up prick. I guess Ben sicced the homeowner's association on them because of Peaches's barking."

"Ben hated that dog," Grace said. "It barked a *lot*. Like, if anybody walked by their house. Or if it was home alone. Which it was, a lot. Plus, your friend and her husband did throw some pretty wild parties. Last year they hired MC Hammer to play at their Fourth of July barbecue. Do you know how many times we heard "U Can't Touch This"? Over and over and over . . ."

"MC Hammer?" Camryn snickered. "Seriously? I did not even know that dude was still alive. How did he survive the nineties?"

"I don't know, but I can assure you, he did," Grace said.

There were three cars ahead of them at the visitors' gate to the subdivision. Grace's pulse skipped wildly as they pulled beneath the security shack's portico. "Here goes," Camryn said, under her breath. Grace pulled on a pair of oversized sunglasses.

The Jaguar's driver's-side window rolled down, and the uniformed security guard stepped forward. Grace sucked in her breath and looked away. It was Sheldon, the same guard who'd turned her away the last time she'd attempted to breach the gate at Gulf Vista.

"Morning, ma'am," Sheldon said, leaning in to look at the Jaguar's occupants.

"Good morning," Camryn said. "We're guests of Marissa and LaDarion Banks?"

Sheldon scanned a sheet of paper on his clipboard, running his finger down the lines of type.

"Ms. Nobles?" he asked, peering into the car's interior. Grace held her breath.

"That's correct," Camryn said.

The guard handed her a guest pass. "Leave that on your dashboard, if you would please, ma'am," he said, and waved her through.

"Nice digs," Camryn said admiringly, as they rolled slowly past the house on Sand Dollar Lane. "What did this place set you back, a million, million and a half?"

"I'm not sure," Grace admitted. "Ben handled all that.

This was one of the model homes. He cut a deal with the developer, and then cut more deals with the contractors who put in the landscaping and the pool and the media room. A lot of the extras, we got at cost, or less, in return for advertising and editorial mention on Gracenotes."

"And you walked away from all that."

" 'Ran away' would be a more accurate way to describe my departure," Grace said.

"And now you're living above a bar on Cortez," Camryn said. "Girlfriend, that is a big change, and I'm not just talking about zip codes."

"Want to know something?" Grace gestured out the window, at the velvety green lawns and lush beds of blooming tropical flowers and palm trees, behind which loomed glimpses of red barrel-tile roofs and white stucco homes. "None of this seems real to me. I lived in this neighborhood for two years. I went to parties, gave parties here, but I haven't heard from a single person since the night I put Ben's car in the pool."

"Mm-hmm," Camryn said. "You broke the rules. Acted ugly, made a mess. Got the law involved." She flipped up her own sunglasses, and grinned. "Welcome to the real world, Grace Davenport."

She turned the corner and pulled into the driveway of a house that dwarfed all the other houses in the subdivision. A wrought-iron gate with curlicued flourishes identified the mansion as Villa Marissa. Camryn opened her window, leaned out, and looked up at the small security camera mounted on the stucco gatepost. "Marissa? It's Camryn. Open sesame!"

The gates swung open noiselessly, and they followed the driveway around to the front of the mansion, an enormous, vaguely Tuscan villa, where a petite woman with long jet-black hair and a complexion the shade of caffe latte waited in a gleaming black golf cart.

"Ladies!" Marissa Banks beamed. She was dressed in a sleeveless hot-pink Nike tank top and matching pink golf shorts, along with pink and white golf cleats. She clapped her hands excitedly. "Welcome to my house."

"Marissa, this is my friend Grace, but I think you've probably already met, right?"

Grace reached out and shook the other woman's hand. "Thanks so much for doing this. You're really sure you want to get involved in my drama?"

"Of course," Marissa said. "You can only get your nails and hair done so many times in one week. I'm dying of boredom. This is going to be fun. Like old times, right, Cammie? Remember that time we snuck onto the grounds at Doral so you could try to interview Tiger Woods?"

"And you distracted the security guards with a phony wardrobe malfunction? How could I ever forget that?" Camryn asked, shaking her head at the memory. "Does LeDarion know you've flashed boob to half the men in South Florida, just to get exclusive interviews?"

"How do you think we met in the first place?" Marissa laughed. "Of course, he thinks he's the only one who ever got a sneak peek. And we're gonna keep it that way, right?"

"Just between us girls," Camryn said. She glanced at Grace. "Are you ready?"

Grace let out a long, shaky breath. "As ready as I'm gonna be. I want this over with. Marissa, are you sure the coast is clear? Ben has a standing golf game at the club Saturday mornings, but you just never know . . ."

"I've been watching the place since eight. He left about eight thirty, and his little girlfriend left maybe fifteen minutes after that." Marissa rolled her eyes. "What a skank! You know she sunbathes nude most of the time, right? Every pool guy and maintenance man in the neighborhood has had a look at her goodies."

"Let's do it," Camryn said.

* * *

After Marissa dropped them off in the golf cart, promising to return as soon as they texted her, Grace and Camryn walked briskly to the rear of the house, where Grace unlocked the kitchen door.

"Wowsers," Camryn said, eyeing the gleaming expanse of black granite countertops, the stainless steel commercial stove, and the glass-front refrigerator. "This kitchen is immaculate. She's a pretty good housekeeper."

Grace glared.

"For a skank, that is," Camryn added.

"Oh, please. J'Aimee doesn't know how to cook," Grace said. "They probably eat at the club every night—or order out for pizza or Chinese."

She went into the dining room and pulled open the top drawer of the mahogany Empire buffet, pausing to run an appreciative finger over her sterling flatware. "Looks like it's all here," she said, after doing a quick count. Grace trotted out to the laundry room and came back with a king-sized pillowcase, into which she unceremoniously dumped all the silver.

"Let's stack everything by the back door," Camryn said, holding up a heavily decorated silver teapot. "That's what professional burglars do. So they can make a quick getaway."

"We're not burglars," Grace said sharply. She took the teapot from Camryn's hand and set it back on the top of the buffet. "I'm not taking anything that isn't mine. The tea service was Ben's grandmother's. The flatware is mine."

When she'd loaded in all the silver, Camryn placed it in the kitchen, near the door.

Grace walked quickly up the back staircase with Camryn following close behind. "How many bedrooms?" Camryn asked.

"Um, six, but we only had furniture in three of them,"

Grace said. She breezed down the second floor hallway toward the master wing, while Camryn opened every door they passed to gaze inside.

"Enough with the sightseeing," Grace urged. "I don't want to stick around here any longer than absolutely necessary. Let's just get the rest of my stuff and go, okay?"

She pushed open the door to the master bedroom. The king-sized bed was unmade, and clothes and shoes and towels littered nearly every flat surface.

"Uh-huh." Camryn nodded, taking in the disarray. "Now we see the girl's true colors."

"Ironic," Grace said. "Ben is a total neat nut. He even colorizes his sock drawer."

"You could put my whole downstairs in this bedroom," Camryn said, slowly doing a 360-degree turn to take it all in. She sat on the bed and fingered the rumpled top sheet. "Are these Pratesi?"

"Yup," Grace said. "We did a giveaway with them."

"Think the skank would notice if I borrowed a set of 'em?"

"In here." Grace jerked her head in the direction of her home office. She opened one of the custom cabinets and began loading her photographic equipment into a black duffel bag she'd brought along for that purpose. Her Nikon camera bodies, her lenses—all of it went into the bag. She scanned the bookshelves holding the hundreds of design books she'd lovingly collected and cataloged over the years, pulling out her favorites and adding them to the duffel bag.

She dragged the duffel bag into the bedroom and dumped it before heading into her dressing room, where Camryn stood, looking bug-eyed at the clothing. She held out the sleeve of a gaudy tie-dyed dress. "This doesn't look like your style."

Grace wrinkled her nose. "None of this stuff is mine.

It's all hers." She opened one of the drawers in the built-in center cupboard and, with her pinkie, held up a hot-pink scrap of lace. "Totally not mine."

She continued rifling through the clothing in the closet. "Damn! This is all J'Aimee's crap. If she threw my clothes out . . ."

"Hey!" Camryn stood in the doorway. "I think I found your stuff. It's in the room next door."

Nearly every item of clothing Grace owned had been dumped on the bedroom floor. Dresses and blouses still on hangers, folding clothes, shoes, handbags—all of it tossed in the corner. Grace stood with her hands on her hips, looking around the room, a lump rising in her throat.

"What a pretty room," Camryn said, looking around.

Grace had spent weeks choosing just the right shade of pale seafoam green for the walls of the bedroom. She'd chosen a natural linen fabric for drapes with a narrow turquoise ribbon trim. The dresser was an old one she'd found at an estate sale in Bradenton, a battered oak chest of drawers that she'd painted a soft white, distressed, then waxed. The only other furniture in the room was an antique wicker rocking chair. She'd reupholstered it herself with a turquoise gingham cushion.

"Where's the bed?" Camryn asked.

"Never got around to buying one," Grace said. Her smile was tight. "This was going to be the nursery."

"Oh." Camryn put an arm around Grace's shoulder. "You wanted kids?"

"Yeah. I had started taking fertility meds, but then . . ." She shrugged. "So it's just as well. I see the crap Wyatt is going through with his ex, and, well, a divorce is tough enough for grown-ups without putting a little kid through all that."

Grace picked out a few items of clothing, a couple pair

of jeans, her favorite little black dress, and a battered leather bomber jacket she'd owned since high school days. "Let's go," she said, turning toward the door.

"That's all you're taking?" Camryn gestured at the mound of clothes and accessories. "You're just going to leave all this stuff here?" She picked up a hot-pink linen dress. "Girl, this is Tory Burch." She added a black-and-white striped patent leather purse. "And this is Kate Spade. You don't walk away from Kate and Tory."

"Take them if you want," Grace said. She looked around the room, searching for an empty suitcase, but found only a lumpy black plastic trash bag. She dumped the contents of the bag onto the floor.

But this clothing wasn't hers. There was a pair of denim shorts, two sizes smaller than Grace wore, a sleeveless black T-shirt, and a pair of new-looking tennis shoes. Everything in the bag was spattered with paint. Bright orange paint. The same memorable hue that had been splashed across the walls at Mandevilla Manor.

"I knew it," Grace said softly, picking up the T-shirt and holding it out for Camryn to see. "I knew it was her."

She heard footsteps on the stairs and froze. A moment later, Ben walked into the room. "What the hell do you think you're doing?"

The two women stared at him. Ben's face was already tanned, but now it was flushed red with anger.

Camryn looked at her in a state of panic. Grace swallowed hard, and then she recalled her mission, and her motive.

"I came to pick up some of my belongings," she said.

"You're burglarizing my home," Ben said. He held up his cell phone. "Sheldon spotted you when you came through the gate, and he called me to ask if I knew you were in the neighborhood. I've got to remember to tip him better at Christmas this year."

"It's still my home, too," Grace said, glaring at him. "And I'm not taking anything that doesn't belong to me."

He pointed at the duffel bag at her feet. "What's in there?"

"My cameras, some of my design books. Nothing of yours."

"I should call the cops on you," Ben said. He picked up the duffel bag and withdrew her macro lens. "This doesn't belong to you."

She snatched it out of his hands. "My dad gave me this for my birthday the last year he was alive. And I'll be damned if I'll let the two of you have it."

"Take it and get out then," Ben said. He glanced at Camryn. "I know you. Camryn Nobles, News Four You. Does your station manager know you're in the habit of breaking and entering?"

Grace shook the paint-spattered T-shirt at Ben. "Do your blog advertisers know you and the slut are in the habit of breaking and entering and vandalizing private property?"

Ben looked at the T-shirt with disinterest. "What's that supposed to be?"

"Your girlfriend was wearing this the other night when she trashed the house I've been working on over on Mandevilla. And don't even try to deny it. This is the same orange paint she splashed all over the kitchen walls. She read my blog posts on TrueGrace, saw that I had a new project, and decided to ruin it for me."

"Ridiculous," Ben said. But he suddenly looked uncomfortable.

"Were you there, too?" Grace asked, her voice rising. "Did you help her break in? I bet you did."

"You're crazy," Ben said. "J'Aimee doesn't even know where that house is."

"Sure she does. Anybody who reads my blog would know it's on Mandevilla. J'Aimee showed up there just last week. To warn me that if I contacted any more of your advertisers, she'd get even with me. And that's just what she did."

"I'm telling you you're wrong. J'Aimee wouldn't do anything like that," Ben insisted.

Grace shoved the T-shirt in his face. "She did it, Ben! And here's the proof. Orange paint. She got it all over her clothes."

He pushed her hand away.

"You really didn't know what she was up to, Ben, did you? She was hiding this stuff from you."

"Take your crap and get out," Ben said, sounding weary.

They heard a door slam from downstairs, and then footsteps.

"Ben?" J'Aimee's voice was shrill, panicky. "Where are you? Call the police! We've been robbed." She was practically running up the stairs.

"I'm in here," Ben called. "And it's not burglars. It's Grace."

59.

"What's she doing here?" J'Aimee looked from Ben to Grace, eyes narrowed with suspicion.

"Picking up some of my belongings," Grace said. She held up the black T-shirt. "But I think you mixed up some of your stuff with mine."

J'Aimee pushed a strand of black hair behind one ear. She was dressed in chic lime-green cropped Lululemon yoga pants and a midriff-baring sports bra, and she was barefoot. She flicked the fabric of the T-shirt. "That's not mine." She gestured around the room. "All this crap is yours. You might as well take the rest of it when you go, because I'm getting ready to redecorate in here."

A shadow passed briefly over Grace's face. J'Aimee knew she'd been planning on using this room as a nursery. She'd even volunteered to help paint it, not even six months ago, shortly after she'd become Grace's assistant.

She swallowed her grief over what might have been and channeled it into anger over what had actually occurred.

"These clothes are yours and you know it," Grace said. She dropped the T-shirt and picked up the paint-spotted sneakers. "These shoes are a size six. And I wear an eight.

Notice the paint? It's the exact same color as the orange you tossed all over the house on Mandevilla."

"I don't know what you're talking about," J'Aimee said, turning to leave. "Ben? I'm gonna hit the shower. Could you make sure she doesn't take anything of mine?"

Grace reached out and snagged the stretchy shoulder strap of J'Aimee's top. The younger woman tried to tug loose of Grace's grip, but she held tight.

"Oh, don't go just yet, J'Aimee. Don't you want to tell Ben about the rest of the sweet stunts you pulled at that house? I mean, besides the paint? Don't you want to brag about how you actually pooped in the bathtub, and then wrote obscenities on the wall with your own excrement?"

"Classy," Camryn muttered.

Ben's face registered revulsion. "Come on, Grace."

"I'm betting you didn't share that happy little story," Grace said. "Fortunately, I've got pictures to prove it." She reached for her cell phone. She didn't, actually, but she knew Ben wouldn't look at them, even if she did have pictures.

"Gross," J'Aimee said, trying to inch away. But Grace pulled her back, keeping a firm hold on J'Aimee's top.

"You should know," Grace retorted. "How about the fire? Did you tell Ben you also set a fire in the living room? If it hadn't been for the neighbor, who saw the flames shortly after you tried to torch the place, it probably would have burned to the ground."

"I didn't!" J'Aimee said stubbornly. She grabbed Grace's hands and wrenched herself loose.

Camryn had been standing quietly on the sidelines, but now she stepped forward. She took one of the sneakers and sniffed it delicately.

"Yup," she said succinctly. "Lighter fluid." She carefully placed both shoes in her oversized pocketbook. "The fire marshall is going to want to take a look at these." She glanced over at Grace. "Let's take the shirt and pants, too. I'll bet they've got traces of lighter fluid, too. It doesn't even take a crime lab."

"Who the hell are you?" J'Aimee demanded.

"Just a friend," Camryn said lightly. "Who happens to be an investigative reporter."

"She's from channel four," Ben said, sounding uneasy. "The same reporter who snuck in after Grace left."

"How did they get in here today?" J'Aimee demanded. "I thought you left instructions at the gate."

Camryn struck a pose and held up the sneaker like an imaginary microphone, saying sotto voce, "News Four You has learned that a local lifestyles blogger, J'Aimee . . ."

She turned to Grace. "What's her last name?"

"Scoggins," Grace said.

"Lifestyle blogger J'Aimee Scoggins is under investigation for breaking and entering, destruction of private property, and arson after she allegedly broke into a residence on Anna Maria Island being redecorated by rival blogger Grace Davenport. Davenport, thirty-four . . ."

"I'm actually thirty-eight," Grace corrected.

"Davenport, thirty-eight, is the estranged wife of local businessman Ben Stanton. Sources tell me that J'Aimee Scoggins and Stanton are romantically involved," Camryn said.

"Very funny," Ben said. He pointed toward the door. "Now, leave. Or I will call the cops."

Grace gathered up the rest of the paint-spattered clothing and slid it into the plastic sack, which she gripped tightly.

"You still haven't asked her if she did it," she said. "But maybe you already know the answer."

Ben turned suddenly and stared at J'Aimee. "Tell me you didn't do any of this. Please."

J'Aimee took a step backward. "She's bluffing. She can't

prove those clothes are mine. She probably put them here herself."

"J'Aimee?" Ben's deep voice was chilly. "Yes or no?"

"Yes! Okay?" J'Aimee said defiantly. "It was just a little joke. God! You people need to lighten up. I didn't mean to break the glass. I was opening the window, which was unlocked, and it just cracked. You can't break into a place that isn't even really locked up."

"What about the paint?" Ben asked.

"Big deal. A little orange paint. The place is a dump. Anyway, she had it coming, writing to my advertisers, telling them I was stealing from her . . . We lost our Kohler ads because of her."

Ben swore softly, under his breath. "And what she said? About the bathroom? Dear God, tell me you didn't actually . . ."

"It was just a joke!" J'Aimee exclaimed. "Okay, maybe it did get a little out of hand. I took a bunch of empty beer cans over there, to make it look like it was kids, and I had a couple of wine coolers of my own, so maybe that wasn't really a cool thing to do." She glanced at Grace. "I'm sorry, okay? Is that what you want to hear?"

"No," Grace snapped. "Sorry doesn't cut it anymore. You could have burned that house to the ground. It belongs to a sweet old man who was getting ready to rent it to me. But after you vandalized the place, he just wants to sell it and be done with it. You and I both know you weren't joking around when you went over there the other night. You wanted to send me a message. Well, you did that, all right. I got the message loud and clear."

Ben was shaking his head. "I can't believe you pulled a stupid stunt like this. Arson! Really? They put people in jail for that, J'Aimee."

"I'm sorry! I told you I was sorry," J'Aimee said, her voice pleading. "Ben . . ."

"Go take your shower," Ben said wearily. "I can't deal with you right now."

J'Aimee turned and slunk out of the room. A moment later, they heard the bedroom door slam.

Camryn edged toward the door, too. "I'll just, uh, be waiting outside. Whenever you're ready."

Ben watched her go. He sighed loudly. "Look, Grace, you have to believe me. I did not put J'Aimee up to this. I would never . . . I mean, we've had our differences." He swallowed and looked away. "The stuff with Gracenotes, that's business. It's not personal."

"It's very personal to me," Grace said. "You and J'Aimee have done your best to put me out of business. You say it wasn't your idea to have her vandalize that house, but you and I both know J'Aimee's never had an original idea in her life. She took her cues from you. Maybe you didn't light that fire, but you sure as hell showed her where the matches were."

He rubbed his jaw. "You're not serious about going to the police with this, are you? J'Aimee's just a kid. Yeah, she did it to get back at you. Because you intimidate her. No matter what, in a weird way, you're still her idol. You heard her. As far as she knew, this was just a prank that got out of hand."

"I'm her idol? That's a laugh."

"It's true," Ben insisted. "She reads every word you write, goes back over your old posts, trying to copy your style. I keep trying to tell her, she's got her own style, which she should develop, but for some reason she's fixated on you, on being bigger, better than you. I guess maybe I should have seen the potential for what happened, should have reined her in before it came to this."

"Ya think?" Grace shot back.

"I'm asking you, please. Don't make a federal case out of this. I'll have a serious talk with J'Aimee. And I'll do whatever it takes to make it right. I'll pay for all the damages, reimburse you for your lost time. I'll fix it. I promise."

"You'll fix it," Grace said, laughing bitterly. "There's that expression of yours again. You just love the idea of covering things up, of pretending they never happened, don't you, Ben?"

"I'm a pragmatist. A businessman," he said calmly. "So, do we have a deal?"

She crossed her arms and gave him a long, hard look. "It's not up to me. It's Arthur's house. I'll tell him about your offer."

"And you'll suggest we settle this without the police getting involved?" he persisted.

Grace saw an opening, and she went for it. "I'll suggest he accept your offer. On one condition."

Ben rolled his eyes. "Here it comes. The blackmail."

"You can call it whatever you like," Grace said. "Here's the deal. You tell your lawyer that you want to settle things fairly with me. I'm not looking to gouge you, Ben. But it's totally unfair that I should have to walk away from this marriage with not a dime to my name. We built a business together, and by rights half of the proceeds from it should be mine. That's what I want. No more, no less."

"And if I don't give you what you want?"

Grace held the garbage bag aloft. "There's always this. And remember, Camryn was standing right here when J'Aimee confessed. I wouldn't put it past her to have recorded the whole thing. You know how sneaky these journalism types are."

60.

By the time Grace emerged from the house, Marissa and Camryn were waiting for her in the golf cart. Camryn held the pillowcase with the wedding silver in her lap. Grace placed the duffel bag with her books and camera equipment on the floor of the backseat and climbed onto the seat, tightly clutching the black garbage bag.

"Let's go," Grace said, glancing back toward the house, half expecting J'Aimee to follow in hot pursuit.

Marissa steered the cart down the driveway and around the corner toward her own house.

Camryn turned around in her seat, one eyebrow raised in question. "So?"

"Mission accomplished," Grace said. "I got what I came for. And more." Marissa turned around, too, and the three women high-fived each other.

"I'm afraid I blew it, though," Marissa said apologetically. "I just went in the house for a minute. They must have slipped right past me. But I hear you got the goods on that little bitch."

"We'll see," Grace said. "The big thing is, we managed to rattle Ben. He's really worried I might go to the cops."

"How worried?" Camryn asked.

"Worried enough that he agreed to talk financial settlement."

"That's great," Camryn said. "You must have done some major cage rattling after I hightailed it out of there."

"I might have mentioned that you were probably secretly taping J'Aimee's confession," Grace admitted.

Camryn smirked, then pulled her iPhone from her pocket, held it up, and tapped an icon. J'Aimee's high-pitched voice floated in the air. "It was a joke," she screeched. Camryn tapped the button and the phone went silent.

"Never underestimate a woman," she advised. "Especially one who's been jerked around the way you and I have."

The two high-fived each other one more time.

"Where's my father?"

Wyatt stood staring down at Callie, still half asleep on the sofa.

She stretched and yawned. "What?"

"Dad. He's not here. Where'd he go?"

Callie sat up slowly. "How should I know?"

"Did he see you here this morning?" Wyatt demanded. "Come on, Callie. This is important. Did he say anything?"

"No. Well, yeah. I mean, he came out of his room, and I heard him banging pots and pans around in the kitchen, making coffee. I went out and asked him if I could have a cup, and he just stared at me. He put the coffeepot down and walked out the door. God! I'm telling you, there is something wrong with that old man. And I'm not talking about diabetes, Wyatt. He's seriously senile."

"Shit," Wyatt said softly. "He's not senile! He can't stand the sight of you, if you want to know the truth. He probably saw you here, dressed in my robe, and got the wrong idea. Which way did he go, did you see?"

"You know how I am before I get my coffee in the morning. He left. That's all I know."

"Hey, Mom."

Callie and Wyatt turned to see their young son, standing in the doorway to the living room, dressed in his Lightning McQueen pajama bottoms.

"Good morning, Bo-Bo," Callie said, her pout turning instantly to a sunny smile. "Come give your mama some sugar."

Bo allowed himself to be cuddled, but only for a moment. Pulling away, he looked at his father's troubled countenance.

"Is Granddad missing again?"

"Not really missing," Wyatt said hastily. "He went out for a walk early this morning, and I'm a little worried, because I don't know whether he remembered to eat some breakfast or take his medicine. I'm going to hop on the cart and take a spin around the park to pick him up. You want to help me track him?"

"Sure!" Bo looked hesitantly at his mother. "I'll be right back, Mom, okay?"

"Take all the time you need," Callie said, yawning again. "I'll be around when you get back."

Grace tried calling Wyatt from the Publix parking lot, but her call went directly to voice mail. It was just as well, she thought, because she really wanted to tell him firsthand how her visit to Gulf Vista played out.

She drove around to the back entrance to Jungle Jerry's and found the nearly hidden driveway that led to Wyatt's trailer. His truck was parked under the carport, in front of a vehicle she'd never seen before, a battered and rust-spotted Jeep.

She tapped lightly at the aluminum storm door. "Wyatt?" she called, and was rewarded with the sound of Sweetie's answering bark, followed by a frantic scratching at the door. She waited another minute. Maybe he was in the shower? Or out in the park, on the golf cart? Grace tapped again, and Sweetie gave another answering bark.

She tried the door. It was unlocked. She pushed the door open and stepped inside. Sweetie threw herself joyously at Grace's ankle, yipping excitedly.

"Hi, little girl," Grace said, scooping the dog up into her arms. "Where are the guys? Huh? Are you the only one home?"

"Not quite."

Grace looked up, startled.

Callie Keeler stood in the doorway from the kitchen, eating from an oversized bowl of cereal. She was barefoot, dressed only in a short, faded bathrobe, loosely belted around her waist.

"If you're looking for my husband, you just missed him," Callie said. "He and Bo are out in the park, looking for Nelson."

"Oh."

Grace's chest constricted. She hugged Sweetie close and blinked. She felt her face growing hot.

Callie laughed at her obvious discomfort and took another bite of cereal. A bit of milk trickled down her chin, and she dabbed at it with her sleeve, revealing, in the process, that she was naked under the robe.

"Awkward moment, huh? I'm guessing you must be the girlfriend Bo's been telling me about. It's Grace, right?"

"Yes," Grace managed to say.

Callie held out the bowl. "You want some cereal? It's Cocoa Puffs. I swear, you're never too old for Cocoa Puffs."

"No thanks," Grace said. She turned and left.

"Don't go on my account," Callie called, chuckling to herself. "I'll tell Wyatt you dropped by."

"Dumb, dumb, dumb." Grace banged her head on the steering wheel with each exclamation. Sweetie whined and crawled onto her lap, licking her chin as a consolation prize.

She started the car and headed down the sandy driveway toward the street. She blinked back tears as she navigated through the thick foliage that lined both sides of the narrow one-way drive.

It was after ten o'clock in the morning, and there stood Callie Keeler, dressed only in Wyatt's robe, calmly eating cereal. Obviously, she'd spent the night there. "You just missed my husband," she'd said. Not "ex-husband," not "Wyatt," but "husband," letting Grace know she'd reclaimed him.

"You can have him," Grace muttered.

No wonder he'd begged off seeing her last night. He'd had a much better offer from his wayward wife. And why should that come as a surprise? Wyatt had made it clear right from the start that his first commitment was to his son's happiness. And like any six-year-old, Bo wanted his parents back together.

How could she have believed he wanted to start a new life with her? How could she let herself get sucked into a relationship on the rebound? Double rebound, if you wanted to be technical, since both she and Wyatt were coming out of ruined marriages. And with a guy she'd met in a divorce-recovery group!

"Stupid, stupid, stupid," she chanted, slapping the dashboard for emphasis.

Sweetie looked up at her with huge, uncomprehending brown eyes.

"Never trust a man, Sweetie," Grace told the dog. "They all lie. Every damn one of them is a liar."

Her cell phone rang. She grabbed it and looked at the caller ID. It was Wyatt.

"This is the liar calling right now," Grace told Sweetie. "Can you believe it?"

She tossed the phone onto the seat, and the little dog sniffed it. The phone rang again. She knew without looking it would be him. And he'd probably keep calling. Why postpone the inevitable? She snatched up the phone and tapped the CONNECT button.

"What?"

"Grace, I just got back to the trailer. Callie told me you came by."

"How nice of her." Grace sneered. "She's a great hostess, Wyatt. She even offered me some of her Cocoa Puffs. I'm sure you two will be very happy. Again."

"Look, it's not like you think," Wyatt said. "I don't care what she told you; we are not back together. We are not getting back together."

"So, last night—was that just a one-night stand? And you think that doesn't count?"

"She slept on the sofa! She broke up with Luke last week, and she called me, hoping I'd let her stay here, but I told her there was no way. So she went to her sister's house, but Luke showed up over there, and they were drinking, so Kendra kicked her out in the middle of the night. You know what it was like last night—it was raining. And then Bo woke up and saw her, so what was I gonna do, kick her out into the rain, with my son standing there, begging me to let her stay?"

"Let me ask you a question," Grace said, her voice oddly cold. "You say this all started last week? Did it ever occur to you to mention to me that your wife was trying to move back in with you? Especially after you told me you couldn't see me last night, because of Bo?"

"That was a mistake on my part, and I know that now," he said, his words tumbling together. "But I didn't tell you because I knew you'd get the wrong idea," Wyatt said. "Which you did. I never had any intention of taking Callie back. It's over between us. And I've told her that. Repeatedly."

"And yet there she was this morning, all cozied up at your place. Was that your robe she was wearing? Or has she already started to unpack?"

"Dammit, Grace," Wyatt said hoarsely. "She slept on the sofa. And she's gone now. I told her she can't come back. And if you don't believe me, you can ask Dad. That's where I was when you came by, out looking for him. He saw Callie asleep on the sofa this morning, and he was so pissed, he just took off, because he can't stand to be under the same roof with her. Or ask Bo. He's in the other room, sulking, because he didn't want his mother to go. But she has. Okay? It is over between Callie and me."

Grace bit her lip. She pulled out of the driveway and into traffic. "You just think it's over," she told him. "But she's not going to let you go, and Bo's not going to let her go. I can't do this, Wyatt. I can't hang around, wondering what will happen with Callie's next crisis. You need to figure all this stuff out by yourself. You're not ready for a new relationship. Not with me, anyway."

"Grace?" His voice was pleading. "I care about you Grace. Don't hang up, please. Just meet me someplace, okay, and let's talk about this. What about Gus's? That doughnut place? Can you just at least talk to me face-to-face?"

"I don't think so," she said sadly. "Not even for doughnuts."

61.

Grace unlocked the door to Mitzi's condo and gently set Sweetie down on the floor. She sank down onto the white sofa and stared out the sliding glass doors at the jade-green surf below. The giddy euphoria she'd experienced earlier in the day, after finally forcing Ben to agree to a financial settlement, was forgotten. Now she felt the gray mist of depression settling over her, like a suffocating woolen blanket.

The bright, buttery-hued sunlight pouring into the apartment was a cruel intrusion. She covered her eyes with one of the colorful throw pillows she'd bought only days earlier and flounced facedown on the sofa.

She heard the muffled sound of her cell phone ringing and ignored it. She let two more calls go directly to voice mail. Time passed. Grace was vaguely aware of the warmth of Sweetie, who'd curled up on the sofa alongside her. She heard the waves rolling ashore outside, and the distant sound of seagulls, and the occasional slamming of a car door.

But the sound of a key turning in the condo's door jolted her back to consciousness. She rolled over and saw the front door swing open, but she did not bother to sit up.

"There you are," Mitzi Stillwell exclaimed. "I've been looking all over town for you. Why didn't you answer my calls? Or your mother's?"

"I just . . . didn't want to deal with anything," Grace said dully. "Why? What's going on?"

Mitzi walked over and sat on the edge of the club chair. "What's wrong with you? Are you sick?"

"I'm okay," Grace said. "Relatively speaking."

Her lawyer gave her an appraising look. "You had a fight with Wyatt, didn't you?"

"It's over," Grace said.

Mitzi groaned. "Oh no. Don't tell me. He's gone back to his wife?"

"Not yet, but he probably will," Grace said. "She broke up with her boyfriend, and she spent the night at his place last night. Which he didn't feel the need to tell me. So it's only a matter of time."

"Did he tell you he wants her back?"

"No," Grace admitted. "He says she slept on the sofa, and the only reason he let her stay was because it was raining so hard last night, and Bo begged him to. He swears they're through, but I don't believe it."

Mitzi patted her arm. "I'm sorry, Grace. I see this all the time in my line of work. Couples go through the worst kind of traumas, file for divorce, then, at some point, they begin to think maybe they ought to give it another try. You especially see it in families with young children."

"No kid wants to see his parents split up," Grace said, thinking about her own reaction to Rochelle's recent disturbing revelation about her marriage to Grace's father.

Mitzi sighed. "Well, that's not exactly true. There are kids who've seen too much—too much violence, hostility, aggression in their parents' marriage. Those kids crave normality; they crave peace. And the smart ones know that's only possible if a toxic marriage does break up."

"I'm just thankful Ben and I didn't have kids," Grace said.

"Speaking of Ben," Mitzi said, raising an eyebrow. "Dickie Murphree called me out of the blue a little while ago, to say they're ready to talk settlement."

"Good," Grace said.

"Good? That's all you can say? Come on, Grace, snap out of it! This is huge. For months now, they've totally stonewalled us. And now, suddenly, they finally want to settle. Any idea what caused this new development?"

"I went over to the house this morning, to get some of my things. And in the process, I found pretty solid proof that J'Aimee really did vandalize Mandevilla Manor."

"How the hell did you get past security?" Mitzi asked. "Please don't tell me you burglarized the place."

"Camryn—my friend from divorce-recovery group? She's friends with the woman who lives directly behind our house, Marissa. She's married to LaDarion Banks, the baseball player. Marissa called the gate and told them she was expecting Camryn as her guest. And I didn't have to break into the house. I still have my key. Easy-peasy."

"And at some point during your unauthorized visit, Ben just agreed to a fair and equitable settlement with you?"

"Ben doesn't want J'Aimee charged with the vandalism—and arson—at Mandevilla Manor. I told him I'd let Arthur know what I'd discovered but that I'd suggest Arthur allow Ben to pay for all the damages and make restitution, without getting the cops involved. Naturally, Ben was grateful," Grace said.

"Naturally," Mitzi said wryly. "I've got news on another front, too. I had a long chat yesterday with Carlton Towne concerning the experience of his client, Harriett, with Judge Stackpole."

"And?" Grace was determined not to get her hopes built up. She'd had enough of an emotional roller-coaster ride for one day. For one year, even.

"Carlton is very old-school. He's been practicing law in this county for more than forty years, and he doesn't like to rock the boat."

"So, that's that," Grace said. "It was worth a try, though."

"Would you stop being so negative! Carlton may be adverse to rocking the boat, but on the other hand, he is also a stickler on the matter of rules and ethics. And he was enraged when I told him how Stackpole has been ordering divorcing parties into therapy—and then steering those same parties to a woman with whom he's romantically involved. He agrees with me that we should file a formal complaint with the JQC."

"Remind me what the JQC actually is?" Grace said.

"Judicial Qualifications Committee. It's the state agency that governs and disciplines judges," Mitzi said. "So that's our next step. First, we document every single instance we know of where Stackpole made attending therapy mandatory for divorcing parties. Then, we assemble an exhaustingly thorough and compelling complaint and take it to the JQC. And if all goes well, they take Stackpole to the woodshed. Metaphorically speaking."

Grace scratched Sweetie's ears absentmindedly. "And you really think this JQC will believe us? And they'll do what?"

"They can do anything from a reprimand to a fine to a suspension from office to removing him from office," Mitzi said. "He could also be 'involuntarily retired due to illness,' although I doubt it would come to that."

"And what do you need from me?" Grace asked.

"We need Paula Talbott-Sinclair on our side. We need her to tell the JQC about her involvement with Judge Stackpole."

"Is that all?" Grace shook her head. "Mitzi, how am I supposed to make that happen? What makes you think I can get Paula to turn on her sugar daddy?"

Mitzi gave her an appraising look. "You're a woman of many talents, Grace, not the least of which is charm. So you do your thing, and I'll do mine. Deal?"

Grace stared out the window for a while. "I'll give it a shot," she said finally.

"Good," Mitzi said briskly. She reached out and patted Sweetie's head. "What'll you do about the dog? I mean, will you still split custody with Wyatt at night?"

"Gaaaawd," Grace said, flopping backward onto the sofa again. "I hadn't even thought about that. I won't take her back to Wyatt's. And I can't take her to my mom's place."

"Well," Mitzi said, looking around the condo. "I guess it wouldn't hurt if the two of you stayed here for a couple weeks. It's really coming along, Grace. I love the bright colors, and the lamps and things. I never would have thought of doing any of this."

"I couldn't just squat here," Grace said uneasily. "It wouldn't be right."

"Why not? You've still got more work to do here, and I'm too busy to use it for the next month or so anyway. The complex is pet-friendly." Mitzi picked up her oversized pocketbook and went to the door.

"I think you should stay," she said, her hand on the doorknob. "You've been through a rough patch. Spend some time here alone, you and Sweetie. If all goes well, Ben will cough up an equitable settlement; we'll get Stackpole out of our hair, if not off the bench; and then you can figure out the next chapter in the Grace Davenport story."

Grace gave her lawyer a rueful smile. "Next chapter? Right now, I can't even figure out the next five minutes."

62.

Grace lolled on the sofa, flipping through channels with the remote control. She paused when she got to *The Real Housewives of Atlanta*. Rochelle watched the show religiously, but Grace had never really seen it. But tonight, she thought, as she dipped a plastic fork into the paper carton of take-out kung pao chicken, and only tonight, she would watch trashy TV reruns and wallow in self-pity.

Her cell phone rang. She picked it up and looked at the caller ID. It was Camryn.

"Where are you and what are you doing?" Camryn demanded.

"I'm at a client's condo, watching *The Real Housewives of Atlanta*," she said warily. "Can I ask you a question? Who are these women? Why do they have their own television show?"

"Girlfriend, I do not have the time to explain RHOA to you. Anyway, you need to turn on channel eight. Now. Because, honey, this is priceless."

Sweetie was sitting directly on top of the remote control. Grace gently slid it out from under the dog's butt and pointed the remote at Mitzi's forty-eight-inch flat-screen.

She was rewarded by fuzzy footage of what looked like two well-dressed women who appeared to be pelting each other with . . . dinner rolls? They were both screeching at the top of their lungs.

"A food fight? On the ten o'clock news? This is why you called?" Grace asked.

"Keep watching," Camryn said, chuckling. "It gets better."

A man's deep voice cut through the shrill din. "Eileen! What the hell?"

"Did you get that?" Camryn asked. "Recognize that voice?"

Grace leaned forward and stared intently at the television, but the camera kept jerking back and forth between the two women. The older of the two, a brunette, lunged toward the other, clawing at her face. Now, a man was tugging at her arm, vainly attempting to fend her off. His back was to the camera, but, once, Grace glimpsed a vaguely familiar profile.

The younger woman, a strikingly attractive African-American woman with short, platinum-blond hair was batting away the other woman's blows. "Get her off of me," she hollered. "Cedric, do something."

Cedric?

"It can't be," Grace whispered, dropping onto the floor, crawling closer to the television until her face was only inches from the screen. The man glanced over his shoulder at the camera, then flung his hand across his face. "Are you filming this? Stop that! Get that thing away from me." He whirled around, and for a moment, just a moment, Grace saw the angry countenance of the Honorable Cedric N. Stackpole Jr.

"Hey, man," another male voice protested. "You can't do that." And then the camera jerked violently, and the footage ended.

"Oh. My. God." Grace was clutching her hand to her chest. "Did I really just see what I think I saw?"

"In living color," Camryn said. "Merry Christmas to us."

"What? I mean, how . . ." Grace sputtered. "What exactly did I just watch?"

"That, Gracie dear, was footage taken last night at a restaurant in Sarasota by an alert diner, who just happened to be talking to a friend on his cell phone, when Eileen Stackpole walked into the restaurant and caught her husband having a tête-à-tête with a pretty young thing."

"I think I've seen her before," Grace said. "The PYT, I mean."

"Mm-hmm," Camryn said. "We have all seen that girl. She's a twenty-three-year-old bailiff assigned to Stackpole's courtroom. Her name is Monique Massey. And I guarantee you the two of them were not discussing tort reform in a cozy little booth in a pricey French bistro at ten o'clock last night."

Grace could hardly take it all in. "How did this end up on the news? What's it all mean?"

"It got on the news because Stackpole flipped his shit when he realized the other diner was filming the whole thing. He knocked the cell phone out of the guy's hand and took a swing at him. One of the waiters pulled the judge off the guy, but, in the meantime, the cell-phone guy's dinner companion called the cops."

"Tell me they arrested Stackpole," Grace begged.

"No such luck," Camryn said. "Stackpole paid his bill and hustled lil Monique outta there before the po-po arrived. And Eileen took a powder, too. The restaurant manager smoothed things over by offering everybody in the place a free drink and dessert. By the time the cops arrived, all was calm. But at some point, the waiter pulled the cell-phone guy aside and whispered to him the identity of his assailant. Apparently, Stackpole is a regular there—and a lousy tipper. Now the cell-phone guy says he's going to sue Stackpole for assault and battery."

"How do you happen to know so much about all this?" Grace asked. "And why isn't this story on *your* station?"

Camryn sighed heavily. "The cell-phone guy e-mailed the footage to me first. But because of my, er, prior history with Stackpole, my news director doesn't want anything to do with the story. I begged and pleaded and threatened, but he won't budge. So I might have tipped off a friend at our rival station. Anonymously, of course. At least the story is out there, and it's hugely embarrassing to Stackpole. So for once, I don't even mind being scooped."

"What else do you know?" Grace asked. "Did Mrs. Stackpole just happen to bump into the judge and this bailiff, or did she know they'd been seeing each other? And what happens now? Will she divorce him? And what about the guy with the camera?"

Before Camryn could answer her barrage of questions, Grace's phone beeped to alert her that she had another incoming call. "Sorry," Grace said. "I better take this. It's my lawyer."

"I'm thinking this calls for a celebration," Camryn said hastily. "Tomorrow night, eight, at the Sandbox. I'll call everybody else. You're in, right?"

"Absolutely," Grace said.

"Did you just see the news on channel eight?" Mitzi asked gleefully.

"Camryn, one of the girls in my divorce group, called to tell me about it," Grace said. "I could just watch it over and over; it's so delicious."

"You totally can. It was on at six o'clock, too. They've already posted the footage on the station's Web site," Mitzi told her. "I've watched it four times, and it gets better with every viewing."

"Better for us," Grace said. "But how would you like to be Eileen Stackpole? Can you imagine the humiliation?"

"I can't imagine marrying the man in the first place. Yeechhh. What a worm! Of course, there's got to be a lot more to the story than what they put on the air tonight," Mitzi speculated. "And the rumors are already flying all over town. Right before I called you, I heard from one of the other lawyers who's tried divorces before Stackpole. She heard Eileen Stackpole didn't just stumble into that restaurant last night. She'd supposedly hired a private investigator. He's the one who let her know Stackpole was playing footsie with his bailiff."

"A twenty-three-year-old!" Grace exclaimed. "And I definitely remember her being in the courtroom that first time we went before Stackpole. Remember, she shushed us?"

"So that's where I've seen her," Mitzi said. She laughed. "Oh, my. Cedric has been a very naughty boy, hasn't he?"

"But is all of this anything that would get him in trouble with your JQC?" Grace asked. "I mean, is being a slimeball enough to get you kicked off the bench?"

"Good question," Mitzi said. "Having your wife attack your girlfriend in a very public place might not be grounds for discipline by the JQC. Although the fact that he's involved with an employee of the court seems unethical. But I wonder how it would sit with Paula? I wonder if she knows Stackpole has *another* other woman—besides her?"

"I guess I'll have to ask her how she feels about it," Grace said, wincing.

"You do that. And let me know what you find out," Mitzi said.

63.

Grace arrived at Paula Sinclair-Talbott's office at eight o'clock on that already-steamy Monday morning, determined that she would be Paula's first client of the day.

She watched idly as the strip shopping center slowly came to life. At nine, a woman wearing a brilliant orange silk sari unlocked the doors at the Diaper Depot. At 9:30 two middle-aged Hispanic women arrived together at the door to the hearing-aid center.

Twice, her phone rang. Both times it was Wyatt. The second time, she was tempted to answer, just to hear his voice, hear him tell her he missed her and wanted her back. She had to grip the steering wheel with both hands to keep from picking up. This was for the best, she told herself.

Finally, at ten 'til ten, she watched as the VW bug zipped into a parking space three cars away. Paula Talbott-Sinclair walked briskly to her office door, unlocked it, and disappeared inside.

Paula was standing in the reception area, staring down at the computer terminal, when Grace walked inside.

"Grace?" Paula looked up and frowned. Her blond curls were mussed and there were dark circles under her unmade-up eyes. She wore a faded, shapeless black jersey dress that hung limply on her slender frame and cheap red rubber flip-flops. There were no tinkly earrings or ankle bracelets this morning. It didn't look like she'd had a fun weekend.

That makes two of us, Grace thought.

"This is a surprise," Paula said. "Is there something urgent you need to discuss?"

Grace cleared her throat. "Uh, yes, actually, there is something kind of important I'd like to talk to you about. That's okay, right? I mean, in the beginning, you told us we could call you about anything."

"Well . . . I suppose I have time," Paula said, hesitantly. "My first group doesn't start until ten thirty. Come on inside."

Grace followed the therapist into the inner office. The heat was stifling. She watched while Paula switched on the lights and then a small window-air-conditioning unit. "Sit down," Paula said, grabbing one of the folding chairs from the semicircle and dragging it over to a position in front of her desk.

"I'm going to make some tea," Paula said. "Would you like a cup?"

What she'd like, Grace thought nervously, was a Xanax, or at least a stiff cocktail. "No thanks," she said politely.

Paula drifted around the room, putting a kettle on a hot plate, rearranging the circle of chairs, and then, finally, when the tea kettle whistled, pouring the water into a lumpy pottery mug.

"Now," she said, settling into the chair behind her desk. "What's happening in your world today, Grace?"

"Um." Grace fidgeted with the strap of her purse. She'd rehearsed her speech half a dozen times at home and in the car this morning, but there was no way she could make this an easy discussion.

"The thing is, Paula," she started. "I think there's something happening in *your* world that we need to discuss."

"Oh?" Paula cautiously sipped her tea. "And how is anything in my world relevant to you?"

Grace felt her face grow warm. "I've been attending your divorce-recovery sessions—for six weeks now—because Judge Stackpole basically made it a condition of granting my divorce. And the others in my group—Camryn, Ashleigh, and Wyatt—Judge Stackpole sent them to you, too."

"That's correct," Paula said. "The judge has been a wonderful advocate for my healing work."

"He's been your lover, too," Grace blurted. "Right?"

Paula looked like she'd been slapped. "I beg your pardon?"

Grace took a deep breath, and the words came tumbling out. "We saw you together! That night the judge dropped in on our session. Wyatt and I came back here to your office. We saw you getting out of his car. You'd obviously had a big fight. You were yelling at him, and then you got out of his car and kicked his tires. You were crying and really upset."

"You're mistaken," Paula said, her voice low.

"We both saw you, Paula," Grace insisted. "And we know it was Judge Stackpole, because after he left you, we followed him back to his house on Longboat Key."

Bright pink splotches of color bloomed on Paula's long pale face. "The judge is . . . a friend. We had a misunderstanding that night. That's all."

"I don't think so. We all noticed how you were around him that night. You were absolutely . . . giddy. Come on, Paula. You're always after all of us about honesty. Why don't you be honest with me? Admit you're having an affair with Stackpole."

Paula's hands shook so violently she had to set the mug of tea on the desktop. "Therapists never discuss their per-

sonal lives with their patients. This is highly inappropriate, Grace." Her voice was stern, but Grace noticed that
Paula was now clasping her hands tightly together in her
lap—probably to stop the shaking.

Grace was shaking, too. But now the fear was gone, replaced by anger.

"Inappropriate? Do you want to talk about appropriate
behavior, Paula? Because that's a subject I'd love to discuss with you. What would you say about a prominent
judge—who, by the way, is married—having an affair with
a therapist? Would you say it's appropriate for that judge
to *require* parties in divorces in his court to attend therapy
with his mistress?"

"Mistress!" Paula yelped. "How dare you?"

Paula's outrage only fueled Grace's refusal to back down.

"Mistress—it's a nasty word, isn't it, Paula? But that's
what you are. You're sleeping with him, and in return he
sends all these shell-shocked divorce disasters right here
to your office, where they pay handsomely for the privilege of listening to your hypocrisy. The five people in my
group are forking over fifteen hundred dollars a week for
this bullshit," Grace said. "How much of that do you have
to kick to Stackpole, Paula? Half? Or does he even let you
keep that much?"

"You've got no right to talk to me like this," Paula said,
pushing back from her desk, looking wildly around the
room for an escape hatch.

"What are you gonna do, Paula? Rat me out to the
judge? Flunk me out of divorce camp? I have every right to
call you out. But what I want to know is, When do you call
him out? Huh, Paula? When do you quit being his victim?"

Paula's eyes flared. "You don't know what you're talking about."

"Sure I do. You moved here from Oregon after your life
went up in flames—a bad divorce, a nasty little pill habit,

then the arrest and then rehab. You moved to Florida to start over again, right? But you can't get licensed to call yourself a therapist here, can you? And then you meet Stackpole, and the two of you cook up this little 'divorce recovery' racket."

"It's not a racket," Paula said fiercely. "I care deeply about my patients. I counsel them and do my damnedest to help them . . ." Her voice trailed off, and her shoulders slumped.

"Avoid what happened to you?" Grace finished it for her. "How are you going to help us, Paula, when you're still so messed up yourself?"

Tears welled up in the therapist's eyes. "That's not fair. I'm sober again. I had a relapse, yes, but that's over now. And it's because of all I've gone through that I can be effective with my patients. I can use my experiences to help them get through their pain and sense of loss."

"Keep telling yourself that, Paula," Grace said. "Maybe part of it's true. But what about the rest of it? You're conspiring with Stackpole. He funnels patients to you—and we don't have any choice in the matter. If we want to get on with our lives, you have to sign off on our therapy. It's fraud."

Paula clasped and unclasped her hands. "I am a *good* therapist. I can help people; I really can. But how was I going to start a new practice? Rent office space, establish myself in the therapeutic community here? Everywhere I looked, I had people slamming doors in my face. After my divorce—it was so humiliating. And unfair. He's the one who slept with a patient and violated his professional oath. But I'm the one who lost everything. He gets to start over with a new life and a new wife, and I get . . ." She looked around the room, with its worn and stained carpet, cheap furniture, and depressing, institutional green walls. "I get this."

Grace sighed. "Yeah, well, welcome to my world. The same thing happened to me—thanks to your boyfriend, the Honorable Cedric N. Stackpole."

Paula lifted her chin defiantly. "You're in a better place now because of me, Grace. I know you don't believe it, but you are. Everybody in your group has made remarkable progress. Look at Suzanne. She's not the same person she was when she walked into this office seven weeks ago."

"Okay," Grace said. "I'll give you that one. Suzanne might be the poster girl for divorce recovery. But that doesn't give you a pass where Stackpole is concerned. He's a creep, Paula. He's a crook and a fraud and a cheater. He cheats on his wife, and he cheats on you. Did you happen to catch the news last night?"

Paula bit her lip but said nothing.

"Did you?"

"I saw," she said, her voice barely above a whisper. "Oh my God. It's all so ugly."

Grace felt sorry for Paula. She felt sorry for Eileen Stackpole, and she felt sorry for herself and everybody in her divorce group. But sorry wouldn't begin to fix what Stackpole had done.

"She's twenty-three, did you know that?" Grace asked. "That girl? The one he was cheating on you with? She's a bailiff in his courtroom. Her name is Monique Massey."

"He was mentoring her," Paula said, her chin quivering as she said it.

"Is that what he told you?" Grace asked. "What a crock! She's a county employee. He's a judge! You don't discuss your career in an expensive restaurant at ten o'clock at night. You talk about it over a cup of coffee in the break room. Or at lunch at the meat and three downtown by the courthouse. Even you couldn't believe a load of bullshit like that."

Paula sprang from her chair. "I have patients coming. You have to go, Grace."

Grace stayed seated. "It's all starting to come apart now, Paula. My lawyer and I have talked to your other patients—and their lawyers. We're going to file a complaint with the state Judicial Qualifications Committee. We can prove Stackpole's bias against women. Wyatt's your only male divorce-recovery patient—right? We know Stackpole had some kind of an unethical arrangement with you. And now we know about the affair with his bailiff."

Paula opened the door to the outer office. "You need to leave. Right now. I won't listen to any more of this."

Finally, Grace got up. "I'll leave," she said, standing just inside the doorway. "But I won't shut up. This isn't going to go away." She studied the therapist's face, looking for some opening, some sense that Paula might switch sides.

"I think you really do care about your patients, Paula. I don't know how you got mixed up with a sleazeball like Stackpole, but you have to know he's been using you. He's betrayed his oath of office, and he's betrayed you. Maybe you should take some of your own advice. Take an honest look at what's happened in your life since you hooked up with Stackpole. Come up with an action plan."

The bell on the outer office door tinkled and a middle-aged woman stepped inside. "Hello, Rachel!" Paula called out. "I'll be right with you."

She lowered her voice to a whisper. "You have to go!"

Grace touched the therapist's wrist. "Think about it, Paula. We need your help. We *are* going to file a complaint against him. There will be an investigation. Questions are going to be asked."

The door opened and another woman stepped inside. Paula looked frantically from Grace to the two women standing in her waiting room.

"Almost done here," Paula called cheerily.

"I'm going to have my lawyer call you," Grace said quietly. "Her name is Mitzi Stillwell. She's a nice person. Will you at least talk to her?"

"Go!" Paula said fiercely.

64.

The members of the Lady Slipper Garden Circle asked endless questions about Jungle Jerry's unusual bromeliad and orchid collection, and Wyatt patiently answered each and every one. By noon he'd marshaled the eleven women through the park and returned them to the gift shop, where they ate their box lunches and listened to the patented garden-club talk his grandfather had written forty years earlier.

Finally, shortly after two, Joyce ushered the last garden clubber out the door and into the parking lot.

Wyatt collapsed onto his desk chair and drained the bottle of cold water Joyce brought him. "How was I?" he asked, as she sat in the chair opposite his.

"You were terrific," Joyce said. "You always are. Every single one of them wanted to adopt you and take you home and feed you. A couple of the younger ones? I think they had better plans."

Wyatt laughed and blushed.

"When is she leaving?" Joyce asked.

"Who?"

"Callie. You know I don't normally poke my nose into

your business, but I have to be honest with you, Wyatt. If she's here for good, I'm leaving."

Wyatt's jaw tightened. "She leaves today. In fact, I told her this morning she had to be gone by lunchtime."

"She's still here. She took Bo over to Scout's house and she was gone for a couple hours, but now she's back again, and your dad is furious. He won't stay in your place while she's there, so he's been out cleaning the birdcages for hours now, and I don't think it's good for him to be out in the heat this time of day."

"Thanks, Joyce. I'll deal with it. Would you please lock up here, then go fetch Nelson and tell him the coast is about to be clear?"

Joyce smiled. "I'll be happy to."

He found Callie in the trailer's kitchen. She was barefoot, humming happily, and stirring something on top of the stove.

"What do you think you're doing?" he demanded.

"What's it look like I'm doing?" She didn't look up. "I'm fixing my spaghetti sauce for dinner tonight. It's Bo's favorite."

"Leave it," Wyatt said.

Now, she turned from the stove, still holding the spoon she'd been using on the sauce. "Oh, for Pete's sake, Wyatt. You know I don't have any place to stay. Why are you being such a complete dick about this?"

He pried the wooden spoon from her hand and dropped it in the sink. "We're getting divorced, Callie. That's what you wanted, and that's what you're getting. Despite your best efforts, I've managed to rebuild my life. Without you. I've tried to be nice, but nice doesn't work with you. So now, I need you to get your stuff and put it in your vehicle and leave."

"And go where?" she said, already pouting.

"I don't care where you go from here," he said, amazed at the fact that he really didn't. "Go back to your sister's, to a motel, whatever. But you're not staying here."

Wyatt reached into his pocket and peeled off four hundred-dollar bills. "This is all the cash I've got. And it's all you're getting until next month, so don't think you can come back here again for more."

She just stared at him. "You're really serious."

He took her hand, pressed the bills into her palm, and closed her fingers over them. "Serious as a heart attack."

"If Bo comes home from Scout's and I'm not here, he'll be heartbroken. I promised him spaghetti and garlic bread tonight . . ."

"Bo's used to you breaking your promises," Wyatt pointed out. "He'll get over it. You can call him after you find a place to stay."

Callie held up the crumpled bills. "And what am I supposed to do when this is gone? Sleep on a park bench? Eat at a shelter?"

Wyatt shrugged. "You might think about a job. But again, not my problem."

It took her two trips to pack her stuff into the Jeep. She banged the screen door as hard as she could both times. Finally, he heard the car's engine sputter and stall, and roar to life again. He heard the spin of her tires on the crushed-shell driveway as she sped down the road and out of his life. For now.

Monday was delivery day at the Sandbox. Grace found Rochelle standing in the dining room, clipboard in hand, as the Budweiser driver unloaded cases of beer and trundled them into the kitchen.

"I was wondering where you'd been," she said as Grace came around the bar to fix herself a cold drink.

"I've been everywhere . . . and nowhere," Grace replied.

"I spent the weekend at Mitzi's condo." She gave her mother an apologetic smile. "Guess I should have called, huh?"

"Would have been nice," Rochelle said. "But you're an adult. I get that you need your privacy." She looked up from her invoices. "If you want to talk about what's going on with you, I'm happy to just listen."

"I'll give you the condensed version. Saturday, I went over to the house and found proof that J'Aimee really did vandalize and set fire to Arthur's house. Then I blackmailed Ben into agreeing to a financial settlement. I broke up with Wyatt. Did you see the news last night? Stackpole's wife caught him with another other woman at a restaurant in Sarasota, and it made the news last night. And then this morning, I dropped in on Paula and tried to convince her she should help us get Stackpole thrown off the bench. It's been a busy time, Mom."

"That's quite a list of accomplishments. Did I hear you say you broke up with Wyatt?"

"Yes," Grace said.

Rochelle sighed and patted her daughter's hand. "Oh, Gracie. Why?"

"His wife wants him back," Grace said. "Bo wants his parents back together." She shrugged. "It was probably inevitable."

"Doesn't Wyatt get a say in any of this?"

"He says he and Callie are never getting back together and that he wants to make a life with me, but . . ."

"But you're ready to give him up anyway?" Rochelle shook her head. "God, Grace. I could have sworn you were born with a backbone."

"This is not about standing up for myself! It's about reality, Mom. Callie will do whatever it takes to get her claws into Wyatt. She spent the night over there Friday, after she'd broken up with her boyfriend, and Wyatt wasn't even going to tell me. In fact, she told me—after I showed up at his place to pick up Sweetie. She met me at the door dressed in his bathrobe. And she made sure I noticed she wasn't wearing anything underneath."

"Do you actually think Wyatt slept with her? Or that he even wanted to?"

Grace took her time answering, slowly peeling the paper wrapper from a drinking straw. "No," she said finally. "But the point is . . ."

Rochelle waved her off. "The point is you don't trust the man. You don't trust his feelings for you. You don't trust his ability to see through his ex. And you don't trust yourself to work through any of this stuff in order to be with him," Rochelle said. "And that's a damned shame."

"I can't have this conversation with you," Grace said, twisting the straw wrapper into a tight spiral. "I appreciate that you like Wyatt, and you want us to be together, but I have to do what's right for me."

"And if I didn't love you so much, I would agree with you and let you alone," Rochelle said. "But I love you too much to watch while you let happiness slip right through your fingers. You walked away from Ben when you found out he was a cheater. And I supported you on that. One hundred percent. But honey, Wyatt's not Ben. Wyatt is good and loyal and true, and when I see the way he looks at you, and the way you look at him when you think nobody is watching, I know he's the one. I think you know it, too."

Grace pushed her drink away. "I don't know anything. That's the problem. Yeah, I think I love him. And I thought he loved me. But look what happened with Ben. I had no clue Ben was sleeping with J'Aimee, and they were literally doing it right under my nose. So how can I be sure Wyatt is the one? We only met two months ago."

"Just trust your feelings for him," Rochelle said gently.

"And remember, nothing in this life is ever going to be one hundred percent for certain. But you can't just hide out, never risk getting hurt again. What kind of life would that be?"

"A safe one," Grace said.

"No." Rochelle shook her head vehemently. "Not safe. Boring. Sad. A total waste."

Grace sat on the bench on Coquina Beach and hugged Sweetie to her chest. The tide was out and a lone gray heron was stalking something in the calm shallow water. It was the same bench she'd sat on with Wyatt only a few days earlier. Sweetie wriggled in her arms, lifted her chin, and licked Grace's chin. She glanced down at the cell phone on the picnic table, for the tenth time in the past hour. Wyatt had called twice that morning and texted her half an hour ago.

His message was short and to the point. *She's gone. I'm not taking her back. You're what I want.*

He seemed so sure. Why couldn't she be like that?

Because, Grace thought. *Because you're the girl who painted her first apartment six different shades of white the first week you were living there. Because you dated Ben for two years and lived with him for another two before finally deciding to marry him.*

She'd waited and waffled after meeting Ben, and still she'd made a mistake. Maybe her mother was right. Maybe mistakes were inevitable. But maybe this time, she really had found *the* one. There was only one way to find out for sure.

Grace snatched up the phone and tapped the icon beside Wyatt's name. She wouldn't give herself any more time to think, wouldn't have second thoughts. This time around, she would just go with her heart.

"Grace?" Wyatt answered on the first ring.

"Don't talk," Grace said hurriedly. "Just tell me where you want to meet."

"Anywhere you want," Wyatt said. "Can it wait 'til I close up the park at five? Bo is at Scout's house. Dad can stay with him after I bring him back here. Are we all still meeting at the Sandbox tonight?"

"Yes, and yes," Grace said. "I'll be at Mitzi's condo."

65.

Grace paced back and forth in the small living room, stopping every five minutes to look out the window at the parking lot, to adjust the drapes, fluff a pillow, or check her makeup in the mirror. She hadn't been this nervous about meeting a man since her first real car date at the age of fifteen. Her palms were actually sweaty.

She'd taken pains with her makeup and had actually changed outfits three times—not that she had that many changes of clothes to begin with—before settling on a pair of blue seersucker capris and a sleeveless white blouse. God help her—she'd even painted her toenails a vivid crimson shade called Sassy Lassie.

Sweetie lay on a throw pillow on the sofa, looking perplexed by Grace's nervous energy.

Grace was midway through her third circuit of the condo when her phone rang. She leapt to grab it, but paused when she saw the caller ID.

Ashleigh Hartounian. Probably, Grace thought, she was calling to ask about that night's get-together at the bar.

"Hi, Ashleigh," she said.

"Graaaace." Ashleigh was sobbing.

"Are you all right?"

"Nooooo," Ashleigh wailed. "I'm not okay. I'll never be okay."

"What is it?" Grace asked. "What's wrong?"

"It's . . . it's . . . Boyce."

Now Grace remembered: today was the day Ashleigh's ex-husband had invited her out to lunch. This was the day Ashleigh expected to win him back and return to her fairy-tale existence as the doctor's wife. Obviously, things hadn't gone as Ashleigh had anticipated.

"Do you want to talk?" Grace asked, hoping she didn't. She was standing in front of the window, craning her neck to see out to the parking lot, watching for Wyatt's car. It was after five.

"No! I'm so upset, I feel like my head is gonna explode."

"Well . . ." Grace started.

"That bitch Suchita!" Ashleigh said. "I should have expected she'd pull a stunt like this. That's all it is, a stunt, to try to trap Boyce."

"Suchita?" Grace was drawing a blank. A truck pulled into the complex's parking lot, but it wasn't Wyatt's.

"You know, Suchita. That little slut drug rep he's been sleeping with. She's the one who got me in trouble with Stackpole in the first place."

"Ohhh," Grace said. "The woman whose house you painted. Now I remember. What's she done to trap Boyce?" As soon as the words were out of her mouth, Grace had a sinking feeling she knew just what Suchita had done.

"She got herself knocked up! Or so she says. It's the oldest trick in the book, but Boyce is such a dummy he never saw it coming. Do you believe this shit?"

"Does this mean he didn't take you to lunch to get back with you?" *Dumb question,* Grace thought.

"He says they're getting married!" Ashleigh screeched. "As soon as our divorce is final. He only took me to lunch because he said he wanted to tell me himself, before one of the girls in the office spilled the beans. Do you believe that?"

Ashleigh was crying again, her wails so loud that Grace had to hold the phone a couple inches from her ear.

"That bitch!" Ashleigh said. "She's five months' pregnant. That explains why she looked so fat when I saw her leaving his office last week. And it's a boy! Boyce is ecstatic. It was all he could talk about, the bastard. I wanted to slug him—I was so upset."

"I'm so sorry," Grace said.

"She's the one who's going to be sorry," Ashleigh said. "I'm not gonna let that bitch ruin my life."

"Ashleigh!" Grace said. "Get a grip. If she's pregnant and Boyce intends to marry her, there's nothing you can do."

"That's what you think. There's plenty I can do. And I will."

"Leave it alone, Ashleigh," Grace warned. "Do not do anything you'll regret. I know you're upset right now, but it's probably for the best."

"You don't know a damned thing, Grace," Ashleigh said, her voice suddenly harsh. "Just because you walked away from your marriage doesn't mean I'm ready to walk away from mine. I should have known better than to expect you to understand what I'm going through. I have no intention of letting that little home-wrecker steal my husband."

Grace felt a chill go down her spine.

"Ashleigh, where are you right now?" she asked quietly. "I don't think you should be alone. Let's talk this through. I've been there, too, remember."

"Thanks anyway, but I'm not really in the mood for a chat right now," Ashleigh said.

"You're coming to the Sandbox tonight, right?"

"What's the point?" Ashleigh asked. "I told you last week I wasn't coming back to group sessions."

"Didn't you see the news the other night?" Grace asked. "Stackpole's wife caught him with another woman and raised a ruckus in a restaurant in Sarasota."

"Was the other woman Paula?" Ashleigh asked.

"No, that's what makes it all so deliciously sleazy. He was with a twenty-three-year-old woman who is one of the bailiffs in his courtroom. Highly unethical, of course."

"Does Paula know?" Ashleigh asked.

"Yup," Grace said. "I had a long talk with her this morning. I think she's this close to helping us file a formal complaint against Stackpole with the Judicial Qualifications Committee."

"And why would she do that?" Ashleigh asked.

"I think she knows he's been using her by referring all these divorcing women to her for therapy group and then forcing her to pay him kickbacks."

"Hah! Can you prove it?"

"Not yet," Grace admitted. "Just come hang out with us tonight at the Sandbox. I'll tell you the whole story then."

"I don't care about any of that," Ashleigh said abruptly. "That's somebody else's problem. Look, Grace, I gotta go now."

"Go where?" Grace asked. "Ashleigh, where are you? Are you at home? Is there somebody you could call to come over and stay with you for a while?"

"I'm in the car," Ashleigh said. "I've been driving around for hours. And I don't need a babysitter. I just wanted to talk to somebody. But I've made up my mind what I need to do."

"Ashleigh?"

The line went dead.

Grace cursed and tapped the redial button.

The phone rang twice.

"Leave me alone, Grace," Ashleigh said. "This is between me and her."

"Her?"

"You know exactly who I mean. Suchita. I'm gonna take care of business. Do what I should have done months ago, before things got out of hand."

"Ashleigh, stay away from that girl. You're angry and upset, but stalking her is not the answer. You'll only get yourself in more trouble."

"I don't care," Ashleigh insisted. "I don't care about anything. Except Boyce. He's all I have. He's the only thing in this world I give a damn about."

"Come on," Grace said. "That's not really true. You have family; you have friends . . ."

"What friends? You mean all those losers in group? Get real. None of y'all give a damn about me."

"We do," Grace said. "We all care about you. I care. You must know that, or you wouldn't have called me."

Silence.

"Ashleigh? Are you still there?"

"I'm here," Ashleigh said. She was crying again. "That's sweet, Grace. Really sweet. I'm sorry. I didn't mean to call you a loser. You're not like the others."

"You're upset," Grace said soothingly. She was looking out the window again, wondering what time it was.

"You said you're in the car. Where are you? Do you want to meet? We could get a cup of coffee and talk."

"I'm . . . oh, hell. I've just been driving around. I guess I'm at Bradenton Beach. But I don't want any coffee. A drink, maybe. Yeah, another margarita."

"Another? You've already had a margarita, and you're driving?"

"Just a couple. But they were little ones, and mostly ice. If you're gonna lecture me about drinking and driving, I'll hang up right now."

"No lecture," Grace said quickly. "Look, why don't you pull into the next gas station you see and call me back. I'm not far away at all. I'll come and meet you. How does that sound?"

"If you want to," Ashleigh said. "But I'm warning you. It won't change my mind."

"Call me right back," Grace said. "I'll meet you, wherever you are."

She left Sweetie napping in the condo and called Wyatt on the fly.

"Grace, hi," he said, sounding out of breath. "I know I'm late, but I had to go through the drive-through at Wendy's to get dinner for Bo. I'll only be another thirty minutes. Promise."

"Actually, that'll be fine," Grace said. "Ashleigh just called me. Today was the day her ex invited her to go to lunch. But instead of asking her to come back to him, he announced that his girlfriend is five months pregnant, and he's going to marry her as soon as their divorce is final."

"Oh, wow," Wyatt said. "And she was so sure he was going to get back with her. How'd she take the news?"

"About like you'd expect," Grace said. "She's obsessed with getting Boyce back, or at least keeping that girl from marrying him. She's been driving around, drinking margaritas, plotting some kind of revenge. I'm really worried she'll do something drastic. I'm going to go meet her and try and talk some sense into her."

"Is that a good idea?" Wyatt asked. "If she's been drinking?"

"I don't know what else to do," Grace said. "She's talking crazy. I'm afraid she might hurt herself—or somebody else."

"Please don't go meet her by yourself," Wyatt said. "Just wait thirty minutes, okay? I'll take Bo straight home, and then come by and pick you up. We can go together. She might listen if we both ganged up on her."

"Maybe," Grace said reluctantly. "But I promised I'd come right away, as soon as she pulls into a gas station. I'll try and stall her. But hurry, can you?"

"I'm ten minutes from home and another fifteen from the condo," Wyatt said. "Stay right there."

66.

"Okay, I'm here," Ashleigh said, without bothering with a greeting. "So, are you coming, or what?"

"Here, where?" Grace asked.

"Um, it's a Hess station on Manatee, but you better get here fast, because I do not like the looks of this place. It's definitely in the hood. The bathroom was so nasty I had to pee standing up."

"I'm trying to think where that is," Grace said slowly. "Like, what block of Manatee is that?"

"How should I know?" Ashleigh snapped. "I don't even know why I agreed to meet you. You can't change my mind, you know. That bitch Suchita is history. She's toast."

"Please don't talk like that," Grace begged. She hesitated, wondering if she should mention that Wyatt would be joining them. Stall her, he'd suggested. But that was no easy feat.

She gazed around the room and spotted Sweetie, who'd hopped off the sofa and was now sitting in front of the sliding glass doors facing the gulf.

"Look, Ashleigh, I just need to let Sweetie out for a potty break before I leave her alone," Grace said.

"Who's Sweetie?"

"My dog. She's a rescue, and I've got her over at a client's condo, but I don't dare leave her alone unless I take her out. Just give me fifteen minutes, okay?"

"You want me to hang around here for fifteen minutes? No way! You said you'd meet me right away. Hell, if I hang around here for another fifteen minutes, I could be carjacked. Shiiiiit," Ashleigh swore softly. "I knew this was a bad idea. Thanks anyway, Grace, but I gotta be moving on."

"No, don't leave there," Grace said hastily. "I'll come right now. You said you're at Manatee, but what's close by? What's the intersection and which corner? Give me a landmark, Ashleigh. I'm not really familiar with that part of town."

"For God's sake. I don't know. Let's see . . . um, yeah, there's a strip shopping center with a Bealls outlet right across from the Hess station."

"If you're worried about the gas station, drive over there," Grace suggested. "You can just go inside and wait until I pull up. Nobody's going to carjack you at a Bealls."

"Maybe." The other woman sounded unconvinced. "Or maybe I'll stay here and get a wine cooler while I wait."

"I really don't think you should have anything else to drink," Grace said.

"And I don't give a flying fuck what you think," Ashleigh retorted. "It's five forty-five right now. If you're not here by six, I'm history."

"I'm coming," Grace said hurriedly. "Stay right there."

Grace called Wyatt from her car. "Sorry, but I can't wait for you," she told him. "I'm meeting Ashleigh at the Hess station on Manatee. She's so antsy, I really couldn't stall her any longer. She's already talking about buying a wine cooler. I'll keep her there as long as I can, and hopefully you can meet us there."

Wyatt sighed loudly. "I don't like this Grace. If she's been drinking like you say she has, I don't think you're going to be able to reason with her. I think maybe you should call the cops and let them handle it."

"Ashleigh respects me. She'll listen to me," Grace said. "Don't worry. I'm just going to talk to her, calm her down, and persuade her to leave her car there and let me drive her home. She's not a maniac, Wyatt. She's upset, and she's talking smack, but I honestly don't think she's capable of really harming somebody—other than herself."

"I hope you're right," Wyatt said. "I just dropped Bo off with my dad. I'll be there in ten minutes. Okay?"

"Hurry," Grace said. And she disconnected.

She spotted the red BMW as soon as she pulled into the gas station. Ashleigh tooted her horn and waved. Grace parked in one of the slots in front of the convenience store and trotted over to Ashleigh's car.

The BMW's engine was running, and when the electric window slid down noiselessly and Grace bent down to talk to her friend, a blast of cold air hit her face. Grace's heart sank when she saw two empty wine-cooler bottles tossed in the passenger seat.

"Hey, Grace," Ashleigh said. Her face was pale and her usually flawless makeup was smeared and tear-streaked. "You know this is a waste of time, right?"

"I don't mind wasting my time," Grace said lightly. "Why don't we go over and sit in my car and talk?"

"Nuh-uh," Ashleigh said, shaking her head vigorously. "I like my car just fine." She patted the leather-upholstered passenger seat. "You can sit here." She reached down to the floor and pulled up a full key-lime-flavored wine cooler. "Look, I bought one for you. We can have a party. A pity party, right?"

"Um, I'm not really thirsty," Grace said. "Come on,

Ashleigh. You've had too much to drink to be driving. Let's go sit in my car, and I'll drive you home. You can plot revenge against Suchita tomorrow."

"No effin' way," Ashleigh said. "Tonight's the night. That bitch is going down!" She tossed her blond hair defiantly over her shoulder. "And if you're gonna be such a buzzkiller, you can just go on to your divorce meeting. Because I've got stuff to do. See ya around, Grace." She rolled the window up.

"Wait!" Grace said, pounding the BMW's roof. She looked over her shoulder, hoping against hope to see Wyatt's truck. Ashleigh was definitely drunk, and in no mood to be reasoned with.

The window slid down again. "You comin' or not?" Ashleigh held up the wine cooler. Grace sighed and took it, crossing to the passenger seat.

Ashleigh popped the lock and Grace moved the empties aside before sliding into the passenger seat.

Ashleigh watched her expectantly. Grace uncapped the bottle and took a sip of the ultrasweet cooler.

"That's more like it." Ashleigh cackled. "Par-tay! Woo-hoo!" She threw the car into reverse and just as quickly into drive.

"Wait," Grace said, the back of her head slamming against the headrest. "Ashleigh, no! You're in no condition to drive."

"Don't be such a nag. I'm fine!" Ashleigh countered. She looked both ways, then zipped out of the parking lot and onto the highway, narrowly avoiding a collision with an oncoming white sedan before crossing the median into the far westbound lane.

Grace glanced over at Ashleigh, who looked back and laughed. "See? I told you. I'm fine. Those wine coolers have almost no alcohol in 'em, and anyway, I've got a really high tolerance. I can drink, like, half a dozen margarias and not feel a thing. We're just a couple of girls, out cruisin', just like in high school. Didn't you and your girl-friends ever get a little buzzed and go cruisin'?"

"You're not fine," Grace said, groping for her seat belt. "And we're not in high school, and you're past being buzzed. Anyway, I thought we were just going to talk. Ashleigh, if you want to drive drunk, that's your decision, but I do not want to go along for the ride."

"Too bad," Ashleigh said. "I keep telling you I'm not drunk. Okay? You wanted to talk, let's talk."

Ashleigh wove the BMW in and out of traffic, twice coming so close to clipping another car, Grace finally just squeezed her eyes tightly and prayed, because she was too nervous to watch where Ashleigh was going.

"I want you to turn around and take me back to that gas station," Grace said through gritted teeth. "Or just pull over and drop me off. This isn't funny, you know."

"You're right; it's not funny. It's fuckin' tragic is what it is," Ashleigh said. Her eyes brimmed over with tears. "I tried calling Boyce while I was waiting for you. The num-ber I had was disconnected. He just called me on it, like this morning. She did that. I just know it. One of her spies probably told her Boyce took me to lunch today. But what she doesn't know is—I've got spies of my own."

She fumbled in the center console of the car and came up with her cell phone. "Here. Grab the steering wheel," she told Grace.

Grace reached over and took the steering wheel with her left hand, grateful that the heavy flow of traffic on Manatee meant that Ashleigh was only doing about thirty miles per hour.

Ashleigh was squinting down at the list of contacts on her phone, scrolling down, looking for something.

"Who are you calling?" Grace asked.

"Here it is!" Ashleigh said triumphantly. She tapped the

number and waited, and then frowned. "The bitch won't pick up. I bet Boyce told her not to talk to me."

"Suchiiiiita." Ashleigh's voice was low and spooky. "Pick up the phone, little mama. I've got a message for you. No? You don't wanna talk to me? That's okay. Cuz I'm coming for you, bitch. Remember? I know exactly where you live. And guess what? You can run, but you can't hide."

She disconnected the phone, dropped it into her lap, and took the steering wheel again.

Grace's mouth felt dry, and she felt beads of perspiration popping up on her forehead, despite the chill from the BMW's air conditioner. She glanced in the rearview mirror, but there was no sign of Wyatt's truck. She felt in the pocket of her shorts for her phone, found it, and slid it into her lap.

She had to call Wyatt, try to let him know what Ashleigh intended. Maybe he could call Boyce Hartounian and warn him that Ashleigh was on a rampage. She glanced over at Ashleigh, who seemed to be watching the road. She managed to thumb down her recent calls and tap Wyatt's number, but then the BMW suddenly swerved into the far left lane and, seconds later, without signal or warning, made a sharp left turn, crossing two lanes of oncoming traffic, earning her a blast of horns from the cars she narrowly avoided T-boning. Grace's phone flew out of her hand and slid down between the seats.

"Ashleigh!" Grace cried. "What the hell are you doing?"

The driver shrugged. "Sorry. Guess I cut it a little close, huh?"

"You nearly got me killed," Grace said angrily. "If you want to kill yourself, that's your business, but I want out of this car, right now. Pull over, dammit."

With her left hand, she tried groping the area beneath her seat, but the small phone eluded her grasp.

Ashleigh laughed. "Don't be such a chickenshit, Grace. Look, I'm barely doing thirty now."

It was true. They'd turned onto a quiet, tree-lined residential street. It was narrow, and cars were parked along the curbs on both sides, dictating a slower speed. Grace wondered if she'd managed to connect the call to Wyatt, wondered if he could hear them right now. She prayed it was so.

"What is this neighborhood?" she asked loudly.

"It's Newtown," Ashleigh said. "The bitch lives right around here, but I can't remember the name of the street. I'll know it when I see it, though."

She was scanning both sides of the street, looking ahead at the street signs.

They were going just slow enough, Grace realized, that she could escape the car without risking her life. She snaked her right hand over toward the passenger door, her fingers clasping the handle.

Click. Grace tugged at the handle, but it was too late.

Ashleigh laughed. "Childproof locks. Great invention, huh? Come on, Grace. Why do you wanna jump ship? I thought you were gonna be my wingman on this mission."

"I don't want anything to do with this," Grace said. "You're scaring me now, Ashleigh. Just pull over and let me out, okay? Or let me drive. You're in no condition to be behind the wheel. You're going to do something stupid and dangerous and end up in real trouble."

"Trouble?" Ashleigh glanced over at her. "What? Stackpole is gonna put me in remedial divorce counseling? Sentence me to community service again? You don't get it, Grace, do you? I don't give a rat's ass about any of that. I just want to give that bitch what she deserves. Once she's out of the picture, Boyce will realize what he's been missing."

Grace clamped her lips together. Finally, the reality of

the situation dawned on her. Nothing she could say would sway Ashleigh's resolve. She glanced again in the rearview mirror. Was that a flash of red, a block back? Wyatt's truck? She said another silent prayer.

Ashleigh drove one block, turned right, drove two more blocks, and turned left. The truck sped up and seemed to be closing the gap between it and the BMW, but then it was forced to come to a halt as an enormous SUV backed slowly down a driveway and into the street, totally blocking it.

Come on, come on, come on, Grace chanted silently.

"This is her street!" Ashleigh muttered. "I knew it was around here." She made a sharp left and slowed the BMW to a crawl, craning her neck to see the numbers on the mailboxes.

If she hadn't been so thoroughly terrified, Grace might have been craning her neck, too. The street was lined with moss-draped oak trees, lawns with thick green grass, and neatly tended beds of flowers. The homes were cozy stucco and wood-frame bungalows built in the twenties and thirties, with welcoming porches and gabled roofs.

It was a storybook street, but Grace had a feeling that this story would not have a happy ending.

"Oh, yeah," Ashleigh said softly. "This is the right block." She glanced over at Grace. "You see this neighborhood? I checked—the cheapest house on this street sold for 377,000 dollars. And I'm living in a dump condo that rents for eleven hundred a month. Ask yourself how a twenty-eight-year-old drug rep affords a house here. I'll tell you how—she hooks up with a rich plastic surgeon and makes him her baby daddy."

She pointed to a house at the end of the street. "That's it. That's her place."

"What . . . what are you planning to do?" Grace checked the rearview mirror. No sign of the truck.

"I'm just going to talk to her, that's all," Ashleigh said, her voice singsongy. "Make her see that she needs to step away."

But as they were talking, they saw a silver Audi back swiftly down the driveway. They were three houses away. As soon as the Audi was on the street, it accelerated so quickly that the tires screeched on the pavement.

"That's her!" Ashleigh said. She sped up, but the Audi zipped through the next intersection without slowing down.

"She knows what my car looks like," Ashleigh muttered. She accelerated, closing the gap between the two cars.

The Audi made two quick turns, and Ashleigh stayed close, flying through stop signs. The Audi managed to stay two car lengths ahead, and never slowed down before making a left.

They were back on Manatee again, heading west. The Audi sped through the thinning traffic, darting in and out of lanes, but Ashleigh gripped the steering wheel and kept on the car's tail. They were doing sixty miles an hour now, somehow managing to make all the green lights. Grace kept looking in the rearview mirror, and when she glimpsed the red truck again, she began daring to hope. Wyatt was there, not far behind. He would think of some way to stop this crazy race.

The Audi sped up again, and Ashleigh did the same. They were only a car length behind now, and the BMW's speedometer was inching over seventy miles per hour.

The GULF BEACHES sign flashed by. "She's headed for Boyce's beach house on Anna Maria," Ashleigh said. "Like he can hide her. Dumb bitch."

Grace saw the fringe of Australian pines, white sands, and the glint of sunlight on the sparkling water of Palma Sola Bay. The Audi was still a car length ahead, but

Ashleigh stomped on the accelerator, and the speedometer needle jumped. They were doing eighty-five now. The Audi wove in and out of traffic, and the BMW stayed right with it. They flew over the first causeway, and Grace held her breath, terrified Ashleigh might somehow send them both flying over the concrete bridge embankment and into the waters below. Her fears eased momentarily when they were over the bridge and into another stretch of causeway, lined on both sides by sandy beaches and the shallow waters of the bay, but not for long.

A lumbering dump truck loomed ahead of them in the right-hand lane, forcing the Audi to slow considerably. Ashleigh veered into the left lane and passed the dump truck. She slowed, waiting for the truck to pass on the right, and laughed triumphantly when she came alongside the Audi.

Grace glimpsed the driver as they pulled alongside the Audi—a long curtain of dark hair, and when the woman looked over and saw who was beside her, her face mirrored the look of shock and horror in Grace's own face.

"Gotcha!" Ashleigh screamed. She jerked the BMW's steering wheel hard to the right, but just as she did so, Grace heard the squeal of the Audi's brakes. The BMW veered off the road.

Grace had the sensation of time slowing. She heard screams—her own, Ashleigh's? She'd never be sure. She was aware of the car slamming through an expanse of corrugated metal fencing, of the windshield shattering, of the splintering of wood on metal as they glanced off a pine tree, and, moments later, of the rush of water.

And then it was quiet.

67.

Wyatt pushed the old truck's accelerator all the way to the floor once he heard the one-sided conversation on Grace's call. He shuddered at the sound of Ashleigh's slurred speech. She was drunk, deranged, out of control. And Grace was strapped into the passenger seat right beside her, helpless.

As he closed the gap between the racing cars and his own, he saw Ashleigh's frenzied pursuit of the silver Audi, guessing the driver was Suchita, Ashleigh's romantic rival. He didn't have a clear idea of what he'd do if and when he caught up to the women, but he knew he would have to do something. He wondered, fleetingly, if Ashleigh had a gun. The only gun Wyatt owned was Nelson's old service pistol—but it was kept under lock and key in the file cabinet in the office. And what if he did have the gun? How would he use it? Shoot out the tires of a moving vehicle? Ridiculous.

A dozen awful scenarios flashed through his mind as he struggled to keep pace.

He wondered if the same scenarios occurred to Grace.

Her voice sounded so calm, so cool on the other end of the phone. "Keep trying, Grace," he murmured.

They crossed the first bay bridge, and he managed to catch up to within two car lengths when a lumbering old dump truck forced everybody to slow down.

But in the blink of an eye, everything changed. He saw the BMW switch lanes, saw it pull alongside the Audi, and then deliberately try and sideswipe the other car.

The Audi's driver slammed on the brakes, and seconds later, to his horror, he saw the BMW veer off the road and plow through the metal fencing. He saw the cloud of sand spewed by the spinning tires, heard the crunch of metal on metal, and, worst of all, heard the hair-raising chorus of screams from inside the BMW.

And then nothing, except the pounding of his own blood in his ears, as he saw the car skimming into the jade green waters of Palma Sola Bay.

Wyatt was out of the truck almost before it stopped, with the only tool he had at hand, the heavy Maglite flashlight he kept under the front seat. He ran through the jagged opening in the fencing left by the BMW and waded into the warm, shallow water. The BMW was immersed up to its hood ornament. He cursed himself for not removing the thick-soled leather work boots that made his trek to the car take what seemed like hours.

Finally, he reached the car. The windshield was shattered, and water was seeping in. He could see that the airbags had deployed and were already deflated. He splashed over to the passenger side, and his heart leapt when he saw Grace's brown hair. He yanked furiously at the door, until he remembered that Ashleigh had locked it.

"Grace!" he shouted. "Grace. Are you all right?" She turned her head slightly to the right, and he could see a thin trickle of blood oozing down her face.

"Turn your head away," he shouted, and began hammering at the center of the window with the butt of the flashlight. He slammed it against the glass again and again, until finally the window seemed to crinkle into a million pieces and fall away.

"Give me your arms," he told her, but she stared at him, dazed or in shock; he wasn't quite sure. "Your arms!" he repeated. "I'm going to pull you out. Come on, Grace. I need to get you out of this water."

"I can't," she said, her voice weak. Wyatt grabbed her by the shoulder. "Come on, honey. You can do this."

She shook her head violently, fumbling with something in her lap. Wyatt stuck his head in the window and saw that her seat belt was still fastened and that water had reached her knees. He leaned in until his torso was in the car and, with shaking fingers, managed to unbuckle it.

"Okay," he said. "Okay. You're good now. Let's go, Gracie. Let's get you out."

Finally, she nodded, turned, and knelt on the seat, reaching her arms for him. He wrapped his own arms under hers. "Put your arms around my neck," he urged. He tugged while she wriggled, and, finally, she came free of the car, collapsing against him in the waist-deep water.

Wyatt stood there for a moment, holding her tightly against his chest, unwilling to let her go. "Are you hurt?" he asked. "Your head, legs, arms, anything?"

"I'm okay," she said shakily. And then, unbelievably, she laughed a little, whispering in his ear. "But I think maybe I peed my pants." He laughed, too, then. "Don't tell anybody, but I might have peed mine, too. Just a little, when I saw the car go airborne."

"Ashleigh," she said urgently. "Get Ashleigh out."

"I need to get you to the shore," he said, starting for the beach, but she pulled away.

"No. I can walk by myself. Get Ashleigh. Please, Wyatt."

He nodded grimly and turned back toward the BMW.

Ashleigh was slumped over in the driver's seat. He broke the window out with his flashlight, calling her name. "Ashleigh? Ashleigh? Talk to me. Come on, Ashleigh. It's Wyatt. Talk to me."

He reached in and touched the base of her neck. She was warm, and he could feel a pulse, but her breathing was shallow. Water was up to her lap and streaming in through the windshield and the passenger window. He wriggled halfway through the window and saw that, unlike Grace, Ashleigh hadn't fastened her seat belt. Which shouldn't have come as a surprise. He grasped the unmoving woman under the arms, in the same way he had grabbed Grace, but she was a deadweight. He backed out a little, trying for the door handle, already knowing it wouldn't open.

The water was still rising. It was chest-high. He grabbed Ashleigh again and tugged, inching her body in an agonizingly slow process. At some point, he was aware of the sound of sirens, of voices coming from the beach.

Finally, a rough arm grasped his. "We got this, buddy."

He turned and saw a pair of uniformed paramedics. "She's breathing, but she's unconscious."

"Thanks," one of them said. "You can step away now."

He found Grace sitting on the tailgate of the ambulance, wrapped in a blanket. A Band-Aid had been applied to the cut over her eyebrow. Sitting beside her, also wrapped in a blanket, despite the August heat, was a stunning brunette, who was shaking and crying uncontrollably.

It was Suchita, the driver of the Audi.

A female EMT had fastened a blood-pressure cuff to Suchita's upper arm. "You're all right," the woman said in a soothing voice. "Your blood pressure's a little high, but not off the charts. And your baby should be fine, too.

But we can transport you to the hospital, if you'd like to get checked out."

"No!" Suchita said. "I want to wait for my fiancé. Boyce is on the way. He should be here soon. He's a doctor; he'll take care of me."

Wyatt nodded in Grace's direction, catching the EMT's eye. "Is she all right? Nothing broken?"

"She's good," the EMT said. "You're gonna want to watch her overnight, make sure she's not concussed, but otherwise the cut over her eye is the only thing. She was damned lucky."

Suchita turned and stared at Grace. "You're her friend? Why? Why did you let her come after me? She tried to kill me. She wanted to kill me and my baby."

"I didn't," Grace said, her voice a whisper. "I tried to stop her. But she'd been drinking . . ."

"She's crazy," Suchita said flatly. "I told Boyce she was dangerous. After she painted my house? I wouldn't stay there again. Not by myself. But she wouldn't leave me alone. She followed me, watched us if we went out together. And then she got my phone number, and she started leaving me messages. I told Boyce. I played him the voice mail messages she's been leaving me. He thought she was just trying to intimidate me. He said she wasn't dangerous." She shivered. "I only went home today to pick up my mail. And that's when she showed up."

Grace looked up at Wyatt. "Is Ashleigh . . . ?"

"She's breathing, but she's unconscious," Wyatt said. "She wasn't wearing her seat belt. I think maybe she hit her head."

"It all happened so fast," Grace said. "And I was so scared. I kept looking back, hoping you were there."

"I got there as quick as I could," Wyatt said. "But that damned SUV had the street blocked, and then, once she got out on Manatee and she was speeding, my old truck couldn't keep up. The whole thing starts to shimmy and rattle after I hit sixty."

"It doesn't matter," Grace said, clutching his hand. "You got here. You got me out of the car. You're here now. That's all that matters."

"I'm here, and I'm staying," Wyatt said, his voice choking with emotion. He looked over at the EMT. "Okay if I take her home now?"

Just then, a short, balding, middle-aged man came rushing up to the ambulance. Wyatt stepped back, but the EMT put out a hand to stop him from coming any closer.

"I'm a physician," he said, puffing out his chest. "Dr. Hartounian. This is my fiancée. Have you checked her vital signs? Did she tell you she's five months' pregnant?"

"She checked out perfect," the EMT said. "Not a scratch on her. Physically, anyway." And she stepped aside.

"Suchita? My God! Are you all right?" Hartounian gestured toward the pair of EMTs who were bundling a stretcher into the second ambulance. "Is that really Ashleigh?"

"I'm . . . I'm . . ." Suchita's voice trailed and broke off into sobs as she threw herself into Boyce Hartounian's arms.

"It's okay, baby. I'm here. Boyce is here," he crooned tenderly, rubbing her back and arms. She was two inches taller than he, but his arms were tanned and muscular. He glanced over at Grace and his eyes narrowed.

"Who are you?" he asked, all business. "You're Ashleigh's friend? I just spoke to one of the police officers. They say the two of you had been drinking. What the hell were you thinking letting her get behind the wheel of a car? If anything happens to our child . . ."

"My name is Grace Davenport," Grace said, feeling her temper flare. "I wasn't the one who was drinking. That was all Ashleigh. And I didn't let her drive. In fact, I was trying to talk her into letting me take her home. She called me earlier, upset after your lunch with her . . ."

Suchita looked up. "You took her to *lunch*? Without telling me?"

Wyatt took Grace's arm and gently steered her away from the ambulance. He meant to take her home, get her in some dry clothes, let the shock wear off. But two uniformed police officers stood beside his truck, waiting for answers.

An hour later, after giving her statement to the cops—and agreeing to a Breathalyzer test to prove she hadn't been responsible for any of the half dozen empty wine-cooler bottles found in the BMW, Grace finally climbed into the front seat of Wyatt's truck.

He'd changed into the spare clothes he kept in a gym bag in the truck—his Manasota Maulers coaches' shirt, shorts, and a pair of baseball cleats.

"What do you think will happen to Ashleigh?" she asked, as Wyatt pulled slowly back onto the roadway.

Wyatt shrugged. "I know you feel sorry for her, but at this point, I hope they throw the book at her. Ashleigh very nearly killed three people today—four if you count Suchita's baby. She'll be charged with drunk driving, for sure. And it sounds like if Boyce Hartounian has his way, I guess they could add attempted homicide, or whatever you call it."

Grace grimaced at the mention of Hartounian. "What a pompous jerk!"

"He must have something the ladies love," Wyatt observed. "To have two hotties like Ashleigh and Suchita fighting over him."

"What he has is a nice big bank account," Grace countered. She closed her eyes and rested her head on the back of the seat. A moment later, she sat up again. "What time is it?"

"Nearly seven," Wyatt said. He closed his hand over hers. "Just rest, okay? I'm going to take you to the condo, let you get changed and showered. I called your mom, just to let her know what happened, so she won't be worried. And I talked to Nelson, to let him know I won't be coming home tonight. The EMTs told me you need to have somebody checking you through the night."

"No!" Grace said. "I mean, that's sweet and all that you want to take care of me. But everybody's meeting at the Sandbox tonight. Mitzi's coming, too. They're expecting me."

"Not a good idea," Wyatt said. "Why don't you just call your mom back and tell her to let everybody know you're not coming?"

"I can't call anybody. Remember? My cell phone is still in what's left of Ashleigh's car. Anyway, I have to go, and you need to be there, too. This is important, Wyatt. If we're going to file a complaint against Stackpole with the JQC, we need everybody to give Mitzi a statement. She's bringing women from Paula's other groups, too. And there's an outside chance Paula herself might show up."

"You think Paula's going to turn against her boyfriend?" Wyatt scoffed. "Now I know you've got a head injury."

Grace proceeded to fill Wyatt in on the Honorable Cedric N. Stackpole's not-so-honorable but very complicated love life.

"I told Paula about the meeting tonight, about what we're doing," Grace said. "She's really conflicted. But I think maybe she's tired of being victimized by him. I think there's an outside chance she'll show up and help us."

"Doubtful," Wyatt said, unconvinced.

"I don't care. Let's go straight to the Sandbox. I can shower and change there." She flashed a smile. "Please? I need you on my team."

He shrugged. "Team Grace? Okay. Sign me up."

68.

Rochelle was carrying a tray of drinks and food to a table of softball players at the back of the room when her bedraggled daughter came scuttling through the side door of the Sandbox, trying not to be noticed.

She dropped the tray on the table, sloshing beer on the shortstop's cheeseburger and sending the catcher's order of hot wings sailing off the plate and into the second baseman's lap.

"Sorry." Rochelle tossed a dry bar towel to the coach, who was, thankfully, a regular.

"Jesus H!" she exclaimed, hurrying over to Grace's side. She hugged her daughter fiercely. "You look awful! Are you sure you don't need to go to the emergency room?"

"I look worse than I feel," Grace said. "I'll be fine after I get a shower." She looked over her mother's shoulder at the table in the corner, where a dozen women chattered away. "Is everybody here?"

"Everybody except you two—and Ashleigh. If that girl's not dead already, I'll kill her myself," Rochelle said.

"Did you tell the others what happened?" Grace asked.

"Just that there'd been an accident and that you were

okay and Ashleigh was taken to the hospital," Rochelle said. "I'll let you fill 'em in. If you're sure you feel like it."

"Wyatt can do it while I get cleaned up." Grace leaned over and planted a kiss on Wyatt's cheek. He blushed, then kissed her back.

"I take it you two patched things up?" Rochelle asked as they watched Grace depart.

"I think so," Wyatt said. "I hope so. I can't go through another day like today. When I realized she was in that car with Ashleigh—the kind of danger she was in . . ."

He ducked his head and swallowed. "If something had happened to her? I honestly don't know what I'd do, Rochelle. I know it's crazy—falling in love with somebody you meet in divorce therapy? But I did. And I think she did, too. And when this is all over, I want us to get married."

Rochelle raised one eyebrow. "You're asking my permission?"

Wyatt laughed and blushed again. "I guess not. Just maybe for your approval. I know I'm not the best financial risk. She'd be going from that mansion she lived in with her ex to a trailer—literally. But I promise you, I love Grace, and I'll never hurt her. I'll spend the rest of my life taking care of her."

"Grace can actually take care of herself," Rochelle said. "Just make her laugh and smile and enjoy life like she used to. Be good to each other. The rest will work itself out."

Mitzi Stillwell dabbed at the beer rings on the tabletop with a paper napkin, then placed a thick file folder on it.

She looked at the eleven women arrayed around the two tables Rochelle had pushed together in a quiet corner of the bar. Camryn Nobles trained a small handheld video camera on Mitzi, then panned around at the other women.

Suzanne passed around the documents Mitzi had prepared: disclaimers, giving Camryn the right to film the women telling their stories and attesting that they were giving their statements of their own free will.

Harriett Porter cleared her throat nervously. Camryn gave her an encouraging nod. "Just pretend you're talking to a friend," she prompted.

Harriett licked her lips and began speaking. "We had our first hearing before Judge Stackpole back in December. I, er, did something I now regret, and Judge Stackpole was very, very angry with me."

"What exactly did you do that made him so angry?" Camryn asked.

"Well, I found out that my husband was having an affair with a stripper . . ." She looked at Camryn. "Is it okay to say it was a male stripper?"

Camryn laughed and nodded.

"Okay, so it was this guy. Named Anubis. I guess that was his stripper name. Anyway, Daryl, that's my husband, was putting tens of thousands of dollars on our American Express card at this place in Tampa called Jeepers-Peepers. I was getting our tax stuff ready for the accountant, which is how I found the AmEx bills. And, well, I, uh, um, I went over to that place one Thursday afternoon, Jeepers-Peepers, and I saw him—Daryl, that is, standing in the parking lot, and he was stuffing money into this guy's—what do you call it? Not a G-string, if it's a man, right? It was sort of a sequined jockstrap."

"Actually?" Thea, an attractive woman in her early fifties raised her hand. "Technically, it's not a jockstrap. It's called a codpiece. I know because I'm from New Orleans."

"Thanks, hon," Harriett said. "He was stuffing fifty-dollar bills into this stripper's codpiece. Right there in broad daylight! And it made me so mad, I lost it. Literally. One minute I was trying to take pictures of Daryl and his boyfriend with my phone, and the next minute I had crashed the car into a Dumpster. The police said I ran over Daryl's foot. I don't remember that part. I do remember he was wearing the four-hundred-dollar Italian loafers I bought him for Father's Day."

Camryn's chest was heaving with silent laughter, and tears were rolling down her face. Harriett was too caught up in her story to notice the reporter's reaction.

"Judge Stackpole called me a renegade!" she said angrily. "My lawyer said I should get half of Daryl's pension plan—I never worked after we married, because he wanted me to stay home with our children. But Stackpole told me I was an able-bodied woman and I should get a job and stop being a leech. And then he told me he wouldn't sign off on our divorce until I completed this divorce-recovery counseling. With a woman named Paula Talbott-Sinclair. Who I later found out isn't even licensed to practice therapy in this state!"

"Did the judge give you the option of seeking treatment with any therapist? Or did he specify Ms. Talbott-Sinclair?" Camryn asked.

"He handed me her business card, right there in the courtroom," Harriett said. "And he said she would have to notify him that I'd completed six weeks of sessions before he would grant our divorce."

Harriett's face was pink with indignation. "She charged me nine hundred dollars a session. Later, after I talked to some other women in the group and we began comparing notes, I found out they were only paying a third of that! And the thing is, I'm still pissed off at Daryl. I haven't recovered from our divorce at all. I don't know if I ever will."

"Thank you, Harriett," Camryn said soberly. She put the camera down and beamed at the women around the table.

"That was great. Who's next?"

Suzanne took a deep breath and a sip of her iced tea. She was wearing a bright orange top and a flattering new shade of lipstick, and she'd had her hair cut and colored.

"Shall I go?" she asked.

"Oh my God," Grace whispered. She was seated, facing the door, when a slender woman with unruly blond curls opened the door of the Sandbox and looked around hesitantly. She stood in the doorway, scanning the room, looking for something.

Grace jumped up and waved. "Paula! We're over here."

Conversation at the table came to an abrupt halt as Paula Talbott-Sinclair timidly approached the table. She stopped a few feet away, looking at Grace for guidance.

"What's she doing here?" one of the women said angrily, jumping up from her seat and snatching up her pocketbook. "Spying on us for Stackpole?"

Paula's already-pale face blanched.

"I invited her," Grace said, standing. She reached out a hand for the therapist. "Paula? There's an empty seat right here, beside mine."

Paula's lower lip trembled. "I don't want to intrude. Maybe it would be better if I didn't stay."

"No," Camryn said. "Stay."

"Please," Suzanne said.

When she was finally seated, Rochelle hurried over to take the newcomer's order.

"Mom?" Grace said politely. "This is Paula. Paula, this is my mom, Rochelle."

"The therapist?" Rochelle looked from Paula to Grace to Wyatt. "You're the therapist?"

"Counselor," Paula corrected. "And I'll just have iced tea, please. Green, if you have it." She lowered her voice and leaned in closer to Grace.

"How's Ashleigh? Have you heard anything?"

"You know about Ashleigh? Already? Has it been on the news?"

Paula shook her head. "Ashleigh called me this afternoon. I guess it must have been before you went to meet her. And then a detective called me just before I came over here. The police retrieved Ashleigh's cell phone, and they were following up on all her recent calls. They wouldn't tell me much—just that she'd made an attempt on another woman's life and nearly killed herself in the process."

Grace stared at the therapist. "Let me get this straight. Ashleigh called you? Today?"

"She called me at the office, and I just happened to pick up. She'd obviously been drinking. She was ranting and raving about getting revenge against—what's the other woman's name?"

"Suchita."

"Right. Suchita. Ashleigh was manic. It was hard to get a word in edgewise. I begged her to come to the office, to talk things over, but she wouldn't hear of it. She was cursing and making all kinds of wild threats. She talked about setting fire to her ex's house or somehow poisoning the woman."

Paula shook her head. "Ashleigh was in a very dark place."

"I still don't understand why she called *you*," Grace said. "No offense, Paula, but she thought you were a quack."

"I'm well aware," Paula said. "She told me that several times today. But I think Ashleigh knew she was spinning out of control. She was desperate for help." Paula looked around the table, recognizing all the faces arrayed around it.

"I failed Ashleigh. And I failed all of these women." She glanced over at Wyatt, who was sitting on the other side of Grace. "And I failed you, too."

Paula squared her shoulders and addressed Grace. "You said your lawyer would be at this meeting. Is she here?"

Mitzi raised her hand. "Mitzi Stillwell, attorney at law."

Paula motioned to Camryn. "You can turn on that camera now. I'm ready to tell my story. All of it. If you're ready to hear it."

"I met Cedric at a cocktail party, soon after I moved down here. We struck up a conversation. He seemed interested in my work—I told him about the seminars I'd done out west and about the book. And—I guess I rattled on a little too long about the end of my marriage. He was sympathetic, and it was clear he was attracted to me . . ."

Paula looked directly into the camera. "I know this sounds incredibly lame—but at the time I had no idea he was married. If I'd known then—I would never have started an affair. Not after the way my own marriage ended. That's no excuse, I know. I should have made it my business to ask more questions, when he never wanted to meet me in public, insisted on meeting at my place. Maybe I didn't really want to know. Cedric is the first man I've been intimate with since my divorce.

"Maybe a month after we'd started seeing each other, he confessed he was married. I was shocked, tried to break it off, but he seemed committed to ending his marriage and being with me. I gave him my book and suggested he read it. Not long after that, he suggested that he should refer clients to me—clients whose divorces he was presiding over.

"It didn't occur to me that this was a breach of ethics. I was flattered and delighted that a distinguished judge thought I could assist these people."

"Oh for God's sake," Camryn said, pausing the video. "Paula, are you trying to tell us that it never occurred to you that you'd hit the motherlode with Stackpole making these counseling sessions mandatory? Come on! You were making fifteen hundred dollars a week just from the people in my little group."

Paula bit her lip and looked away. Rochelle brought her iced tea. She took a long sip. "I'll answer that on camera, if you like."

"When I moved here, I was very nearly destitute. I'd been in rehab and lost my license to practice in Oregon. When my husband and I divorced, we sold our home there at the very bottom of the market, for what amounted to pennies on the dollar, and, of course, he got half of that. I moved to Florida with my clothes, my car, and very little else. I was living in a motel room and working part-time as a social worker in a nursing home when I met Cedric.

"Cedric thought I should go into private practice again. He suggested I could get around Florida's tough licensing laws by not calling myself a therapist or a marriage counselor. He loaned me the money to rent my office space and buy a computer and some secondhand office furniture. Start-up funding, he called it. He was hearing so many divorce cases. He said there was a real need for the kind of therapy I offer. And he said it could be very lucrative."

"I'll say it was lucrative," Harriett put in. Camryn swung around in her seat and focused the camera on her. "With what I paid you alone in the past six months, you could have bought a nice midsized sedan. And yet you're still driving that dinky little toy car and operating out of that dump office. What happened to all the money? We heard you had a drug problem. Is that where it all went?"

Camryn chuckled, as did several other women at the table, although not Grace and not Suzanne.

Paula winced.

"That's a fair question, Harriett. I'm guessing by mentioning my drug problem you're referring to my arrest for forging prescriptions for tranquilizers in Oregon. I completed my court-ordered rehab out there, and I was doing reasonably well until I got involved with Cedric.

And then . . . well, I can't sugarcoat it, can I? I had a relapse. Obtaining drugs is much easier in Florida. I went to a storefront clinic, got a scrip, and I was in business again.

"You want to know where the money went? Not to drugs. I'm clean again. Most of it went to Cedric. Right off the bat, he told me my fee schedule was a joke. He said the patients he was referring to me were screwed up and desperate to get out of their lousy marriages. Why shouldn't they pay, and why shouldn't he be compensated for all those referrals? Especially since he'd already 'loaned' me all the money to get on my feet again."

"Kickbacks," Mitzi said succinctly. "You were paying him kickbacks? How much?"

"I can't give you a precise figure," Paula said. "But I only kept roughly a third of my fees. The rest I handed over to Cedric."

"How did you pay him?" Mitzi asked. "Cash, check? Do you have any records?"

Paula looked puzzled. "You mean receipts? Don't be absurd. Remember, Cedric was a lawyer before he was a judge. He's really quite brilliant."

"Then, how did you pay him?" Camryn asked from down the table. "If we're going to be able to make charges stick against Stackpole, Mitzi here is going to need some proof."

"I understand," Paula said. "I was getting to that, Camryn, if you'll just be patient."

"Sorry." Camryn flashed a grin and started filming again.

"Cedric's wife kept all their household accounts. He said she watched every penny he earned or spent. I know she was pretty wealthy in her own right, and he resented that—she didn't work, but she controlled the purse strings. He was very careful. He set up a janitorial business called Clean Sweep. All the money I paid him, I wrote out the checks to Clean Sweep. It was supposed to be for nightly cleaning and paper supplies, things like that."

"But it was a dummy corporation?" Mitzi asked.

"As far as I know, I was Clean Sweep's only client," Paula said. "And I never got any janitorial services. I cleaned the office myself."

"Sounds like you got taken to the cleaners yourself, girlfriend," Thea chimed in.

Paula sighed. "He said he loved me. But he'd signed a prenup before marrying his wife. If he left, he'd be living on a judge's salary. Peanuts, he called it. The money I gave him, he called it our nest egg. We were going to buy a cottage on Anna Maria. I was going to work on getting my licensing back. He'd leave the bench, start his own law firm. We'd give our own version of my old divorce diversion seminars and travel all over. We'd write a book together. He even had a title: *De-Toxing After Divorce*."

"Damn!" Camryn said. "That's a fabulous title. I'd buy a book called that. You know, if it was written by somebody other than Stackpole."

"And me," Paula said. She shrugged. "That's all I came to say, really. I'm sorry I allowed all of this to happen. Sorry I was a party to Cedric's scheme. Sorry I failed all of you. Could you turn the camera off now, please, Camryn?"

Camryn set the camera down carefully on the tabletop.

"Thank you, Paula," Grace said. "I mean it. Your coming here tonight and telling your story, that took a lot of courage. We all appreciate it, don't we, ladies?" She looked around the table, but the women returned only blank stares.

Suzanne stood up. She clapped her hands together. Slowly. Grace nodded and stood, too, and began clapping, as did Wyatt. They looked expectantly at Camryn, who nodded, stood, and joined in. Slowly, one by one, all the women at the table stood and joined in the polite applause.

69.

Wyatt tiptoed into the bedroom and set the teacup on the nightstand. He hurried to the windows to draw the curtains. The EMTs had versed him in postconcussion rules—no bright sunlight, sharp noises, or too much physical activity. Plenty of sleep, plenty of fluids, plenty of watchfulness. Grace had fallen asleep in the truck the previous night, just minutes after they'd left the Sandbox.

He'd hurried her into bed, and spent the night on the armchair beside it, waking occasionally, to listen to her soft, steady breathing, gently touch her hair, and to reassure himself that she was here and she was safe.

It was nearly ten now. Sweetie trotted into the room and sat expectantly at his feet. He tossed her a treat, and she chewed noisily.

"Shh," he cautioned.

Grace turned on her side and sat up slowly. "Oh, stop tiptoeing around! I'm awake, and I'm fine." She patted the bed and Sweetie jumped up, did a quick circle, and then settled herself into a nest just under Grace's arm.

Wyatt dropped a kiss on Grace's forehead and sat down on the few inches of bed the little dog hadn't claimed.

"How's the head?"

"A little achey, but better than it felt last night." She glanced at the clock on the nightstand. "It's ten already! Why didn't you wake me?"

"You needed to sleep," he said. "And the EMTs told me you should take it easy for the next few days."

"But I don't need a babysitter. And you need to get to work. So move along, mister," she ordered.

He held four fingers in front of her face. "How many?"

"Four."

"How did you get hurt?"

She rolled her eyes.

"Humor me," Wyatt said. "I'm supposed to test your memory."

"I was in a speeding car driven by a maniac. We went off the road and into the bay. Things get a little blurry after we hit the water. I do know you pulled me out and saved my life."

"And then you promised to love me forever and be my sex slave," Wyatt prompted.

"That part I don't remember," Grace said.

He shrugged. "It was worth a shot."

Wyatt pulled a bottle of Tylenol from his pocket and gestured to the tea. "Drink that and take two of these. And then drink some more. You're supposed to stay quiet today. I've already walked Sweetie, and there's some cereal and fruit in the kitchen. I've got to get over to the park now, but your mom will be by after the lunch rush is over."

"Run along now," Grace said. "You're sweet, but I really don't need babysitting and I hate being fussed over."

"Humor me," he said. "I nearly lost you yesterday." He thumped his chest meaningfully. "I love you, Grace. Really, deeply, truly."

"I know it." She yawned and her eyelids drooped. "I think I love you, too. But I think I need another nap."

70.

Grace slept. And then she slept some more. Despite her protests and much to her annoyance, Wyatt and Rochelle continued to cosset her.

After a week had gone by she'd had enough. When Wyatt showed up at the condo after work that Friday afternoon, he found her fully dressed, tapping away at her laptop at the dining room table.

"Hey you," he said, unsnapping Sweetie's leash and setting down the bag of take-out Chinese. "What's that?"

"My blog. I haven't written a word in nearly two weeks. I'm afraid my readers will think I'm dead."

He tried to read over her shoulder, but she shielded the screen with both hands. "It's not ready for public consumption yet. My writing has gotten sort of . . . rusty. I'll let you read it after I've cleaned it up and edited a little."

"Okay." He opened one of the white paper sacks. "Which do you want for dinner? Kung pao or sizzling shrimp?"

"Neither, thanks," Grace told him. "I've been stuck here for what feels like forever. Let's go out. I don't care where, just as long as I'm not staring at these four walls and eating Tylenol."

Wyatt nodded at the view out the French doors. "You're bored looking at the Gulf of Mexico?"

"I don't want to *look* at it anymore," Grace said. "I want to walk in it, splash in it, get wet, sweaty, sandy—anything but safe and sleepy, which is what I've been all week long."

"You're sure you feel like that?" Wyatt looked at her anxiously. "No headaches? Funny smells?"

"I am absolutely symptom-free and bored to tears. And I am truly grateful for all the loving care you and my mom have given me this week. I know you must have been neglecting Bo and your dad, not to mention work."

"We aren't exactly swamped at Jungle Jerry's this time of year," Wyatt said. "Yesterday we did exactly sixty-two dollars in admissions. Anyway, Dad understands, and Bo's just happy he's gotten to spend so much time with Sweetie. In fact, he sent you this."

Wyatt reached into the pocket of his shorts and handed her a carefully folded sheet of paper.

"Awww," Grace said softly. It was a crayon masterpiece, vividly rendered in black and orange and green and red, with spiky objects erupting from what looked like either a garbage can or a spaceship. Written in exuberant red letters across the bottom was a caption reading, "GRACE, GET BETTER SOON. Luv, Your Freind Bo."

"We're working on the spelling thing," Wyatt said. "But you'll notice he spelled your name correctly. And his, too."

Grace outlined the drawing with her fingertip. "I love it. What's it supposed to be?"

"Silly girl," he chided her. "That's a bouquet of red roses. He wanted to buy you some from the QuikTrip, but since they were plastic, which I assumed would offend your sensibilities, I suggested he draw you some instead."

"I'm going to have this framed and keep it forever. He really is the sweetest, most thoughtful boy."

"He gets that from me," Wyatt said modestly. "And lest

the son outshine the father, I brought you a present from me, too." From the other pocket he produced her cell phone.

"My iPhone!" She touched the ON button and the screen lit up. "It works! How did you manage this?"

"The cops told me where Ashleigh's car was towed, and Tuesday morning, after I left you, I bribed, er, tipped the salvage guy twenty bucks to let me retrieve it."

"But it must have gotten wet. It was ruined."

"It did get wet. But I went online and read some stuff about how to save it. Turns out, if you don't turn the thing on, which I didn't, and just put it in a plastic bag full of uncooked rice and let it sit for a couple days, to let the rice absorb the moisture, there's a good chance it might still work."

Grace turned the phone over and over. "It's ridiculous how much I missed this thing. I've felt like I was in solitary confinement without it."

Wyatt looked a little guilty. "I actually powered it up yesterday. I couldn't help but notice, you had some missed calls. And some voice messages."

Grace scrolled down her call log. Lots of missed calls. One from Paula Talbott-Sinclair, one from Arthur Cater, some out-of-area numbers she didn't recognize—and three calls from Ben, and two voice mails. She gave Wyatt a questioning look.

"I didn't listen to any of them, I swear. Although I'll admit I was tempted. If you want to listen now, or call anybody, I can come back in a little while."

Part of her was tempted to send him away, to hunker down with the phone, catch up with the world—and find out why her soon-to-be ex had called her more times in the past week than he had in the previous three months. And then she glanced out the window, at the sun sparkling on the water, at a handful of late-afternoon beach strollers.

"It can wait," she said, tucking the phone into the pocket of her shorts. She whistled for Sweetie. "Let's go."

They picked up grouper sandwiches and a couple of $1.50 beers at the Rod and Reel Pier, eating them on the lower deck, watching the fishermen, and chatting about life. Sweetie sat expectantly at their feet, waiting for her share of their dinner.

"Betsy called me today to say a new judge has been assigned to my divorce," Wyatt told her. "Charlie Davis. She says he's fairly young but has a good reputation. And he's speedy. His nickname is Rocket Docket Davis. She thinks it'll only be a matter of weeks now."

"That's good," Grace said, trying to sound noncommittal. "Mitzi dropped by earlier today. She says we finally got the luck of the draw with Catherine Chandler. She's the senior judge—and what Mitzi calls a card-carrying feminist. She expects Dickie Murphree and Ben will squawk about it, but there's not a damned thing they can do about it." While she spoke, her hand hovered unconsciously over the pocket with her cell phone.

"Go ahead and listen to your messages and voice mails," Wyatt said. "I know the suspense is killing you. I'm gonna go back upstairs and get a slice of key lime pie. Text me when you're done, and we can go for that walk I promised."

"You sure?" Grace flashed him a grateful smile.

"Grace?" Arthur Cater seemed to be shouting into the phone. "Are you there? Listen, I had a visit from your, uh, husband. I guess he's still your husband? Anyway, he straightened me out on a couple of things, and afterward, the wife and I got to talking. She's got her heart set on you finishing up your work on the house on Mandevilla. The upshot is, we'd like to sell you the place if you're still interested. You better call me quick, though, before I list it with an agent."

"Yippee!" Heads turned as Grace stood and did a modified happy dance, right there in the middle of the Rod and Reel Pier.

She took a swallow of beer and hit the call-back button.

"That you, Grace?" Arthur was still shouting. "I was beginning to think maybe you'd found another project for yourself."

"Not at all, Arthur! My phone and I were out of commission for a few days, so I just now got your message. I would absolutely love to talk to you about buying Mandevilla." Her heart was racing—she was so excited—but she knew she had to ask the hard question. "Do you have any idea how much you'd want for it?"

"What I want and what I'll take are two different matters," he said, chuckling. He named his price, and Grace's pulse blipped and her mouth went dry.

"You still there?" he hollered.

"I'm here, Arthur. But you must know, the house is worth at least fifty thousand more than that."

"It's probably worth seventy-five thousand more than that," he corrected her. "But my accountant says if we make too big a profit, I'm gonna get screwed over at tax time. More importantly, my wife swears she'll nag me into the grave unless I see to it that you finish what you started with that little old cracker house."

"I really want to meet your wife, Arthur," Grace said.

"That can be arranged. So . . . what do you say?"

She chose her words carefully. "I want to say you've got a deal. Right now. But to be honest, my divorce settlement is still up in the air. We've got a new judge, though, and my lawyer thinks everything should be settled pretty soon."

"Fair enough. You call me when it's all settled, then, will you?"

"The minute I know something, I'll call. And thanks, Arthur. Really. Thanks."

Grace took another sip of her beer and stared out at the water. A school of fingerling mullet slashed just below the surface of the green water, and a couple of screeching gulls swooped in to pick off a few.

Arthur said Ben had paid him a visit. Whatever he'd told the old man, it had been enough to change his mind about selling her the house. She wondered if her own mostly idle threats to tell the police about J'Aimee's involvement in vandalizing the house had prompted the visit to Arthur.

She turned the phone over and over in her hand. Part of her was dying of curiosity, part of her dreaded hearing Ben's voice. There was only one way to find out what he wanted. She listened to the first voice mail he'd left—which had been Monday evening.

"Hey, uh, it's me. Give me a call."

Tuesday morning, he'd left another message.

"Okay, Grace, if you're trying to be coy, it's not working. Call me, okay? I've, uh, got a proposition for you."

A proposition? Did she even want to know? Yes. She did want to know exactly what Ben was up to. Without giving it much more thought, she touched the redial.

"Grace?" Ben sounded . . . different. "Listen, I didn't know about the accident. Your lawyer just called Dickie about getting together to finalize the settlement, and she mentioned you'd had a head injury. What a hell of a thing. Are you all right?"

"I am now. Are we finalizing a financial settlement? Is that the reason you called?"

"It's one of the reasons. Uh, there have been some

changes around here, and I thought I should let you know about them. Before it's final and everything."

"Oh-kayyy," she said slowly. Where was this going? Why was he being so civil? Maybe he'd been hit on the head, too?

"First off, I'm getting ready to list the house and move," he said briskly. "Dickie informs me that the new judge will probably make me split the proceeds with you, so he says I have to let you know, in case you have any interest in buying out my half."

"You're moving? Where? Why?"

"It's time," he said. "I've had a job offer from a big-time agency in New York. They're opening a new media division, and it's too good an opportunity to pass up. But they want me up and running right after Labor Day, which doesn't give me a lot of time to sell the house and find a new place."

Her mind was racing. "What about the blog? What about J'Aimee? Will she move with you?"

There was a long stretch of dead silence on the other end of the phone.

"No. J'Aimee is not part of the new package," Ben said. "If you must know, she's gone. As for the blog, well, that was another reason for my reaching out to you."

"I see."

"If you've been following it, you probably noticed that our sponsorships were down, and the numbers had stagnated. I won't get into the reasons for that."

A smile played across Grace's lips. Of course Ben wouldn't get into the reasons why Gracenotes had tanked. It had tanked because it was Graceless. Not that she'd rub that in his face.

"I still think it's a good business model," Ben was saying. "For the right person. Somebody like you. Anyway, if you want it back, it's yours. I'll send you the new passwords and the contact info for the current advertisers. We can work out a payment schedule as we go."

Was that a compliment he was sneaking in under the radar?

"Where is all this going, Ben?" she asked.

"Shit." He sighed.

"Ben?"

"What? You want me to grovel? Beg for forgiveness? Not my style, Grace, and you know it."

"You sure know how to charm a girl," Grace said, her tone acidic.

He sighed. "Sorry. This isn't easy for me. A lot's happened, Grace. Do I regret what happened? Yeah. I do. J'Aimee was a mistake. Huge mistake. And I take responsibility for that. I'd like to think I'm a better man than that."

"You used to be a better man than that," Grace said quietly. "But there's a lot I regret, too. Drowning your car was not one of my finer moments."

He laughed. "Nor mine. But I guess I probably had it coming."

"So. Where does this leave us?" she asked.

"I guess you don't want to buy out my share of the house?"

She shuddered. The fact that Ben had just given her the closest thing to an apology she'd ever get from him didn't mean she ever intended to spend another night in the house where he'd betrayed her.

"No thanks."

"Didn't think so. I'll e-mail you the listing agreement. You can let me know if you think the asking price is realistic. I'd like to get out from under it as quickly as possible."

"Whatever you want," Grace said. "The faster it sells, the faster I can buy a house for myself."

"Yeah. About that. I went to see the old man over there on Mandevilla."

"Arthur. He told me. And he offered to sell it to me for a price I can't pass up."

"Good," Ben said gruffly. "You should have a house of your own. And that place suits you, Grace."

She was touched. "Thank you, Ben. That's the nicest thing you've said to me in a really long time."

"See? I'm not a jerk one hundred percent of the time."

"I know you're not."

"You might share that thought with Rochelle. She doesn't have a very high opinion of me."

"Mom? Have you talked to her recently?"

"Saw her today, as a matter of fact. After Dickie told me you'd been in an accident, I took flowers for you over to the Sandbox. She told me you weren't there, but she wouldn't say where you were staying. I'm guessing you've moved in with the new guy?"

Was that a note of jealousy she detected?

"No, I'm not living with Wyatt," she said.

"None of my business, but are things pretty serious between the two of you?"

She couldn't resist. "I'll answer that if you'll tell me what happened to J'Aimee. You said she's gone? Did she leave before or after you accepted the new job?"

"You first," Ben said.

"Yes, things are fairly serious between us. But his divorce isn't final yet, either, and he has a young son, and there are complications with his ex. All that aside, he's a great guy, and I think we have a future together. Now, you."

"Christ," he grumbled. "J'Aimee's moved to California. End of story."

"Nuh-uh, you don't get off that easy," Grace chided. "What's she doing in California?"

"Auditioning for some crazy reality show she read about on the Internet. Look, Grace, I gotta go."

"Not before you tell me what kind of a reality show," Grace said. "You owe me at least that much, Ben."

He mumbled something incoherent.

"What's that?"

He mumbled again.

"I can't make out what you're saying, Ben."

"It's called *Homewreckers*. Got that? I came home from golf last week and she'd packed her crap and loaded up her car and announced she was going to Hollywood to get a part in a reality show about women who sleep with married men. In other words, homewreckers."

Grace laughed so hard, she couldn't catch her breath.

"Glad you're amused," Ben groused.

"Sorry," she said, gasping for air. "Very sorry. Goodbye Ben."

Wyatt came back and shared his key lime pie with her, and it was so good, she made him buy her a second slice. Then they got in the truck and drove up the beach. They didn't discuss it, but Grace had a feeling she knew where they were headed.

He parked the car at Coquina Beach. "We're still not supposed to have a dog on this beach," Grace pointed out, nodding at Sweetie, who was perched in her lap.

Wyatt opened his door and then came around and opened hers. "I won't tell if you won't tell."

They left their shoes on the soft carpet of pine needles and walked down to the water's edge. Grace stood still and let her toes sink into the pale gray sand. She looked down at the warm water swirling around her ankles, at the foam frosting the waves as they lapped at the shore. A lifetime ago, she'd felt a suffocating panic, strapped into Ashleigh's car, with the water rising around her knees. Now, with

Wyatt's hand clasped in hers, she felt as light as the gull's feather that floated past.

She inhaled and exhaled. "This is good. This is what I needed."

They walked for nearly an hour, until the brilliant orange sun hovered just above the tops of the Australian pines. Then they found a picnic bench and settled in to watch the show.

"I talked to Ben," she said, with Wyatt's arm thrown casually around her shoulders.

"Oh?"

"He's ready to settle. I think his lawyer saw the handwriting on the wall. Anyway, it turns out he's accepted a new job in New York. He's moving immediately, and he wanted to know if I wanted to buy out his share of the house."

"The mansion?"

"Whatever. There's nothing there for me now."

"Is the girlfriend going with him?"

"No. She's gone to seek her fame and fortune in Hollywood. Ben didn't sound too heartbroken about it. In fact, I think he was relieved."

Wyatt turned to look at her. "How about you? Are you relieved? To have her out of the picture?"

She shrugged. "Funny you should ask. I find myself curiously apathetic about J'Aimee. Guess I've let go of the anger. I wonder what Paula would say about that."

"I think she'd say you've had a growth moment," Wyatt said, making two-fingered quote marks in the air.

"Maybe I have," Grace mused. "I'll have to write about that in my journal." She reached over and laced her fingers through his. "How 'bout you? Had any growth moments of your own lately?"

"As a matter of fact, I have. A couple of them, actually."

"Wanna share?" She kept her tone light.

"Dad and I had some long talks this week. Turns out,

he's not opposed to my selling Jungle Jerry's to the state for a park."

"Really? So . . . it's a done deal?"

"We're dealing with the state of Florida, Grace. Everything works at a snail's pace with them. But it turns out they've got some kind of federal grant to develop what they call urban parklands. Smaller parks, under fifty acres, like ours, where the emphasis will be on community education rather than recreation. We'd keep the original gardens, get rid of the old playground equipment, and, in its place, develop demonstration gardens for heirloom Florida fruits, vegetables, and flowers. The guy with the state seems to think there's a good chance I'd be offered the job as park superintendent, or whatever they call them these days."

"That's great, Wyatt!" she said, beaming. "It sounds perfect for you."

"I know. If I had to write my dream-job description, this would be it."

Sweetie perked up her ears and gave a low growl. They both looked up and saw an elderly man inching slowly down the beach toward them. He was shirtless and his sun-browned skin gleamed in the dying sunlight. Baggy black shorts hung from his hips to just above mahogany-colored knobby knees. Below these he wore what looked like white surgical stockings and thick-soled black rubber sandals. He didn't appear to see or hear them—or Sweetie.

The old man wore a pair of enormous earphones connected to an unwieldy metal detector, and his eyes were glued to the sand as he waved the detector's wand back and forth over a three-foot-wide swath of sand.

Grace nodded in his direction. "You think he ever finds anything valuable? From the looks of him, he must spend hours and hours with that thing."

"He probably finds lots of bottle caps and pennies. Maybe the occasional set of keys or a piece of jewelry.

Probably just enough to keep him in gas and beer," Wyatt said.

"But he never gives up. And he walks for miles. I've seen him every day this week, on the beach outside Mitzi's condo. I guess it gives him something to do," Grace said.

"You said you had a couple of growth moments this week?" Grace asked idly, her eyes following the treasure seeker's progress. "What was the other one?"

"Mm-hmm," Wyatt said. He rested his lips briefly against her right temple. "Callie showed up at the park again yesterday, begging me to give her a job. And another chance."

Grace half stood and tried to pull away, but Wyatt gently tugged her back down beside him.

"I told her no," he said, placing his hand on her cheek. "Hell, no. What you said just now—that there's nothing there for you—back at your old house, with Ben. That's how it is with me and Callie. I wish her well, for Bo's sake, but that's it."

"You're sure?" Grace held her breath.

"Never surer," Wyatt said. "It's you and me now, kid, if you'll have me." Slowly, he slid off the thick gold band on his left ring finger. He stood up, cocked his throwing arm back, and made his pitch.

"This is me, letting go," he said.

The wedding band spiraled and looped, the dull gold catching glints of the fading sunlight. It landed fifty feet away, in the soft sand, maybe twenty yards in front of the old man, who seemed not to see it.

"Good arm, huh?" Wyatt said, admiring his own prowess.

Grace wrapped her arms around his neck and kissed her approval. "Good arm, good man," she murmured. "Good everything."

Epilogue

True Grace, Feb. 14

The old rules of etiquette for second marriages were stern and absolute. In her starchy 1957 Complete Book of Etiquette: A Guide to Gracious Living, Amy Vanderbilt opined that the second-time ceremony must be small, and that the "mature" bride should never wear white or a veil, or, heaven forbid, expect wedding gifts. She cautioned, too, that many ministers would actually refuse to perform a second wedding in a church! Invitations should not be engraved, as with a formal first wedding, but a handwritten note would be acceptable.

Thankfully, wedding rules these days have been relaxed, or sometimes, totally discarded. Although I'm a traditionalist at heart, for our own second wedding, my intended and I wanted something intimate and meaningful, with just a few close friends and family members.

We actually didn't tell our guests that they were coming to a wedding at all. Instead, we invited them to what we simply billed as a garden party. Of course, we have the good fortune to have access to one of the most beautiful settings I can imagine, Wyatt's family's small but charming botanical park, here on Florida's Gulf Coast.

The party was to be the last private family party at Jungle Jerry's, an old-timey Florida tourist attraction founded by Wyatt's grandparents shortly after World War II, before the park is turned over to the state of Florida.

Our guests arrived at the park's front gate at dusk and were ferried to the party site by golf carts. When they reached the small enclosed butterfly garden, they were greeted with glasses of pink champagne, iced tea, or locally brewed beer.

Wyatt and I mingled with our guests and enjoyed the food he and I prepared together from local farms and fishermen—stone crab "martinis," chilled shrimp and avocado gazpacho, and crab beignets with pineapple-mango salsa. All the food was set out on rustic wooden picnic tables that were hand-built years ago by Wyatt's grandfather, with centerpieces of hibiscus, lilies, orchids, and other flowers picked right from the gardens.

Shortly before sunset, a small string quartet arrived and began to play classical music. At that point, we invited everybody to be seated in a semi-circle of battered vintage lawn chairs and proceeded to the surprise event of the evening—our wedding!

The minister, a family friend who happens to be a regular at my mother's bar, stepped in front of a weathered wooden trellis, which was lit by hundreds of tiny white fairy lights and blooming with pale pink New Dawn roses.

When the wedding march started, I joined Wyatt in front of the makeshift altar.

Amy Vanderbilt says that for a second-time-around wedding, the attendants should be limited to one each for the bride and groom and should be the bride and groom's age. But, since Amy's long gone, we broke the rules—just a little.

The bride (that's me!) wore a 1960s vintage lace-over-silk minidress dyed the same exact hue as the roses. My bouquet was one made for me by Wyatt, from flowers he grew at the park, including hot-pink lilies, deep-violet hydrangeas, and my favorites—heavenly white gardenias. No other flowers were necessary, since the scent of the orange blossoms from the citrus gardens blanketed the late-afternoon air.

I promised Wyatt I wouldn't ask him to get too dressed up, so he chose his own khaki slacks, a nice white dress shirt—and in a major concession to the importance of the occasion, a navy blue blazer, which he promptly ditched right after the ceremony. He also wore a boutonniere—of rosemary and white phlox clipped from the garden at our tiny newly restored cottage.

Since my own father is deceased, Wyatt's dad, Nelson, agreed to give me away. Wyatt chose his six-year-old son Bo as his best man. Nelson wore his best (and only) good gray suit, and Bo was heartbreakingly adorable in his own khakis and blue blazer.

I'd begged my mother to be my maid of honor, but she gracefully declined with the excuse that she didn't want anybody to mistake her for a maiden. As if!

Instead, my friend Camryn agreed to be my at-

tendant. Camryn loves fashion, so she wore a chic one-shouldered deep-violet silk dress by a designer so trendy I'd never heard of her. And spike heels— Camryn says she feels barefoot unless she's wearing at least four-inch heels—even during a garden wedding in February.

Amy Vanderbilt probably never considered the idea of including a pet in a wedding party, but since our little rescue dog, Sweetie, is such an important part of our blended family, she had to have a role in our big day. Bo was proud and happy to walk her down the aisle, although he did state loudly that he thought the pink tulle ruffle I fastened around her neck was "disgusting."

After we said our vows, my mother revealed her masterpiece—a three-tiered lemon pound cake with strawberry cream cheese frosting—topped with an ingenious bride and groom crafted by Bo—from Legos.

We cut the cake, had some toasts, and, when it got dark and chilly, we all repaired to the after party at the Sandbox, my mother's bar in nearby Cortez.

I don't know what Amy Vanderbilt would have thought of our second-time-around wedding, but I know, for us, it was definitely an affair to remember.

Grace was rushing around the bar, greeting guests, when she spotted a newcomer out of the corner of her eye. She threw her arms around the woman.

"Suzanne! You came back. I'm so happy to see you."

"There's no way I would have missed your garden party—and then to sneak in a wedding, well, what can I say? It was beautiful, unexpected, and so romantic, Grace. Like something out of a fairy tale."

"Thanks," Grace said, beaming. She gestured to the willowy young woman at Suzanne's side. "And this must be Darby."

"It is. Darby, meet our beautiful, blushing bride, Grace."

Wyatt wandered up and wrapped an arm around Suzanne's and Grace's waists. "And don't forget the blushing bridegroom."

Darby was a slender brunette, two inches taller than her mother, but with the same striking olive-green eyes. "Congratulations," she said shyly. "Mom's told me all about you, and the rest of the group."

"Look who's here," Camryn shrieked, enveloping Suzanne in a hug before standing back to critique her appearance. "You look amazing," Camryn said. "How's life in North Carolina? And the new job?"

"It's good," Suzanne said. "I'm slowly getting used to winter. And snow! I had to actually go out and buy a wool coat and boots. The job is good." She glanced at Darby, who'd drifted off and was chatting with Camryn's daughter, Jana. "Elon is a good fit. For both of us."

Camryn leaned in, her eyes dancing with a mischievous glint. "And what about men? Are you getting any action?"

Suzanne blushed violently. "I've actually had a couple real dates. The men's soccer coach. He's a good bit younger, but . . ."

"Ooh, Suzanne. You're a cougar!" Camryn linked her arm through Suzanne's and Grace's. "Look at us now, y'all. Grace and Wyatt married. Suzanne moved off and prowling around up there in North Carolina . . ."

"What about you?" Suzanne asked. "Grace says you left News Four You."

"I sure did," Camryn said. "There was a senior producer's slot open, but I got passed over, so I up and left. I'm producing the six o'clock news at channel two. The money's not quite as good, but I get to sleep in for the first time in twenty years. And I sub-in on camera when somebody's out sick or on vacation."

"Men?" Suzanne raised a quizzical eyebrow.

"I was seeing somebody, but it didn't work out," Camryn said. "That's one thing I learned from my divorce. If it's not right, it's not right. Cut your losses and move on."

"Has anybody heard from Ashleigh?" Suzanne asked, looking around the room.

"Oh, sure," Camryn said. "You can't keep that girl down. She did some work-release thing as part of her sentence for trying to kill her ex's baby mama. She's working for another plastic surgeon and living down in Naples. She has to wear one of those electronic-monitoring bracelet things, which she hates, 'cuz she says it makes her ankles look fat, so she has to wear pants and can't show off her legs anymore."

"Ashleigh would have been here today, except the idea of being around all the party stuff —you know, with liquor and everything, made her a little anxious," Grace said. "She's been clean and sober for six months now."

"Really?" Suzanne looked taken aback. "I mean, you two are on speaking terms? After everything that happened?"

"Grace has a much more forgiving heart than I do," Wyatt said. "I'm good with Ashleigh now, although Grace is banned from ever getting in a car with her again."

Grace laughed. "She's changed a lot since that day. I think it was a turning point for her."

"You'll never guess who Ashleigh's AA sponsor was," Camryn said.

"Who?" Suzanne was still scanning the room, looking for familiar faces.

"None other than Paula Talbott-Sinclair," Camryn said.

578   *Mary Kay Andrews*

"I wondered what happened to Paula," Suzanne admitted. "I know you all might disagree, but I really think she did eventually help all of us in our group."

Wyatt pulled Grace into his arms. "I, for one, am eternally grateful to Paula. Without her, I might never have met the love of my life."

Grace rewarded her new husband with a kiss, then looked at her friends. "He's a sweet-talking fool, but he's right about Paula. If she did nothing else, she brought us all together, at the lowest point in our lives, and forced us to look at our attitudes and expectations about love."

"Don't forget what we did for *her*," Camryn chimed in. "She might still be mixed up with that parasite Cedric Stackpole if we hadn't exposed him for the scum-sucking dog he really is. I bet she never would have had the nerve to rat him out to the state if it hadn't been for us. And she damn sure wouldn't have been able to reinvent herself like she has without me."

"Paula reinvented herself?" Suzanne looked puzzled. "How? And what did you have to do with that?"

"Paula is now a certified laughter coach," Camryn said. "She works with people dealing with depression, terminal illness, and severe emotional problems. I did a feature story on her before I left News Four, and now she's got her own syndicated radio show."

"Any news about dear old Stackpole?" Suzanne asked.

"He's actually been in the news a good bit recently," Grace said, not bothering to suppress her glee. "The feds raided his new law office and seized all his tax records. My lawyer says the IRS is going after him big-time for falsifying tax records and tax evasion, among other things."

"That's one story I would have loved to have been in on," Camryn said. "What I wouldn't give to stick a live microphone in his sorry face."

"Just his face?" Wyatt asked. "And don't forget, Stackpole still has to deal with the lawsuit filed by that guy who filmed his wife and girlfriend's hair-pulling match in Sarasota. Couldn't happen to a nicer guy, huh?"

As they chatted and caught up on each other's lives, music began to filter into the room. Chairs scraped against the wooden floor as they were cleared out of the way, and guests began to edge onto the makeshift dance floor.

"You hired a DJ?" Suzanne asked, looking around the room.

"Better," Rochelle said, joining the group. "When Grace was making me clean up the place, I finally got rid of Butch's old Ms. Pac-Man game. It was broken, and I couldn't get anybody to fix it. Instead, I found an old jukebox at the flea market and had it restored. I put in all the records he and I used to dance to."

"And even some music from the last half century," Wyatt teased.

Grace tugged at his arm. "Okay, enough talk, mister. This is our wedding night, and you are going to dance with me, and that's final."

"Gladly," Wyatt said, leading her into the middle of the cramped floor.

Suzanne looked at Camryn. "Dance?"

"Damn straight," Camryn said. "But just so you know, I always lead."

The party was still in full swing at ten o'clock, when the two grizzled barflies known as Miller and Bud approached the Sandbox door. Miller pushed on the door, but it didn't move.

"Hey," he said, puzzled. "The lights are on, but it's locked. What's up with that?"

Bud pointed to a small hand-lettered note taped to the door.

CLOSED DUE TO PRIVATE PARTY

"They can't do that to us," Miller protested. "It's Sunday night. We always watch the games on Sundays."

Bud pressed his bulbous pink nose against the glass door and peered inside. "Man! They got all kinds of food on the tables, and balloons and decorations and shit, and some kind of fancy pink drinks in martini glasses."

Miller shoved him aside and took a gander for himself. "They're dancing!" He turned to Bud in astonishment. "They're actually dancing in there." He frowned. "I see a couple guys—there's an old dude in a suit, and a younger guy dancing with Rochelle's daughter, and some little kid—hey, the kid is dancing with Rochelle."

"Lemme see." Bud elbowed him out of the way. He looked disgusted. "It's mostly women in there. And they're not even watching the game."

"Must be a ladies' night thing," Miller concluded sadly as he turned away from the door. "Looks like we're gonna have to find ourselves someplace new, Bud."

Acknowledgments

Gale H. Moore of Largo, Florida, and Jean Higham of St. Petersburg, Florida, as well as Beth Fleishman of Raleigh, North Carolina, gave me good legal advice for the research for this book—but in the interest of fiction and plotting, I kept some of what they gave me and made up my own rules of law where needed, so don't blame them if you don't think my plot is plausible! Many women were generous with tales of their own divorce wars, but Martha Woodham and Melita Easters were especially gracious with their time. On the homefront, Grace Quinn was as essential and good-natured as always— in the face of looming disasters and tax deadlines. The women of Weymouth— where this book was initially conceived and eventually delivered, were amazing, and I owe them all—Alexandra Sokoloff, Bren Witchger, Diane Chamberlain, Katy Munger, Margaret Maron, and Sarah Shaber, a huge debt of gratitude. Thanks also to the amazing team at St. Martin's Press, including but not limited to Sally Richardson and Matthew Shear, my fabulous editor Jennifer Enderlin, publicist John Karle, and many more, including Michael Storrings, who always gives me such a delicious book jacket. Meg Walker at Tandem Literary gets huge thanks for her marketing genius and great Facebook advice. I am so blessed to have the best damn literary agent in the business—Stuart Krichevsky, and to him and the folks at SKLA, including Shana and Ross, I send hugs and kisses—and virtual pound cakes. Lastly but never last, the biggest thanks go to my family, Tom, Katie and Mark, Andy, Molly and Griffin, who make everything possible. I may write about divorce and heartache, but in real life, my champion, my hero, my best friend, Mr. MKA, aka Tom Trocheck, is the inspiration for every good guy in every book.

Read on for an excerpt from

THE WEEKENDERS

by Mary Kay Andrews

Available in trade paperback from St. Martin's Griffin

1.

Wendell Griggs was big on promises. Always had been. On their first date, he'd promised Riley Nolan she'd never want to date anybody else. When he'd presented her with her engagement ring—a three-carat diamond bigger than any of her girlfriends had—he'd promised it was the start of a life that would be big and rich and exciting. No doubt about it, her husband was a dreamer. And a schemer.

But lately, Wendell's promises meant nothing. Just talk. Hollow words meant to placate or stall. Nothing more. What was it her grandfather used to say?

"All hat, no cattle."

Like today. Wendell had promised—sworn—he'd meet them at the ferry dock at Southpoint in time to make the last boat over to Belle Isle.

It was Memorial Day weekend, a tradition they'd established even before they'd gotten married, kicking off the season on the island where Riley's family had summered for the past hundred years.

And yet, here she stood. She brushed a stray lock of dark brown hair from her eyes and squinted down at the screen of her smartphone. Still nothing.

Her fingertips raced over the keys.

WHERE R U?

All caps. It was the texting equivalent of screaming. And that's how she felt, like screaming.

The late afternoon sun shimmered off the water's surface, and the light breeze whipping the surface of the river carried the faint scent of honeysuckle. It was the prettiest day in weeks, but Riley Nolan Griggs was oblivious to all of that.

She glanced again in the direction of the parking lot, willing his car to appear. The black Jeep CJ. *What a stupid car for a grown man.* Vehicles were streaming into the lot now, station wagons, big SUVs, all of them carrying people intent on making the last ferry of the day. All of them with the distinctive oval BI sticker connoting membership in the tribe of Belle Isle. Vehicles pulled to the curb in front of the ferry terminal to unload everything needed for another summer on the island. Passengers spilled from the cars, lugging coolers, wheeled suitcases, bicycles, leashed dogs, and fishing gear. Deckhands, most of them deeply tanned college boys in navy blue BI-logo golf shirts and baggy cargo shorts, scurried around the baggage area, loading all the freight into aluminum carts that would be rolled onto the ferry.

Women greeted each other with that peculiar high-pitched Southern squeal of delight. "Heeeeyyy!" *What did Wendell call it? Oh, yes.* "The mating call of the ivory-breasted Tri-Delt."

It was six thirty. The boat would leave at seven on the dot. He knew that, knew how crazy it made her when he cut things this close. But there was no sign of the black Jeep. She checked to make sure she hadn't missed a call, and checked her e-mail too, but there was still no word from him.

Selfish bastard. He was doing this to torture her, she was sure. Waiting until the last possible minute to make an appearance. She could already picture the moment. He'd stroll across the pavement, just as the *Carolina Queen* was blasting the "last call" horn, maybe make a quick dash before the deckhands pulled up the metal gangplank.

Her face reddened, her stomach twisted, and she felt the familiar acid taste in her mouth.

He'd promised. Sworn to her he would make the last ferry today, no matter what. Most importantly, he'd sworn it to Maggy. Even with things as crappy as they were between them, he didn't usually break a promise to their daughter.

"Heeeeyyyy, Riley!"

She turned. The woman was bearing down on her with laser-like intensity. She wore a pink-and-lime-green cotton Lilly Pulitzer shift and pink Jack Rogers sandals. Riley, trapped, managed a weak greeting in return.

"Oh, hey, Andrea."

"It's so great to see you!" Andrea Payne gushed. "You look terrific. I swear, I wish I had your metabolism. Have you lost a ton of weight over the winter?"

Without waiting for a reply, Andrea wrapped her slender arms around Riley's neck and hugged her close. Too close. Riley was already tense and overheated, and the last thing she needed right now was a volley of nosy questions.

Riley managed to subtly loosen herself from Andrea's grasp. She took a step backward.

Andrea turned to her companion. "Melody, doesn't Riley look fantastic?"

Andrea's friend Melody Zimmerman dutifully nodded her head in agreement. "Fantastic." She gestured at the handbag slung casually across Riley's shoulder. "Is that a Michael Kors? OMG, I love it so much."

"Um, maybe," Riley said, glancing at her bag. It was an oversize leather number in trendy turquoise, with a large, dangling gold-monogram charm that Riley secretly found just the tiniest bit gaudy. But she knew the gift had been expensive, and besides, it did hold a lot of stuff. "I mean, I'm not sure. Wendell gave it to me for my birthday last year."

"It's adorbs!" Andrea pronounced. "Are y'all going to the full-moon party tonight? Is Maggy here, or did she decide to do summer camp this year? Where's Wendell?"

Riley deliberately sidestepped the issue of Wendell's whereabouts. "I haven't really been dieting. Maybe just eating healthy. And yes, Maggy's here. For now, anyway." She looked around for an escape route and conveniently spotted her daughter weighted down with tote bags and a backpack, struggling to keep Mr. Banks, their unruly pug puppy, under control.

"Maggy, hold on. I'm coming!" Riley called out. "We'll catch up later, ladies."

"You and Wendell *have* to come over for drinks, before the party," Andrea burbled. "Right, Melody?"

"Absolutely!" Melody agreed, bobbing her head.

"I can't wait for you to see my new kitchen tonight," Andrea said.

"OMG—she got an eight-burner Wolf range," Melody said. "And a Sub-Zero fridge. It's my dream kitchen!"

"Oh geez," Riley said, looking in the direction of the parking lot. "Sounds great. But I really need to go give Maggy a hand with that crazy dog of hers."

Andrea tapped Riley's arm. "So, I won't take no for an answer. You're coming for drinks. Right?"

"We'd love to."

"Said nobody, ever," Riley muttered under her breath. She hurried away from the ferry dock, the soles of her rubber flip-flops slapping against the furnace-hot asphalt.

"Maggy!"

Her daughter had come to a dead stop in the middle of the parking lot and was tapping furiously on her cell phone, oblivious to the oncoming stream of cars, her mother, and Banks, who was squatting down on one of the carefully manicured landscape islands, amidst the grass and pink Knock Out roses, doing what puppies liked to do.

"Maggy! Don't let him . . ."

But it was too late. Banks finished his toilette and came scampering toward his mistress, his plump little body wriggling with happiness and relief.

Now Maggy looked up. "Huh?"

Riley picked up the pair of overstuffed totes and nudged her daughter out of the path of a looming white Mercedes SUV. "Sweetie, pay attention! While you were busy Snapchatting with your girlfriends just now, you nearly got run down. And Banks managed to drop a deuce on those rosebushes over there." Riley rummaged around among the groceries in the tote bag until she found a roll of paper towels. She tore off a sheet and handed it to her twelve-year-old daughter.

Maggy recoiled. "Gross. No way."

Riley took her daughter's hand, deftly removed the phone, and replaced it with a paper towel. "Way. He's your dog. Your responsibility. Your poop. Now go clean it up before somebody rats us out and we get issued a littering citation."

Maggy rolled her eyes but handed the dog's leash to her

mother before stomping off in the direction of the landscaped island.

Riley was struck by how much her daughter had grown
over the past year. Micro short shorts showed off Maggy's
long, tanned legs, and the tank top that left bare a two-inch
strip of her abdomen also revealed a modestly developing
bustline. She'd let her taffy-colored hair grow out over
the spring, and although she wore it now in carelessly
fashioned pigtails, Maggy was already starting to raid
Riley's bathroom for her expensive salon shampoo, conditioner, and styling products.

No more sweet-smelling baby shampoo for Maggy. No
more baby anything, for that matter, Riley thought ruefully. In October, Maggy would officially be a teenager.

Despite the heat, a shiver ran down Riley's spine. Banks
pressed his muzzle between Riley's sweaty calves. She absentmindedly scratched the dog's ears and glanced down
at her daughter's phone.

It was the latest model iPhone, of course, ensconced in
a neon purple case with a florid monogram on the back,
and the screen was littered with a dizzying array of unfamiliar app icons. Riley's own phone was at least two years
old. She'd told Wendell it was ridiculous to buy such an
expensive cell for a kid who'd already managed to lose two
phones in one year, but Wendell, being Wendell, had over-
ruled Riley's objections.

"I want her to have a good phone. What if her blood
sugar gets low? Or she needs to get in contact with me?"

Maggy's diagnosis earlier in the year with juvenile onset type 1 diabetes had thrown them both for a loop.

Riley remembered that particular "discussion" with
crystal clarity. She'd stared back at Wendell, startled by
what she was suddenly seeing.

Her husband had changed in the past two years. His
thick black hair was streaked with silver. He'd started wear-

ing it longer, letting it brush his shirt collar. He'd stopped wearing the business suits she'd always enjoyed picking out for him, instead buying his own skinny designer jeans and Armani designer shirts. His blue eyes, made brighter by new contact lenses, narrowed.

"What if *I* need to get in contact with you?" Riley asked.

"What's that supposed to mean?" Wendell demanded. "Are you going to start in on this again? I call you every night. I talk to Maggy every morning. I'm working, Riley. I'm trying to save Belle Isle. Trying to make a living for my family. For *us*. You think I want to work all these crazy hours? Think I don't miss spending time with my kid?"

Snippets of those tense conversations over the past year played in an endless loop in Riley's mind.

Maggy was back. "Hey! No snooping." She snatched the phone out of Riley's hand.

"I wasn't snooping," Riley said. "Who were you Snapchatting with?"

"Nobody."

Riley raised one eyebrow.

"Okay," she relented. "I was texting Daddy, letting him know we're here at the ferry dock."

"Did he text you back?"

"Not yet," Maggy admitted. "But the ferry doesn't leave for another twenty minutes. He'll be here."

Riley squeezed her daughter's narrow shoulder. "I wouldn't get your hopes up. You know how busy he's been. He'll probably have to catch the morning boat."

"He's coming tonight," Maggy insisted. "He promised. For the full moon party."

"I just don't want you to be disappointed if he doesn't make it. . . ."

But Maggy wasn't listening. "Parrish!"

The leggy redhead in a white tank top and black capri pants darted across the parking lot toward them, teetering dangerously atop stylish, red, alligator-skin, three-inch, cork-soled, platform sandals.

Maggy flung herself into Parrish's outstretched arms. "You dyed your hair! I love, love, love it!"

"Thank Gawd somebody does," Parrish drawled. "Your uncle Ed detests it. He says I look like a hoochie mama."

She grinned at her best friend over the top of the child's head. "What's your verdict?"

Riley lifted a lock of hair and considered. "It's different."

"Always the diplomat," Parrish said, laughing. "Tell the truth. You hate it, too."

They started to make their way back toward the ferry dock, arm in arm, with Maggy and Banks bringing up the rear.

"No, really. It's cute. You just took me by surprise, that's all," Riley said. "This is definitely not a hoochie-mama shade. I think it suits you. What made you decide to go red?"

"No special reason. I was bored with being blond."

"You're the only woman I know who could get tired of being a blond bombshell."

"More like a cherry bomb than a bombshell," Parrish corrected. "Hey. I spotted you chatting with Belle Isle Barbie when I pulled into the lot. What did your new best friend want?"

Riley didn't want her daughter to overhear the two of them dishing up a serving of snark on Andrea Payne.

"Mags, it's too hot out here on the asphalt for Mr. Banks. Why don't you take him over to the shade of the loading area and pour some cool water into his bowl? It's in that tote with the blue handles."

"Okay."

Parrish watched the girl and her dog lope toward the dock. "My Lord. She's grown another inch just since I saw her at Grayton on Easter. And did she just now sprout boobs, or is that my imagination?"

"She's growing like a weed and already wearing an A-cup bra, although she'd kill me if she knew I'd told you that. She's so self-conscious about her body right now. I think she's going to take after Wendell's side of the family."

"Let's hope she's not a hundred-percent Griggs," Parrish said, rolling her eyes. "How's that going, by the way? Is Wendell coming, or do you think he'll be a total no-show?"

"He promised both me and his daughter that he'd be on the ferry with us this afternoon. But so far, no sign of him. He hasn't returned any of our calls or texts or e-mails. Not even Maggy's, which isn't like him."

"He'd never break a promise to Maggy," Parrish agreed. "But to his wife? Different story. Right?"

Riley wiped a bead of sweat from her brow. "All too true."

"Typical passive-aggressive bullshit. He doesn't want to be the one to break his kid's heart."

2

Shitheel," Parrish said. She shook her head. "I know. You don't have to remind me. It's all my fault, right?"

Riley shrugged. "If you hadn't made me go to that stupid barbecue . . . "

It was the summer of '97. Riley was working as a reporter for the local CBS affiliate in Raleigh, living in a tiny, bug-infested garage apartment in Cameron Park, while Parrish had gotten a job clerking at a local law firm.

After a messy breakup with her senior-year boyfriend and a series of laughable one-night stands and blind dates, Riley had sworn off men—at least for the summer. But Parrish had insisted on dragging Riley to a law-firm party at the managing partner's country house.

At first, Riley had flatly refused to go. "No way," she'd told Parrish. "No offense, but your work friends are either boring, stuck-up, or ancient. I'd rather stay home and give myself a facial."

"This party is different," Parrish said. "It's a pig-picking, and it's at Boomer Grayson's farm. He's having a bluegrass band play, and besides, it definitely won't be all lawyers. Boomer's son, Bryan, played shortstop at Wake Forest and he even played a season in the minor leagues for the Boston Red Sox farm team until he hurt his throwing arm. He's moved back home and is in his third year of med school at Duke. So there'll be plenty of hunky baseball players and hot doctor types. You gotta come!"

"Why do you need me?" Riley had asked, her suspicions aroused by Parrish's insistence. "Why not save all the hunky medics and jocks for yourself?"

"Okay, well, I might have a little crush on Bryan. But I don't want to go to the farm for the weekend by myself, because that would look too obvious."

"So I'm your wingwoman?" asked Riley.

"You got it."

"I'll go. But you're driving, and if you take off with this guy to go play doctor and leave me alone with a bunch of boring lawyers, I'll never speak to you again."

Despite Riley's threats, Parrish had totally snuck off with the jock-doc almost the moment they'd arrived at the pig-picking.

But the band was great and, left to her own devices, Riley found herself drawn into a circle of partygoers clustered around the fire, tapping her toes to "Little Liza Jane."

He'd materialized by her side, seemingly from nowhere. Tall, preppy looking, singing along to all the verses. He was sunburnt, which made his blue eyes look bluer, sipping on a red Solo cup of what he swore was moonshine.

"I say we name our first kid Little Liza Jane. That okay with you?"

She'd turned to this brash stranger and frowned. "What if it's a boy?"

He had an easy answer, of course. "Liza James?"

His breath on her cheek was warm and boozy.

"Do I know you?" she'd asked, amused.

"Not yet. My name's Wendell Griggs, but I already know yours," he confided, leaning in. "You're Riley Nolan."

"And how do you know me?" Riley asked.

"I see you every night on channel nine," he replied. "You're the girl who did all the stories about that puppy mill over in Kinston, right?"

"Well, I'm not on every night. More like once or twice a week. But, yeah, I did the puppy mill stories."

"I actually went over to the Humane Society and tried to adopt one of those beagle puppies, but the shelter wouldn't approve me because I live in a condo without a yard."

"Those little guys were soooo cute. I just wanted to scoop one up and run away with him," Riley confided. "But, let me tell you, beagle puppies are *loud*! And my landlady doesn't allow pets. Anyway, I'm gone all day, so I guess it doesn't make sense for me to have a dog right now. But someday . . ."

"I know, right? We always had black Labs growing up. I can't wait to get a real house with a yard so I can get another Lab."

A little while later, after some more pleasant chatter—and a lot more moonshine—Wendell had a sheepish look on his face. "We have something else besides puppies in common," he admitted. "I actually work for your dad."

"No! You work for Belle Isle Enterprises? How come we've never met?"

"I just started working as a leasing agent for the new retail shopping village a couple of weeks ago. I'm mostly working in the Wilmington office right now."

Wendell had been so easy to talk to in the beginning, so charming. So much fun. He'd been interested in everything. They'd stayed talking by the bonfire that night until finally Parrish had emerged from the shadows, hand in hand with Bryan Grayson, her hair mussed and her clothes askew, sometime around 3 a.m.

Early Saturday morning, Riley had gotten called back to the station to fill in for an ailing reporter, but somehow,

Wendell had finagled her phone number from Parrish, who'd stayed over for the rest of the weekend.

He'd called that Monday, and she hadn't bothered to call back. Then he called again the next day, and the day after that, had a huge bouquet of sunflowers delivered to her at the station, with a note that read, *You Are the Sunshine of My Life.*

Tamika, the noon anchor, had read the note over Riley's shoulder and given her nod of approval. "A dude who sends something besides roses? And quotes Stevie Wonder? That's a dude worth keeping."

It didn't take long for Wendell's charm—and persistence—to erode Riley's resolve to take a hiatus from dating.

But it had been her father who'd swayed her opinion on the matter.

Although her parents always spent the summers on Belle Isle, her father had made a special trip to Raleigh on a weekday, called her ahead of time, and invited her to lunch at the Carolina Country Club, an unusual move for him.

"I understand Wendell Griggs has been trying to wangle a date with you," her father had said, sipping on his usual pre-lunch scotch and water. "He claims you've shut him down every time."

"He told you that?" Riley blushed.

"He casually mentioned that you'd met at a party, and that he was very taken with you," W.R. said. "I guess he was just trying to figure out why you won't go out with him."

"Casually. Right," Riley said, her voice dripping with sarcasm. "Okay, I'll tell you what I told him. I'm not dating anybody right now. I'm concentrating on my career."

"Your career," W.R. scoffed, putting the phrase in finger quotes. "Covering the Miss Carolina tobacco pageant and cow-milking contests."

"I'm the newbie at the station right now. They always give rookies the crap assignments," Riley said. "But that story I did on the puppy mills got picked up by *The News and Observer* and by the wire service. And I'm working on a piece about the county foster-care system."

"Good for you," W.R. said, nodding his head. "But I still don't see why you shouldn't have a little fun on your own time. Wendell Griggs is a nice guy. A real go-getter. Your mother likes him, too."

"What is this?" Riley asked, half-amused and half-annoyed. "You and Mom are now taking votes on who I should date?"

W.R. tipped his glass and emptied it. "And why not? Who knows you better than your own parents?"

"Forget it," Riley said flatly. "Sorry, Daddy, but I am not currently in the market for a boyfriend. And when I am in the market, I doubt I'd choose a guy like Wendell Griggs."

W.R. had sighed and shook his head, then signaled the waiter for the lunch ticket, which he'd signed with a flourish. "That's what your mother said you'd say. But I had to try."

The next time Wendell Griggs called, for reasons she still couldn't remember, Riley had finally said yes.

He took her to dinner at the most expensive restaurant in Raleigh, insisted on ordering champagne, and afterward, as he walked her to the door of her garage apartment, he'd given her a chaste kiss on the cheek.

Which had come as a surprise to Riley, considering how hotly he'd pursued her.

She'd been intrigued, enough to say yes when he'd called the next night to ask her out for the coming weekend.

Things were not nearly as innocent that night. And the following week, he'd insisted she move out of what he referred to as her "roach motel" and in with him. Two months later, he'd surprised her with the most magnificent diamond she'd ever seen. A diamond so big it took Riley's breath away.

Wendell Griggs, Riley quickly learned, was all about the grand gesture.

It took several years before she realized that her husband wasn't quite as attentive when it came to the nagging little details of daily life.